Nicholas Evans was born and grew up in Worcestershire. Before writing his first novel, *The Horse Whisperer* – later made into a film directed by Robert Redford – he worked as a journalist, film producer and screenwriter. Nicholas Evans lives in Devon.

'Compelling . . . a love story . . . The issues raised in Nicholas Evans's book are fascinating. Whenever men and wolves have met, the wolves have lost . . . the descriptions of the lupine way of life is fascinating'

Bernard Cornwell, *Daily Mail*

'The real power of the story lies in the details of lupine life, and in the scenes high up in the mountains where the wolves stalk, fight and mate. The silence and the cold nurture an existence older than ours and are described here with a passion that provides a touchstone'

Elizabeth Buchan, *The Times*

'*The Horse Whisperer* . . . conveyed a genuine and personal emotional charge which resonated with millions of readers. *The Loop*, Evans's second novel, confirms that he is that rare phenomenon, a natural storyteller'

Mail on Sunday

'*The Loop* focuses on the brutality of men and the nobility of nature: emotive stuff'

She

Nicholas EVANS

The Loop

sphere

SPHERE

First published in Great Britain in 1998 by Bantam Press,
a division of Transworld Publishers
Published in paperback in 1999 by Corgi Books
This paperback edition published in 2006 by Time Warner Books
Reprinted by Sphere in 2007, 2010

A CIP catalogue record for this book
is available from the British Library.

ISBN 978-0-7515-3937-0

Typeset in Bembo by M Rules
Printed and bound in Great Britain by
Clays Ltd, St Ives plc

Papers used by Sphere are natural, renewable and
recyclable products sourced from well-managed forests and certified
in accordance with the rules of the Forest Stewardship Council.

Mixed Sources
Product group from well-managed
forests and other controlled sources
www.fsc.org Cert no. SGS-COC-004081
© 1996 Forest Stewardship Council
FSC

Sphere
An imprint of
Little, Brown Book Group
100 Victoria Embankment
London EC4Y 0DY

An Hachette UK Company
www.hachette.co.uk

www.littlebrown.co.uk

For my mother, Eileen,
and in memory of my father,
Tony Evans

Acknowledgements

Of the books that helped in my research, I am most indebted to: *Of Wolves and Men* by Barry Lopez, *War Against the Wolf* edited by Rick McIntyre, *Wolf Wars* by Hank Fischer, *The Wolf* by L. David Mech, and *The Company of Wolves* by Peter Steinhart.

Of the many people who helped, I would particularly like to thank Bob Ream, Doug Smith, Dan McNulty, Ralph Thisted, Sara Walsh, Rachel Wolstenholme, Tim and Terry Tew, Barbara and John Krause, J. T. Weisner, Ray Krone, Bob and Ernestine Neal, Richard Kenck, Jason Campbell, Chuck Jonkel, Jeremy Mossop, Huw Alban Davies, John Clayton, Dan Gibson, Ed Enos, Kim McCann and Sherry Heimgartner.

I am especially grateful to the Cobb family, Ed Bangs, Mike Jiminez, Carter Niemeyer, Bruce Weide, Pat Tucker and Koani, the only wolf I can plausibly call a friend.

Finally, for their patience, support, advice, acuity and friendship while I wrote this book, warmest thanks must go to the following: Linda Shaughnessy, Tracy Devine, Robert Bookman, Caradoc King and my wonderful editors, Carole Baron and Ursula Mackenzie.

Everything the Power of the World
does is done in a circle. The sky is
round and I have heard that the earth
is round like a ball and so are all the stars.
The wind, in its greatest power, whirls.
Birds make their nests in circles,
for theirs is the same religion as ours.
The sun comes forth and goes down
again in a circle. The moon does the
same and both are round. Even the
seasons form a great circle in their
changing and always come back again
to where they were. The life of a man
is a circle from childhood to childhood.
And so it is in everything where power moves.

BLACK ELK, Oglala Sioux
(1863–1950)

SUMMER

1

The scent of slaughter, some believe, can linger in a place for years. They say it lodges in the soil and is slowly sucked through coiling roots so that in time all that grows there, from the smallest lichen to the tallest tree, bears testimony.

Perhaps, as he moved silently down through the forest on that late afternoon, his summer-sleek back brushing lower limbs of pine and fir, the wolf sensed it. And perhaps this vestige of a rumor in his nostrils, that here a hundred years ago so many of his kind were killed, should have made him turn away.

Yet on and down he went.

He had set out the previous evening, leaving the others in the high country where even now, in July, there lingered spring flowers and patches of tired snow in gullies shy of the sun. He had headed north along a high ridge then turned east, following one of the winding rocky canyons that funneled the snowmelt down from the divide to the valleys and plains below. He had kept high, shunning the trails, especially those that ran along the water, where sometimes in this season there were humans. Even through the night, wherever it was possible, he had stayed below the timberline, edging the shadows, in a trot so effortless that his paws seemed to bounce without touching the ground. It was as though his journey had some special purpose.

When the sun rose, he stopped to drink, then found a shaded nook high among the sliprock and slept through the heat of the day.

Now, in this final descent to the valley, the going was more difficult. The forest floor was steep and tangled with blowdown, like tinder in some epic fireplace, and the wolf had to weave his way carefully among it. Sometimes he would double back and find a better route so as not to puncture the silence with the telltale snap of a dead branch. Here and there, the sun broke through the trees to make pools of vivid green foliage and these the wolf would always skirt.

He was a prime four-year-old, the alpha of the pack. He was long in the leg and almost a pure black, with just the faintest haze of gray along his flanks and at his throat and muzzle. Now and again he would pause and lower his head to sniff a bush or a tuft of grass, then lift his leg and make his mark, reclaiming this long-lost place as his own. At other times he would stop and tilt his nose to the air and his eyes would narrow and shine yellow as he read the scented messages that wafted on thermals from the valley below.

Once while doing this, he smelled something closer at hand and he turned his head and saw two white-tailed deer, mother and fawn, no more than a dozen yards away, frozen in a shaft of sunlight, watching him. He stared at them, connecting in an ancient communion that even the fawn understood. And for a long moment, all that moved were the

4

spores and insects that spiraled and glinted above the deers' heads. Then, as if deer and insect were of equal consequence to a wolf, he looked away and again assessed the air.

From a mile and a half away came the mingled smells of the valley. Of cattle, dogs, the acrid tang of man's machines. And though he must have known, without ever being taught, the peril of such things, yet on again he went and down, the deer following him with inscrutable black eyes until he was lost among the trees.

The valley which the wolf was now entering ran some ten miles due east in a widening, glacial scoop toward the town of Hope. Its sides were ridged and thick with pine and, viewed from above, seemed to reach out like yearning arms to the great sunbleached plains that stretched from the town's eastern edge to the horizon and countless more beyond.

At its widest, from ridge to ridge, the valley was almost four miles wide. It was hardly perfect grazing land, though many had made a living from it and one or two grown rich. There was too much sage and too much rock and whenever the pasture seemed about to roll, some coulee or creek, choked with scrub and boulders, would gouge through and cut it off. Halfway down the valley, several of these creeks converged and formed the river which wound its way through stands of cottonwood to Hope and on from there to the Missouri.

All of this could be surveyed from where the wolf now stood. He was on a limestone crag that jutted from the trees like the prow of a fossilized ship. Below it, the land fell away sharply in a wedge-shaped scar of tumbled rock and, below that, both mountain and forest gave way grudgingly to pasture. A straggle of black cows and calves were grazing lazily at their shadows and beyond them, at the foot of the meadow, stood a small ranch house.

It had been built on elevated ground above the bend of a creek whose banks bristled with willow and chokecherry.

There were barns to one side and white-fenced corrals. The house itself was of clapboard, freshly painted a deep oxblood. Along its southern side ran a porch that now, as the sun elbowed into the mountains, was bathed in a last throw of golden light. The windows along the porch had been opened wide and net curtains stirred in what passed for a breeze.

From somewhere inside floated the babble of a radio and maybe it was this that made it hard for whoever was at home to hear the crying of the baby. The dark blue buggy on the porch rocked a little and a pair of pink arms stretched craving for attention from its rim. But no one came. And at last, distracted by the play of sunlight on his hands and forearms, the baby gave up and began to coo instead.

The only one who heard was the wolf.

Kathy and Clyde Hicks had lived out here in the red house for nearly two years now and, if Kathy were honest with herself (which, on the whole, she preferred not to be, because mostly you couldn't do anything about it, so why give yourself a hard time?), she hated it.

Well, hate was maybe too big a word. The summers were okay. But even then, you always had the feeling that you were too far away from civilization; too exposed. The winters didn't bear thinking about.

They'd moved up here two years ago, right after they got married. Kathy had hoped having the baby might change how she felt about the place and in a way it had. At least she had someone to talk to when Clyde was out working the ranch, even though the conversation, as yet, was kind of one-way.

She was twenty-three and sometimes she wished she'd waited a few years to get married, instead of doing it straight out of college. She had a degree in agri-business management from Montana State in Bozeman and the only use she'd ever made of it was the three days a week she spent shuffling her daddy's paperwork around down at the main ranch house.

Kathy still thought of her parents' place as home and often got into trouble with Clyde for calling it that. It was only a couple of miles down the road, but whenever she'd spent the day there and got in the car to come back up here, she would feel something turn inside her that wasn't quite an ache, more a sort of dull regret. She would quickly push it aside by jabbering to the baby in the back or by finding some country music on the car radio, turning it up real loud and singing along.

She had her favorite station on now and as she stood at the sink shucking the corn and looking out at the dogs sleeping in the sun by the barns, she started to feel better. They were playing that number she liked, by the Canadian woman with the ball-breaker voice, telling her man how good it felt when he 'cranked her tractor'. It always made Kathy laugh.

God, really, she should count her blessings. Clyde was as fine a husband as any woman could hope for. Though not the richest (and, okay, maybe not the brightest either), he'd been, by a long way, the best-looking guy at college. When he'd proposed, on graduation day, Kathy's friends had been sick with envy. And now he'd given her a beautiful, healthy baby. And even if this place was at the back end of nowhere, it was still a place of their own. There were plenty of folk her age in Hope who'd give their right arms for it. Plus, she was tall, had great hair and even though she hadn't quite got her figure back after having the baby, she still knew her looks could crank any tractor she chose.

Self-esteem had never been a problem for Kathy. She was Buck Calder's daughter and around these parts that was about as big a thing to be as there was. Her daddy's ranch was one of the largest spreads this side of Helena and Kathy had grown up feeling like the local princess. One of the few things she didn't like about being married was giving up her name. She had even suggested to Clyde that she might do what those big-shot career women did nowadays and go double-barreled, call herself Kathy Calder Hicks. Clyde had said fine, whatever, but she could see he wasn't keen on the idea and so as not to hurt him she'd settled for plain old Kathy Hicks.

She looked up at the clock. It was getting on for six. Clyde and her daddy were down in the hay fields, fixing some irrigation, and they were all coming over for supper around seven. Her mom was due any minute with a pie she'd baked for dessert. Kathy cleared the mess out of the sink and put the corn into a pan on the stove. She wiped her hands on her apron and turned the radio down. All she had left to do was peel the potatoes and, when they were done, Buck Junior out there on the porch would no doubt be hollering for his feed and she'd do that then get him all bathed and brushed up nice and smart for his grandpa.

The cows in the top meadow looked up as one when the wolf came out from the trees. He stopped where the grass began, as if to give them the chance to inspect him. They had never before seen such a creature. Perhaps they placed him as some larger, darker kind of coyote. Coyotes were only a real danger when a calf was freshly born. Perhaps he seemed more like one of the ranch dogs who wandered among them sometimes and the only time you had to pay heed to them was when they snapped at your heels to make you go some place you'd rather not.

In return the wolf barely graced them with a glance. All his senses were locked on something else, something down at the house, and he lowered his head and started down the meadow toward it. He moved more slowly now, with greater caution, not skirting the cattle but passing right through them. But so clear was his disinterest that none moved away and all soon went back to their grazing.

As the sun slid behind the mountains, a line of shadow came creeping across the grass in front of the house and up and onto the porch, like a rising tide, so that first the wheels and then the base of the baby's buggy were engulfed and the oxblood wall behind it congealed to a darker red.

The wolf by now was at the foot of the meadow and here he stopped by the fence where Clyde had rigged up a pipe and an old enamel bathtub to water the cattle if the creek dried up. A pair of magpies broke from the willow scrub down by the creek and came up toward him in a series of fluttering swoops, scolding him, as if they knew his business here and didn't much care for it. The wolf ignored them. But from the shelter of his buggy, now only some twenty yards away, the baby did a passable imitation of the birds, shrieked with delight at how it sounded then did several encores. Inside the house a phone started to ring.

It was Kathy's mother. She said the pie had burned but not to worry because she had something else in the freezer that they could microwave.

'Oh and Luke says he'll come, if that's okay.'

'Of course it's okay.'

Luke, Kathy's brother, had just turned eighteen. He was sweet with the baby whenever she bumped into him down at the ranch, but he and Clyde didn't get along too well and since she'd been married, Luke hadn't been up here to the house more than a couple of times. As kids, they had never really been close. But then no one was close to Luke. Except, of course, their mom. She was the only one, in the end, who could handle his stutter.

Kathy had always been too impatient. Even when she was old enough to know better, she couldn't help finishing his sentences for him when he blocked. Since he'd graduated from high school, a couple of months ago, she'd hardly seen him. He was getting to be more of a loner than ever, it seemed to Kathy, always off on his own in the wilderness with only that funny-looking horse of his for company.

Anyway, he was coming to supper and that was fine.

Her mother asked how the baby was and Kathy said he was just great and that she'd better get off the phone because it was coming up toward his feed time and she still had things to do.

It was just as she hung up that the dogs started barking.

Normally, she wouldn't have given this a second thought. The dogs were forever hollering and taking off after some varmint or other, But there was something about the noise they were making now that made her look out of the window.

Maddie, the old collie, had her tail tucked under her and was slinking off around the side of the barn, muttering over her shoulder. Prince, the yellow Labrador that Kathy's father had given her when they first moved up here, was pacing to and fro with his hackles up. His ears alternately pricked and flattened as if he were unsure of himself and he punctuated his barking with worried little whines. His eyes were fixed on something beyond the house, something up toward the meadow.

Kathy frowned. She'd better go see what was spooking them. The pan in which she was cooking the corn started to hiss and she went over to the stove and turned down the heat. When she came out through the kitchen screen door and stepped down into the yard there was no sign of the collie. Prince seemed relieved to see her.

'Hey you, what's going on here?'

The dog started to come toward her, then seemed to change his mind. Perhaps her presence gave him that little extra courage he'd been lacking, for now he took off in full cry around the side of the house, kicking up the dust as he went.

It was only then that the thought struck her. The baby. There was something on the porch, getting at the baby. She started to run. It must be a bear. Or a mountain lion. God, how could she have been so dumb?

As she came around the corner of the house, Kathy saw, directly below the porch, what at first she took for a big, black dog, a German Shepherd maybe. It turned to face the Labrador's charge.

'Get out of here! Git!'

The animal glanced at her and she felt the yellow flash of his eyes upon her and knew in that instant this was no dog.

Prince had skidded to a halt before the wolf and had lowered himself, his front paws splayed so that his chest was just inches from the ground. He had his teeth bared and was snarling and barking but with such timid bravado that it seemed he might at any moment roll over and submit. The wolf stood very still, but somehow at the same time seemed to make himself bigger so that he towered over the dog. His tail was bushy and raised high. Slowly, he curled back his lips and snarled and his long incisors showed white.

Then, in a single lunge, he had his jaws on the Labrador's throat and swung him off his feet and through the air as if he were no heavier than a jackrabbit. The dog yelped and Kathy had a sudden image in her head of the wolf having already done the same with her baby and she screamed and jumped onto the end of the porch.

The buggy was at the far end and it seemed like a hundred miles away as she ran toward it.

Oh God, please. Don't let him be dead. Please don't let him be dead.

She couldn't tell whether the buggy had been disturbed, but even through the dog's shrieking, she knew her baby inside was silent and the thought of what she would find made her sob.

When she got there she hardly dared look. But she forced herself and saw the child staring up at her, his face breaking into a gummy grin, and she cried out and reached down and snatched him up. She did it with such sudden violence that the child began to cry and she held him to her so hard that he cried even louder. She turned, pressing her back to the wall, and looked down from the porch.

The wolf was standing with his head lowered over the Labrador. Kathy could see right away that the dog was dead. His hind legs gave a final twitch, just like they did in his dreams when he slept in front of the fire. His throat had been torn out and his belly gaped like a gutted fish. The bleached grass under him rivered red. Kathy screamed again and the wolf started, as if he'd forgotten she was there. He stared right at her and she could see the glisten of blood on his face.

'Get out of here! Go on! Get out!'

She looked around for something to throw at him but there was no need. The wolf was already running off and within moments he was ducking under the fence and loping up among the cattle who had all quit their grazing to watch the spectacle below. At the top of the meadow he stopped and looked back to where Kathy still stood over the dead dog, clutching her baby and crying. Then he turned and vanished into the shadow of the forest.

2

The offices of the US Fish and Wildlife Service Wolf Recovery team were on the third floor of a plain red-brick building in a quiet part of Helena. There was no sign outside that told you this and if there had been it probably wouldn't have lasted long. There were people around here who didn't much like any federal agency, least of all one whose sole purpose was to protect a creature they considered the most loathsome God ever came up with. Dan Prior and his team knew from experience that when it came to wolves it was best to keep the profile low.

In the outer office stood a glass case from which a stuffed wolf looked, more or less benignly, on their labors. The plaque on the side of the case said its occupant was *Canis Lupus Irremotus, Northern Rocky Mountain Wolf.* But, for a reason no one in the office could now recall, the wolf was more informally known as Fred.

Dan had gotten into the habit of talking to Fred, particularly on those long nights when everyone else had gone home, leaving him to unpick yet another political tangle in which Fred's more animated brethren had snagged him. On such occasions Dan would often come up with other, more vibrant names for his silent companion.

Tonight was definitely not going to be one of those nights. In fact Dan, for the first time in living memory, was leaving early. He had a date. And because he'd made the mistake of mentioning it, everyone in the office had been teasing him about it all week. As he came out of his office, stuffing some papers into his bag, they all chanted in rehearsed unison, 'Have a nice time, Dan!'

'Thank you very much indeed,' he said, through clenched teeth. Everyone laughed. 'Will someone tell me, what's so goddamn fascinating about my private life?'

Donna, his assistant, grinned at him. She was a big, gutsy woman in her late thirties, who ran the office with a calm good humor that even in the most frenzied moments never seemed to desert her. She shrugged.

'I guess it's just that you never had one till now.'

'You're all fired.'

He gave them a dismissive wave, told Fred to wipe that grin off his face and was just reaching for the doorknob when the phone rang.

'I'm gone,' he mouthed to Donna and out he went.

He pushed the elevator button and waited while the cables clunked and whirred behind the stainless-steel doors. There was a ping and the doors opened.

'Dan!'

He waited with his finger on the button, keeping the doors open, while Donna hurried down the corridor toward him.

'You know that new private life of yours?'

'You know, Donna? I was just thinking of giving you a raise.'

'I'm sorry, but I thought you'd want to know. That was a rancher called Clyde Hicks from Hope. He says a wolf just tried to kill his baby boy.'

Twenty minutes and half a dozen phone calls later, Dan was in his car and on his way to Hope. Four of the calls were to game wardens, Forest Service rangers and other Fish and Wildlife people in case any of them had heard anything about wolf activity in the Hope area. None had. The fifth was to predator-control agent Bill Rimmer, asking him to meet him in Hope to do a necropsy on the dog.

The last call was to the lovely and formidable Sally Peters, the newly divorced marketing director of a local cattle feed company. It had taken Dan all of two months to summon the courage to ask her out. After her reaction just now when he'd told her he wasn't able to make dinner, next time, if there was one, it would take longer.

It was about an hour's drive from Helena to Hope and as he swung west off the interstate toward the mountains, now darkening against the pale pink of the sky, Dan reflected on why it was that anyone who worked with wolves ended up getting screwed by them.

Over the years, he'd met a lot of biologists who specialized in other animals, from pygmy shrews to penguins, and though there were one or two damaged souls among them, on the whole they seemed able to stumble well enough through life like the rest of humanity. But wolf biologists were walking disaster areas.

In every league – divorce, nervous breakdown, suicide – they came out tops. By these standards, Dan himself had nothing to be ashamed of. His marriage had lasted nearly sixteen years. It was probably some kind of record. And even if Mary, his ex, didn't speak to him, Ginny, their daughter – who was fourteen, going on twenty – thought he was an okay

15

dad. Hell, she adored him; and it was mutual. But apart from Ginny, what, really, at the age of forty-one, did he have to show for all these years of devotion to the welfare of wolves?

To avoid answering his own question, he leaned forward and switched on the radio. Hopping through the commercials and the relentless country music (which, after three years in Montana, he still hadn't learned to like), he settled on the local news. The last item did little to improve his mood.

It was about a 'wolf attack' on a ranch near Hope and how the baby grandson of one of the community's most prominent figures, Buck Calder, had only escaped certain death because a pet Labrador had bravely laid down his life instead.

Dan groaned. The media had it already. That was *all* he needed. But it got worse. They already had a phone interview with Calder himself. Dan knew of him but had never met him. He had the deep, seductive voice of a politician. All daggers dripping with honey.

'The federal government let loose all those wolves down there in Yellowstone and now they're everywhere and threatening mothers and babies. And are we allowed to defend them and defend our livestock and our property? No sir, we are not. And why's that? Because the federal government tells us these animals are still an endangered species. I tell you, there's no more sense than justice in it.'

The report ended and Dan switched off.

The guy had a point. Until recently, the only wolves in the region had been the few that had ventured down the continental divide from Canada. Then, after years of furious debate between environmentalists and ranchers, the federal government decided to give wolf recovery a boost. At huge expense, some sixty-six wild Canadian wolves were captured, trucked to Yellowstone Park and Idaho, and released.

In response to local anger, ranchers who lived in these so-called experimental areas were allowed to shoot any wolf they

16

found attacking their livestock. But the released wolves had multiplied and because they weren't too good at reading maps (or perhaps because they were), they had spread to places where shooting them earned you a $100,000 fine and even a spell in jail.

Hope was one of these places. What's more, it was wolf-hater heartland. If a wolf had indeed shown up there today, it needed its head examined.

About ten years ago, Fish and Wildlife had held public meetings all over the state so that people could vent their feelings about federal proposals for wolf recovery. Some of these meetings had apparently gotten pretty stormy. But the one they'd held in Hope community hall beat all records.

A group of young ranch hands and loggers had stood outside with guns and yelled abuse all the way through. Those inside, where guns were banned, were just as scary. Dan's predecessor, a legendary diplomat, had managed to keep the lid on. But afterward, two loggers had shoved him against a wall and threatened him. He came out several shades paler than he'd gone in, only to find someone had poured a gallon of red paint over his car.

In the far distance now, Dan saw the town looming.

It was the kind of town you could drive through and barely know you'd been there. One straight street, a couple of hundred yards long, fishboned with a few side alleys. At one end stood a rundown motel and at the other a school, and in between you could find a gas station, a grocery, a hardware store, a diner, a laundromat and a taxidermist.

Many of the town's five hundred or so population lived scattered along the valley and to service their various spiritual needs there were two churches and two bars. There were also two gift shops, which said more about optimism than sound business sense; for although summer tourists often passed through Hope, few chose to linger.

In an attempt to remedy this and to meet demand from the modest but growing band of subdivision newcomers, one of these shops (and by far the better) had last year installed a cappuccino bar.

The shop was called Paragon and on those rare occasions when Dan was passing through, he always made a point of dropping in, not so much on account of the coffee, which was good, as of the woman who owned it.

She was a handsome New Yorker called Ruth Michaels and, from their two or three encounters, he'd so far established that she used to run an art gallery in Manhattan and had come to Montana on vacation after her marriage broke up. She'd fallen in love with the place and stayed. Dan could imagine knowing a lot more about her.

Cappuccino hadn't exactly taken off with the locals who mostly preferred their coffee weak and stewed, the way they did it over the street at Nelly's Diner. As he drove by, Dan was sad, but not altogether surprised, to see Ruth had a FOR SALE sign stuck in the front window.

Ahead, he could see Bill Rimmer's pickup parked where they'd arranged to meet, outside a forlorn bar, aptly named The Last Resort. Rimmer got out to greet him. He was a born and bred Montanan and with his Stetson and droopy, blond mustache, looked it. At six foot six, he always made Dan feel like a midget. He was a few years younger than Dan and better-looking too; in fact, come to think of it, Dan couldn't figure why he liked the guy so much.

He got out of his car and Rimmer slapped him on the shoulder.

'How're you doing, old friend?'

'Well, Bill, tell you the truth, I had a better date than you lined up for tonight.'

'You could break a man's heart, Dan Prior. Shall we head on out there?'

'May as well. Everybody else is. Did you hear the radio?'

'Yep. And I heard there's a TV crew up there too.'

'Terrific.'

'That old wolf sure chose a good spot to make his debut.'

'Come on, Bill. We don't even know it was a wolf yet.'

They climbed into Rimmer's pickup and pulled out down Main Street. It was nearly seven-thirty and Dan was starting to worry about the light. It was always easier to check out the scene of a depredation in daylight. He was even more worried about all the people who had been trampling over the scene of the so-called wolf attack. If there were any tracks they were probably all scuffed up by now.

He and Rimmer had started their jobs at virtually the same time. Their predecessors had both been centrally involved in the release program and had quit not long after for more or less the same reason. They were 'wolfed out' – tired of being yelled at by ranchers for not doing enough to control the spread of wolves and by environmentalists for not doing enough to help it. You simply couldn't win.

Rimmer worked for Animal Damage Control, a division of the Department of Agriculture, and was usually the first person to get the call when a rancher was having trouble with predators, be it bear, coyote, mountain lion or wolf. He was judge, jury and, where necessary, executioner. A trained biologist, he kept his love of these animals to himself. And that, along with his skill with rifle and trap, had helped him earn the respect even of those who harbored a natural mistrust of all federal employees.

He dressed like a cowboy, and that, along with his easy, laconic manner, gave him the edge over Dan when it came to placating irate ranchers who'd lost (or thought they'd lost) a calf or a sheep to a wolf. To such people, Dan would always be an East Coast outsider. Their main difference, however, was that while ranchers saw Rimmer as the man who could

19

help solve their problem, they saw Dan as the one who'd caused it. Dan always felt happier when he had Rimmer alongside, especially in situations like the one they were headed for now.

They swung off the last stretch of blacktop and onto the gray gravel road that wound up the valley toward the mountains. For awhile they traveled without talking, listening to the scrunch of the car's wheels that left a drift of dust behind them. Through the open windows the evening air was warm on Dan's forearm. Between the road and the darkening green of the cottonwoods along the river a hawk scoured the sagebrush for an evening snack. It was Dan who broke the silence.

'You ever hear of a wolf trying to take a baby?'

'Nope. Likely it was the dog he was after all the time.'

'That's what I figured. What about this Calder guy. Have you met him before?'

'Couple of times. He's quite a piece of work.'

'What's that supposed to mean?'

Rimmer grinned, without looking at him, and with one finger eased the brim of his hat up his forehead a little.

'You'll see.'

The gateway to the Calder ranch was a massive structure of weathered lodgepole, its crossbar mounted with the skull of a longhorn steer. It reminded Dan of the entrance to a wild west rollercoaster ride called the Canyon of Doom on which he and Ginny had scared themselves witless last summer in Florida.

They rattled over a cattle guard and past a wooden sign that said CALDER RANCH. There was a smaller one beside it, freshly painted, which said simply HICKS. Dan assumed there was no pun intended.

They drove beneath the skull and followed the road for another mile, winding among small, scrub-covered hills, until the Calder ranch house loomed ahead of them. It stood assertively on the south-facing slope of a low bluff which no doubt afforded shelter from the winter blizzards as well as a commanding view of the best pastures of the Calder domain. The house was built of stout, whitewashed timber and though it was on two stories, its great length made it seem low and anchored immutably to the land.

Below it lay a wide cement yard, on one side of which stood an imposing set of freshly painted white barns, and on the other three silver feed silos which towered like missiles above a network of corrals. In the pasture that fell away beyond, a wide-crowned cottonwood grew from the shell of a Model T Ford, rusted the same shade as the horses that grazed around it. They lifted their heads to watch the pickup and its train of dust go by.

They forked left and two miles farther up the road they crested another hill and saw, in the gathering dusk, the dark red shape of the Hicks' house. Rimmer slowed so they could take in the scene.

There were six or seven vehicles parked in front and though partly obscured by the corner of the house, a small crowd could be seen around the rear porch. Someone seemed to have a spotlight on and every so often there was the flash of a camera. Dan sighed.

'I want to go home.'

'Sure looks like a circus.'

'Yeah. And here come the clowns.'

'I was thinking more of the Roman kind, you know, where they feed you to the lions.'

'Thanks a lot, Bill.'

They parked along with the other cars and made their way up to the house and around to the back where all the people were. Someone was talking and Dan recognized the voice right away.

Up on the porch, in a flood of light, a young TV reporter

21

was interviewing Buck Calder. She was wearing a red suit that looked a good two sizes too small for her. Calder towered above her. He was tall, almost as tall as Bill Rimmer, and much more powerfully built. His shoulders were as wide as the window behind him.

He wore a light-colored Stetson and a white snap-button shirt that set off his tan. His eyes gleamed a pale gray-blue in the TV lights and Dan realized it was the eyes even more than the man's physique that gave the impression of power. They were locked on the young reporter with such smiling intensity that she seemed mesmerized. Dan had expected to see the grandfather he knew Calder to be. But here instead was a man in his prime, who clearly knew the effect his confidence had on others.

Alongside him, looking a lot less comfortable, were Kathy and Clyde Hicks. Kathy was holding the baby who was staring at his grandfather, eyes wide with wonder. There was a table beside them with something bulky and yellow on it and it took Dan awhile to realize it was the dead dog.

'The wolf is a killing machine,' Calder was saying. 'He'll take anything he can. And if it wasn't for this poor, brave dog here he'd have taken my little grandson. Though I reckon Buck Junior here might have given him a sock on the jaw first.'

The crowd laughed. There were about a dozen people there. The photographer and a young man taking notes were from the local newspaper; Dan had seen them before. Who the others were, he had no idea. Probably neighbors and family. There were two faces that he kept going back to: a graceful woman, in her mid-forties, Dan guessed, and a tall young man, probably in his late teens, beside her. They were standing in the shadows, a little way back from the rest. Dan noticed how neither of them joined in the laughter,

'Calder's wife and son,' Rimmer whispered.

The woman had thick black hair, streaked with gray and loosely pinned up to show a long, pale neck. There was a kind of melancholy beauty about her that was echoed in the face of her son.

Everything had suddenly gone quiet up on the porch. The TV reporter, entranced by Calder's gaze, had blanked. Calder grinned at her with teeth white and perfect as a movie star's.

'You going to ask me another question, sweetheart, or are we about done here?'

The laughter this time made her blush. She looked around at the cameraman, who nodded.

'I think we're done,' she said. 'Thank you Mr Calder. Very much. That was really, really . . . great.'

Calder nodded then looked over the heads to where Dan and Rimmer were standing and gave them a little wave. Everyone turned to look at them.

'I can see a couple of fellas over there who you might like to ask a few questions too. I know I've got one or two for them.'

From the darkness of the barn, Luke Calder looked out across the yard to where they were doing the necropsy. He was just inside the open door, kneeling beside Maddie and stroking her. She was lying with her head on her paws and every now and then she would whimper and lift her head and look up at him, licking her grizzled old lips, and Luke would stroke her some more till she settled again.

Rimmer had the Labrador laid out on clear plastic sheeting on the tailgate of his pickup. He'd rigged up some lamps so he could see what he was doing with his knife. The other guy who'd come with him, the wolf expert, was videoing it, while Luke's father and Clyde stood to one side, looking on in silence. His mother and Kathy were inside getting supper ready. Everyone else had at last, thank God, gone home.

That nightmare of a woman from the TV station had asked if she could stay and film the necropsy too but Rimmer had said no. The wolf guy, Prior, had agreed to answer a few of her dumb questions, basically telling her nothing, then politely sent her packing because they needed to get on with the job while the dog's corpse was still fresh.

They were skinning him like a deer, Rimmer talking all the while for the video, saying out loud what he was doing and what he could see. Luke could see him peeling Prince's hide away like elastic from the bloody pink muscle.

'Severe internal hemorrhaging and more bite marks here at the base of the neck. Real deep puncture wounds. Can you see that Dan? Here, I'll measure them. These incisor holes are nearly two inches apart. That's a big animal.'

It must have been the alpha male, Luke thought, the big black one.

Luke had known for many months that there were wolves up there. He'd first heard them in the deep of winter when the backcountry lay thick with snow and he was out on his skis where he most liked to be, as far away from the world as you could get.

He'd found tracks and knew at once they were too big for any coyote, and he'd followed them and found the carcass of a fresh-killed elk.

Then, one day in April, he'd seen the black one.

First on skis, then on foot, he'd climbed to the top of a high ridge and had stopped there to rest. It was a cloudless day, still icy but with a promise of spring. And as he sat there on a rock, gazing down into the next valley, he saw the wolf trot out from the trees. It made its way across a small meadow of melting snow at the higher end of which was a slope, cluttered with sliprock and blowdown. The wolf had simply vanished into it, leaving Luke to wonder if he'd dreamed the whole episode.

It was where the mother had denned. And in the weeks that followed, Luke saw the others. When the snow melted, he would ride up there, always making sure to stay downwind, tying Moon Eye a good way off and climbing to the top of the same ridge. He would slither the last few yards on his belly, with binoculars ready in his hands, elbowing his way through the rocks until he could see down into the meadow. And he would lie there for hours at a time, sometimes seeing none, sometimes all of them.

He had told no one.

Then, one afternoon in the first week of May, he saw the pups. They were still fluffy and dark and none too sure of their feet and all five of them had come stumbling out from the den, blinking in the sunshine. Their mother with her drooping teats stood proudly by while the father and the two other, younger adults greeted the little ones and nuzzled them, as if welcoming them into the world.

Toward the end of June they disappeared and for awhile he was afraid someone had killed them. But then he found them again in another meadow, farther up the canyon. It seemed to Luke a safer place, fringed with trees and sloping gently to a stream where the pups would splash and wrestle. And it was there one morning that he saw one of the younger adults come trotting back from a hunting trip, looking all proud, as if he'd won the lottery or something, and all the pups came running across the meadow to greet him, jostling him and licking his face until he kind of grinned and yawned and retched up meat for them to eat, just like the books said they did.

As the meadow filled with flowers, Luke watched the pups chasing bees and butterflies and learning how to hunt mice and it was often so comical he found it hard not to laugh out loud. Sometimes when their mother or their father lay dozing in the sun, the pups would stalk them, creeping on their bellies through the paintbrush and shooting stars and the lush, long grass. Luke was sure the parents knew what was going on and were just playing along, pretending to be asleep. When they got real close, the pups would pounce and everything went crazy and the whole pack would go chasing around the meadow, tumbling and nipping each other and the game would go on and on until they all collapsed in one big, exhausted heap of wolf.

And witnessing this, Luke would silently say a little prayer, not to God, of whose existence he'd had scant evidence so far, but to whoever or whatever decided these things, pleading that the wolves be smart enough to stay up there where they were safe and not venture down to the valley.

But now it had happened. One of them had come.

And just now, watching his father lapping up the limelight on the porch, Luke had felt angry at the wolf, not for killing his sister's dog, whom he had always loved well enough, but for being so utterly reckless with the lives of the others. Didn't the fool of an animal know how people around here felt about wolves?

His father was aware how well Luke knew the mountains, how he was always going up there, off on his own, when he should have been helping out on the ranch, like ranchers' sons were supposed to. And earlier that evening, before all the people showed up, his father had asked him if he'd ever seen any sign of wolves up there.

Luke had shaken his head and, instead of leaving it at that, for some stupid reason, had tried to say no, he never had. The lie made him block on both the *no* and the *never* even worse than usual, and his father walked off before the sentence was out.

Luke just let it die unspoken, with the other million dead sentences he had inside him.

Across the yard, the necropsy was over now and Dan Prior had turned off his camera and was helping Rimmer clean up.

Luke's father and Clyde stepped closer and the four men started to talk, their voices low, so that Luke could no longer hear. He gave the old dog one last stroke, stood up and walked out of the barn toward them, stopping a short way off in the hope that no one would spot him.

'Well, there's no doubt it was a wolf,' Rimmer said.

Luke's father laughed. 'Was there any doubt before? My daughter saw it with her own eyes. I reckon she can tell a wolf from a woodpecker.'

'I'm sure she can, sir.'

His father caught sight of him and Luke cussed himself for leaving the barn.

'Gentlemen, this is my son, Luke. Luke, this here's Mr Prior and Mr Rimmer.'

Fighting an instinct to turn and run, Luke walked over and shook hands with them. They both said hi but Luke just nodded, avoiding their eyes in case they tried to get him to talk. As usual, his father steamed right on with the conversation, simultaneously rescuing him and consigning him to yet another failure. Luke knew the real reason his father always stepped in so smartly; he didn't like folks knowing he had a stutterer for a son.

'So, how come you fellas never told us there were wolves around here?'

It was Prior who answered.

'Well, Mr Calder, we've always known wolves do sometimes travel along the continental divide. As you know, there's a growing population of them in the state—'

His father gave a mocking laugh. 'I had heard tell.'

'And as they do travel, sometimes, quite long distances, it's not always easy to know where they all are at any given time or—'

'I thought you were supposed to have radio collars on them all.'

'Some, yes sir, but not all. Your daughter's pretty sure this one didn't have a collar. We've had no indication, until today that is, of any wolf activity in this area. This one may be a dis-perser, a single wolf who's broken away from some other pack, maybe many miles from here. Maybe he's hanging out with others that are collared. That's what we're going to try and find out. In fact, as of tomorrow morning, we'll be out there looking.'

'Well, I surely hope so, Mr Prior. And so does Clyde here, as you can imagine.' He put his arm around his son-in-law's shoulders. Clyde didn't look too comfortable about it, but managed a stern nod.

'What are you planning on doing once you've found them?'

'I think we need to know a little more before we decide on that,' Prior said. 'I can sure appreciate how upset you must be, but if it's any consolation, there's never been a case anywhere in North America of a healthy wild wolf killing a human being.'

'Is that a fact?'

'Yes sir. In all probability this one was only ever after the dog. It's kind of a territorial thing.'

'Oh is it now? Tell me, Mr Prior, where do you come from?'

'I live in Helena, sir.'

'No, I mean originally. Where you were born and grew up. Somewhere back east is my guess.'

'Yes, as a matter of fact. I come from Pittsburgh.'

'Pittsburgh. Hmm. Grew up in the city.'

'Yes sir, I did.'

'So that's *your* territory?'

'Well, in a manner of speaking, yes, I guess it is.'

'Well, let me tell you something, Mr Prior.'

He paused and Luke saw the look in his father's eyes, that

flash of smiling contempt which all his life Luke had dreaded, for it always heralded some crushing remark, some witty, withering flourish of words that left you wanting to crawl away and hide under a rock.

'This here is *our* territory,' his father went on. 'And we've got "kind of a territorial thing" about it too.'

There was a tense space of silence across which his father held Prior in a vise-like gaze.

'We don't want wolves here, Mr Prior.'

3

Buck Calder was baptized Henry Clay Calder III but he had never been too keen on the idea of being third or even second to anyone, and both to those who liked him and to those who didn't, he'd always been much more a Buck than a Henry.

The nickname came when, at fourteen, he carried off every prize on offer at the high school rodeo, revealing only when all was safely won that he had two broken fingers and a cracked collarbone. Even back then, the name's more carnal connotation was not lost on the more knowing of his female classmates. He was already the object of wide-eyed whispers and once of a stern and exclusively female inquisition when his name was found on a wall of the girls' toilets, coupled in rhyme with a word from which it differed by only one letter.

Had any of these girls seen fit to share such secrets with their mothers, they would perhaps have found less surprise than they might have expected. For a previous generation of

Hope schoolgirls had flushed with similar feelings for his father. Henry II, by all accounts, had practiced a particular method of kissing that a girl never quite forgot. A winning way with women, it seemed, swam strongly in the male Calder gene pool.

Of Buck's grandfather, Henry I, no such intimate detail endured. History bore witness only to his great resilience. It was he who in 1912 had loaded a few cows and chickens, a young bride and her upright piano onto a train in Akron, Ohio, and headed west.

When they got there, they found all the best land had already gone and Henry ended up filing a claim way out by the mountains where no one had yet been rash enough to try. He built his homestead where the big ranch house now stood. And while countless others gave up, driven out by drought, wind and winters that killed even the hardiest stock, the Calders somehow survived, all but the piano, which after the journey never quite sounded the same.

Henry bought the land his neighbors couldn't make pay and, little by little, the Calder ranch spread wider and deeper down the valley toward Hope. With dynastic ambition, he named his first son after him and set about making the linked HC brand something to be proud of.

Buck's father never went to college but every moment he wasn't chasing women, he spent reading everything he could lay his hands on about rearing cattle. He would have the library order special books he'd heard about and get livestock magazines shipped all the way from Europe. His father thought some of the articles the younger Henry read to him too newfangled but he was always smart enough to listen. It was at his son's urging that he switched from a commercial to a purebred Hereford operation. And the more he handed over decisions, so the more the herd thrived.

Buck grew up with all the confidence and not a little of the

31

arrogance such status can give a child. No ranch was bigger than theirs, no rancher smarter than his daddy. There were some who expected – and others who secretly hoped – that the legendary Calder drive might dissipate in this third Henry's veins. Instead, it seemed to redouble. He had two older sisters and two younger brothers but it was clear from the start that he was the only proper heir to the empire.

Buck went to college in Bozeman and learned all about genetics. And when he came back, he helped take everything a step farther. He started keeping an individual file on every animal they reared, charting its performance in minute detail. Birthing ease, mothering skills, weight gain, disposition and much more were scrutinized and ruthlessly acted upon. The progeny of those who made the grade flourished; those found wanting went swiftly to the wall.

As a philosophy, it differed little from the one to which ranchers and farmers had adhered for years. Weeding out poor stock was hardly revolutionary. But the rigor with which it was applied on the Calder ranch was. Buck's changes improved performance dramatically in every area and soon had stockgrowers talking across the state. The first Henry Calder died content that his line would stretch strong and glorious to the century's horizon.

But Buck had only started. With the old man gone, he argued that they should switch from raising purebred Herefords to Black Angus. He argued that they made better mothers and soon everyone would be going for them. His father said he must be out of his mind. It would be throwing away everything they'd worked for all these years. But Buck persuaded him to let him try raising some Black Angus of his own, just to see.

Almost immediately his small herd was outperforming the Herefords on every count. His father agreed to switch the whole herd, and within a few years, their reputation for pure-bred Black Angus surpassed all competition. Calder-bred bulls and the richness of their seed were renowned throughout the West and beyond.

With his own seed, the young Buck Calder was somewhat less discriminating. He was generous with his favors and traveled widely to bestow them. There wasn't a decent whorehouse from Billings to Boise that he hadn't graced with a visit. He would boast that a real man had three unalienable rights: life, liberty and the pursuit of women.

There were two kinds of women he pursued and the ones he dated knew nothing of the ones he paid. What made this surprising was that several of the former had brothers or male cousins who knew all too well about the latter. One or two of these young men had indeed witnessed Buck unbuckling and roared at the Calder motto, coined in his cups one bawdy night, that all you had to do with women was 'Buck 'em and chuck 'em'.

His friends' silence on these matters, born less of loyalty perhaps than fear of self-incrimination, allowed Buck to be seen, throughout his twenties, as nothing worse than what some still quaintly called a 'lady's man', which did little to prevent him simultaneously being seen, except by bad sports and the inordinately perceptive, as Hope's most eligible bachelor.

By the time he turned thirty, most women his age, including those he'd so excited at high school, had sensibly looked and found elsewhere. All were married and most were mothers and Buck by now was dating their younger sisters. Like his father before him, his eyes came at last to settle on a young woman ten years his junior.

Eleanor Collins was the daughter of a hardware store proprietor from Great Falls and had just finished her training as a physical therapist. Buck was one of her first patients.

He had strained a shoulder hauling a broken hay wagon from a creek. The last time he had come to the clinic he'd been stretched and pummeled by an older woman whom he'd

33

later mocked as having the looks and charm of a Russian tank commander. So when he saw this young goddess step through the door of the consulting room, he thought she must be an assistant or nurse.

She wore a white coat that fitted close enough to show Buck's practiced eye the kind of figure he liked best, slim and lithe and full-breasted. She had skin like ivory and long black hair, held up with tortoiseshell combs. She didn't return his smile, just fixed him with her wonderful green eyes, asked him what the trouble was and told him to take off his shirt. Dear Lord, Buck thought, as he unbuttoned, it's like something you read about in *Playboy* magazine.

Had Eleanor Collins succumbed to the charm he instantly applied, had she agreed to meet him for a cup of coffee at lunchtime, had she so much as smiled even once, things might have turned out differently.

Months later she would tell him that she'd been nervous as a chipmunk that day; that as soon as she'd laid eyes on him, she'd thought this was the man for her and how hard it had been to mask her feelings with professional cool. As it was, Buck left the clinic with both his shoulder and his heart aglow. And from the latter alone, he knew this was more than just another buck-and-chuck, for normally he felt the glow in a baser place. No. He had met, at last, the woman he would marry.

Of the cautionary signs to which Eleanor might have paid heed, perhaps the most telling was the quiet, resigned sadness in the eyes of Buck's mother. It could have shown her what grim toll there was to pay for living with a firstborn male Calder. But Eleanor saw in her future mother-in-law only a shared and understandable adoration for this handsome, charming power-house of a man, a man who had chosen her from all the women in the world to share his life and bear his children.

Her refusal to sleep with him before they were married only stoked Buck's passion all the more. Eleanor remained a virgin until their wedding night, whereupon she dutifully conceived. It was a boy. His name was not up for discussion. Two daughters, Lane and Kathy, followed at intervals of roughly two years.

'Only breed your best cow every other year,' Buck said to his drinking pals at The Last Resort. 'That's the way to get prime beef.'

It was a description that he could honestly apply to the first three of his children. Henry IV was a firstborn Calder to the core and sometimes when the two of them were out hunting or rounding up cattle or fixing a fence, Buck would shake his head with pride at the boy's easy, unwitting emulation.

Dear Lord, he thought, the power of the seed. And then he'd look at young Luke and think again.

This second son didn't look like a Calder at all. It had taken Eleanor four years to have him and during that time something seemed to have happened to the Calder genes. The boy was the image of his mother: the pale Irish skin, the dark hair, the same watchful green eyes.

'Well, he sure is his mother's son,' Buck joked in the hospital when he first laid eyes on the child. 'No telling who his daddy is though.' And ever since, even in front of the boy, he'd gone on referring to Luke as 'your son'.

It was said in jest, of course. He was far too proud to think that any man would dare cuckold him or that any woman of his would allow it. But secretly he felt his genes had somehow been denied access to the boy. Or worse, that they had been admitted and failed. And he felt this even before Luke began to stutter.

'Ask for it properly,' Buck would tell him at the table. He didn't shout. He'd say it gently, but firmly. 'Say, "Please may I have the milk." That's all you have to say, Luke.'

And Luke, just three years old, would sit there and try and fail and keep trying and keep failing and he wouldn't get the milk until he cried and then Eleanor would go and hug him and give it to him and Buck would yell at her, because how the hell was the boy supposed to learn if she did that every time, for Christsake?

As Luke grew, so did his stutter. And the space between his words seemed linked in some organic process to the space that opened little by little in the midst of the family, he and his mother on the one side, everyone else on the other. More than ever, he became Eleanor's son and soon he was to be her only one.

On a snowy November day, when Luke was seven years old, two Henry Calders, his older brother and his grandfather, were killed in a car wreck.

Young Henry, just fifteen years old, was learning to drive and it was he at the wheel, when a deer sprang out before them. The road was like greased marble and when he swerved, the wheels locked and the car slithered and launched itself into a ravine like a wingless bird. The rescue team reached it three hours later and with flashlights found the snow-sprinkled bodies in a tree, frozen and entwined, as if in some fabulous balletic leap.

With seventy-six years on the clock, the older Henry's death was the more easily absorbed. But the loss of a child is an abyss from which few families return. Some claw their way again toward the light, perhaps finding a narrow ledge where, in time, memory can shed its skin of pain. Others dwell in darkness forever.

The Calders found a kind of nether twilight, though each by a different route. The boy's death seemed to act on the family with a force that was centrifugal. They could find no comfort in collaborative mourning. Like shipwrecked strangers, they each struck out for shore alone as if fearful that in helping others they might be dragged beneath the waves of grief and drown.

Lane and Kathy fared best, escaping as often and for as long as they could to the homes of their separate sets of friends. Their father meanwhile, like a brave pioneer, strode forward in manly denial. Unconsciously impelled, perhaps, to spread some compensating genes, Buck sought sexual solace wherever he could. His philandering, only ever briefly curtailed by his marriage, took on new zeal.

Eleanor retreated to a distant inner land. She would sit glazed for days before the TV. Soon she knew every character in every soap and saw the same issues and faces come around again and again on the morning shows. She would watch wives yell at cheating husbands and daughters berate mothers for stealing their clothes or their boyfriends. She shocked herself sometimes by yelling along too.

When she grew tired of that, she tried drink. But she could never quite get the hang of it. Every kind of liquor she tried tasted terrible, even if she drowned it in orange or tomato juice. It made her forget, but only the wrong things. She would drive all the way to Helena or Great Falls only to find she had no idea why she was there. She drank with such graceful discretion that no one ever suspected, even when they ran out of bread or milk or she served the same meal two nights running or, once, forgot to serve one at all. In the end she decided she wasn't cut out to be alcoholic and simply stopped.

It was Luke who felt her distance most keenly. He noticed how she often forgot to come and kiss him goodnight and how she rarely hugged him anymore. She still protected him from his father's rage, but wearily and without passion, as if it were a duty whose purpose she had forgotten.

And so the boy's quiet harvesting of guilt went undetected.

On the day of their death, his brother and grandfather had been on their way to fetch him from his speech therapist in Helena. And with the unsullied logic of a seven-year-old, this fact alone made the accident his fault. With one stroke he had slain his father's father and best-beloved child, the ancient king and heir apparent of the Calders.

It was indeed a splendid burden for a boy to carry.

4

The red and white Cessna 185 banked steeply against a cobalt dome of morning sky, then seemed to hang weightless for a moment above the rim of the mountains. As he tilted the starboard wing at the sun and pointed the nose for the twentieth time toward the east, Dan looked directly down at the plane's shadow and saw it falter then fall, like the ghost of an eagle down walls of ancient limestone a thousand feet deep.

Beside him in the narrow cockpit, Bill Rimmer sat with the radio receiver on his lap, going methodically, again and again, through the list of frequencies of every collared wolf there was from Canada to Yellowstone. There was an antenna on each wing and he constantly switched between them, while both men strained their ears for the unmistakable cluck-cluck-cluck of a signal.

It wasn't the easiest country for spotting wolves. All morning they'd combed the peaks and the canyons, using their eyes as much as their ears, squinting into the shadowed spaces between the trees, scanning ridges and creeks and lush green meadows for some telltale sign: a carcass in a clearing, a flock of ravens, a sudden flight of deer. They saw plenty of deer, both white-tail and mule, and elk too. Once, flying low over a wide ravine, they startled a grizzly bear feeding with her cub in a patch of buffaloberries and sent them bounding for the shelter of the forest. Here and there they came across cattle, grazing the 'allotments', high summer pastures that many ranchers leased from the Forest Service. But of the wolf or wolves there was no trace.

Last night Rimmer had driven Dan back into Hope to get his car and they'd gone into The Last Resort for a beer both felt they'd earned. The place was dark, its walls crowded with trophy heads whose unseeing eyes seemed to follow them as they took their glasses to a table in the corner. At the other end of the room a couple of ranch hands were playing pool and feeding a jukebox. The music had to compete with the ball game on the TV above the bar, where a lone drinker in a sweat-stained hat sat recounting the details of his day to the barmaid. She was trying to sound interested and overdoing it a little. Dan and Rimmer were the only other customers. Dan was still seething from his encounter with Buck Calder.

'I told you he was a piece of work,' Rimmer said, wiping the froth from his mustache.

'Piece of something, anyway.'

'Oh, he's okay. Reckon his bark's bigger than his bite. He's one of these guys likes to test you, see how tough you are.'

'Oh, that's what he was doing.'

'Sure it was. You stood up pretty good.'

'Well, thanks Bill.' He took a long drink from his glass and put it down with a clunk. 'Why the hell couldn't he wait before calling all those goddamn reporters?'

'They'll all be out there again soon enough.'

'Why's that?'

'He told me they're gonna bury the dog, you know, give it a proper hero's funeral, tombstone and all.'

'I don't believe it.'

'That's what he said.'

'What do you reckon they ought to put on the tombstone?'

They both thought awhile. Dan got there first.

'Maybe just, "Labrador formerly known as Prince."'

They laughed like a couple of kids and far longer than such a dubious joke deserved, but it felt good and that and the beer soon put Dan in a better mood. They had another and stayed until the ball game finished. By then the place was getting busier. It was time to go.

As they headed for the door, Dan heard a voice on the TV say, 'And in the Hope Valley, a baby's narrow escape from death when Mr Wolf comes to call. That story coming up. Stay with us.'

So they did, but stood in the shadows by the door in case they were spotted. And true to his word, after the commercials, the local anchorman came back with the story and Dan felt his hackles rise at the sight of Buck Calder's crocodile smile.

'The wolf's a killing machine. He'll take anything he can.'

'The guy ought to run for president,' Dan said in a low voice.

Then, over a shot of Dan and Rimmer, trying to keep a low profile at the back of the crowd, just as they were doing now, the report went on to say that federal officials were 'embarrassed' by what had happened. They used a snippet of the short interview Dan had given, in which he proved the point before he even opened his mouth. He was squinting furtively into the glare of the lights, like a man on trial for unspeakable crimes.

'Could this wolf be one of those wolves you released into

Yellowstone?' the reporter in the red suit asked him, shoving the microphone up his nose. The *you* hurt.

'It's really too early to know that. Until we've had a chance to examine the body, we can't even confirm it *was* a wolf.'

'Are you saying you don't think it was?'

'No, I'm not saying that. I'm just saying we can't confirm it yet.' His attempt at a disarming smile just made him look shiftier. Dan had seen enough.

'Let's get out of here,' he said.

Flying over from Helena this morning, with the sun bouncing off the mountain front, things hadn't seemed quite so bleak. He and Rimmer had talked optimistically about the chances of picking up a signal. Maybe, in her panic, Kathy Hicks hadn't registered that the wolf was wearing a radio collar. And even if he wasn't, maybe he was teamed up with others who maybe were. That was a whole bagful of maybes. In his heart, Dan knew the chances weren't great.

As a matter of policy, over the past couple of years, they had deliberately scaled down the number of wolves they'd collared. The idea of restoring a viable breeding population to the region was that the animals should be truly wild and live as naturally as possible. When there were enough breeding pairs, they could be taken off the list of endangered species. It was Dan's personal view that collars weren't necessarily going to help this happen.

It was a view not shared by everyone. There were even those who advocated using capture collars, fitted with darts you could trigger anytime you wanted to put the wolf to sleep. Dan had used them himself a few times when he worked in Minnesota and they sure did make life easier. But every time you captured a wolf and drugged him and handled him and took a blood sample and tagged his ear and gave him a shot, you made him a little less wild, a little less of a wolf. And in the end you had to ask yourself whether this kind of

41

remote control by humans made him that much different from a toy boat on a park pond.

However, if a wolf started getting himself into trouble, killing cattle or sheep or people's pets, you needed to get a collar on him pretty damn quick – for his own sake as much as everyone else's. You tried to give ranchers the impression that you knew the address of every wolf in the state and then, when one stepped out of line, you had to scramble like hell to find him before someone beat you to it with a gun. If you could get a collar on him, at least then you knew where he was. And if he got into trouble again, you could relocate or shoot him.

Now, as the sun climbed higher in the sky, the two men in the Cessna's cramped cockpit were as silent as Rimmer's receiver. If any wolf down there was wearing a collar, they should have found him by now. Finding an uncollared wolf – or wolves – in country like this was a much tougher job. The question was, who was going to do it? And then, who was going to monitor them once they had been found?

It was a job Dan would happily have done himself. The only wolf he ever got to see nowadays was Fred. He'd become so much of a desk biologist, he often joked about doing a PhD on the breeding habits of memos. He longed to be out in the field again, like the good old days in Minnesota, where the phone and the fax couldn't get you. But it was out of the question. He had too much to do and no one except Donna to off-load it on. Bill Rimmer had generously volunteered to help with any trapping, but in truth he was more overworked than anyone.

Wolf recovery had long been a political football but lately all the goals seemed to have been scored by those politicians who opposed it. As the wolf population grew, so did the controversy surrounding it. The more incidents like this there were, the harder it became to argue for more tax dollars and manpower to handle them. Dan had seen his budgets cut to the bone. Now even the bones were going. Sometimes, in an emergency, he managed to shuffle someone from another job for a month or two or borrow a research student or one of the volunteers they used down in Yellowstone.

The trouble was, this was more than just a trap-and-collar job. Hope could easily turn out to be the most severe test yet for the whole recovery program.

With the town's deep hatred of the wolf and the fact that the media were already making a meal of it, whoever Dan sent in wouldn't simply have to be good at trapping and tracking wolves. He, or she, would have to be a skilled communicator, sensitive to local feelings yet strong enough to stand up to bullies like Buck Calder. Biologists with such an array of talent were hard to find.

The Cessna reached the end of another eastward run and Dan turned it once more and, as it tilted, looked down to see the town of Hope laid out like a surveyor's model. An eighteen-wheeler cattle truck that looked small enough to pluck with your fingers was pulling out of the gas station. The bends of the river flashed like chrome between the cottonwoods.

Dan glanced down at the fuel gauge. There was just enough juice for one more pass, then they'd call it a day.

This time he flew directly over the Calder ranch where a few cattle stood out like black ants on the sunbleached grass. A car was winding its way through the hills toward the Hicks place. Another damn reporter, no doubt.

Once they reached the forest, he flew lower, as low as he dared, the tree and canyon tops skidding away crazily beneath the plane's shadow. Then, just as he was lifting the nose for the final climb, he caught a glimpse of something up ahead, a pale gray form slipping out of sight over a rocky ridge. His heart leapt and he looked at Rimmer and knew he'd seen it too.

Neither one of them spoke and the ten seconds it took to

43

reach the place seemed much longer. Dan swung the plane out to one side and dipped the inside wing as they crested the ridge and they both peered down its far side where the animal had gone.

'I got him,' Rimmer said.

'Where?'

'Just going into the trees by that long slab of rock.' He paused. 'It's a coyote. Real big fella though.' He turned to Dan and gave him a consoling grin. Dan shrugged.

'Time we were headed home.'

'Yep. Looks like a job for the trap man.'

Dan put the Cessna into a final turn and the sun dazzled briefly through the windshield. Then he leveled the wings and set course for Helena.

And somewhere below, in a wild place that was still a young man's secret, the wolves heard the drone of the plane's engine fade and die.

5

Helen Ross hated New York. And she hated it even more when it was ninety-four degrees and the air was so humid you felt like a clam being baked in traffic fumes.

On her rare visits here, she always resolved to approach the place like a biologist, to observe the behavior of the curious species who trod its sidewalks and try to deduce why some actually seemed to enjoy its relentless glare and blare. But she always failed miserably. And after a customary moment of childish exhilaration upon arrival she would feel her face rearrange itself into a defensive cynical scowl.

The scowl was firmly in place right now. And sitting at the cramped table on what the restaurant manager had laughably called the *terrazzo*, by which he meant the dustily hedged display pen out on the street, Helen poured another glass of white wine, lit another cigarette and wondered why the hell her father always had to be late.

She searched for his face among the lunchtime crowds

along the sidewalk. Everyone looked impossibly cool and beautiful. Tanned young businessmen in linen suits, jackets tossed with studied nonchalance over one shoulder, chatted to women who all had perfect teeth, legs a mile long and probably several Ivy League degrees apiece. Helen hated them all.

The restaurant was her father's choice. It was in an area called SoHo which she had never been to and which, he said, was *the* chic place to live. It was full of art galleries and the kind of stores that sold just one or two exquisite items, exquisitely lit amid acres of space, patrolled by assistants who had stepped straight from the pages of *Vogue*. They were uniformly thin and disdainful and looked as if they might well refuse you admission simply on aesthetic grounds if you had the nerve to venture inside. Helen already didn't like SoHo. It was even written stupidly.

It wasn't that she was, by nature, mean-spirited. Quite the contrary, she lived her life normally at the danger end of generosity, prepared to give the benefit of even the most doubtful doubts. Today, however, several factors had conspired, along with the city and the weather, to put her out of sorts. Not least among them was that she was about to turn twenty-nine, which seemed to her a colossal, quaking milestone of an age. It was the same as thirty, only worse, because at thirty at least the crash had happened. Once you were thirty, you might as well be forty or fifty. Or dead. Because unless, by then, you had a life, you almost certainly never would.

Her birthday was tomorrow and, barring divine intervention, when it dawned she would still be unemployed, unmarried and unhappy.

It had become a ritual that her father took her out for a birthday lunch, no matter where either of them was living at the time, which was usually several hundred miles apart. It was inevitably Helen who did the traveling because her father was always so busy and still under the impression that as she spent most of her life in the back of beyond, coming to the city was a treat. By the time the event came around every summer, Helen had quite forgotten that it wasn't.

A month in advance, an air ticket would arrive in the mail, with details of how to get to some fashionable restaurant, and Helen would phone around and fix up to see friends and get excited. She loved her father and their birthday lunch was about the only time she ever got to see him nowadays.

Her parents had divorced when she was nineteen. Her sister Celia, two years younger, had just gone away to college and Helen was studying biology at the University of Minnesota. Both girls came home to Chicago for Thanksgiving, and after the meal, their parents pushed their plates aside and calmly announced that now their job of bringing up their children was done, they were going their separate ways.

The marriage, they revealed, had been wretched for years and they both had someone else with whom they would rather live. The family home would be sold, but the girls would, of course, have their own rooms at the two new homes that would replace it. It was all being done rationally and quite without rancor. Which, to Helen, made it infinitely worse.

It was devastating to discover that a household she had always assumed to be, if not exactly happy, then only averagely unhappy, should all along have secretly sheltered such misery. Her parents had always rowed and sulked and needled each other with countless petty vengeances; but this, Helen had assumed, was the kind of thing, surely, that everybody's parents did. And now it turned out that all these long years they had loathed each other and suffered each other's company only for the sake of their children.

Celia had behaved perfectly, as Celia always had and always would. She wept and went and hugged them both, which made them both weep, while Helen looked on in amazement.

47

Her father had reached out and tried to rope her in as well so they could all weep together in some ghastly communal act of absolution. She dashed his hand away and screamed, 'No!' And when he begged her, she screamed even louder, 'No! Fuck you! Fuck both of you!' and stormed out of the house.

At the time, it had seemed a reasonable response.

Her parents appeared to believe that not getting divorced earlier constituted a permanent, indestructible gift to their children, and that the illusion of having had a happy childhood was as good as the real thing. Their true gift was a starker and more durable thing by far.

For Helen had never since been able to rid herself of the notion that she was to blame for all the mutual pain her parents had endured. It couldn't be more clear. Had it not been for her (and Celia, of course, but since Celia didn't much go in for guilt, Helen had to generate enough for both of them), her parents could have 'gone their separate ways' years ago.

Their divorce confirmed her long-held suspicion that animals were infinitely more reliable than people. And, on reflection, it seemed no coincidence that around that time she had begun to develop a passionate interest in wolves. With their devotion and loyalty to each other, the way they cared for their young, they seemed superior to human beings in almost every respect.

Ten years had allowed her feelings about the divorce, if not to mellow, then at least to mingle with all the other doubts and disappointments with which Helen had since managed to fill her life. And except on rare, uncharitable days, when the world itself seemed swept by a bleak, recriminating wind, she was pleased her parents had at last found happiness.

Her mother had remarried immediately after the divorce came through and now lived a life of golf, bridge and apparently galvanic sex with a short, bald and hugely attentive real estate agent called Ralphie.

48

It turned out Ralphie had been her Someone Else for six years. Her father's Someone Else didn't see out six months and had since been superseded, over the years, by a string of Other Someone Elses, each younger than the last. His work as a financial consultant (what exactly that meant, Helen had never managed to figure out) had taken him from Chicago to Cincinnati to Houston and from there, last year, to New York City where, this summer, he had met Courtney Dasilva.

And this was the other main factor that had helped render Helen's mood today less than ebullient. Because this coming Christmas, Howard and Courtney Dasilva were to be married. Helen was about to meet her for the first time.

Her stepmother-to-be, so her father had told her on the phone last week when he'd broken the news, worked for one of the biggest banks in America. She was also, he said, a Stanford psychology major and the most drop-dead gorgeous human being he had ever laid eyes on.

'Daddy, it's wonderful. I'm so happy for you,' Helen had said, trying to mean it.

'Isn't it? Baby, I feel so . . . oh, God, so *alive*. I'm dying for you two to meet. You'll adore her.'

'Me too. I mean, meet her.'

'Is it okay if she joins us for lunch?'

'Of course! That'd be . . . wonderful.'

There was a short silence and she heard him clear his throat.

'Helen, there's just one thing I ought to tell you.' The voice was suddenly confiding, a little tentative.

'She's twenty-five years old.'

And there she was, a block away, locked onto his arm, her great mane of black hair bouncing and shining in the sun as she strode beside him. She was talking and laughing, a talent which Helen had never mastered, while her dad just beamed like a king and subtly scanned the faces of passing males for any trace of envy. He seemed to have lost about thirty pounds and had a different, shorter haircut. Courtney was wearing a no doubt hugely expensive black linen shift with a wide red belt. Her high-heeled sandals were red too and made her taller than he was, which was about five-ten. Her lips were painted to match the belt and the shoes.

Helen was wearing a dress too, her best in fact: a mud-colored cotton print dress, bought two summers ago at The Gap. She briefly considered crawling under the table.

Her father saw her and waved and pointed her out to Courtney and Courtney waved too. Helen quickly stubbed out her cigarette and as they arrived outside the dusty hedge of the *terrazzo*, she stood up and leaned over it to give her dad a hug and, in so doing, knocked the table so that the wine bottle toppled, emptied itself over the skirt of her dress, then rolled off and shattered on the floor.

'Whoa there!' said her father.

A waiter torpedoed to the rescue.

'Oh God, I'm sorry,' Helen wailed. 'I'm so stupid.'

'No you're not!' insisted Courtney and Helen almost snapped back, *What the hell do you know? I'll be stupid if I want.*

Her father and Courtney had to go around and in through the door of the restaurant to get out to the *terrazzo*, so Helen had a few moments, with some rather too intimate assistance from the torpedo-waiter, to dry her dress. He was on his knees in front of her, rubbing her thighs with his cloth. Everyone was staring.

'That's fine, thank you. That's fine, really. STOP!'

Mercifully, he did and disappeared and Helen stood there damply, shrugging and grinning like an imbecile at the people at the neighboring tables. Then she saw her father and cranked her face into what she hoped resembled a smile. He opened his arms and she let him hug her.

'How's my baby girl?'

'Wet. Hot and wet.' He kissed her. He was wearing cologne. Cologne! He stood back, pinning the tops of her arms so that he could inspect her.

'You look fabulous,' he lied.

Helen shrugged. She had never known how to react to his compliments. Nor anyone else's, come to that, not that she got that many. Her father turned to the lovely Courtney, who stood to one side, looking warmly on.

'Baby, I want you to meet Courtney Dasilva.'

Helen wondered if they were expected to kiss and was relieved when Courtney held out a tanned and elegant hand.

'Hi,' Helen said, shaking it. 'Great nails.'

They matched the belt, the shoes, the lips and, probably, the underwear too. Helen's own nails were like a trucker's, all stubby and chipped from working all summer in the kitchen at Moby Dick's.

'Why, thank yooou,' Courtney said. 'You poor thing, is your dress ruined? Howard, honey, we should go buy her another. There's a great store just around—'

'I'm fine. Really. Actually, I always do it, to cool off. And if we run out of wine I'll just wring some out.'

Howard-honey ordered champagne and after a couple of glasses Helen started to feel better. They talked about the weather, New York in the heat and about SoHo, where Courtney, of course, wanted to get a loft. Helen couldn't resist asking her with a straight face what she was going to keep in it, Christmas decorations or what? Courtney patiently explained that loft, in this context, meant a sort of large apartment.

The waiter reappeared and told Helen she wasn't allowed to smoke which, considering they were sitting *alfresco* on the *terrazzo* breathing traffic fumes, seemed less than logical. It was disappointing too because she had already noted Courtney's disapproval and wanted more. She had only just taken the habit up again after quitting for seven years and drew perverse pleasure out of being the only biologist she knew who smoked.

They ordered. Helen went first, opting for the fish terrine then a heavy-duty pasta number to follow. Then Courtney said all she wanted was an arugula salad with lemon juice, no dressing, and then her new, svelte father, who had already confided, with a proud pat of his stomach, that he went crack of every dawn to a gym where all kinds of famous people worked out, ordered the striped bass, grilled, no oil, no sauce, and nothing to start. Helen felt not just a klutz but a glutton now too.

While the waiter heaped a mortifying amount of spaghetti carbonara onto her plate, her father leaned nearer and said,

'Guess where we're getting married.'

Helen wanted to say Vegas maybe? Or Reno, or wherever it was you could get divorce papers out of a machine the very next day.

'I have absolutely no idea.'

'Barbados.'

He took Courtney's hand and Courtney smiled and kissed him on the cheek. Helen wanted to throw up.

'Wow,' she said instead. 'Barbados. Wow.'

'But only if you promise to come,' said Courtney, wagging a long red nail at her.

'Well, sure. I'm often cruising around down there, so why the hell not?' Helen saw a flicker of hurt in her father's eyes and told herself to stop. Be nice, for heaven's sake, just be nice.

'You pay, I come.' She beamed at them both and went on, 'No, seriously, I'd love to. I'm really happy for you both.'

Courtney seemed touched. She smiled and her eyes went all watery. She probably wasn't so bad, thought Helen, although why she should want to marry a man more than twice her age was a mystery. For heaven's sake, the guy wasn't even rich.

Courtney said, 'I know stepmothers are supposed to be like the wicked Queen in *Snow White* or something—'

'Right!' Helen cut in. 'But give it time, you can grow into it. I mean, hey, you've already got the nails.' She boomed with laughter. Courtney smiled uncertainly. Helen poured herself the last of the champagne, feeling her father's eyes on her. He and Courtney had already switched to mineral water. Klutz, glutton, why not drunken bitch too?

'You're a biologist,' Courtney said. Boy, she was trying hard.

'I wash dishes. Or used to wash dishes. I quit last week. Technically, at the moment I'm, as they say, "between jobs".'

'"Available."'

'That too.'

'And you're still up on Cape Cod?'

'Yup. Stranded on the Cape. Good a place as any to wash up.'

'Why do you always put yourself down so much?' her father said. He turned to Courtney. 'She's a brilliant wolf biologist. This PhD thesis she's finishing is ground-breaking stuff.'

'Groundbreaking!' Helen scoffed.

'It's true. Your supervisor said so.'

'He doesn't know a thing. Anyway, that was three years ago. By now the whole species has probably evolved into tree-dwelling herbivores.'

'Helen lived among them in Minnesota for a number of years.'

'"Lived among them." Dad, you make me sound like Mowgli or something.'

'Well, you did.'

'Not "lived among". You hardly ever got to see the damn things. I just did research, that's all.'

In fact, her father wasn't far wide of the mark. Whether her research was 'groundbreaking' was debatable, but it was

53

certainly one of the most intensive studies ever carried out into why some wolves kill livestock and others don't. It was about the age-old issue of nature versus nurture (which had always intrigued her) and seemed to suggest that cattle-killing was more learned than inherited.

Helen was damned, however, if she was going to perform a party piece and share any of this with Courtney, who now had her pretty chin propped on one hand, trying to look fascinated.

'Tell me what it was like. I mean, what did you do?'

Helen emptied her glass before answering, nonchalantly.

'Oh, you kind of follow them around. Follow their tracks, trap them, radio-collar them. Find out what they're eating.'

'How?'

'Basically you examine their shit.'

A woman at the next table gave her a look. Helen smiled sweetly at her and went on, louder.

'You pick up every piece of shit you find and poke around in it for hairs and bone and stuff and then analyze what it came from. When they've just been on a kill, the shit's all kind of black and runny which makes it more difficult to handle. And really, really smelly, you know? God, that kind of wolf shit, can it stink! It's better when they haven't eaten in awhile, you know, the turds are kind of firmer. Easier to pick up. With your fingers.'

Courtney nodded sagely. To her credit, she hadn't flinched once. Helen knew her father was giving her his hurt stare and she told herself off for being so childish. She'd had way too much to drink.

'Anyway, that's enough of that shit,' she said. 'Courtney, why don't you tell me about your shit? You're a banker right?'

'Uh-huh.'

'Got any money?'

Courtney smiled, easily. She had class, this girl.

'Only other people's,' she said. 'Unfortunately.'

'And you're a psychologist.'

'Well, I never practiced.'

'Practice makes perfect and you seem pretty damn perfect to me.'

'Helen . . .' Her father put a hand on her arm.

'What? What?' Helen looked at him, all innocence.

He was about to say something, then gave her a sad little smile instead. 'Who'd like dessert?'

Courtney said she needed to go to the bathroom, though after how little she'd consumed, Helen couldn't imagine why, except to touch up her nails maybe. When she had safely gone, Helen's father said,

'What's the matter with you, baby?'

'What do you mean?'

'There's no rule that says you have to hate her, you know.'

'Hate her? What on earth do you mean?'

He sighed and looked away. Helen felt her eyes suddenly fill up with tears. She reached out and put a hand on her father's arm.

'I'm sorry,' she said.

He took her hand in both of his and looked, with great concern, right into her eyes.

'Are you okay?' he said.

She sniffed and fought back the tears. God, she couldn't make yet another scene in this place, they'd have her committed.

'I'm fine.'

'I worry about you.'

'There's nothing to worry about. I'm fine.'

'Have you heard from Joel?'

She had prayed he wouldn't ask. Now she was sure to cry. She nodded, not trusting her voice for a moment, and took a deep breath.

'Yep. He wrote me.'

No, she wasn't going to cry. Joel was thousands of miles away and it was all over, anyway. And here came dear old Courtney, heading out toward them through the restaurant, smiling with new resolve and freshly glossed lips. Helen resolved to give her a break. She wasn't so bad. In fact there was something tough and sassy about her that Helen found appealing.

Who knows, she thought, someday they might even be friends.

6

Helen flew back to Boston that same evening. She had planned to stay the weekend with friends in New York but she called them from the airport and made some excuse about having to get home. In truth, she simply wanted to get out of the stifle and clamor of Manhattan.

The rest of the lunch had been better. Her father gave her a beautiful Italian leather purse that Courtney had helped him choose. Courtney had a present for her too, a bottle of perfume, and redeemed herself vastly in Helen's estimation by eating a giant slice of chocolate gateau.

To her father's obvious pleasure, the two women had even kissed goodbye, with Helen undertaking to be in Barbados for the wedding, though refusing flatly to be a bridesmaid. Not even Matron of Dishonor, she said.

It was getting on for ten o'clock by the time she'd driven down from Boston and swung east onto Route 6, which would take her all the way up the Cape to Wellfleet.

In her haste to get out of New York, she had forgotten it was a Friday night, when the going was always slowest. Most of the way it was bumper to bumper with weekenders and tourists, their car roofs stacked high with bicycles, boats and boogie boards. Helen longed for the fall when the place would empty out and even more for winter when the wind roared across the bay and you could walk the ocean shore for mile upon mile and the only living things you saw were birds.

The house she had lived in for the last two years was a rental on the bay side, a mile or so south of Wellfleet village. She still thought of it as Joel's house. To reach it you had to leave the highway and negotiate a labyrinth of narrow, wooded lanes, then a steep dirt trail that led down to the water.

Driving through the woods, away from the traffic at last, Helen turned off the air-conditioning of the ancient Volvo station wagon and wound down the window to get the warm smell of the woods. It was probably no cooler than New York, but the heat here was different, the air clean and there was nearly always a breeze.

The car bumped its way down the trail until she could see the black expanse of water below her through the trees and the three small houses she had to pass before the final descent to her own. She stopped beside her mailbox but there was nothing in it. He hadn't written for over a month.

There was a light still on at the Turners' who looked after Buzz when she was away. She could hear him barking a welcome as she pulled up outside. He was inside the screen door of the kitchen, wagging his tail and watching her. Mrs Turner appeared and let him out.

Buzz was a neutered scruff of uncertain parentage that Helen had got from a dog pound in Minneapolis, the Christmas before she met Joel. Which, except for her father and an ill-tempered hamster – one of the menagerie of pets

Helen had kept as a child – made it the longest relationship with a male she had ever had. His coat was shaggy now, which made nonsense of his name. When she'd first laid eyes on him, he'd had an all-over crew-cut to rid him of a frightful infestation. Covered in blotches of purple disinfectant, he'd been, without even a close rival, the ugliest dog in the pound. Helen simply had to have him.

'Hiya Trouble. How're you doing? Get down now, get down.'

Buzz jumped into the car and waited in the passenger seat while Helen thanked Mrs Turner and chatted for a minute or two about the horrors of summer in the city. Then she and Buzz drove down the last quarter of a mile of bumps and potholes to the house.

It was a big old place, clad in rotting white clapboard that rattled when the wind blew, as it often did, from the west. It stood on its own like a beached liner at the water's edge, overlooking a marshy inlet of the bay. It seemed yet more like a ship inside, its every wall, floor and ceiling paneled in narrow, darkly varnished tongue and groove. Upstairs, twin gable windows surveyed the bay like portholes. The bridge of the ship was a long bay window in the living room where at high water you could look out and imagine you were at last afloat and setting sail for the Massachusetts mainland.

Helen could happily stand at that window all day, if she let herself, watching the weather rearrange the shapes and colors of the bay like a restless, perfectionist painter. She loved the way the wind and clouds made traveling patterns through the marsh grass and how, when the tide slid out, the air filled with a salty, primordial tang and the mud flats hummed and scuttled with armies of fiddler crabs.

The time-switch light above the back door was on and a welcome-home party of bugs was whirring around it, casting shadows five times their size on the stoop. Helen dumped her

59

bag outside the door She would take a quick walk along the shore to give Buzz a run She was tired, but the kind of tired you get from sitting in a plane and a car too long. It was also an excuse to delay going inside. The house seemed so big and silent now that it was only she and the dog who lived there.

She walked down the curve of broken boardwalk and then down the steps to the strip of sand that ran beside the marsh grass all the way to the end of the inlet.

The breeze felt good on her face and she took the salt air deep into her lungs. Across the bay she could see the lights of some small boat heading out on the tide. A waning moon was looking for gaps among the clouds, and when it found one, lit a path across the water. Buzz ran ahead, stopping now and then to pee or sniff the line of fresh debris that the tide had left.

When Joel was around, they had taken this walk every night before turning in. And early on, in the days when they couldn't keep their hands off each other for five minutes, they would stop and find a hollow in the dunes and make love, while Buzz went off on his own, foraging for crabs in the marsh grass or chasing birds he'd sprung, then coming back sodden and making them shriek by shaking himself all over them.

About half a mile along the shore was the hull of an old yawl that someone had once perhaps intended to rebuild but that had now rotted beyond salvation. It had been hauled onto the shingle above the reach of all but the highest tides and lay tethered uselessly by moss-bearded ropes to two old trees. It was like the skeleton of some less ambitious Noah's ark, abandoned by all but rats, to whom Buzz paid nightly visits. He was in there now, growling and scuffling in the dark. Helen sat on a driftwood log and lit a cigarette.

She and Buzz had first come to the Cape on vacation in early

June the summer before last. Her sister had rented a house for the whole season, one of the million-dollar places set high above the water, with a stunning view over to Great Island and its own steep, wooden staircase down to the beach. She had invited Helen to stay.

Celia had married her college sweetheart, bright but boring Bryan, whose software company had just been bought out by a California computer giant for a mind-boggling amount of money. Even before that, they had been predictably happy and had produced, with no trouble at all, two perfect, blond children: a boy and a girl, Kyle and Carey. They lived in Boston, in a waterside development that, naturally, had won several design awards.

Helen had spent most of the previous five years roughing it in the wilds of Minnesota and it took her awhile to get used to the luxury. The 'guest suite' at Celia's Cape Cod rental even had its own jacuzzi. She had planned to stay for a week, then go back to Minneapolis to work on her thesis, for which her supervisor was already nagging. But the week became a fortnight, then the fortnight a month.

Bryan would drive down each weekend from Boston to join them and once, for a few days, their mother and Ralphie came to stay, managing to break one of the beds. The rest of the time it was just Helen, Celia and the children. They got on well and it was good to have time to get to know the kids, though her sister remained the enigma she always had been.

Nothing seemed to faze Celia. Not even Buzz eating her best straw hat. Her clothes were always clean and pressed, her figure trim, her hair washed and neatly bobbed. On those rare occasions when Kyle or Carey howled or threw a tantrum, she would just smile and soothe and hug them until they felt better. She did charity work, played elegant tennis and cooked like a dream. She could lay on an impromptu banquet for ten at half an hour's notice. She never had headaches or sleepless nights or got grouchy with her period and even in the privacy of her own bathroom, Helen surmised, seldom, if ever, broke wind.

Helen had long ago discovered there was little fun to be had in trying to shock her sister. It was impossible and anyway they were grown-ups now and you didn't do that to someone who washed your underwear and brought you a cup of coffee in bed every morning. They talked to each other a lot, mainly about nothing, though just occasionally Helen would try to find out what Celia felt about the important things in life, or at least what she herself considered important.

One night after supper, when Bryan wasn't there and the kids were in bed, Helen asked her about their parents' divorce. They were sitting at the table under the trees, finishing the wine which Helen, as usual, had drunk most of, and watching the sun sink beyond the island into the black band of the Massachusetts coast. She wanted to know if the divorce had been as traumatic for Celia as it had been for her.

Celia shrugged. 'Oh, I guess I always felt it was for the best.'

'But doesn't it ever make you angry?'

'No. That's just the way they were. They wanted to stay together till we were old enough not to be too upset by it.'

'And you weren't "too upset" by it?' Helen asked incredulously.

'Oh sure. I was mad at them for awhile. But you can't let these things get to you. It's their life after all.'

Helen had persisted, trying to find some crack in what she thought might only be a protective veneer, but she couldn't. Maybe it was true that this same event that had torn her own guts apart and sent her, in her love life at least, spiraling almost out of control for years, had left her sister untouched. Whatever, there was no point talking about it. But how strange, she thought, for two people with the same genes to be so different. Perhaps one of them had been swapped at birth.

62

After a month of swimming, reading and playing with Kyle and Carey on the beach, Helen had grown restless. A friend of hers in Minneapolis had given her the number of a friend, called Bob, who was working at the Marine Biological Laboratory at Woods Hole, farther down the Cape, and one evening Helen called him.

He sounded nice and asked her if she would like to come to a supper party he was holding that weekend. He and a few friends were going to be watching some 'amazing footage' that one of the Woods Hole guys had shot inside the womb of a sand tiger shark. It wasn't exactly Helen's idea of a great night out but what the hell, she thought, why not?

She noticed Joel Latimer as soon as she walked in.

He looked like one of those Californian surfbums from the sixties, tall and thin and tanned with a mop of sunbleached blond hair. He caught her staring at him while Bob was telling her about Woods Hole and he gave her such a direct smile she nearly spilled her wine.

It was a help-yourself-in-the-kitchen kind of dinner and Helen found herself at the vegetarian lasagne alongside him.

'So you're the woman who runs with the wolves,' he said.

'Actually it's more of a flat-footed shuffle.'

He laughed. He had the bluest eyes and the whitest teeth she'd ever seen. She felt something contract in her stomach and told herself not to be ridiculous. He wasn't even her type, though quite what was her type she'd never been quite sure. He helped her to some salad.

'You're on vacation here?'

'Yes, I'm staying with my sister. Up at Wellfleet.'

'Then we're neighbors.'

Joel was from North Carolina and she could hear it in his accent. His father ran a fishing business. He told her he was doing a PhD on horseshoe crabs, which he said weren't really crabs at all, but arachnids, distant cousins of the spider. They were a kind of living fossil, ancient even when dinosaurs roamed the earth; they had been around for about four hundred million years without changing.

'Sounds like my supervisor,' she said. He laughed. God, she felt witty. Normally in the presence of good-looking men she either lost the power of speech or babbled like a loon. She asked him what the crabs looked like.

'You know those helmets the Nazis wore? Well, they're like that, only brown. And inside it's kind of like a scorpion.'

'Definitely like my supervisor.'

'And it has this spiked tail sticking out the back.'

'He keeps his tucked away.'

He told her that horseshoe blood had all kinds of important medical applications, was even used to diagnose and treat cancer. But they were a species under pressure and one of the problems here on the Cape was that eel fishermen killed them for bait. His research was to find out how serious an impact this was having on the local horseshoe populations. He lived in a big old rented place, just south of Wellfleet. It looked like a ship, he said. She must come by and visit.

They took their food off to a corner and he told her who the other guests were and about the video they were going to see. She asked him how you got to shoot a movie inside the womb of a shark.

'With great difficulty.'

'I guess you have to find a really big shark—'

'Or a really small cameraman.'

'Right. Who's also a gynecologist.'

Later, watching it, sitting crammed on the couch between Joel and someone else, she wondered if he was as aware of the press of their bodies as she was. His jeans were torn and she couldn't stop herself sneaking looks at the patch of tanned thigh that showed through.

The guy who'd shot the video (who was of normal size)

talked them through it, explaining that when a female sand tiger has mated, several fertilized egg capsules form in two separate wombs, developing rapidly into embryo sharks complete with teeth. In each womb, one shark fetus emerges as the strongest and then sets about murdering and devouring its brothers and sisters. Only these two are born, already well versed in the art of killing.

As he talked, the tiny endoscope camera traveled the glutinous pink caves and tunnels of the mother shark, like a Steadicam in a cheap horror movie. You could see a swilling soup of dead baby sharks but no sign of the infant from hell who'd killed them all. Then, at the far end of the womb, a yellow eye suddenly surfaced in the soup, looking right at the camera and a room full of case-hardened biologists screamed in unison. In the laughter that followed, Helen was embarrassed to find she had grabbed hold of Joel's arm. She quickly let it go.

Afterward, Bob took her away to meet some other people and every so often she would glance across the room at Joel. And even though he was deep in conversation, he would see her and smile. When they said goodbye, he asked if she would like to meet some horseshoe crabs and, far too promptly, she said she would. He said how about tomorrow and she said fine.

Within a week they were lovers and a week later Joel asked her to come and live with him. He said he felt he had known her forever, that they were 'soul mates', that if she moved in, they could spend the winter side by side, writing their theses. Helen had never heard anything so romantic in all her life. But men weren't supposed to go around making such rash offers of commitment. So she said no, it was out of the question, ridiculous in fact; and the next morning moved in.

It was as close to shocking Celia as she had ever come.

'You're going to *live* with him?' she said, watching her pack.

'Yep.'

'After knowing him only two weeks?'

'Sister, if a girl can't find Mr Right, sometimes she's got to settle for Mr Right Now.'

Since her parents' divorce, she had stumbled from one bad affair to the next. Not that she'd been exactly promiscuous. Even if she'd wanted to be, that would have been tricky, living out in the wilds most of the year. It was just that she seemed to have this uncanny knack of picking the most unsuitable men available. There were exceptions, but mainly they were men that other women saw coming a hundred miles away, who had jerk or cheat or bastard written in neon letters on their foreheads, men she didn't like or lust after but still somehow ended up with.

Quite why she chose so badly, Helen had never been able to figure out. Perhaps she set her sights low because, deep down, she was sure no good man could ever possibly see anything in her. Not that the bad ones seemed to see much either, for it was rarely Helen who ended the affair, except when she sensed she was about to be dumped and managed to beat him to it.

Normally, she stuck in there, even with the worst of them, trying to make it work, striving desperately for their approval, until they drifted off or started cheating on her or announced over a last, lousy dinner in a cheap restaurant, trying to break it gently, saying maybe, honey, we should call it a day.

She'd never lived permanently with any of them. And so when Joel made his proposal, she went into a spin of panic. For weeks, she would wake up in the middle of the night with her heart pounding and an absolute certainty roaring in her head that tomorrow this gentle, golden man who lay warm and softly snoring beside her would tell her it had all been a mistake and would she please pack her bags, take her dog and get the hell out of his life.

But it didn't happen. And after awhile she relaxed. And soon it seemed as if they weren't even separate people. She had read about such things in books but never believed it could be so. But it was. They often knew each other's thoughts without need of words. They could spend a whole night talking or a whole day silent.

Normally when people asked her about her work she would give a few jokey answers, putting it down, and would then switch the conversation around by asking questions of her own. Who could possibly be interested in what she did? But with Joel, it was different. You couldn't deflect him. She found herself telling him more about her work than she had ever told anyone and he made her realize that her supervisor was right: she was good; hell, she was brilliant.

The first time he told her he loved her, she didn't know how to react. She just murmured and kissed him and the moment passed. She couldn't bring herself to say it back, although it was true. Maybe he was the kind of man who said it to every woman he slept with. But that wasn't all that restrained her. There seemed something fearfully final about saying it back, like joining two ends of a string to make a circle; she would be completing something. Ending it.

But as fall gave way to winter and the Cape cleared of tourists and its skies of the great flocks of migrating birds, Helen found herself somehow clearing too. Free of doubt and self-consciousness, she came to accept what she and Joel had found. He loved her and she must therefore be lovable. He told her she was beautiful and for the first time in her life she truly felt she was. And though surely he must know it, why should she not now tell him that she loved him in return? So the second time he said it, she did.

They moved the long kitchen table into the living room and arranged it by the big bay window, setting up their laptops and piling it high with papers. But little work got done. They talked too much or gazed too long at the wind scything spume from the gray waves of the bay. There was a wood stove which they kept going all the time and each day they took Buzz for long walks by the water's edge in search of driftwood.

Joel had a way with animals and the hitherto unruly Buzz was soon his devoted slave, sitting and staying to command and fetching sticks thrown seemingly impossible distances out into the surf. Helen watched in mounting panic while the poor dog got tossed and swamped and dragged under. She was convinced he would drown. But Joel just laughed. And soon, a bedraggled head would bob up somewhere in the foam, teeth clenched on the stick that, miraculously, he always managed to find and he would struggle back with it and drop it at Joel's feet, begging for more.

Joel had just discovered opera, which Helen had always claimed to hate. She groaned every time he put on a disc and even more when he sang along. Then he caught her one day humming something from *Tosca* in the bathtub and she was forced to admit that some of it was bearable. Not as good as Sheryl Crow, but not bad.

There was a bookcase stuffed by the landlords, inexplicably, with musty translations of Russian classics, books Joel said he had always meant to read but had never gotten round to. He started with Dostoevsky and moved rapidly on through Pasternak and Tolstoy to Chekhov, whom he discovered he liked best of all.

He liked to cook and in the evenings, as he did so, he would tell her what was happening in the story, while she sat smiling and watched him work. They ate by the fire and afterward they would curl up together on the couch and read or talk about places they knew or wanted to know.

He told her that when he was a kid, his father used to take all the kids crabbing at night. They'd row out into the bay, drop the pots, then come back and light a fire on the beach. Then they'd row out again and haul up the pots and his father would just empty them into the boat.

'It was only a little rowboat and we were all in swimsuits and no shoes or anything. And these crabs and lobsters were scuttling around in the dark over our feet in the bottom of the boat. God, we used to shriek.'

Once, he said, they'd pulled up a pot and found a plastic bag with a bottle of whiskey in it and a note saying, *Thanks for the lobster!* Some people on a yacht must have left it, he said.

She loved listening to his stories. Later they would make love, while the clapboard rattled and the salt wind moaned in the eaves.

That winter, for the first time in years, snow fell heavily and stayed for the best part of a month. It was so cold that the bay froze over. From the frosted window, they watched it stretching away like tundra to a gray horizon. Joel said they were like Zhivago and Lara, marooned in their palace of ice. All they needed, he said, were some of her Minnesota wolves to howl for them at night.

The spring and summer were the happiest of Helen's life. They borrowed a dinghy and Joel taught her how to sail. Sometimes at night they would hike through the woods to a freshwater pond and swim naked. Their bodies undulated pale as muslin in the black water, still warm from the sun. They would hold each other and listen to the frogs and the muted roar of the ocean beyond the dunes.

Instead of doing her own work Helen helped with his. Wolves now seemed to belong to a distant age, some desolate place in her past. This was her life now, this place with its teeming shores and vivid skies and air so full of salt and ozone it scoured the inside of your skull.

That second fall, at last, she got down to work on her thesis. Just as he'd promised a year ago, they worked side by side in the big bay window. Sometimes they would spend a whole day discussing a problem one of them had run into. On other days they hardly spoke. Joel would go out to the kitchen and make tea and bring it to her at her desk and kiss the top of her head while she worked and she would kiss his hand and smile and go on with her work without a word being uttered.

Then, subtly at first, things began to change. Joel grew quieter and corrected her sometimes when she was talking. He would criticize her for little things, how she'd left something unwashed in the sink or forgotten to turn off a light. It didn't bother her too much, but she took note and tried not to make the same mistakes again.

They had long disagreed about the issue that lay at the heart of Helen's research: nature versus nurture. Joel believed the actions of any living creature were almost entirely conditioned by its genes, while Helen thought learning and circumstance often counted just as much. They had debated the subject endlessly and quite amicably. But now when it arose, Joel would get impatient and one evening he shouted at her and said she was stupid. He later apologized and Helen made light of it. But she felt shocked and hurt for days.

They went to Celia's for Christmas and Joel and Bryan got into an argument about a new catastrophe that was unfolding in Central Africa. Every TV news program was showing footage of hundreds of thousands of starving refugees, fleeing from tribal butchery through knee-deep mud and filth. A carload of American aid workers had been ambushed and hacked to death with machetes. And watching the report from his leather recliner, in the big living room, Bryan said casually that he didn't understand why we bothered.

'What do you mean?' Joel said.

Helen caught the tone of his voice from the hallway. She'd been reading the children a bedtime story and had just kissed them goodnight. Carey had asked her if she and Joel were

70

going to get married and have babies and Helen had made a joke and avoided giving a proper answer.

Bryan said, 'Well, it's none of our business, is it?'

'So, what, we just let them all die?'

'These guys have been killing each other for centuries, Joel.'

'Does that make it okay?'

'No. But it has nothing to do with us. In fact, I think it's kind of patronizing for the West to get involved at all. You know, like we're the civilized ones. We don't even understand why these people are killing each other in the first place. And if you don't understand it, you just end up making things worse.'

'How's that?'

Helen was hovering in the doorway. Celia came out of the kitchen and made a face at her as she went past into the living room. She asked breezily if anyone wanted coffee, which meant, *Okay fellas, merry Christmas, that's enough.* Both men declined.

'We always end up backing the wrong side,' Bryan said. Helen could see Joel nodding, as if considering what Bryan had said. He didn't say a word and had an icy look in his eyes that she had never seen before. The TV news moved onto a story about a fifteen-foot python that had been found under an old couple's house in Georgia. It had been living there happily for years and was only discovered after someone thought how remarkable it was that so many of the neighborhood's dogs had gone missing.

Bryan seemed a little disconcerted by Joel's silence.

'So, what do you think?' he asked.

Joel looked at him for a moment then said quietly,

'I think you're an idiot.'

The holiday never quite recovered.

They came back to the Cape and for awhile things seemed

71

more or less normal. But, as the new year settled in, Helen became aware of a growing restlessness in him. She would look up from her computer and catch him staring into space. She could tell that little things she did irritated him, like when she tapped her nails on the keyboard while thinking something through.

Soon she felt that everything she did was being silently judged and found wanting. He would suddenly get up and snatch his coat and say he was going for a walk and Helen would sit there, wondering what she had done and blaming herself. She would watch him from the window as he strode away along the shore, shoulders hunched against the wind, ignoring the sticks that Buzz dropped for him to throw, until the dog got the message that the game was a thing of the past.

In bed one night, staring at the dark ceiling, Joel said he wanted to do something worthwhile with his life.

'You don't think what you're doing at the moment is worthwhile?' she said. He gave her a look and she quickly added, 'I don't mean, you know, *us*. I mean your work.'

She meant both actually, but he took her at her word and said, sure, of course it was worthwhile, in its own way.

'But saving a few crabs isn't really going to change things. I mean, the oceans are dying, the whole planet's being destroyed. Helen, all over the world people are starving and slaughtering each other and actually, when you think about it, what the hell am I doing? What the hell do a few crabs mean alongside all of that? It's like fiddling while Rome burns.'

She suddenly felt very cold. He made love to her, but it was different, as if he'd already gone.

One night in late April, he told her over supper that he had applied to a foreign aid charity to go and work for them in Africa. They wanted to interview him. Helen tried not to look hurt.

'Oh,' she said. 'That's great.'

'Yeah. Well, you know. It's just an interview.'

He took another mouthful. He wouldn't look her in the eyes. There was a pause in which Helen's head screamed inside with accusation. She tried to find a tone of voice that wouldn't show it.

'So, do they have starving crabs in Africa?' The words just slipped out, she couldn't help it. He looked at her. It was the first bitchy thing she'd ever said to him. She went on, trying to make it seem like a real question, 'I mean, they need biology graduates, do they?'

'I think the two years of med school I did maybe impresses them more,' he said coldly.

There was another long silence. He started to stack the plates.

'You didn't mention you were applying.'

'I wasn't sure I wanted it.'

'Oh.'

'I mean, I'm not even sure now.'

But she could tell he was. The following week he flew to Washington for the interview and they called the next day to say they wanted him to start in June. He asked Helen what she thought he should do and she told him what he wanted to hear. He should take it. Of course he should take it.

It was a long while before they could talk about it, or about anything else, come to that. Outside the air was growing warm. You could hear the call of piping plovers and see sanderlings again on the shore, playing their tireless tag with the waves. But, in the house, winter endured. They were clumsy with each other now, colliding in the cramped kitchen, whereas once they had known each other's moves, effortlessly, like dancers. A cool politeness had settled, under which Joel stifled his guilt and she her anger.

Reason told her she had no cause. God, it wasn't as if they were married or had even discussed it as a possibility. Why shouldn't he go and do something *worthwhile* with his life? It was fine. More, it was laudable. He was a 'disperser', that was all. It was 'in his nature'.

Then anger gave way and creeping upon her came that same old sense that, yet again, she had failed. But she knew it was worse, for this time she had not just sought to please but had opened every corner of herself. There was no part of her he didn't know, nothing with which she could console herself and say, had he but seen this in me, then surely he never would or could have gone.

She had given all and still been found wanting.

In May, when the water warms along the Cape, the horse-shoe crabs return in droves from their deep winter haunts. And when the sun and the moon align and the highest tides of the year flood in, they swarm to the shallows to breed.

At this time, for the last two years, Joel had tagged several hundred of them, pressing numbered stainless-steel tacks into the rear of their shells. The idea was to see how many returned. Now, just a fortnight before he was due to leave for Africa, he planned to do it one last time.

Tentatively, for that was how things now were between them, he asked if Helen would like to come along, as she had last year, to help. To show him how little (or how much) his departure bothered her, she had taken a job as a kitchen hand at Moby Dick's, a seafood place out on the highway. But it was her night off. Fine, she said, if he needed her help, she didn't mind coming.

It was a cool, cloudless night with all but the brightest stars doused by a full moon, around which there hung a ring of umbral haze. Later, Helen heard such a ring was considered by some to be an omen of disaster.

They loaded the tagging gear into two large packs and, leaving Buzz in the house, set off in their waders along the strip of sand that traced the lip of the estuary. The sand glowed pale as bone dust and although they walked apart, the angle of the moon made their shadows merge.

They could see from a long way off that the crabs had come. Along the shore's edge the water seethed and as they drew nearer they saw hundreds of domed and barnacled shells jostling in the shallows. The water swirled around them in galaxies of phosphorescent foam.

From the previous year Helen knew what to do. With barely a word, they took what they needed from their packs and got to work. Joel waded in among the crabs, putting on a pair of tough rubber gauntlets. One by one, he carefully hoisted the crabs and held them to the beam of the flashlight that hung on a cord around his neck. The crabs bucked and struggled in his hands, the hinged rear part of their shells thrashing as they tried to stab him with their dagger-tails. When he found one that was tagged, he called out the number and Helen, beside him, noted it down on a pad. With those that weren't tagged, he called out their sex and size and she duly recorded them and handed him tags to clip to their shells.

Occasionally, as they worked Joel would point something out and explain what was going on. How the males, sometimes as many as a dozen of them, were fighting to latch onto a single female, but how only one would succeed. He pointed the flashlight at a female for Helen to see. The crab had dug herself a shallow nest in the sand, as near to the water's edge as she dared. You could see the eggs streaming from her, thousands of them in shiny gray-green clusters and the male, hooked to her, spreading his sperm on them, while the other males fought to do the same, oblivious to the humans who stood among them.

Helen started to ask him something but suddenly heard her voice crack and she stopped in mid-sentence and realized that her eyes were running with tears. Last year she had watched

75

this same scene in wonder. But the frenzy, the blind, primal ferocity of this ancient creature's will to survive, to propel its genes across the centuries, for millions and millions of years, the immense, implacable power of it, now struck her with a fearful sadness.

Joel saw her face contort and splashed toward her and took her in his arms. And she clung to him and sobbed into his chest like a desolate child.

'What?' he said, stroking a tangle of hair from her face. 'What is it?'

'I don't know.'

'Tell me.'

'I don't know.'

'It's only a year, Helen. It'll go so fast. I'll come back and this time next year we can be here again. Tagging crabs together.'

'Don't joke.'

'I'm not. I mean it. I promise.'

She looked up at him and thought she saw a hint of tears in his eyes too.

'I love you,' she said.

'I love you too.'

She would never forget how he looked at that moment. Like a frail ghost and suddenly somehow a total stranger. Then he smiled and the image was gone. And he kissed her, while the horseshoes churned and clattered heedlessly around them, their black backs glistening at the moon.

He had been gone, now, for nearly two months.

Helen finished her cigarette and called Buzz. He had been in the ark nosing for rats long enough and she was getting cold. She called him and started to walk back along the shore. Above her, high in the woods, an owl was uttering the same plaintive message over and over again.

She picked up her bag outside the back door. The bug party around the outside light was still going strong. Buzz barked at them a couple of times and she told him to hush and nudged him through the screen door into the kitchen.

She didn't turn on the lights. There was too much of Joel everywhere you looked. In a vain attempt to convince her he was coming back, he had left a lot of his belongings. Books, a pair of boots, the Discman with its state of the art speakers, all his opera CDs. Since he had gone, she hadn't trusted herself to listen to music of any kind.

The red light on the answering machine showed there were three messages. She listened to them in the dark, looking out at the path of moonlight on the bay. One was from her father, hoping she'd gotten home safely and saying he was sure that she and Courtney were going to be friends. The second was from Celia, just to say hi. And the third was from her old wolf-buddy Dan Prior.

They'd had the briefest of flings one summer when they were tracking together in northern Minnesota. He'd been one of the rare exceptions to the catalog of jerks she normally dated, but it had still been a mistake. They were cut out to be friends, not lovers. And like all the best men, Dan was happily married. Worse still, Helen knew – and liked – his wife and daughter.

They hadn't talked in about three years and it was good to hear his voice on the machine. He said he had a job for her, in Montana. Would she please give him a call.

Helen looked at her watch. It was a quarter to one. And she remembered that it was her birthday.

7

Dan Prior stood sipping his third cup of coffee, apparently unaware of the giant Alaskan brown bear that towered right behind him. Both man and bear were looking toward the gate where the first disgruntled passengers from Salt Lake City were emerging. The flight had been delayed and Dan had already been there an hour, which wasn't as long as the bear, who'd been shot on Friday, 13 May 1977, stuffed and set here on his hind legs to scare all visitors to Great Falls.

Dan had spent most of the weekend cleaning up the cabin in which Helen would be living and trying to fix the carburetor of the old Toyota pickup he'd found for her to use. He hoped she wasn't going to be too shocked by the state of either. The cabin belonged to the Forest Service and stood beside a small lake way up in the wilderness above Hope. No one had spent more than a night or two there for several years and, from the look of it, birds, insects and assorted small rodents had been throwing regular all-night parties.

The pickup belonged to Bill Rimmer's brother who kept a hospice for terminally ill vehicles in his backyard. Even with a new carburetor, its chances of seeing out the winter were slim. He would need to find her a snowmobile too.

Dan scanned the faces coming through the gate and wondered if she still looked the same. He'd dug out a photograph the other night, taken five years ago in northern Minnesota, when they were working together. She was sitting in the front of a canoe, looking over her shoulder at him and giving him one of those slow, sly smiles of hers. Her eyes were a clear golden brown and slightly angled, so that she seemed almost elfin. She was wearing that old white T-shirt with the sleeves cut off and *Danger: Alpha Female* in red letters on the back. Her long brown hair had gone blond in the sun and she was wearing it the way he'd always liked best, tied up in a pony-tail, so you could see the tanned nape of her neck. Dan had forgotten how stunning she was and sat staring at the picture for a long time.

What had happened between them didn't really qualify as an affair. Just one night at the end of a long summer's field-work, the kind of thing that could happen when two people worked together out in the wild, living in such intimate conditions that it seemed almost perverse not to go that final step.

Dan had always been attracted to her, more so, he knew, than she had ever been to him. It wasn't just her looks. He loved her quick wit, that spiky sense of humor she used to deflect attention from something vulnerable. She mainly used it to mock herself. She also happened to be the smartest wolf biologist he'd ever worked with.

At the time he'd been running a wolf research program at the university and Helen was one of the volunteer workers. He'd taught her how to trap and in no time at all she was better at it than he was.

That one night, camping by a lake under a star-riddled sky,

79

was the only occasion Dan had been unfaithful to Mary since they'd been married. He'd made the mistake of telling that to Helen the next day and that was the end of it. In hindsight, perhaps he should have casually conveyed that he did that kind of thing all the time. It had taken him a fair while to get over her, but in the end he had and they'd managed to remain friends and colleagues until he left to take up another post.

Now, watching for her face in the crowd, he wondered if there might be a chance of rekindling things, at the same time telling himself not to be so damn stupid.

Then he saw her.

She was coming out of the gate, blocked behind a harassed woman with two small children, both bawling their eyes out. Helen saw him right away and waved. She was wearing blue jeans and a baggy beige army shirt. The only real change was the hair which was cut short, like a boy's. She stayed blocked by the bawling kids all the way to where Dan stood waiting.

'What did you do to them?' he asked.

Helen shrugged. 'I said look at that guy over there by the bear and they just started to cry.'

He opened his arms and they gave each other a hug.

'Welcome to Montana.'

'Thank you, sir.' She leaned back, still holding on to him, and inspected him.

'You're looking okay, Prior. Power and success don't seem to have changed you. I thought you'd be wearing a suit.'

'I dressed down for the occasion.'

'But no cowboy hat yet.'

'You know, I've got two of them at home and now and again I try one on and look in the mirror and see this funny guy looking back at me.'

She laughed loudly. 'It's good to see you.'

'It's good to see you too, Helen. What happened to your hair?'

80

'Don't. I did it last week. Big mistake. You're supposed to say how nice it looks, Prior.'

'It could grow on me.'

'I wish it would on me.'

They went down the escalator to the baggage claim area and stood chatting by the carousel while they waited. He asked her if she'd ever been out here before and she said only once, when she was a kid. They'd come on a vacation to Glacier Park and her sister had gotten food poisoning and spent the whole week in bed.

Helen's bags appeared on the belt, two big duffel bags and a battered trunk which weighed about a ton and which she said had once belonged to her grandfather. They loaded them on a cart.

'Is that it?' Dan asked. She gave him a guilty look.

'Well. Almost.'

An airline official was making his way toward them with a crate that was barking loudly. Helen bent down and opened the caged door and one of the oddest-looking dogs Dan had ever laid eyes on came out and started washing Helen's face.

'This is Buzz.'

'Hi, Buzz. Funny, Helen, but on the phone I don't recall you mentioning Buzz.'

'I know. Sorry. Listen, I'll have him put down immediately.'

'I've got a gun in the car.'

'Fine. Let's go do it.'

Buzz was giving Dan a quizzical look.

'Go on, admit it,' Helen said. 'Isn't he cute?'

'Yeah, well. Let's hope that wolf thinks so.'

When she stepped outside the terminal, the heat hit her in a wave. The temperature gauge in Dan's car said it was in the low nineties but it wasn't humid and Helen felt embraced by it. She kept the window down as they headed out onto the interstate and pointed south toward Helena. She was dying for a cigarette but too ashamed to light one up in front of Dan. Instead she made do with the smell of sun-baked grass that carried on a hot wind from the plains. Buzz sat blinking and licking at it with his head poked out of the window behind her head.

'You see, we even named a town for you,' Dan said.

'You mean Hope?'

'We all live in hope, Helen.'

'Funny how they never named these places Despair or Misery.'

'My dad grew up in a place in western Pennsylvania called Panic.'

'You're kidding.'

'I swear. And just down the road was a place called Desire.'

'Where the streetcars come from.'

He laughed. He'd always laughed at her clunky jokes.

'My mom always used to say, never marry a man out of Panic, but my old man claimed the church where they got hitched was technically nearer the other place so in fact she'd married him out of Desire.'

'Are they still together?'

'You bet. They get more in love every year.'

'That's nice.'

'Yep. It is.'

'And how's Mary?'

'She's fine. We got divorced two years ago.'

'Oh, Dan, I'm sorry.'

'Yeah, well. I'm not and she sure isn't. And Ginny's okay, thank the Lord. She's fourteen now. Mary's still living in Helena, so it all kind of works out, you know, Ginny gets to spend time with us both.'

'That's good.'

'Yeah.'

82

There was a pause and she knew what was coming.

'How about you? I mean, have you . . .'

'Don't be shy, Prior. You mean how's my love life?'

'No. Okay, yeah.'

'Well, let me see. We've been together, what, just over two years now.'

'Really? That's great. Tell me about him.'

'Well. He's got long, sandy-colored hair, brown eyes, does-n't say a whole lot. And he's got this thing about sticking his head out of car windows and thwacking the back of your legs with his tail.'

Dan smiled.

'No, I was living with a guy for a couple of years on the Cape. But he's, well, kind of gone off somewhere. I guess you'd say it's on hold.'

She swallowed and looked away out of the window. There were mountains in the distance. Dan, bless his heart, seemed to sense he was on fragile ground and changed the subject. He started to fill her in on all that had happened since the wolf had first shown his face in Hope almost a month ago and soon had her laughing again with his account of the funeral Buck Calder had staged for Prince, the Hero of all Labradors.

Calder had organized a preacher to come from Great Falls and do the honors, in front of family, friends and, of course, the press and TV cameras. The tombstone was made of black marble and had probably cost the best part of five hundred dollars. Instead of Dan's idea for the epitaph, which Helen liked a lot, they had gone with something more resonant:

Here lies Prince
Who kept the wolf from the door
And laid down his life for a child.
Good Dog!

Since then, Dan said, things had quieted down some. Every so often he would get a call from a reporter asking if he had located the wolf yet and he would play the whole thing down, giving the impression that it was all under control, that they were monitoring the situation constantly and that the fact that this wolf hadn't been seen again almost certainly meant he was a lone disperser and was by now probably a hundred or more miles away, which Dan wanted to believe but didn't. Just two days ago a Forest Service ranger hiking the backcountry due west of Hope had reported finding tracks.

At the office he introduced Helen to Donna, who gave her a big welcome and said it was great that at long last Dan had seen sense and hired a woman.

'And this is Fred,' Dan said, patting the top of the glass case. 'The only one who does any work around here.'

A few minutes later, Helen bumped into Donna having a quiet cigarette in the restroom and gratefully lit one herself. One of life's lesser-known truths, Donna confided, was that only the best kind of women smoked – and only the worst kind of men.

Dan sent out for sandwiches and the two of them adjourned to his office where they spent the next couple of hours, with the help of maps and charts and photographs, going through what Helen would be doing once she got to Hope.

They had flown the backcountry three times now, Dan said, and hadn't picked up so much as a hint of radio signal. Whatever was out there almost certainly wasn't collared, so Helen's job was to trap, fit collars and then track to find out what was going on. Bill Rimmer, who was due back any moment from his vacation, had volunteered to help her set the traps.

If there turned out to be a whole pack, Helen was to find out its size and range, what it was preying on, all the usual

84

stuff, Dan said. As well as that, of course, the important thing was to try to build a rapport with the local ranchers.

Finally, he sat up and put on a mock official voice while he went through the terms of her employment. The only way he was allowed to hire her, he explained, was on what was known as a 'temporary' basis. That meant she was employed for a fixed term of a hundred and eighty days, which he could then renew. She was to be paid a thousand dollars a month, no benefits.

'No health insurance, disability or retirement pay, no rehire entitlement. Basically, being temporary means you don't exist in the federal system. You're invisible. We have temporary people who've been working for us for years.'

'Do I get to have a scarlet letter T painted on my forehead?'

'That's entirely optional, Miss Ross.'

'Do I get a truck or is it just a bicycle?'

He laughed. 'I'll show you. Want to take a drive out there?'

'To Hope?'

'Sure. Not right up to the cabin. We can do that tomorrow. But I thought maybe you'd like to have a look at the town, then maybe we could go get something to eat. If you're not too tired.'

'Sounds good.'

As they went out to the parking lot, Dan said they could either check her into a hotel for the night or she could stay at his place. Ginny was at her mother's, he said, so Helen could have her room.

'Are you sure? That'd be great. Thank you.'

'And this is what you've really been waiting to see.'

He stopped by the old Toyota pickup. In the sunshine it didn't look too bad. He'd taken it through the car wash and discovered that the paintwork when cleaned was more or less the same color as rust, which was handy. The chrome was even trying to shine. He slapped the hood affectionately and the wing mirror fell off. Helen laughed.

'This is mine?'

Dan bent down and picked up the mirror and handed it to her.

'Every last bit of it. In fact it has to be. All federal vehicles have to be of US manufacture and I don't have one available. I can only give you mileage. Thirty-one cents a mile.'

'Gee, Prior, you sure know how to spoil a gal.'

She drove. The steering felt like dancing on rollerskates, you had to plan each turn well in advance to have any chance of making it. But Helen soon got the hang of it and followed Dan's directions out of town, heading with the sun toward the mountains.

They had talked all afternoon and it didn't feel wrong to be quiet for awhile. It was cooler now and the wind had blown itself out. On either side of the road, the land stretched away as far as she could see, cropped a pale gold and scattered with hay bales like giant Tootsie Rolls.

Both sky and earth seemed to Helen immense, their every angle boldly drawn. The roads ran straight and purposeful to ranches confidently placed. She found herself both thrilled and daunted and somehow inconsequential to it all. And she thought of Joel, as she still did a dozen times each day, and wondered whether he felt anchored in his new world or detached as she now was in hers, a watcher wanting to belong but somehow always floating past.

As the mountains loomed larger, the land before them crumpled into a badland sprawl of rocky bluffs, sliced randomly by sudden scrub-filled creeks. Cresting a hill, she saw a line of cottonwoods converging from the south and through their foliage the glint of water.

'That's the Hope River,' Dan said.

The blare of a car horn made them both jump. Looking at the river, Helen had let the pickup wander and in the mirror now she saw a black truck right behind them. She yanked the steering wheel so hard to the right that they lurched and shuddered briefly onto the verge. She quickly got control again. She narrowed her eyes and didn't look at Dan.

'One crack about women drivers and you're dead.'

'I've never seen a woman drive better.'

'You're dead.'

The black truck pulled out to pass. As it drew alongside, Helen turned and beamed her sweetest apology at the two inscrutable cowboy faces that surveyed her. They were maybe in their early twenties but with an attitude that made them look older. Dan gave a friendly wave. The one in the passenger seat touched the brim of his hat and almost smiled, while the driver just shook his head and drove on by, his disdain shared by a dog who rode windblown in the back. Once they were ahead, the passenger turned briefly to look at them through the gun rack in the cab's rear window.

'You know them?'

Dan nodded. 'They're Abe Harding's boys. They ranch a little spread up near the Calder place. You'll be neighbors.' Helen looked at him and saw he was grinning.

'Are you serious?'

' 'Fraid so.'

'Well, there's me off to a great start.'

'Don't worry, it's not your driving they'll hate you for. See the bumper sticker?'

She had to lean forward and squint because the truck was accelerating ahead, but she could still make out a wolf's head crossed out in red and, beside it, the words *No Wolves, No Way, No Where*.

'Terrific.'

'Oh, you'll soon have them eating out of your hand.'

The road followed the bends of the river for another four miles until Helen saw a white church on a low hill, then other buildings rear above the trees. There was a narrow, railed bridge that crossed the river and a sign saying HOPE (POPULA-TION 519) after which some cryptic soul had added three clean bullet holes of perfect punctuation, consigning both town and people to a state of perpetual suspense.

'I always get this childish urge to spray "abandon" on it.'

'Dan, you're doing a really great job selling this place to me.'

'Like I told you, it has a history.'

'So when do I get to hear it?'

They were coming over the bridge and he pointed ahead.

'Take that turn there.'

She pulled off the road and down into a small gravel parking lot beside the river. There were a couple of other cars there and Helen stopped beside them and turned off the engine.

'Come on,' Dan said. 'I'll show you something.'

They left Buzz in the pickup and walked into a small park that stretched beside the river. It was a pretty place, its grassy slopes kept lush by sprinklers. Their spray made rainbows in the sun that was shafting the shade of several tall willows. There were swings and a climbing frame for children, but those there now were playing chasing games through the sprinklers. Their mothers sat chiding them halfheartedly from one of half a dozen wooden picnic tables.

Below, at the water's edge, silhouetted against a molten reflection of sky between two cottonwoods, an old man in red suspenders and a dusty blue feed cap tossed crusts to a family of swans. Helen could see their feet churning to hold steady in the current.

Dan led the way along the raised path that snaked from the parking lot to the white clapboard church on the hill at the far end of the park. He seemed to be scanning the ground. Then he stopped and pointed down.

'Look.'

88

Helen stopped beside him. She couldn't see what he was pointing at.

'What?'

He bent and picked up something small and white from the path. He handed it to her and she examined it.

'It's like a piece of shell or something.'

He shook his head and pointed again to the ground.

'See? There's some more.'

There were flecks of it along the edge of the path, like a snowy residue, scuffed there and scrunched to ever finer fragments by the constant passage of sneakers and bicycle wheels.

'Sometimes you can find bigger pieces,' he said. 'Deep down the soil must be full of it. I guess that's why the grass grows so well.'

'What is it then?'

'It was from an old road that was here once.'

Helen frowned.

'It's wolf bone. The road was paved with wolf skulls.'

She looked at him, thinking he must be kidding.

'It's true. Thousands of them.'

And while, across the park, the children played on among the sprinklers, their laughter floating on the balm of the evening air, as if the world had ever been thus, Dan sat her down at one of the tables beneath the willows and told her how there came to be a road of skulls.

8

It was a hundred and fifty years since white hunters and trappers first arrived in any number in this valley. The first of them came in search of beaver when the land farther east was trapped out, making their watchful way along the Missouri in mackinaw boats piled perilously with store enough, they hoped, to see them through a winter. Paddling west then south, they found a narrow tributary, nameless to all but 'savages', that led toward the mountains and they followed it and made their camp.

Along the slopes of the hill where the church now stood, they dug cave-like shelters, roofing them with timber, brush and sod so that all that showed were stumplike chimneys of stacked stone. The following spring, when they sailed back to Fort Benton with their pelts, word began to spread of the great killing to be had. And over the next few years others followed, bringing horses and wagons, until soon there was a small village of hunters and trappers, a veritable colony of carnage to which someone, not in aspiration but rather in memory of a drowned child, gave the name Hope.

In a few seasons the beaver were all gone, their pelts sold for proceeds soon squandered on Indian whiskey and women and shipped east to warm the fashionable heads and necks of city folk. It was only when the beaver ponds stood stagnant that Hope's earliest inhabitants switched their attention to the wolf.

The valley had been a special place for wolves since ancient times. Honored as a great hunter by the Blackfeet who had long lived here too, the wolf knew it as a winter shelter for deer and elk and as a passage from the mountains to the plains where, in great packs, he trailed herds much greater still of buffalo. By 1850 the white man had begun his grand massacre of these herds. Over the next thirty years he would kill seventy million head of buffalo.

Ironically, at first, this made life easier for the wolf, for all the hunters wanted was the hide and maybe the tongue and a little prime meat. Wolves could dine in style on what was left. Then, from across the eastern ocean, came a great demand for wolfskin coats. It didn't take a genius to find a way of meeting it. Like thousands of others all across the West, the good, the bad and the downright demented, the trappers of Hope turned to wolfing.

It was easier than killing beaver, provided you had the two hundred dollars to set yourself up. A bottle of strychnine crystals cost seventy-five cents and it took two to lace a buffalo carcass. But set the carcass in the right spot and it could kill fifty wolves in a single night and still be fit to use the next. With good wolfskins now fetching two dollars apiece, a winter's poisoning might net you two thousand dollars. That kind of money made the risks seem worth taking. A man could freeze to death with no trouble at all and lose his scalp too, for of all the white invaders, the wolfer was the most reviled and the Blackfeet killed him when they could.

Each day the wolfers of Hope rode out in search of bait. As buffalo grew rare, they improvised with any creature they could find, even the smallest songbirds, whose breasts they delicately slit and stuffed with poisoned paste. The line of bait might stretch for many miles and was laid in a circle. When they rode its circumference the next morning, the wolfers would find it littered with the dead and dying of any bird or beast that had happened across it. As well as wolves, there would be fox and coyote, bear and bobcat, some still retching and convulsing. Their vomit and drool would poison the grass for years, killing any animal that grazed it.

A wolf might take an hour to die and the wariest among them, those who only sniffed and lightly licked while their brothers and sisters gorged, might take much longer. The strychnine went to work slowly in their gut until their fur fell out and left them wandering the plains, like naked ghosts, to howl and perish in the cold.

When winter tightened its grip and the daily harvest froze too hard for skinning, the wolfers stacked the bodies in the snow like firewood. It made the evenings easier but meant all could be spoiled by a sudden thaw. And it was one such thaw that gave birth to the road of skulls.

The winter of 1877 saw one of the longest freezes Hope had ever known. By March, more than two thousand unskinned wolves were piled in towers above the wolfers' caves and around the sprawl of cabins where most now lived.

Then, one morning, there came a whisper of warmth in the air. The trees began to drip and the ice at the river's edge to crack and soon a full chinook was blowing hot from the mountains. The cry went up and the wolfers, frantic with the fear of a whole season's loss, set to work with their snicker-snack knives, like demons on the day of reckoning.

By sunset every stockpiled wolf in the village was skinned and not a pelt lost and the wolfers of Hope, giddy with triumph, danced up to their knees in a mire of melted snow and blood.

For years they had dumped their skinned carcasses on the lower ground beside the river to be picked clean by ravens and buzzards, many of which promptly died from the strychnine ingested by the wolves. Now, as a monument to their brave day's doing, the wolfers raked all the bones together and, along with the headless remains of those just skinned, laid the footings of a road. Then they took the heads and boiled them and later, with great artistry, cobbled it with clean white skulls. And from that day forth the skull of every wolf they killed was added.

On a clear night when the snow was gone from the ground you could see the road from the mountains, many miles away, gleaming pale in the moonlight.

Eventually the skulls wound their way more than half a mile to where – perhaps to find more fragrant air, perhaps more fragrant company – those who had followed on the wolfers' heels preferred to live.

By now the valley was filling with the moan of cattle and the town grew proportionate with every herd that came, servicing the rancher's every need. Blacksmith, barber, hotelier and whore, all thrived in their several ways.

So too, at the other end of the road of skulls, did Hope's wolfers, their daily deeds now overlooked, from its own Golgotha, by a fine white church (overlooked in senses both literal and metaphoric, for wolves, like all animals, of course, were not deemed to possess souls).

Even before the church was built, the wolfers had not gone in want of spiritual guidance, thanks in large part to a self-styled preacher, wolfer and former Indian fighter by the name of Josiah King, better known to his flock as the Reverend Lobo.

On Sunday mornings, depending on the weather and the

amount of whiskey consumed the night before, Josiah would tell those assembled that the wolf was no mere varmint but the walking apotheosis of all evil. And he preached its annihilation with such infectious zeal that the wolfers of Hope came to see themselves as latter-day crusaders, reclaiming the frontier from this infidel beast and wreaking holy vengeance.

The work of the Lord brings just reward. Wolfing was better paid than ever. There was a state bounty of a dollar for every wolf killed, topped up by cattlemen whose hatred of the species needed no priestly prompting. For now that the buffalo was gone and the deer and elk grown scarce, wolves had acquired a taste for beef. Cows, moreover, were slower and dumber and easier to kill.

In truth, the elements were always better and more brazen in their killing than the wolf had ever been. The arctic winter of 1886 killed almost every herd in the valley. Only Hope's hardiest ranchers survived, but with grievance etched in ice on their hearts.

Yet whom could a man blame for the cold? Or for sickness and drought or the pitiful price of beef? And why curse government, weather or God, when the devil himself was at hand? You could hear him each night out stalking the range and howling the stars from the sky.

So the wolf became Hope's scapegoat.

And sometimes, for his crimes, they would catch him alive and parade him in shame through the town. Children would throw stones and the braver among them poke him with sticks. Then folk of all ages would gather by the river and watch while the Reverend Lobo's most ardent inquisitors torched him like a witch.

Most of the wolfers drifted away with the century. There was no longer a living to be made. Some turned to different trades, others traveled farther north and west where easier killing persisted awhile. The livestock industry had gained huge political clout and, spurred by a rancher-president, who declared the wolf to be 'a beast of waste and desolation', the federal government took over the crusade.

Rangers in every national forest were ordered to kill every wolf they could find and in 1915 the US Biological Survey, the agency entrusted with nurturing the nation's wildlife, methodically went to work on a well-funded policy of 'absolute extermination'.

Just as they had followed the buffalo across the plains, wolves now followed it, in a few short years, to the brink of extinction.

In Hope, with its great hinterland of wilderness, some lingered on. They hid high in the forests, too wise and wary to be caught by a crassly poisoned carcass. They could smell a poorly set trap from half a mile and would sometimes dig it up and spring it to register their contempt. To catch these animals, a man had to be more than cunning; he had to think like a wolf, had to know every shade and scent and tremor of the wild.

And there was only one now in Hope who could.

Joshua Lovelace had first come to the valley from Oregon in 1911, attracted to Montana by a new state law that increased the bounty on wolves to fifteen dollars. He was so much more skilled than any of his rivals that soon the local cattlemen's association hired him full-time. He built himself a home, five miles out of town, on the north bank of the Hope River.

He was a taciturn man who preferred his own company and guarded closely the subtle secrets of his profession. He was known, however, for two special trademarks. The first (for which many thought him either eccentric or excessively principled) was that he never used poison of any kind. When asked, he would proclaim his loathing of it, saying it was only for imbeciles who didn't care what they killed. Wolfing, to him, was an art of the utmost precision.

95

His second trademark was a working illustration of this, a device he had invented himself and for which he had applied, unsuccessfully, for a patent. He claimed to have gotten the idea as a boy, in Oregon, watching salmon fishermen lay nightlines in the mouth of a river.

He called it the 'Lovelace Loop'.

It was used only in the spring when wolves were denning and consisted of a circle of thin steel wire, some fifty feet in length, to which were attached, on traces of thinner wire, a dozen spring-loaded hooks. Each hook was baited with a bite-sized piece of meat (almost any kind would do, though Joshua's personal preference was chicken). The loop would then carefully be laid around the outside of the den and anchored with an iron stake.

Timing was critical. For optimum results the loop needed to be laid between three to four weeks after the mother had given birth, and knowing this, through discreet observation, was part of the skill. An adult wolf would rarely be fool enough to take the bait. But it wasn't to catch adults that the loop was designed.

At the age of two weeks a wolf pup's eyes opened and a week later his milk teeth broke through and he could hear. This is when he would first venture out into the world and be ready to eat small morsels of meat, brought home and regurgitated by the adult wolves. Joshua used to pride himself on knowing the exact moment that the loop should be laid. He wanted his chicken to be the pups' first taste of meat. And their last.

He would lay it as the sun was starting to go down and then retire to some high place and, for as long as there was light, keep watch with the brass army telescope he had once traded from an old Indian who claimed to have plucked it himself from General Custer's body at Little Bighorn.

Sometimes, if Lovelace got lucky, he might see one or two

pups emerge that same evening, lured from the den by the smell of the chicken. Once, in Wyoming, he caught a whole litter of six before nightfall. Normally, however, they came out of the den when it was too dark to see and you only knew you'd got one from the squeal they made when the triple-hook snapped open in their throats.

At dawn you would find five or six pups, hooked like fish around the den and still alive, though too tired by now to make more than a whimper. More often than not, their mother would be there, nuzzling and licking them, all her wariness lost in distress.

And therein lay the beauty of the loop. For if you were smart, if you had found yourself a good spot and didn't go blundering in at first light, you could catch the whole pack, shoot the other adults one by one, as they came home from their night's hunting. Only when you were sure you had them all, did you go in and finish the pups off with an ax or the butt of your gun.

Lovelace eventually married a woman much younger than himself and she died a year later, giving birth to their only child. The boy was christened Joseph Joshua but was known by his father from an early age simply by his initials.

By the time the boy was born, Lovelace had virtually eliminated Hope's wolves. The ranchers kept him on a retainer to clear up the occasional disperser and any other lesser varmints they were bothered by. His reputation had spread, however, and he had offers of work from far afield, wherever wolves persisted. Almost as soon as J.J. could walk, Joshua took him on his travels and taught him about killing.

The boy was an eager pupil and was soon adding refinements of his own to his father's techniques. He inherited a hatred for poison. For the next seventeen years, the two of them spent half the year in Hope and the other half traveling the continent, from Alaska to Minnesota, Alberta to

Mexico, going wherever there was a wolf that no one else could catch.

From the mid-fifties onward, when the traveling became too much for his father, J.J. worked on alone and, of necessity, once wolves were protected by law, in ever greater secrecy.

The site of the old wolfers' camp in Hope remained so toxic that for many years the County fenced it off. The road of skulls crumbled and succumbed beneath a tangle of bushes whose berries mothers of successive generations forbade their children to pick.

Then, long after the last howl of the last wolf had echoed in lament across the valley, bulldozers came to level the land for a park. While the work went on, several dogs died mysteriously from bones they brought home.

But only Hope's oldest guessed why.

Indian folklore had it that the spirits of all America's slaughtered wolves lived on. They were gathered, so the legend said, on some far-off mountain, beyond the white man's reach.

Awaiting a time when they might safely walk again upon the earth.

9

Luke Calder leaned back in his chair and waited while his speech therapist rewound the videotape. She had just taped him reading a whole page of *This Boy's Life* and he had managed it with only one block, and although it was a big one, he felt pleased with himself.

Through the window he watched a double trailer-load of cattle that stood shuddering at a red light, a row of pink noses poking wetly through the slatted sides. It was only a little after nine in the morning but already the streets of Helena were shimmering in the heat. On the way in, he'd heard the radio weatherman promising rain. Barely a drop had fallen all summer. The traffic lights went green and the cattle truck rumbled off.

'Okay, kiddo, let's have a look.'

Joan Wilson had been helping him with his stutter for about two years now. Luke felt easy with her. She was a tall, genial woman, maybe a few years older than his mother, with rosy cheeks and eyes that disappeared behind them when she smiled. She seemed to have an endless supply of exotic earrings, which Luke thought was odd because otherwise she dressed like a Sunday school teacher.

Joan worked for a cooperative that covered some of the more remote schools in the area. Luke had always looked forward to her weekly visits. At the start he'd had joint sessions with a younger boy, called Kevin Leidecker, which Luke had found hard because the boy's stutter was nowhere near as bad as his own.

He'd liked Leidecker well enough, until he overheard him in the locker room one day doing an imitation of 'Cookie' Calder, blocking on *To be or not to be*. It was pretty good; had the other kids almost wetting themselves. Luke's nickname (some preferred 'Cooks' or 'Cuckoo') came from the stabbing stutter he often got into when asked to say his name.

A year ago, the Leideckers had moved to Idaho and since then Luke had had Joan to himself. During school vacations, instead of her coming to see him, he came to see her and, every Wednesday morning, drove himself to this private clinic.

They had used the video a few times before, usually to practice some new technique or to help him see what he was doing physically. when he blocked. Today it was because lately, in addition to the tightening he always felt around the mouth, he'd found himself blinking and skewing his neck to the left. Joan said this was quite normal. It was what they called 'secondary characteristics'. She was videoing him so they could both examine what was going on and see if they could do something about it.

The first time they used the video, she'd been worried it might upset him to see himself on the screen, but it didn't. It was like looking at someone else. His voice sounded weird, especially when he came near to a danger word and did that nerdy, smiling thing. Joan always told him how handsome he was, which was nice of her but, of course, just therapist bull-shit. To his own eye he looked like a frightened bird, likely at a second's notice to spread his wings and fly away.

Screen-Luke was doing pretty well. He was sailing through words that often knocked him flat, M words and P words like *music* and *Paris*. He even got through *Hohner Marine Band* but that was only because everything was easy compared with what was coming.

He'd already spotted it up ahead and as it got nearer and nearer he knew he wasn't going to make it. He heard Screen-Luke's voice begin to brace itself, like the engine of a car straining on a mountain pass. And then, as he came up to the M of *Moulin Rouge,* he took a great gulp of air and his mouth locked and pushed forward and he started to blink. He'd run smack into the brick wall and for five, six, seven seconds he was stuck there, his face pressed into it.

'I l-look like a fish.'

'No, you don't. Okay, let's stop it there.'

Joan pressed pause and froze Screen-Luke pouting in mid-blink, confirming what he'd just said.

'Look. Fish.'

'You saw the words coming.'

'Yeah.'

'Was it something to do with it being in French maybe?'

'I don't know. I don't think so. It's no b-big deal. I just wish I didn't b-blink like that.'

She wound the tape back and played it again, and this time showed him where he was tensing up. You could see the mus-cles in his face and neck contract. She got him to say the phrase several times over and think about what his tongue and his jaw were doing as he said it. Then she got him to read the whole thing again and this time, although there were a couple of minor blocks and repetitions, he didn't blink or twist his neck once.

'See?' Joan said. 'You were right. No big deal.'

He shrugged and smiled. They both knew that success here was one thing; doing it in normal life was another. Sometimes he could spend a whole hour talking with Joan and not block at all. Then he'd go home and his father would ask him a simple question and he would completely seize up, even if the answer was yes or no.

Talking with Joan didn't count. Just like it didn't count when he talked with animals. He could talk all day to Moon Eye or the dogs, as if he'd never stuttered in his life. But it didn't count. Because it wasn't like the real world where words had such terrifying importance. Apart from Joan, there was only one person in the world he could talk with easily (well, two, if you counted Buck Junior who didn't yet understand a word, which was probably why it was okay) and that was his mother.

She was the only one who didn't look away when he got into trouble. And if he blocked, she just waited patiently and the tension would slip out of him like water from a tub. It had always been like that.

He could remember her grabbing him up from the supper table and carrying him away to safety when his father was insisting he ask properly for something. Luke would sit there going redder and redder while the wall in front of the word he was trying to say got higher and higher and then he would start crying and his mother would leap up and take him away to another part of the house where they would sit in the dark and listen to his father ranting and raving until the door slammed and his car roared off into the night.

That was the real world. Where a little word like *milk* or *butter* or *bread* could raise a hurricane that would sweep through the whole house and leave everyone in it sobbing and hollering and quaking with terror.

After the video work, Joan got him to do some voluntary

stuttering, doing it deliberately to get him used to having control over his speech. She said this might help with the blinking too and he might try practicing it on his own along with his other exercises. The one he'd been working on lately was to make meaningless sounds, get the voice flowing like a river, then just let the words float out on it.

Then they did some role-playing which was more for fun than anything and normally ended up with them both helpless with laughter. Joan was a frustrated actress and always gave it all she'd got. Last week she'd been the bad-tempered owner of a concession stand at a ball game and Luke had to chat about the game and order some popcorn and two Cokes. He could always make her crack up by throwing something in, like last week, when he'd asked her to marry him. Today she was a mean traffic cop who had just stopped him for speeding. She checked his papers, handed them back and then leaned toward him and sniffed.

'Have you been drinking?'

'Not much, ma'am.'

'Not much. How much?'

'Just five or six beers.'

'Five or six beers!'

'Yes, ma'am. And a bottle of w-whiskey.'

Luke could see her lips begin to quiver.

'Okay, that's it. You're booked.'

Joan always avoided eye contact when she was about to laugh and now she shook her head and pretended to write something on a notepad beside her on the desk. Then she tore off the sheet and handed it to him. Luke studied it. It was her shopping list.

'Ma'am, I d–don't understand.'

'What?'

'You've booked me for Po–Pop-Tarts and p–pantyhose.'

That did it. She started to shake and by the time they'd

stopped laughing it was ten o'clock and the session was over. They both stood up and she put an arm around his shoulders.

'You're doing okay, kiddo. You know that?'

Luke smiled and nodded and she stood back and gave him a look. Nodding, like all avoidance tricks, was strictly forbidden.

'I'm d-doing okay,' he said. 'Okay?'

'Okay.'

She walked him out and along the corridor that led to the lobby.

'How's your mom?'

'She's fine. She said to say hi.'

'Are you still planning on putting college off till next year?'

'Uh-huh. My dad thinks it's a g-good idea.'

'And what do you think?'

'Oh, I don't know. I g-guess so.'

She peered at him as if something in his face might show this to be a lie. He smiled.

'I do. Really,' he said.

Joan knew about him and his father. They'd talked about it right from the start and though Luke, through some baffling sense of loyalty, had spared her much, she clearly believed his father was largely to blame for his stutter. Luke often got the feeling, however, that her dislike ran deeper and was maybe colored by what had happened with one of her predecessors, a much younger woman than Joan, to whom his father had taken a shine. Her name was Lorna Drewitt and she had been Luke's speech therapist for about a year before he discovered what was going on.

It was during the Christmas vacation when Luke was twelve years old. His father had come to collect him from the clinic and told him to wait in the car while he 'settled up' with Miss Drewitt. Luke had been sitting in the dark parking

104

lot for ten minutes when a man knocked on the window and said his car was boxed in and could they move theirs to let him out.

Luke ran back into the clinic to tell his father and didn't think to knock on Lorna's door. Like a total jerk he just burst in and, in that splinter of a second before they sprang apart, he caught the two of them pressed together against the filing cabinet and plainly saw his father's hand up inside her hoisted sweater, cupping her breast.

Lorna quickly rearranged herself and pretended to be searching for something in the cabinet while Luke stood there, feeling his face begin to glow, and tried to say that there was a man outside who wanted to move his car. But he ran aground on the first M and stayed stranded there like a beached whale until his father came over and said quietly,

'It's all right, son. I'm coming.'

They drove all the way back home in silence and no mention was ever made of what his father must have known Luke had seen. That was the last he saw of Lorna Drewitt, though later he heard she had moved to Billings, a town his father still often visited on business.

Whether Joan knew of this particular incident or of some similar one, Luke wasn't sure. Perhaps all she knew was his father's famed womanizing, which Luke later discovered at school was common knowledge. Whatever the reason, Joan took little trouble to hide her feelings and when Luke had first told her he wasn't going straight to college that fall, she'd gotten all worked up and said that the sooner he got away, the better he and his stutter would be.

They said goodbye in the clinic lobby and Luke put his hat on and stepped out into the blast of white sun and across the parking lot.

Driving out of Helena, he mulled over what Joan had said about him needing to get away. She was probably right. He knew full well why his father wanted him to do a year's work on the ranch before going to college.

Luke had his heart set on studying wildlife biology at the University of Montana in Missoula, a place his father thought infested with liberals and 'bunny-huggers'. He wanted Luke to follow Kathy's example and do agribusiness management at rancher-friendly Montana State in Bozeman and was hoping that a year of practical ranching might make his son see sense.

Luke was happy enough to go along with it, though for an entirely different reason.

It meant he could go on watching the wolves. And if the need arose, as he feared it might, perhaps he would be able to protect them.

There was no one to be seen when he got back to the ranch. His mother's car was gone and he figured she must be up at Kathy's or had maybe gone into town. There was another car Luke recognized as belonging to the local vet, Nat Thomas. He parked the old Jeep beside it and got out. Their two Australian cattle dogs came rushing to greet him and bounced beside him as he walked up the dusty slope to the house.

He called hello when he came through the screen door into the kitchen but there was no reply. His mother had left something cooking in the oven. It smelled good. Everyone would soon be coming in for lunch. Wednesday, after his session with Joan, was now the only day he got to eat with the others. Every other day, since his father had given him the job of riding the herd up on the allotment, he just took sandwiches and ate them on his own. It suited Luke just fine.

He headed up to his room to change into his work clothes so he could ride out directly after eating.

His room was upstairs on the southwest corner of the house. From the west-facing window you could see the head of the valley where the forest began and, beyond it, the mountains whose tops were often veiled with cloud.

It was really two rooms, knocked into one. The other half, through an open archway, had been his brother's. And though, over the years since the accident, Luke had gradually colonized some of it, Henry was still very much present.

Some of his clothes still hung in the closet. There were shelves crammed with his high school photographs, sport trophies and his collection of hunting magazines. Hanging from a hook on the bottom shelf was what had once been his most treasured possession: a baseball mitt autographed in faded ink by some superannuated star. *Go Henry,* it said, *Hit 'em big.*

Luke sometimes wondered if his parents had ever discussed clearing it all away. He guessed it must be hard to know what to do with a dead child's possessions. Hiding them might be as bad as leaving them.

The shelves in Luke's half of the room were filled with books and a museum-like clutter of things he had picked up in the mountains. There were rocks of strange color and pattern and shape, gnarls of old wood like the faces of trolls and fossilized fragments of dinosaur bone. There were bear claws and feathers of eagles and owls and the skulls of badger and bobcat.

There were stacks of books, some of which he read again and again – Jack London, Cormac McCarthy and Aldo Leopold – and books about animals of almost every kind. Hidden among them, as others might hide raunchy magazines, were the ones about wolves. He had more than a dozen of them, some by old-timers like Stanley P. Young, but mostly those of more modern writers, like Barry Lopez, Rick Bass and the great wolf biologist David Mech.

Luke looked at his watch. He had about an hour to kill before the others showed up for lunch, so he decided to do some of Joan's voice exercises. He lay down on his bed and closed his eyes and began what she called the 'body scan'. Breathing slowly and deeply, he consciously relaxed every muscle in his body. Each time he breathed out, he 'sounded it' with a soft moan. Little by little, he felt the tension slacken.

Then he pictured in his mind, as Joan had told him, that his voice was a river, flowing from his mouth, and that he could let words, any words, whatever nonsense came into his head, gently float upon the river and out into the world.

'Me oh my, how I love cherry pie. Float with the pie, let the pie float by . . .'

The river flowed out through his open door and along the corridor where particles of dust glittered in a wedge of sun, then on and down, to the listening house below.

'My mom's cherry pie floated up to the sky.'

After awhile his voice grew sleepy and slow, as if the river were forming a lake and the water slowly swirling, filling the house until at last he fell asleep and the silence regathered, stirred only by the lowing of a distant calf.

It was how the house mostly was nowadays: silent and empty of all but memories. It had been that way since Luke's sisters had moved out, first Lane, who had married a real estate agent from Bozeman, then Kathy.

You noticed it most of all in the living room, from which all the other downstairs rooms radiated. It was a large room, with a broad-plank cedar floor and walls of swirled white plaster, framed in pine. At its far end stood a stone hearth where, on winter nights, great logs would crackle and roar and still be there glowing at dawn. Above it, a hooded black iron flue towered toward heavy beams, burnished by decades of smoke to the color of molasses.

The walls of the living room were hung with samplers and tapestries, stitched with mystical patience by Luke's grandmother and her mother before her. Here too, as well as photographs of all the Henry Calders, were the antique wall clocks that Luke's mother had once collected.

The cases of these clocks were oblong and made of maple. On their glass-paneled fronts, below the dial, each was decorated with its own hand-painted scene, mostly depicting animals or birds or flowers. There were four clocks now and once there had been five, until Luke's brother managed to smash one showing off his roping skills to the girls and earning himself a thrashing from his father.

There was a time when their mother had kept all the clocks in time and good repair. Every Sunday she would wind and adjust them so they chimed the hour in unison. Visitors had often expressed wonder that anyone could bear to live amid such clang and clatter but Eleanor would laugh and say no one in the family ever heard it, which was mainly true, although Luke could remember once having a nightmare about them when he was little. It was when he was having one of his regular bouts of tonsillitis and in his fever he had dreamed that the ticking was really the snicker of cutlasses and that a band of bloodthirsty pirates was creeping up the stairs to get him.

All of these clocks were now silent. They had been that way for more than ten years. Whether it was a deliberate symbolic gesture or simple neglect, no one dared ask, but since Henry's death, his mother had never again wound them. And because they were hers alone and maybe served some private purpose in her grief, no one else had touched them. Dustily, they registered the several times of their own demise.

There were other adornments on the walls, both here and elsewhere in the house, which, for Luke at least, carried greater significance. These were the mounted heads of animals killed by four generations of Calders, all of whom had been great hunters. His brother had shot his first elk at the age of ten, which was both illegal and a great source of pride to his father. The head was mounted above the door to the kitchen and one of Henry's favorite tricks was to toss his hat onto the antlers from twenty feet across the room. It hung there still.

As a child Luke had always found these trophies disturbing. When he was four years old, his brother had confided to him that the animals weren't in fact dead and that even though they couldn't move, their brains and eyes still functioned.

For the best part of a year Luke believed his every move was being watched, his every deed assessed. The most important of the heads, his brother told him, was that of a huge moose their grandfather had shot and which had pride of place at the foot of the stairs.

'If any of the others see you doing something bad they tell the old moose,' Henry had whispered. Luke was aware that his sisters were looking on with great seriousness, but he kept his wide eyes locked on Henry. 'And the moose keeps a count of all these bad things and when you've done too many, he'll come and get you.'

'How m-m-m-men—'

'How many bad things do you have to do?'

Luke nodded.

'You know, Lukey, I'm not sure. But I tell you, when I broke that old clock of Mom's, he came to my room in the middle of the night and boy, did he give me a whupping.'

'W-w-what w-with?'

'Those great big antlers of his. Uses them like a paddle. And I tell you, they hurt a hell of a lot worse than Daddy's belt. I couldn't sit down for a whole week.'

Every night when he went upstairs to bed, Luke made a silent confession to the moose and told him he was sorry for everything he had done wrong that day, a list which by now, often as not, included stuttering in reply to his father's mealtime demands and any consequent eruption. And even after his mother found him doing this one bedtime and assured him it wasn't true and Henry got another thrashing from his father, it

110

was a long time before Luke could again walk comfortably beneath the moose's nose or sit in any room where there were heads on the wall and feel certain he wasn't being watched.

It wasn't that he was afraid of them. He'd never been afraid of any animal. Already he had found that it was easier to make friends with them than it was with human beings. The ranch dogs, cats and horses, even the calves, always seemed to come to him rather than to others. When his stutter started, he used to get around it by talking through Mo, an old glove-puppet that had once looked like a fox but became so worn and darned that it soon didn't look like anything. Through Mo's mouth, he could talk as fluently to people as he could through his own to animals. In the end it drove his father mad and Mo was banished to a locked closet.

Perhaps because of his brother's joke about the trophies, perhaps because of those defiant genes that made him so unlikely a Calder, all that Luke had ever feared in animals was their judgment. Not simply of himself, but of all his species. He saw the wrongs they suffered at man's hands and knew, by virtue of his own strictured tongue, how it felt to be unable to speak out against oppression.

A ranch was not the easiest of homes for one of such sensibility, though Luke had always done his best to conceal it. He helped with jobs that his conscience abhorred, such as holding calves down at branding time while their balls were chopped off and the smoke of their seared flesh filled his nostrils with nausea. He ate meat, although its taste and texture often made him want to gag.

To find favor with his father, he had even gone hunting and in so doing achieved the opposite.

Six years after his brother's death, his father had asked him if he wanted to try for his first elk. Luke was thirteen and had been dreading the invitation while at the same time feeling hurt that it had taken so long to come.

111

The two of them rode out before dawn under a mottled November moon that lit the breath of the horses and made shadows of them on the sequined snow. An hour later they were up in the forest, standing silent with the horses on a high crag while they looked back to see the sun scale the world's rim and turn the snow-swept plains to a sea of crimson.

His father always knew where they were most likely to find elk. It was the place where Henry had shot his first buck, a hidden canyon where a herd would often shelter and feed when the snow lay thick. Luke had come here on his own many times to watch. But never, until this day, to kill.

They left the horses and went the final mile on foot, taking care to stay on the safe side of what little wind there was. The snow was fresh and fluffy and not deep enough to bother them, though now and then one of them would sink to the hips in a hidden drift. They barely spoke and when they did it was in whispers. Otherwise, but for their breathing and the creak and crunch of their boots in the snow, the forest was still. Luke's heart was thumping and he prayed, crazily, that his father couldn't hear it and that the elk could and would take flight and save themselves.

His father carried the rifle. Usually he hunted with a 30-06 Springfield or the .300 Magnum he had bought the previous fall. But today he had brought only the .270 Winchester, the same weapon that Henry had used to fell his first elk six years earlier. It had less recoil than the others and in practice a few days earlier Luke had hit the target time after time. His father had been thrilled.

'You shoot darn near as straight as your brother,' he said.

It took them more than an hour to reach the lip of the canyon. They crawled into the sheltered hollow of an old pine and peered through the gap between its lowest branches and its girdled drift of snow. His father handed him the binoculars.

The elk hadn't heard his heartbeat. Across the canyon,

there was a herd of maybe twenty cows. A little way off, a solitary bull with five-point antlers was nibbling bark in a stand of quakin' asp. He was less than two hundred yards away. Luke handed the binoculars back to his father and wondered if he dared say that he didn't want to go through with it. But he knew that even if he were to try, the words would never come out; their effect would be too catastrophic.

'Not a six-point like Henry's, but he'll do,' his father whispered.

'M-m-maybe we should w-w-wait till we find a s-s-six-point.'

'Are you crazy? That's a fine animal. Here.'

He carefully passed the rifle. Luke knew that a single touch on the tangle of branches above them would dislodge a pile of snow and maybe spook the elk. He toyed with the idea of doing it.

'Take your time, son. Take it real slow now.'

His father helped him ease the barrel out through the gap. The hollow of the tree smelled strongly of resin and Luke wondered why it should make him feel sick when it never had before. He pressed the butt of the rifle into his shoulder.

'Get yourself comfortable now. Find a good place for your elbows. How does that feel? Okay?'

Luke nodded and put his eye to the scope. The eyepiece felt clammy against his skin. For a moment all he could see was a racing blur of snow-covered trees and the striated gray rock of the canyon wall above.

'I c-c-can't find him.'

'See that patch of blowdown? The cows are directly below it. Can you see them?'

'No.'

'Take your time, it's okay. He's at two o'clock from where the cows are.'

Now he saw them. They were stripping moss from the

bark of the fallen trees. He could plainly see their eyes when they lifted their heads and stood chewing. The crosshairs of the scope moved from one animal to another, panning their pale bellies inside which by now calves were starting to form.

'Got him?'

'Yes.'

The bull was tugging a piece of bark from a sapling and when it came free the tree quivered, sprinkling his head and antlers with snow. The intimacy of the scope was shocking. Luke could make out individual hairs on the dark neck. He could see the grinding of the jaws as the elk chewed, see the paler patches around the liquid black eyes that impassively surveyed the cows, see droplets of melted snow on his nose.

'He looks k-k-kind of young to have his own herd. M-m-maybe there's a b-b-bigger bull around somewhere.'

'Hell, Luke, if you won't take him, I will.'

Half of Luke's brain screamed at him to hand his father the gun right then. But the other half assessed this moment for what it was: a final chance to *be* something in his father's eyes. He must take this creature's life for his own to have any value.

He was breathing fast and only in the very top of his chest as if his lungs were three-quarters closed. His heart was pumping so hard he thought it might burst and he half hoped it would. He could feel his blood pulsing in the flesh pressed against the eyepiece of the scope. The crosshairs moved on the elk's head and body like a yo-yo.

'Easy now, son, easy. Take a deep breath.'

He felt his father's eyes on him, judging him. Comparing him, no doubt, with how Henry had been that day.

'Do you want me to take him?'

'No,' Luke snapped. 'I c-c-can do it.'

'You've still got the safety on, Luke.'

With twitching fingers, Luke felt for the catch and clicked it off. The elk had lowered his head to the tree again and was about to strip more bark when something made him hesitate. He raised his head and lifted his nose to the air. Then, suddenly with every sense alert, he turned and seemed to look directly into the lens of the scope.

'Has he seen us?'

His father was looking through the binoculars and didn't answer for a moment.

'He's sure gotten a whiff of something. If you're going to do it, Luke, do it now.'

Luke swallowed.

His father went on, his whisper urgent now, 'The rifle's sighted in at two hundred and that's about where he's at. There's no wind, so it's line of sight, just the way you see it.'

'I know.'

'Take him just behind the shoulder.'

'I know!'

The elk was still looking at him. The blood was roaring in Luke's ears. It was as if the world had become a tunnel with only two living creatures in it, he at one end and the elk at the other, staring back at him, into his mind and deeper still, as if scouring the darkest corners of his heart. And finding there perhaps a glimpse of death, the animal jerked in alarm and began to move away.

And at that precise moment, Luke pulled the trigger.

The elk jolted and stumbled. Below, the herd of cows erupted and headed as one for the cover of the trees.

'You got him!'

The bull was on his knees but then he stood again and moved off in a broken, uncertain run through the aspens. Luke's father was pushing himself headfirst out of the tree hole.

'Are you sure?'

115

'Sure I'm sure. Come on!'

Luke followed, pushing himself out through the snow into the glare of the sun. His father was already standing up.

'Here, I'll take the rifle. Let's get over there. He's not going far.'

And his father set off down the slope, wading strongly through the snow with the rifle held high and Luke followed in his tracks, half blinded by the sun and falling so often that soon he was covered in snow and all the time saying, whether out loud or to himself, he didn't know and didn't care, *Oh God, please don't let me have done this and if I have, please let him live, please let him get away. Oh please.*

When they got to the stand of aspen they found blood in the snow and they followed its spattered trail up into the ribbon of pine that fringed the foot of the canyon wall.

They heard the elk before they saw him. It was a sound Luke had never heard before and would never forget, a kind of low, throaty scream, like the broken door of a derelict house creaking in the wind. From the tracks, it seemed that the elk had stumbled and disappeared over a ledge of rock. Luke's father carefully edged his way along it through a snow-drifted tangle of scrub and peered down.

'Here's your baby, Luke. You got him in the neck.'

Luke felt his chest contract. The elk's screaming was relentless now and its echo in the canyon so terrible that he had to fight not to block his ears.

'Come on, Luke. You've got to finish the job. Careful as you go, it's steep here.'

Luke walked along the ledge not caring if he fell, dreading with every step what he was going to see. He came alongside his father and peered down. The ground fell away steeply in a tumble of sliprock. About halfway down there was a dead tree which had snagged the elk's fall and he lay wedged there, watching them, while his hind legs thrashed useless in the air below. There was a dark hole in his neck. His shoulder and chest ran slick with blood.

His father racked another bullet into the chamber and handed him the rifle.

'There you go, son. You know what to do.'

Luke took it and, as he did so, felt his mouth quiver and the tears flood in his eyes and he tried so hard to stop it but he couldn't and his whole body started to shake with sobs.

'I c–can't.'

His father put an arm around his shoulders.

'It's okay, son. I know how you feel.'

Luke shook his head. It was the dumbest thing he'd ever heard. How could anyone know how he felt? Least of all his father who must have seen this kind of thing a dozen times.

'You've got to do it, though. He won't be yours unless you do.'

'I don't w–w–want him!'

'Come on, Luke. He's in pain—'

'You think I d–d–don't know that?'

'Then finish the job.'

'I can't!'

'Of course you can.'

'Y–y–y–you do it.' He handed back the rifle.

'A hunter finishes what he's started.'

'I'm not a g–g–goddamn hunter!'

His father looked down at him for a long moment. It was the first time Luke had ever cussed in front of him. Then, in what looked more like sadness than anger, his father shook his head and took the rifle.

'No, Luke. I don't think you are.'

His father shot the elk through the neck again and they watched it jerk and kick its legs in the air as if its soul was flying to some far-off place. Then, with its eyes never leaving them, it stiffened and gave a long, gurgling sigh and at last was still.

117

But that wasn't the end of it.

They got a rope on the carcass and pulled it out of the tree from below. And there his father made him help skin it out and field-dress it. This was the deal, he explained, as he slit the belly and reached up inside to sever the windpipe and haul out the elk's steaming heart and liver and lungs. If you hunted, this was what you had to do. It was a sacred moment, he said. And they sawed off the head and then cut the body into pieces so that they could pack it out. And Luke wept in silence all the while, wept at the feel and smell of the elk's warm blood on his hands and wept for himself and his shame.

They hung what they couldn't carry from a high branch so coyotes or any late-denning bears couldn't get it. And when they left the place, with the antlered head swaying crazily above the meat strapped to his father's shoulders and more meat strapped to his own, Luke looked back and saw the gut piles and the snow soaked wide with blood and it occurred to him that if there were indeed such a place as hell, this was how it must look and where surely now he belonged.

The elk's head was never hung on the wall with the others. Perhaps his mother forbade it, after hearing what had happened; Luke never knew. But even now, five years later, he still sometimes conjured it in his dreams, leering at him from some unexpected place. And he would wake whimpering and soaked with sweat, among the twisted sheets of his bed.

10

Hope, that Wednesday morning, looked like the set of an out-of-control movie. The whole of Main Street was jammed with cows, cars and children about to bludgeon each other with musical instruments. Overhead, two young men, precariously perched on ladders, were trying to hang strings of colored flags from one side of the street to the other. The town was getting ready for the annual fair and rodeo.

Eleanor Calder stood in the doorway of Iverson's grocery store and watched. All along the street others were doing the same.

The high school band had been practicing all morning and now, marching in the street in the glare of the noon sun, tempers had started to frazzle. They were supposed to be playing 'Seventy-six Trombones', which was probably someone's idea of a joke for there was only one trombonist among them and even his survival was now in doubt because a cornet player, a girl twice his size, had just threatened to waste him if he poked her one more time in the back. Ignoring the shrill pleas of Nancy Schaeffer, their distraught teacher, everyone in the band was taking sides and screaming at each other while the cattle streamed like philistines around them.

Quite what the cattle were doing there, nobody seemed to know. Either they had misread their calendars and were on their way to the fairground or else someone had picked an inspired moment to move them to a pasture on the far side of town. Whichever it was, the men hanging the flags weren't impressed. Their ladders were being jostled by the cattle until at last one of them took a head-on shove and toppled and the man had to leap for safety onto the porch roof of Nelly's Diner just in time to watch his line of flags flutter down to garland the heads of the cows and be swept merrily away out of town.

Old Mr Iverson clucked and shook his head.

'Gets worse every year,' he said. 'Even the band can't play a half-decent tune anymore.'

'Oh, they've got a couple of weeks to get it together,' Eleanor said. 'The cows don't help.'

'They sure make a better noise though.'

Eleanor smiled. 'Well, I'd better be getting home. Some hungry men'll be wanting their lunch.'

She said goodbye and made her way with her two sacks of groceries along the cracked sidewalk to where she had parked. Except for a few stragglers, the cattle had almost gone. Two young hands Eleanor didn't recognize were bringing up the rear on horseback and taking abuse from storekeepers and some of the less patient drivers who'd been blocked in their cars. Band practice appeared to be over and the squabbling factions were dispersing.

Eleanor dumped her groceries into the back of her car and shut the tailgate, chiding herself for having bought so much. Like most of her neighbors, she normally went once a week to the big supermarket in Helena and only used Iverson's for the odd thing she had forgotten to put on her list. On these rare visits, like today, she was always stricken with guilt and ended up buying all kinds of things she didn't need. She was sure the Iversons, the lugubrious couple who had owned the place for as long as anyone could remember, recognized this as a syndrome and adjusted their expressions accordingly when anyone came in. They probably whooped and danced with glee when they had the place again to themselves.

Eleanor got into the car, wincing at the scald of the seat through her cotton dress. She was about to start the engine when she noticed the FOR SALE sign was still in the window of Ruth Michaels' gift shop across the street. She thought yet again about what Kathy had said.

It was about a month ago, when they were changing little Buck's diapers. Kathy mentioned that Paragon was up for sale and suggested Eleanor should consider buying it. Since she had gotten married, finding projects for her mother to get involved in was one of Kathy's favorite pastimes. Eleanor had variously been told she should go to college, open a restaurant, start a mail-order business, take up yoga; maybe even do all of these at the same time. Now it was buying Ruth Michaels' gift shop.

'Don't be silly,' Eleanor said. 'I wouldn't have the first idea how to run it, let alone make a cup of cappuccino.'

'You used to help out in Grandpa's store. Anyhow, you wouldn't have to. Ruth doesn't want out. She's just borrowed too much and can't afford to keep going. You could buy into the business and let her go on running the place. Be involved as much or as little as you wanted.'

Every excuse she put up, Kathy neatly demolished and though it was never mentioned again, Eleanor had thought about it many times since. It might be just what she needed. With both girls now married and Luke soon off to college, she could do with something to fill the void.

In the old days, before Henry died, she used to handle a lot of the ranch paperwork that Kathy now looked after. And apart from cooking – which Eleanor was amazed to think she had once actually enjoyed – she barely got involved at all. She got so bored and lonely sometimes, she worried for her sanity.

She didn't know Ruth Michaels, except to say hello to, but had always thought she seemed bright and pleasant. People had been both intrigued and a little suspicious of her when she'd first arrived in town some five years ago. To be more precise, the men had been intrigued and the women suspicious and for the same two reasons: her dark, exotic looks and the fact that she was single. By now she was accepted (or as much as any New Yorker ever would be) and generally liked.

On the few occasions Eleanor had gone into the shop, she had been impressed. It wasn't the usual western tourist trash – plastic dream catchers, snowshakers and jokey cowboy T-shirts. Ruth had taste. You could see it in the selection of jewelry, books and pieces of artwork.

Before she had finally made up her mind, Eleanor found herself crossing the street, picking her way with care between what the cows had left behind and the last few bickering band members.

Ruth allowed people to stick notes and posters on a board in the shop window, announcing yard sales, unwanted puppies or upcoming events such as potlucks or weddings to which the whole town was invited. Most at the moment were to do with the fair and rodeo, including one that made Eleanor smile. *Trombonists Urgently Wanted,* it read. *Call Nancy Schaeffer – NOW!* Below it, a black cat basked asleep in the filtered sunshine.

There were bells on the door that clanked when it opened and closed. After the glare of the street, Eleanor's eyes took a moment to adjust to the shadowed clutter of the shop. It was cool and calm and soothing music floated on the air along with a rich smell of coffee. There was no one to be seen.

Eleanor stepped carefully between tall dressers stacked with pottery and handmade toys and brightly colored Indian blankets, taking care not to knock the jungle of mobiles and chimes that hung from the ceiling, tinkling as they turned and touched. There were baskets of bracelets made of dyed and plaited horsehair and glass cabinets crammed with silver jewelry.

There were clunking and hissing noises coming from the rear of the shop, where the cappuccino bar was, and as Eleanor got nearer she heard Ruth's voice.

'Do it, you stupid bastard! *Do* it!'

There was nobody to be seen. Eleanor hesitated. She didn't want to blunder into a private altercation.

'I'll give you one more chance and then I'm going to beat the living shit out of you, okay?'

There was a huge chrome coffee machine on the counter and suddenly it erupted with a terrifying squall of steam.

'You shit! You lousy, useless godforsaken heap of shit!'

'Hello?' Eleanor said tentatively. 'Is that Ruth?'

Everything went quiet.

'Not if you're from the bank or the IRS, it isn't.'

Ruth's head lifted slowly into view above the machine. There was a smudge of black oil on her cheek. When she saw Eleanor, her eyes seemed briefly to fill with panic. Then she beamed.

'Mrs Calder! Hi! I'm sorry, I didn't hear you. This machine will, probably literally, be the death of me. What can I do for you? Can I make you a coffee?'

'Not if it's going to explode.'

'Oh, he only behaves badly when he thinks no one's here.'

123

'You've got something on your . . .' She pointed to the smudge.

'Oh. Thanks.'

She found a tissue and, using the coffee machine as a mirror, wiped it off.

'Do you believe in ghosts?'

'Yes, I think I do. Why?'

'I swear this thing is haunted. I got it from a place that was closing down in Seattle, really cheap. Now I know why. How about that coffee?'

'Do you have decaf?'

'You bet. Skim milk or regular?'

'I'll have skim.'

'Why bother.'

'Well, I . . .'

'No, I mean, that's what I call it. No caffeine, no fat, so why bother?' She laughed. It was a catchy, throaty laugh, almost scurrilous, and it immediately had Eleanor laughing too.

'Did you get caught in the stampede?'

'Very nearly. Those poor children.'

'Please, take a seat.'

Eleanor settled herself on one of the little bar stools while Ruth coaxed two cappuccinos from the machine. She was wearing faded jeans and a baggy purple T-shirt emblazoned with the shop's name. Her black hair was bundled up in a red bandanna. Eleanor guessed she must be in her mid to late thirties and was struck by how attractive she was.

She wondered about that look of panic when Ruth saw her just now. Maybe she really had been expecting a visit from the IRS. She placed Eleanor's coffee in front of her.

'So, have you found a buyer yet?' Eleanor asked. 'Kathy said you were hoping to find a partner to come in with you.'

'Did you see them all lining up outside? Nobody's interested.'

Eleanor sipped her coffee. It tasted good. Go on, she told herself, say it. She put the cup down.

'Well,' she said. 'I might be.'

Buck figured the calf must have been dead a good few days. There wasn't a whole lot left of it. But for a few bones and chewed-up strips of hide, its hindquarters had all but disappeared. The remains were lying exposed at the top of a steep gully and what the birds and other varmints hadn't taken, the sun had baked stiff. Nat Thomas was having a hard time working out what had happened.

He was kneeling beside it, probing among the flies and maggots with his knife and forceps. The ground around him was alive with grasshoppers. Nat and his father before him had been vets to the Calder ranch for years and Buck had called him right away. He wanted to get an independent opinion before the feds got their itchy hands on the carcass. They'd come clean about it being a wolf that had killed Prince, but given that Kathy had seen the damn thing with her own eyes, they hadn't had much choice.

Buck didn't like the guy from Fish and Wildlife, Prior or whatever he called himself. He didn't trust him either. The other one, Rimmer, the predator-control fellow, seemed okay, but when it came to the crunch, whatever they might pretend, feds were feds and wolf lovers, every goddamn one of them.

Buck was standing with Clyde, looking over Nat's shoulder. It was noon and the heat shimmered off the rocks that dotted the pasture. The only sounds were the flick of the grasshoppers and now and again the call of a cow farther up toward the forest. Buck was still sweating from the steep walk up here. They'd left Nat's car down at the house and the three of them had driven up as far as they could get in Clyde's truck. They'd had to leave it about a half-mile farther down the slope where the land got too rough. It would have been better to come up on horseback.

It was Clyde who had found the calf this morning and what riled Buck was why Luke hadn't found it earlier. He had given the boy the job of riding the herd up here on the allotment as soon as Prince got killed. If there were wolves around, someone needed to keep watch on the cattle and as Luke knew the lie of the land and wasn't a whole lot of use at much else, it might as well be him.

Buck had told him to keep an eye out for exactly this kind of thing and the boy hadn't found it. Probably because he spent most of the time with his head in the clouds, dreaming and reading books or scrabbling around for bits of old bone or whatever. How Buck was ever going to make a half-decent rancher out of him, he had no idea.

'Well, Nat, what d'you reckon?'

'Sure ain't too much to go on.'

'How long's he been dead?'

'Oh, three, four days maybe.'

'Reckon it was a wolf?'

'Well, he's been chewed up real good. See these teeth marks here on the neck? That's a predator with a fair-sized jaw and it sure doesn't look like a bear. Could be a wolf or a coyote. Have you looked around for tracks?'

'Too dry,' Clyde said. 'And you can't see the ground for grasshoppers.'

'Could be he was already dead and whatever it was has just been chewing on him.'

'My cows don't go falling over dead of their own accord, Nat. You know that.'

'Sure, but from all that's left of him here, he could have been struck by lightning, anything—'

'Struck by lightning. Give me a break, Nat.'

'Well.'

126

Buck looked down at the carcass. He noticed something and bent to pick it up. It was a scrap of hide, hardened by the sun. On it was the linked HC brand of the Calder ranch. He blew a grasshopper off it and turned it over in his fingers.

Sure, you got to lose a calf from time to time up here. Sometimes one got sick or got himself stuck in a gulch somewhere. A few years back they'd lost a couple to an old grizzly and a predator-control agent had come and taken it out. If you were ranching this kind of country, losing the occasional calf was part of the deal.

But for the last two falls every animal that had summered on the allotment had come back safe and sound. And seeing his brand on this piece of hide, Buck felt a surge of anger.

He knew in his bones that a wolf was to blame and he was damn well going to prove it. It was probably the same one that killed Kathy's dog, one of those varmints the goddamn feds had let loose in Yellowstone. And they expected you to stand by and serve it five-hundred-dollar calves for its dinner! It made a man sick. Buck wasn't going to stand for it.

He slung the piece of hide away and watched it curve like a skimming stone down into the gully.

'So, Nat, are you prepared to back me on it being a wolf or not?'

The vet stood up and scratched his head. Buck could see how uncomfortable he was, being put on the spot. The two men had known each other since they were kids. Both were aware that Nat and his father had made good money from the work the ranch provided.

'Well, Buck, you know, it's a tough call.'

'Well, he sure didn't die of old age.'

'Maybe not, but—'

'And you said it wasn't a bear.'

'I can't say for sure it wasn't.'

127

Buck put his arm around the vet's shoulders. Nat was short and Buck towered over him like an uncle.

'You're a good friend, Nat, and I don't want to put words in your mouth. But you know what these bunny-huggers are like. They'll do all they can to pretend it isn't one of their precious wolves that did it. All I want is your best opinion, just a little ammunition.'

'Well, maybe.'

'Maybe isn't going to cut a lot of snuff with these fellas. What are you saying, that it's ninety percent certain it was a wolf? Eighty? You tell me.'

'That's pushing it, Buck.'

'Seventy-five then.'

'Well, I dunno. Maybe.'

'Seventy-five. Okay.' Buck took his arm off the vet's shoulders. He'd got what he wanted. 'Well, thank you Nat. I appreciate it, old buddy. You can put the tarp back now, Clyde.'

They'd brought an old green tarpaulin up in the truck and Clyde swung it over the carcass, sending up a cloud of grasshoppers. Nat Thomas looked at his watch and said he was already running late on his calls and had better get going. Buck knew the poor fellow just didn't fancy being around when the feds got here. Buck slapped him on the back and they set off down the hill.

'I'll drive you down. Come on Clyde, let's go call the bunny-huggers.'

'Luke? Are you coming to eat?'

Luke opened his eyes and saw his mother standing beside the bed, looking down at him.

'Are you all right?'

'Yeah, I was doing some exercises and must have dropped off.'

She stroked the hair from his forehead and smiled, but he could see in her eyes that something was wrong. He sat up, swung his legs off the bed and started pulling on his boots.

'What's the matter?'

She looked away and sighed.

'Mom?'

'Clyde found a dead calf. Your father's making a big thing of it.'

'W-where?'

'Oh, somewhere, I don't know.'

'Up on the allotment?'

She looked at him and nodded.

'And he thinks it's a w-w-wolf?'

'Yes. And so does Nat Thomas. Come on, everybody's down there. Let's get it over with.'

He followed her out and along the corridor toward the top of the stairs. What was he going to say? He knew his father would blame him. How on earth had Clyde found it? And what was he doing checking up on him anyway?

Luke had come across the carcass two days ago. There were fresh wolf tracks in the dust and some scat too. He'd dragged the calf down into the gully and covered it with rocks. He'd broken off a branch of limber pine and brushed away the tracks, then gotten rid of the scat. He'd figured no one was going to know anything until the fall when the cattle came down and got counted.

As he walked toward the kitchen doorway, Luke could hear them all chatting. Clyde was laughing and telling the two hands who were helping with the haying, Ray and Jesse, what Nat Thomas had said. But he stopped as soon as Luke stepped into the room. Everyone looked up at him. His father was sitting at the head of the table.

'Hi, Luke,' he said. 'Had a good sleep?'

'I w-w-was—'

129

'Come and eat. It's going cold.'

Luke sat next to Ray, who gave him a nod.

'How're you doing, Luke?'

'G-g-good. '

His mother was cutting him a slice of meat loaf, which was one of the few meat dishes he actually enjoyed, though right now he didn't feel hungry at all. Everyone else had almost finished.

'Anyhow,' Clyde went on. 'He's scratching his head and getting all fidgety and saying how it's a real tough call and all, and so Buck here says, "Well, Nat, he sure didn't die of old age!"'

Clyde bellowed with laughter and the ranch hands laughed too. Luke knew his father was looking at him, but he kept his own eyes on his plate while his mother piled it with salad and potato. She put it down in front of him and started serving second helpings to the hands.

'So, Luke,' his father said. 'You heard we found a dead calf.'

Luke had his mouth full so he just nodded. His father waited for the reply.

'Yes sir. W-w-where did you f-f-find it?'

'Over by Ripple Creek,' Clyde said. 'You know the gully that runs along the foot of the meadow there?'

'Uh-huh.'

'Just up there.'

The hands were concentrating hard on their food, sensing this was family business. His father's eyes hadn't once left him.

'I thought you said you checked along there every day,' he said.

'Not down in the g-g-gully always. I ride al-along the t-t-top.'

'That's where it was. Along the top, lying there right out in the open.'

Something had found it and hauled it up there again, Luke

130

thought. What would do that? Maybe the wolves had come back.

'Wh–wh–what k–k–k—'

'What killed it?'

'Yes.'

'Nat Thomas reckons it was a wolf. That Prior fella's trying to get hold of Bill Rimmer to come up this afternoon. What bothers me is how many more dead calves have we got up there?'

'I d–d–don't think there are—'

'You wanted that job, Luke. If you're going to do it, you're going to have to do it properly. Okay?'

Luke nodded. 'Y–y–yes, sir.'

'Or we'll just have to put Jesse here onto it.'

'Phew,' said Ray, wiping his brow and grinning. 'That's good. Least I ain't going to get chewed up by wolves.'

Everyone laughed and the tension loosened a little. His father stood up and, as if attached to him by invisible strings, so did Clyde.

'Probably wasn't a wolf anyhow,' his mother said.

'That's not what Nat Thomas says,' Buck said, putting on his hat. Luke's mother was cleaning pans at the sink, not looking at him.

'Nat Thomas would swear it was the Easter Bunny, if you gave him ten dollars.'

When his mother said things like that, Luke realized how much he loved her.

Dan had told her a lot about Buck Calder, but nothing he'd said had quite prepared Helen for the shock of the real thing. The sheer physicality of the man was overwhelming. He made those around him seem like suckerfish to a shark.

Dan had introduced them down at the house, telling him Helen had just come on board to help find the wolf, taking care to keep it singular. She and Buck had shaken hands. His hand was huge and strangely cool and he had held on to hers just a little too long, fixing her with those pale eyes. The gaze was so direct, so immediately intimate, that Helen had found herself blushing. He had asked her to ride up here to the pasture with him in the truck and she'd replied, a little too quickly, that no, it was okay, she would ride up with Dan and Bill Rimmer. Dan had teased her about it on the way up.

'Sure missed your chance there, Helen.'

'Whoa! My mom calls eyes like that *bedroom* eyes.'

'Bedroom eyes?' Bill said.

'Yeah. First time I heard her say it I was only little and I thought she meant, you know, sleepy or something. And one day she heard me tell Eddie Horowitz, the kid next door, that he had bedroom eyes and she gave me a slap.'

Bill Rimmer laughed loudly. He seemed a nice guy.

Calder's son-in-law had called the office in Helena just as she and Dan were about to set off up to the cabin and were packing the Toyota with Helen's gear and the ton of provisions they had just bought at the supermarket. It was still all stacked in the back.

Now they were standing around this supposed wolf-kill with grasshoppers jumping all over their boots.

Bill Rimmer was on his knees beside it, inspecting it and taking his time. Helen stood beside Dan who was videoing it. Facing them across the carcass, Calder and his son-in-law stood waiting for the verdict.

It was a farce. Dan clearly thought so too. She had caught his eye briefly when Clyde swung the tarpaulin off and the flies cleared enough for them to see what was left of the calf. It was so far gone, nobody could possibly say how it had met its end. It could have been shot or died of a broken heart.

A horse snickered somewhere below them and Helen looked down into the gully and saw Calder's son riding up

132

toward them through the rocks. She had seen him down at the house but no one had bothered to introduce him. She had been struck immediately by how good-looking he was and wondered why he had hung back, listening while his father and Clyde did all the talking.

Once Helen had caught him staring at her with those intense green eyes and she'd smiled but he looked away immediately. They had passed him on his horse coming up here and Dan had told her who he was.

Luke got off his horse when he was still some way off and stayed there, standing beside it and stroking its neck. Helen smiled again and this time he gave her a little nod before looking away to where the others stood around the carcass.

Rimmer was standing now.

'So?' Calder said.

Rimmer took a long breath before answering.

'You say Nat Thomas saw this just this morning?'

'About three hours ago.'

'Well, I don't see how he can say this animal was killed by a wolf.'

Calder shrugged. 'Experience, I guess.'

Rimmer ignored the insult. 'You see, sir, there's just not enough to go on. We can take it away and have some tests done—'

'I think Nat's the man to do that,' Calder cut in.

'Well, that has to be your decision, sir. But, frankly, I don't reckon tests would give us anymore of an idea. Dan and Helen here have both seen a fair number of cattle predations. Dan?'

'I'm afraid I have to agree.'

'Well, there's a surprise,' said Calder sarcastically. 'Miss Ross? Would you care to venture an opinion?'

Helen felt the power of his stare again and she cleared her throat, hoping her voice wasn't going to show how nervous he made her.

'You can't say it wasn't a wolf, but there's no sign left that it was. Did anybody look for prints before the ground got all scuffed up like this?'

'Course I did,' Clyde said, defensively. He darted a look at his father-in-law. 'The ground's too hard. Too much rock and stuff.'

'Or scat maybe? You know, droppings—'

'I do know what scat is.' He gave a little humorless laugh. 'There wasn't none of that either.'

Dan said, 'Maybe, Mr Calder, if you'd called us first, we could have—'

'Who I choose to call first is my business, Mr Prior,' Calder snapped. 'And with all due respect, I reckon Nat Thomas's opinion is a sight more objective than others' around here.'

'What I meant is, I can understand why you might want Nat to come and have a look too, but if—'

'Oh, you can?'

'Yes, sir.'

'Seems to me you government fellows don't understand a damn thing. You let these wolves loose, let them kill our pets and now our cattle, and then try and pretend they're not to blame.'

'Sir, I—'

'Don't make an enemy of me, Prior. It's not a good idea.'

He looked away, down the valley, and for a long moment, no one spoke. Somewhere way above them in the mountains an eagle called. Calder shook his head and looked at the ground, nudging some sage with his boot. The grasshoppers scattered.

Helen thought it amazing. Here they were, all adults, and he had them hanging on his every word like naughty schoolkids hauled before the principal. But they all went on watching him and waiting for him to speak and at last he seemed to reach some conclusion.

134

'Okay,' he said, and after a moment more looked up at Dan. 'Okay. You tell me this young lady here is going to be working full-time on this.' He didn't grace Helen with his eyes when he said this, just tilted his chin in her direction.

'Yes, sir.'

'Then she'd better do a good job and do it quick. Because I tell you, Mr Prior, if I lose another calf, we may have to do something about it ourselves.'

'Well, I'm sure I don't need to remind you of the law about—'

'No sir, you sure as hell don't.'

They were glaring at each other, neither one prepared to be the first to look away. Helen could see Dan was seething. She'd never seen him so angry. It wouldn't have surprised her if he'd stepped over the carcass and punched the rancher on the jaw. Then Calder suddenly flashed his white teeth and turned to Helen, clicking on the charm again, as if nothing had happened.

'So you'll be living up by Eagle Lake?'

'Yep. Going up there right now.'

'It can get kind of lonely up there.'

'Oh, I'm used to being alone.'

Calder gave her a look that said plainly as any words, *How could that be? Pretty little thing like you.* It was like a lustful uncle putting a hand on your knee.

'Well, Helen, you must come down to the house and have supper with us some time, tell us how you're getting along.'

She gave him a blithe smile.

'Well, thank you,' she said. 'That'd be nice.'

135

11

It took Helen the rest of that day and most of the next to unpack her things and get the cabin into some kind of livable condition. And it would have taken longer if Dan hadn't helped.

Compared with some places she had to stay in, it wasn't too bad. It was twelve feet square and built of logs, with a screened window in each wall and a roof that would soon need some serious attention. In one corner stood a pot-bellied stove with a top you could cook on. Dan had filled a box beside it with a month's supply of firewood and given her a chain saw for when it ran out. There was also a Coleman gas stove with two burners.

'Hey, I can throw dinner parties,' she said.

'Yeah, for your new friend Buck Calder.'

'Please!'

Stacked on rickety shelves beside the stove were assorted cups, bowls and plates, all of them chipped and emblazoned with the Forest Service logo, in case anyone was desperate enough to steal them. Apart from the cobwebbed curtains, which looked as though they might fall apart if you touched them, the only decoration was a laminated map of Hope and some blackened cast-iron pans that hung from nails above the cracked enamel sink. The sink itself was rigged with an elegant pitcher pump and drained into a somewhat less elegant slop pail below.

In the opposite corner were two bunk beds, for the bottom one of which Dan had thoughtfully provided a new mattress, blankets and pillows. The only other pieces of furniture were an old wardrobe and a plain wooden table with two chairs.

Sunk into the planked floor was a trapdoor.

'What's down there?'

'Oh, that goes down to the basement. You know, laundry room, sauna, that kind of thing.'

'No hot tub?'

'They're installing it next week.'

She opened the trapdoor and found a bare, cement-lined root cellar, some three feet square and four feet deep. It was to keep food from freezing in winter and getting too hot in summer.

The one luxury was the neat little Japanese generator that Dan had rigged outside the door so she could recharge her laptop, stereo and the cell phone Dan had supplied her with. In theory, he said, she should be able to hook the phone up to her laptop and get e-mail. The trouble was, cell phones didn't work too well up here in the mountains; often as not you couldn't get a signal. The prospect of isolation didn't bother Helen at all. As backup, Dan was also going to set up a voice-mail number for her.

Around the back of the cabin was a logbuilt outhouse and, beside it, a kind of improvised shower – a metal bucket with holes in the bottom. Birds had been nesting in it, but with a little maintenance Helen would soon have it working.

'I tried to clear things up a little,' Dan said.

'It's terrific. Thank you.'

'And whatever your friend Buck Calder says, I can guarantee you're not going to be lonely.'

'How do you mean?'

He showed her the mousetraps he'd set behind the stove and under the beds. They were all sprung, bait taken, no mouse.

'I see you're still no better at trapping, Prior.'

'That's why I took the desk job.'

'What bait did you use?'

'Cheese, what else?'

'Hey, buddy, you know better than to ask a trapper her trade secrets.'

That first night she was too tired to be bothered with trying to catch mice and regretted it almost as soon as she shut her eyes. Buzz spent the whole night scrabbling around for them and made so much noise that in the end she took him out and shut him in the Toyota. Left to their own devices, the mice scuffled in and out of her dreams till daybreak. By the time Dan arrived the next day Helen had set up an elaborate trap which had him in fits.

It was a method Joel had taught her their first year together on the Cape when the ship-house suddenly became the neighborhood refuge for homeless rodents. All you needed was a bucket, a length of wire and a tin can, drilled at both ends. You fed the wire through the holes in the can and rigged it so that it hung across the top of the bucket into which you poured a few inches of water. All that was left to do was prop a stick against the side of the bucket, smear the can with peanut butter, lock the dog away and retire. The mice climbed up the stick, crawled along the wire and when they stepped onto the can it spun and dumped them in the drink.

'It never fails,' Helen said.

'No way.'

'I'll bet you dinner on it.'

'You're on.'

That night she caught three mice and had them proudly on display when Dan showed up in the afternoon with all the radio collars, trapping gear and some mapping software for her computer. He'd halfheartedly accused her of cheating, but true to his word, after another day getting the cabin straight, took her that same evening to Nelly's Diner.

Helen was now struggling to finish the biggest steak she had ever laid eyes on. The menu called it a *T.Rex bone* and even that didn't do it justice.

The diner was wallpapered throughout with huge photo-panoramas of the Rocky Mountains which once must have made the real thing, glimpsed from the small front windows, look like poor imposters. Over the years, however, the colors had grown saturate and dark and the joins had split open with the heat, so that now the landscape seemed to be in shadow, ominously riven with seismic cracks. Against this background of imminent doom, the tables with their paper cloths of red and white check and candles afloat in little red glasses strove bravely to make the place cheerful.

Only two other tables were occupied: one by a family of German tourists whose monster Winnebago was blocking all view from the front windows and the other by two old men in matching white Stetsons, who were arguing about hearing aids.

The only waiter was a friendly giant with blue-tinted aviator glasses and long gray hair tied in a ponytail. From the voice that hectored him from backstage in the kitchen (Nelly's, perhaps), they gathered his name was Elmer. The tattoos and the black T-shirt with *Bikers for Jesus* emblazoned on the front proclaimed him the owner of the Harley that stood gleaming outside. When Helen and Dan had first walked in, he'd said, 'Angels on your body.' It took them a moment to realize it was a greeting. They'd avoided catching each other's eye until they were safely alone at their table.

Helen pushed her plate away and leaned back.

'Dan, this steak's got me beat.'

She wondered if she would lose all credibility with him if she were now to light a cigarette. She decided not to risk it.

They had spent most of the meal reminiscing about the good old days in Minnesota. Helen reminded him of the time his hand had slipped while he was trying to give a trapped wolf a shot of sedative and emptied the syringe into his own thigh instead. He'd gone out like a light. They laughed so much the two little German kids kept turning to stare at them with big blue eyes.

No mention had been made of that one time they had briefly become more than just friends and for this Helen was grateful. The news that Dan was now divorced had bothered her a little. Whether there was anyone new in his life, she didn't know, but she hoped so.

Dan couldn't finish his steak either. He took a drink of beer and sat back, silent for a moment, smiling at her.

'What are you grinning at?' she said.

'Oh, I was just thinking.'

'What?'

'Just that it's good to have you out here.'

'Hey, I'll go anywhere for a free dinner.'

She could tell from the way he was looking at her that there was more to it than that. She hoped he wasn't going to voice it and spoil things.

'You know, Helen, after Mary and I broke up, I nearly called you.'

'Oh?'

'Yeah. I thought about you a lot. And how, you know, that summer, if I hadn't been—'

'Dan, come on.'

'I'm sorry.'

'Don't be sorry.'

She reached across the table and took his hand and smiled at him. He was such a sweet guy.

'We're friends,' she said softly. 'And that's really how it always was.'

'I guess.'

'And, right now, I really need a friend more than, well, more than anything else.'

'I'm sorry.'

'Say that once more and I won't ever share my mouse-trapping secrets with you again.'

He laughed and let go of her hand. Elmer loomed to the rescue and asked them if they were done with their steaks and did they want cream pie or death by chocolate? They settled for coffee.

'You're the new wolf lady, huh?' he said when he came back to pour it.

'That's me. How did you know?'

He shrugged. 'Whole town knows.'

Buck took another good look in his rearview mirror and then checked up ahead again to make sure the road was clear both ways. If he ever saw another car when he reached her driveway, he would just keep on up the road.

It was real handy, her living out here on the edge of town where there were no snoopy neighbors and he could park his car around the back where it couldn't be seen from the road. It was certainly a whole lot better than doing it in some seedy motel on the interstate or up in the forest, bare-assed to the elements, or in the back of a truck in winter, which was all fine and dandy when you were young with the sap rising so fast it was a job keeping the lid on it. But as

141

a man got older, love, like most things, required a little comfort.

Some time ago they had worked out a system. If she closed the curtains in the little window nearest the road, it meant she had company and he should drive on by. He was glad to see that tonight they were open. He could see a light on inside and imagined her in there, showered and smelling all fresh and ready for him. The thought made his pants tighten a little at the crotch.

Buck never had trouble finding an excuse to be away from home. There was always a meeting to attend or neighbor to visit or a deal to do in town. On those rare occasions when things got tricky, there were always friends he could count on for cover. Tonight he was supposed to be – and indeed had been, for awhile anyhow – at a stockgrowers' meeting in Helena. Mostly, he didn't even have to lie because Eleanor never asked where he was going or how late he would be and she was always in bed asleep when he got home.

The road was clear and he swung the car into the driveway and parked behind the old station wagon. The door to the house opened as he was getting out and he saw her in her black bathrobe lean her shoulder against the door frame, smiling that knowing smile of hers and waiting for him. She watched him walk toward her, neither one of them saying a word, and when he reached her, he slipped his hands inside her robe and held her by her naked hips while he kissed her neck.

'Ruth Michaels,' he said. 'You're the sexiest goddamn woman this side of the Missouri River.'

'Oh yeah? So who is it you're seeing on the other side?'

Later, at home, as he shed his clothes for the second time that night, Buck's mind ran with matters much less steamy. From the narrow closet area that linked bedroom and bathroom, he watched Eleanor's sleeping shape in their big brass bed and wondered what in God's name she thought she was playing at, offering Ruth the money.

Ruth seemed to find it amusing. She'd broken the news about half an hour after he arrived, when they were lying sticky and sated and he was thinking, for no particular reason, about that pretty young biologist all alone up there in the forest and wondering what his chances might be in that direction. And as if to punish him for his thoughts, Ruth had said, almost matter-of-fact, that Eleanor was going to bail her out and become her business partner. He'd almost fallen off the bed.

'Your business partner!'

Ruth laughed. 'You know, when she came in I was so nervous, I thought uh-oh, here it comes, she knows. But then she sits there with her cappuccino and offers me the money.'

'She can't do that. For Christsake, Ruthie, I've told you, I'll give you the damn money.'

'I couldn't take your money.'

'But hers is okay?'

'Yes.'

'Well, I don't get it.'

'Well, Buck honey, you think about it.'

Then she'd laughed, which made her breasts move in a way that was disconcerting when a man was trying to assess important news. He'd asked her what was so funny and Ruth told him Eleanor had said she'd want to be more than just a 'sleeping partner'.

Buck didn't think that was funny at all.

He stood in the shower and sluiced the smell of sex from his body while he considered things. He couldn't say a word, of course, until Eleanor chose to tell him. And hell, after all, it was her money. Her daddy had left it to her and she could flush it down whichever toilet she pleased. But if it happened,

143

it was bound to make life more complicated. One of the basic rules of adultery was that wife and mistress be kept as far apart as possible. Ruth, to his amazement, didn't seem to think it was a problem.

He dried himself in front of the mirror, routinely admiring his body and checking it for any mark she might have made on him. He was all clear. Then he cleaned his teeth, flashed himself a humorless smile and walked back through to the bedroom, avoiding the floorboards that creaked. He switched off his bedside light which Eleanor always left on for him and slipped quietly into bed beside her.

As always, she was turned away, facing the wall, and didn't so much as stir. He couldn't even hear her breathing. Sometimes he thought she only pretended to be asleep.

'Goodnight,' he said quietly. But there was no answer.

Women, Buck thought, as the ceiling dimly configured itself in the darkness above him. Even after all these years, with all the work he'd put in trying to know as many and as much about them as possible, they remained, in the end, one of God's great unraveled mysteries.

Eleanor listened to him sighing and shifting and knew he was lying on his side, facing her, perhaps even watching her for any sign that she was awake. She lay still. Soon he would sigh again and turn the other way and then, in about five minutes, would settle on his back and his throat would click and he would start to snore.

She envied him the ease with which he could slip away from the world. Long ago, in the days when she still believed sleep was at least a possibility, she had tried the ritual herself: left side, right side, back. But it never worked.

His snoring wasn't loud, except when he had been drinking. It was more of a rushing sound, like the bellows he used on the living-room fire in winter. The rhythm of her own breathing was faster than his and every night she fought to maintain it. But she always gave in. She would lie there, holding the spent air uncomfortably in her lungs, resenting with every accelerated beat of her heart that even in sleep her husband's will should so prevail.

Sometimes, when she was sure he was asleep, she would turn quietly and lightly, so as not to move the mattress, and lie studying him. She would watch the rise and fall of his great chest, the quiver of his open lips as he exhaled. Slackened by sleep, his upturned face was oddly childlike, almost touching. There was a pale band across his forehead, like a halo, where his hat shielded him from the sun. Eleanor would search her heart for some vestige of love and try to remember how it was to feel more for him than pity or contempt.

She had known about Buck's record with women before they married, though not its full extent. A friend of a friend had firsthand experience and conveyed a warning that was easy to misconstrue as sour grapes. When Eleanor confronted him, he disarmed her with what passed for a full confession then proceeded to convince her that his wilder oats had only been sown in a lonely quest that had led at last to her.

Even had she not believed him, she would probably still have married him. His appetite for women was a weakness and, in one so visibly strong, weakness of any sort could be appealing. It stirred in Eleanor's Catholic blood some deep, redemptive urge. She was not the first woman, nor would she likely be the last, to marry a man in the belief that she might save him.

The fact that Buck Calder was either unready for salvation or perhaps incapable of it took only a few short years to emerge, though it took several more for Eleanor to acknowledge.

His work as a state legislator and champion of the livestock industry gave him ample opportunity to play away from home

145

and what her eyes couldn't see, her heart could safely eschew. He was a skilled and thoughtful deceiver, selecting his women with care to avoid those who might later come screaming vengeance in the night. Those he lay with always seemed to know the rules. They never called him at home or smeared make-up on his clothes or seemed to mark him, even in their wildest throes, with their teeth or nails.

Denial is a creature of infinite resource, wriggling its way into the finest crevices of the mind to spin its cocoons around fear and suspicion. And Eleanor, being spared much of the routine ignominy of the cheated wife, was a willing host.

Even when, by chance at the hairdresser's, she saw a photograph in a local magazine of Buck at a cattlemen's dinner, entwined with a young rodeo queen, she readily gave him the benefit of the doubt. He was a man whom women found attractive, for heaven's sake. It wasn't his fault. And he was hers and the father of her children. And he loved her, she *knew* he loved her, for he told her so and showed her.

It was Kathy's birth that changed things.

Eleanor's waters broke a fortnight early, when Buck was at a livestock conference in Houston. Everything happened in such a rush it wasn't until late that night, with the baby safely swaddled in her arms, that she called his hotel from her hospital bed and was put through to his room. A woman answered the phone, one to whom he obviously hadn't yet had time to explain the rules.

'Mr Calder's bed,' she purred, before the phone was snatched from her.

Buck came home and came clean. And for the sake of the children, but also because he was as good at contrition as he was at cheating, Eleanor was prepared to forgive him for what he promised was his only transgression. Nothing could excuse what he'd done, he said. But there he'd been, away in a strange city, all on his own, and after a few drinks too many, a man could sometimes go astray. And with Eleanor being pregnant and all and it being awhile since they'd last well, you know.

She put him through six months of purgatory, banished him from her bed and tried not to feel sorry for him while he played the penitent husband, taking his proper punishment like a man. He tended to the children as well as all the work on the ranch, while she looked after the baby.

Careful to remain aloof and stony, Eleanor was secretly impressed by how much he knew about the many tedious details of what had always been her domain. He coped; he more than coped. He got Henry and Lane up in the morning and got them fed and bathed and to bed at night. He got the groceries in without having to ask her what they needed. He bought her flowers and cooked special suppers for her, which she ate without comment. He was courteous and considerate, giving her a chastened little smile if ever she should deign to look his way.

Eleanor didn't know how many Hail Marys adultery deserved, but she was just starting to think he might have done enough when two commiserating friends made the mistake of thinking she should now hear what they had always kept from her. Over coffee one morning, they gave her chapter and verse about others Buck had bedded in the past few years, including some Eleanor had counted as friends.

She should, she now knew, have followed their advice and left him. But in some diminished corner of her heart, she felt that Buck might yet be saved. Sometimes she would look out from the kitchen window at the snowbound pasture and see the cottonwood growing from the rusting Model T and she would tell herself that anything was possible, that the good Lord brooked no wreckage that did not contain at least a seed of hope.

Eventually she allowed him back into her bed, though it

would be another three years before she allowed him to make love to her again. Not that she didn't want him. There were times when she woke hot and wet in the night and felt the need of him so badly that it took all her strength not to reach out for him and wake him and take him into her in lustful absolution.

It was in precisely this way that Luke was conceived. And during the months that followed, as their last child grew in her womb, Eleanor and Buck found a passion in their coupling that seemed to surprise and excite him as much as her. He was the only man who had ever made love to her, but not until then had her flesh fully woken to him.

Thinking back on that time, even now, so many years later, Eleanor could almost feel the bruise and ache of their love-making and be ashamed that she should have let herself be so carnally consumed. If only she had been decent and restrained herself, perhaps the pain of his subsequent betrayals would have been more bearable. It would have been better never to have known him in this way. For, with the arrival of Luke – *her* son, as unlike a father as a boy could be – their passion ended.

For Buck, she later thought, it probably seemed merely like the end of another affair.

She took his criticism of Luke as criticism of herself, for the boy was indeed the image of her and his frailty and failings must thus be hers.

Their other children had learned early to sleep through the night. Only if they were sick did they ever sleep in their parents' bed. But Luke cried and cried and cried and the only way to make him stop was to bring him to her bed and hold him till he fell asleep.

At first Buck would make her carry him back to his crib, but Luke would always jerk awake and cry again and soon, despite Buck's protests, she let the child stay all night.

148

Thus was the new geometry of their life conformed: Eleanor, tired and defensive; her husband ousted and angry and soon back to his wanderings (which, from this point on, she would do her best to ignore and try – try so very hard – to pity him for); and this new boy child, who had so literally come between them.

And so the long winter of their marriage began. Devoid already of desire and soon of friendship too, there wasn't even warmth enough for mutual comfort when young Henry died. The closest they came to connecting in their grief was the row they'd had on the day after the funeral. Buck had found her ironing her dead son's laundry and called her a fool. What did he expect, she asked, that she should throw the boy's clothes away?

She heard her husband turn now and adjust his pillow.

Soon he was snoring and she lay listening to him, wondering whose bed he had been in earlier. And doing her best, after all these years, not to care.

Dan escorted Helen to her pickup outside The Last Resort where they'd gone for a beer after leaving the diner. She thanked him for a great evening and gave him a kiss on the cheek.

'Angels on your body,' she said as she drove away.

'And on yours.'

It was getting on for midnight and the town was deserted. She headed out to where the pavement ended and turned onto the gravel road that led up the valley. Buzz, who had been sleeping in the pickup, rode shotgun in the front seat.

It was the first time she had driven the route in the dark, and after leaving the main road near the top of the valley it became a little complicated. There were no signs and she knew she had to take two right turns and one left but she got one wrong and ended up at a ranch where dogs came barking and someone peered out, silhouetted in yellow light, from an upstairs window. She waved and turned the pickup around then stopped a little way back down the road so that she could study the map with a flashlight.

At last, at the forest's edge, she found the row of five mail-boxes, her own among them, that marked a turning, all but hidden by trees. Here the gravel road turned to dirt and wound through the forest for another four steep and rutted miles to Eagle Lake. The mailboxes were all different colors. Hers was white. The others belonged, she supposed, to cabins or houses she had yet to discover. The only other signs of human life she'd so far seen up here were a solitary hiker and a huge logging truck that had nearly run her off the road that afternoon.

As the old pickup lurched and creaked its way through the trees, she thought about what Dan had tried to say at dinner. God, a woman could do a whole lot worse than Dan Prior. She'd proved it herself several times over. She was touched and even, for a moment, flattered that he should still feel that way about her – until her other self, the one that always sliced her off at the knees when she started to feel remotely good about herself, clicked in and told her not to be stupid; the poor guy was divorced, lonely and probably just plain desperate.

Eagle Lake lay in a clearing, a shallow bowl of meadow half a mile long that in early summer erupted in a blaze of moun-tain flowers. The cabin stood on the bowl's western rim some thirty yards from the water at the top of a gentle slope that was divided by a stream where mule deer came at dawn and dusk to drink.

Helen's headlights found them there now, eight or nine of them, as the pickup came up and out of the trees. They looked up as one, quite unafraid, and Helen stopped and for a few moments they watched each other, while Buzz, alert and watching too, quivered and made little whining noises.

Then the deer turned and slowly moved away until the white of their tails merged into the trees and disappeared.

She parked the pickup beside the cabin and while Buzz went off to forage, she leaned her back against the hood and looked up at the sky. There was no moon and every far-flung star in the firmament was pitching for the job. She had never seen a sky so incandescent. The air was still and smelled of pine.

Helen filled her lungs and coughed. She was definitely going to quit smoking. Forever. She would just have one last cigarette and that would be it. Absolutely definitely.

She lit up and walked down beside the stream, surprised that starlight alone could make a shadow of her. On a spit of gravel at the lake's edge there was a wooden boat once presumably used for fishing but now rotten and colonized by reeds. She tested its bows as a seat and found them solid and she sat there to smoke her final cigarette and ponder the sky's reflection in the glass of the water.

Now and then, above her in the trees, she could hear Buzz exploring and once she thought she heard the footfall of some larger animal. But all else was silent, not the croak of a frog nor the flicker of an insect's wing, as if the world this night were in suspended deference to the sky. Gazing at the water, she saw the mirrored fall of a meteor and fancied that from that distant shore of the universe she also heard its roar.

She hadn't seen a shooting star since her last night on the Cape and she closed her eyes now and wished the same convoluted cheat of a wish that she had wished then, three rolled into one, that Joel was safe and would come back as he had promised and that he would want (which she doubted most of all) to be with her.

She stood up and crushed the burning tip of her cigarette between her fingers. Then she put the filter in her pocket, speculating on what special kind of cretin it was who cared

151

more for the health of the planet than of her own coked lungs.

Tomorrow she would start her new life and the search for the wolf. She wondered where in the wilderness the animal was right now. Hunting somewhere, no doubt, wetly nosing the black air, waiting and watching with yellow eyes or stalking like a liquid shadow through the forest.

Perhaps she should howl, she thought, and see if she got an answer. Dan had always said she had the best howl in the business, that no wolf in Minnesota could resist returning her call. But she hadn't howled in years and though Buzz was her only audience, she felt self-conscious. Then she thought, what the hell, and cleared her throat and tilted her face to the sky.

She was so out of practice that the first howl was a mess. It sounded like a donkey with a sore throat and the second wasn't much better. Then, on the third attempt, she found it: the low start, that rose in a slow, expanding, mournful curve and tailed away into the night.

If any wolf heard it, none replied.

All it found was an echo in some remote recess of the mountains. But the sound made Helen shiver. For in it she heard the cadence of her own bereft soul.

FALL

12

They reached the ridge and stood among slabs of lichenous rock, shielding their eyes against the sun and squinting into the canyon that stretched away in a crooked arm below them. She could hear the rush of the creek and see flashes of foam where it hustled among the thickets of willow and alder lining the canyon bed. Helen swung her pack off one shoulder and pulled out her water bottle.

The last part of the climb had been steep and hot in the midday sun but at least up here they had found a breeze. Helen felt its cool press on the sweaty patch her pack had made on the back of her T-shirt and watched it shimmer the leaves of the aspens below them. She drank, then handed the bottle to Bill Rimmer. As he took it he nodded toward the other side of the canyon and Helen followed his gaze and saw a herd of bighorn sheep standing like sculpture, staring back at them.

It was three weeks since they had laid the traps. Dan had

taken her up in the Cessna so she could get an idea of how the land looked. There had been no hint of a radio signal. The following day, Helen and Rimmer had scouted out the best places to set the traps.

He had turned up at Helen's cabin bearing gifts of wolf scat and urine and his famous bait which Dan had warned her about. Rimmer called it 'kitty candy'. He opened the jar and held it out for Helen to smell. She nearly passed out.

'My God! What *is* that?'

Rimmer grinned. 'You really want me to tell you?'

'I don't know. Do I?'

'Putrefied bobcat and fermented coyote anal glands.'

'Thanks for sharing that with me, Bill.'

Buzz, who'd gotten a whiff too, was beside himself and ever since had viewed the (mercifully) airtight jar with quivering interest.

In this remote canyon, where they now were, they had found wolf tracks and scat, though neither was fresh. It seemed the most promising place of all, a rocky funnel down which any wolf traveling the divide might choose to use, and they decided to set ten of the twenty traps in and around it. The rest, with Buck Calder in mind, they laid along the two most likely routes down through the forest toward the allotments Calder and his neighbors leased for summer grazing.

Aware of Rimmer's high reputation as a trapper, Helen had been nervous about him watching her at work. But he had been easy and generous, even complimenting her on her technique and choice of trapping spots. After seeing her make her first dirt-hole set he'd joked that he might as well go home.

She enjoyed his company. He knew the country well and, without in any way patronizing her, taught her how wolves behaved in this kind of mountainous terrain, what they mostly preyed on and where they might choose to den. He had a gentle way about him and talked a lot about his wife and kids.

He had two boys, five and six years old, and a girl of eight who, he said, ruled the household and gave him stern lectures on how wicked he was to kill animals, which she knew to be part of his job.

The traps they were using were modified number 14s, very like the old Newhouse traps Helen had always used in Minnesota, which had a low risk of damaging a trapped leg. Rimmer was a little sniffy about them, saying they were too soft and gave the wolf too good a chance of escape. He personally preferred to use traps that had a firmer leg hold and were made down in Texas by a legendary trapper called Roy McBride.

Each trap was attached by a cord to a radio collar hidden nearby, in a tree if possible. As soon as the trap was dragged from the ground, the cord pulled a little magnet off and the collar would start to transmit a signal. Helen set half of the traps and Rimmer the other half and they bet a beer on who would catch the first wolf.

The result, after three weeks, was that neither of them had.

Every day Helen had scanned the frequencies and hadn't heard a single beep. Morning and evening, she went out and checked all three traplines. The two down in the forest were easy enough because she could use the logging roads and get close with the pickup. Checking the canyon trapline took longer. The old Toyota nearly shook itself to pieces until the last road ran out and from there it was a good hour's hike.

Each time she had reached the ridge where she and Rimmer now stood, she would convince herself that this was the day. And as she walked down through the trees, she would listen for the telltale clink of the drag chain or a rustle in the bushes where a trapped wolf might have taken cover. But each time it was the same.

Nothing. No wolf, no new prints or scat, not even a tuft of hair on a thornbush.

She started to think that maybe she had lost her touch or was doing something wrong. So after about ten days she moved the sets around, changed the way she made them and tried different kinds of places, not just along the side of trails, where normally you would expect a wolf to travel. She placed them high on the ridge and down by the creek, out in the open and deep in the scrub.

It had no effect.

Then she got to think that perhaps the traps were too new or smelled too metallic and so she took them back in batches to the cabin, scrubbed them with a wire brush then boiled them in creek water and logwood crystal. She pulled them out slowly through melted beeswax and hung them in a tree to let them dry, taking care all the while not to touch them with ungloved hands.

It made no difference.

Then she wondered if Buzz was the problem. He normally came along with her and sometimes even contributed his own pee to the wolf pee that she sprayed around the set. It had seemed like a good idea, both to Helen and to Rimmer when she told him. The scent of any trespassing canine, be it a wolf or a castrated dog, normally helped attract a wolf's attention. But perhaps Buzz's efforts were putting them off. So lately, much to his annoyance, Helen had left him in the truck or back at the cabin. She even gave up smoking for a few days in case it was the smell of that which was bothering them.

And still the traps stayed defiantly empty.

Not that she didn't have plenty of other things to fill her days. She'd loaded all the GIS (Geographic Information System) software Dan had given her into her computer and could now call up maps of the whole area. There were separate maps for watercourses, roads, different types of vegetation, and you could layer them on top of one another in any combination. Onto these she entered not just the precise location

158

of every trap, but any other information that might prove useful, such as sightings or signs of elk or deer or any other animal a wolf might be preying on – including the cattle on the grazing allotments.

She knew how important it was to keep herself busy. Because whenever she stopped, even if it were only for a few moments, some random thought of Joel might steal up behind her and grab her.

The nights were worst. It was usually dusk when she got back from checking the traps and her routine from then on was always much the same. If her cell phone had recharged (it often didn't seem to want to) and if she could get a signal, she would check her voice mail and return any calls. She had already more or less given up on e-mail. Because of the cell phone's analog transmission, downloading from the Internet was excruciatingly slow; a mere page could take five minutes.

Every time she checked her phone messages, she hoped, foolishly, that she might hear Joel's voice. But it was usually just Dan or Bill Rimmer, to see if she'd had any luck with the traps. Lately, even they had stopped calling, embarrassed, per-haps, about always getting the same answer. Occasionally, Celia or her mother left a message and Helen would do her best to call them back.

Then she would feed Buzz, take a shower, cook herself some supper and spend the rest of the evening on the com-puter, making notes and reading. And as it got dark, and silence lowered itself like a murderer's pillow over the forest, pierced only by the scream of an owl or a dying animal, it became harder and harder to keep Joel at bay.

She had tried playing music to deflect him, but everything she played only lured him closer. She would hear him coming in the hiss of the Coleman lanterns or the flutter of an insect's wing against the screen door. And even if she managed to keep him for awhile from her head, he would creep into her body and hang like a deadweight inside the cavity of her chest and force tears into her eyes until she couldn't bear it any longer and she'd get up and storm out of the cabin and down to the lake and sit there, sobbing and smoking and hating herself and him and the whole sorry world.

And when the sun rose again, without fail, she would feel what a fool she'd been and be ashamed, as if her idiotic grief were some dreadful man she'd somehow ended up in bed with. The practical biologist in her told her that such aberrant behavior could become habitual and that what she needed to do was break her routine.

So, she tried doing a howling survey, hiking up to the high canyon. But it was hopeless, even worse than that night she'd tried howling by the lake. She managed to get out a couple of reasonable howls – to which, naturally, there was no reply – then started to cry.

More successful were her evening trips into town, where she was gradually getting to know people. She would eat at Nelly's and usually get chatting with somebody, though she hadn't yet plucked up the courage to go alone into The Last Resort.

By now she had visited with most of the local ranchers and done her best to charm them. She had explained what she was there to do and asked them to get in touch with her if they saw any sign of a wolf. She would phone them and arrange to visit them at some convenient time of the day, usually around midday. Mostly those she met had been courteous and welcoming, though the women rather more so than the men.

The Millwards, who raised purebred Charolais bulls, had made a big fuss of her and insisted she stay for lunch. Even Buck Calder's daughter, Kathy Hicks, had been friendly enough, considering what had happened to her dog. Most of the ranchers, though not all, gave her permission to go on their land if she needed to, provided she didn't make a nuisance of herself or leave any gates open.

160

She had managed to see almost everyone except Abe Harding.

She had tried phoning his ranch but got no reply. Then she saw him in town one day outside the grocery store and smiled and said hi and he walked right past her as if she didn't exist. Helen was a little shaken. Harding's two boys, the ones in front of whom she'd made a fool of herself driving to Hope that first day, were loading something into the back of their truck. She could see them smirking.

'Oh, don't worry about Abe Harding,' Ruth Michaels said, when Helen told her what had happened. 'He's like that with everyone. The guy's a creep. Actually, that's not fair. He's just sad, sour and maybe a little unhinged. But with two sons like that, who wouldn't be?'

Helen liked Ruth and whenever she went into town she made a point of stopping at the gift shop for a coffee. Ruth's wicked sense of humor always got her laughing, which was as good a tonic as the coffee. It was useful too to have someone who could tell her the local gossip and fill her in on all the town characters.

As the weeks had gone by, Helen's failure to catch the wolf was becoming something of an embarrassment. People were starting to make wisecracks. She'd bumped into Clyde Hicks at the gas station two days ago and he'd leaned out of his car window and asked her how things were going, had she caught that old wolf yet, knowing full well she hadn't. No, she said. She hadn't.

'Know the best way to do it?' he said, grinning unattractively.

Helen shook her head.

'But I think you're going to tell me.'

'You get a big rock, sprinkle some pepper on it, wolf comes along, sniffs it, sneezes, knocks himself clean out. Bingo.'

Helen smiled, with gritted teeth.

161

'Is that so?'

'Yup. You try it. Tell you that for free.' And the smartass drove off.

At night she would lie awake, wondering why she was having no luck. Maybe it was people, she thought. Maybe there were others up in the forest who were somehow deterring the wolf from stepping into one of her traps? Not deliberately, just by being there. She had never seen anyone else up here, but she knew hikers came to the canyon and then there were the loggers who worked for the post and pole business farther down the valley.

She sometimes found bootprints in the dust or in the mud down beside the creek, though not often enough to make her worry about snagging someone in a trap. Lately she had also found hoofprints and horse dung. But wolves weren't normally put off by hikers or horses. Sure, they were shy, but no more so than grizzlies or mountain lions, both of whose tracks she had found. It was strange.

Stranger still, lately she had found traps sprung, with no sign of what might have done it. It looked as if it happened all by itself for they weren't dragged from the ground, which would have activated the radio transmitters. Helen had tried adjusting the pan tension to make them less sensitive and still it happened. Then yesterday she had found three of them sprung and that's when she had called Bill Rimmer and asked him to come out with her this morning.

Typically, they hadn't found a sprung one yet. All the ones down in the forest were untouched.

'You'll be thinking I imagined it,' she said now as they started down the slope into the canyon.

'It's like having a noise in your car and you take it in to get it fixed and the wretched thing won't do it.'

'With mine they wouldn't know where to start.'

The first two traps they checked in the canyon were just as

162

Helen had left them last night. The next one, at last, had been sprung.

She had set it at the side of a narrow dust trail which looked as though it was used mainly by deer. Rimmer walked around it, scanning the ground before each step. The trap lay exposed in its set, its jaws shut on nothing. He picked it up carefully on the end of a stick and examined it before handling it and checking the mechanism.

'There's nothing wrong with the trap.'

He put it down again and walked away about twenty yards along beside the trail, his eyes fixed on the ground. Then he came back and went the same distance the other way. Helen just stood and watched him.

'Come and have a look,' he said at last.

She walked over and Rimmer pointed down at the trail.

'See these deer tracks and how they just stop?'

'I guess he could have turned off.'

'I don't think so. Look over here.'

They walked together past the trap to where Rimmer had first stopped.

'See how the tracks start again here? That's the same animal, going in the same direction.'

'Are you sure?'

'Yep. Whatever sprung the trap brushed the trail clean afterward. I've met some pretty smart wolves, but none that smart.'

They hunted for tracks off the trail but the ground was too full of rock and scrub. It was the same at the site of the next trap: the trap was sprung and the ground completely clear.

Then, at the third, they found wolf tracks and fresh scat right on top of the sprung trap. Helen whooped.

'Well, at least he's still around.'

Rimmer was frowning at the ground.

'Yeah. But I don't reckon he sprung it. See these tracks

163

here? There's no sign of him pawing at it or jumping when it went off. Looks like he's just sauntered up and sniffed it, done his business, then gone on his way.'

'You think it was sprung before he came along?'

'Reckon so. Looks like the dust's been brushed before he came along. That's why you can see his prints so well.'

He pulled a plastic bag out of his pocket and put it over his hand to pick up the scat. Then he turned the bag inside out and handed it to Helen.

'At least he left you a present.'

They combed the area around the trap. Rimmer squatted down and sniffed at a tuft of grass.

'Sure is a strong smell around here. Like ammonia or something.'

He broke it off and handed it to Helen to smell.

'Yeah. And something else too. Gasoline maybe?'

They went on looking. Then Rimmer found a freshly broken piece of sagebrush, covered in dust. He held it up for her to see.

'Here's his broom. Somebody around here's playing games.'

Standing under the shower that evening, she was still no nearer to solving the mystery.

She had the shower working perfectly now and was proud of the modifications she had made: new screens, a hinged door that was low enough for her to see the lake and, heaven forbid, any visiting bears. Best of all was the five-gallon plastic tub that she had mounted in the tree above the shower bucket. To one side of it she had tied a rope and all she had to do was pull the rope and the tub would tilt and fill the shower bucket. She was sure one day the whole thing would collapse on her, but it gave her a much longer shower, even if the water was so damn cold you came out blue.

Her teeth were chattering by the time she grabbed her

towel and started to dry her hair, which took all of five seconds and was the only thing she liked about her new haircut.

Why on earth would anyone want to tamper with her traps?

All the ranchers she had met had been only too eager for her to catch any wolf that might be around. It didn't make sense. Unless it was someone's idea of a joke. She wrapped the towel around her and headed back to the cabin.

Once she was dressed, she made herself some tea then switched on her computer and logged the locations of the six traps she and Bill Rimmer had reset. She sat for a long time looking at the map of the canyon where they'd found the ones that had been most recently sprung. She clicked on the mouse to get the adjoining map. With her eyes still on the screen, she sipped her tea then took a bite of a big red apple that looked a lot better than it tasted. Then something on the map caught her eye.

On the south side of the canyon there was an old logging road she hadn't noticed before. She always came from the north and hadn't so far bothered to explore over there. She clicked again and zoomed wider to see where the road led. It snaked through the forest for about five miles, working its way down through a deep defile to a house high in the valley. She knew whose place this was, but clicked on it just to make sure. The words came up 'Harding Ranch'.

It was odd that it hadn't occurred to her before: perhaps it was those two boys who were playing tricks on her. Not that she had any grounds for suspicion, other than that they were by a long way the least friendly folk she'd met since she'd been here.

Half an hour later she was swinging the Toyota past a broken sign that said PRIVATE PROPERTY – NO HUNTING – KEEP OUT, and started to negotiate the potholes of the Hardings' driveway. Buzz, bouncing beside her, looked almost as nervous as she was and soon she saw why. Two dogs about twice his size and ten times meaner came hurtling out of the trees toward the pickup, their hackles bristling like sharkfins. Buzz whimpered.

Helen parked beside a rusted cattle trailer that lay with several other pieces of antique machinery, stitched to the ground by weed and grass, along the edge of the driveway. She switched off the engine and sat for a moment wondering what to do.

She was good with dogs but there was something about these two that made her reluctant to push her luck. One of them reared up and put his paws against the side of the pickup, barking and snarling and salivating all at the same time. Buzz gave an unconvincing woof and lowered himself onto the seat.

'Coward,' Helen said. She looked toward the house.

It was a forlorn sight, little more than a shack that had been added to over the years, presumably as money allowed. Ugly, makeshift extensions sprouted from it like architectural cancer, unified only by a mildewed whitewash. The roof was patched with blistered tarpaper. Even some of the patches were patched. It huddled against a cliff of bare rock as if fearful of being swallowed by the wilderness.

There were two trucks parked nearer to the house, one of them the black truck the boys drove. But the dogs were the only sign of life.

The light was fading fast and inside Helen could see the flicker of a TV, the remote world finding its way to this outpost via a giant satellite dish, bolted precariously to the cliff face above. From a line strung between two dying fir trees, the pale shapes of old shirts and underwear hung unstirring in the twilight.

Suddenly Helen heard a shout and the dogs immediately stopped their barking and ran back toward the house. A torn screen door opened and Abe Harding stepped out onto the porch. He yelled again at the dogs and they cowered and circled below him toward the side of the house.

Helen expected Harding to come over toward her, but instead he stayed where he was, just stood there, looking at her.

'Oh well,' she said, under her breath to Buzz. She opened the pickup's door. 'Here goes.'

She swung the door shut and headed out over the weed-studded gravel toward the house. She had already worked out how to play it. There was no way she was going to start accusing anyone about the traps. She wasn't even going to mention it. She was going to be sweetness and light.

'Evening!' she called out in her cheeriest voice.

'Uh-huh.' It was hardly friendly, but it was a start.

As she came to the foot of the steps that went up to the porch, one of the dogs growled invisibly from around the side of the house and without taking his eyes off Helen, Abe told it sharply to shut up. He was a gaunt, wiry man with eyes deep-set and troubled. He was wearing a pale, stained hat, jeans and a longsleeved undershirt. He wasn't wearing boots and his toes showed through a hole in one sock.

Helen put him somewhere in his mid to late fifties. Ruth Michaels had told her that he'd bought this place after coming back from Vietnam. Whether it was the war that gave him his wary, hunted look, Helen could only guess. Perhaps it came from living cornered in this dismal place, his back forever to the wall.

Helen held out her hand. 'Mr Harding, I'm Helen Ross, from the—'

'I know who you are.'

He looked at her hand and she thought for a perilous moment that he wasn't going to shake it. Eventually, as if it were against his better judgment, he did.

'Pretty place you've got here.'

He sniffed his contempt. She didn't blame him.

'Want to buy it?'

Helen laughed, a little too enthusiastically.

'Wish I could afford to.'

'What I hear, you government people get a pretty good deal. All the tax dollars you squeeze out of folk like us.'

'Yeah, I wonder who *does* get all that.'

Harding turned his head to one side and spat out a mouthful of black tobacco juice. It hit the dust beside the steps with a smack. Things weren't going as well as Helen had hoped. He looked at her again.

'What yer want?'

'Mr Harding, as you know, I've been given the job of trying to catch that wolf who killed Kathy Hicks' dog not so long ago and I just wanted to drop by, like I have with all your neighbors, and, you know, just say hi and introduce myself and . . .' She felt so *stupid*. As if a drunken frog had taken over control of her tongue.

'So you ain't caught him.'

'Not yet. But, boy, I'm trying!' She laughed nervously.

'Uh-huh.'

She could hear the sound of the TV from inside the house. It was a comedy show and, judging by the regular roars of studio laughter, a really good one. Helen suddenly became aware that she was being watched from inside. One of Harding's sons was looking out from the screen window of what she supposed was the kitchen. Soon his brother joined him. She ignored them and soldiered on, as brightly as she could.

'Obviously, to find out if he's still around and what he's up to—'

'Feeding on our cows, up on the allotments, I imagine. Had one of Buck Calder's calves already, I heard.'

'Well, it wasn't clear from the carcass—'

'Shit.' He shook his head and looked away. 'You people.'

Helen swallowed. 'Some of the other ranchers, including Mr Calder actually, have very kindly said they'll allow me to go on their land. You know, to look for tracks, scat, things like that.' She laughed, though why, she had no idea. 'Provided, of course, I'm very careful, shut gates and so on. And I wondered if you'd mind if I—'

'Come snooping around my land?'

'Well, not "snooping", but—'

'Like hell, you can.'

'Oh.'

'You think I'm going to let the goddamn federal government go tramping over my property, poking their noses into my business?'

'Well, I—'

'You must be out of your goddamn mind.'

'I'm sorry.'

'Git out of here.'

The two dogs appeared around the side of the house. One of them gave a low growl and Abe told it to shut up. Out of the corner of her eye, Helen could see the two boys grinning on the other side of the kitchen screen. Helen smiled bravely at their father.

'Well, I'm really sorry to have troubled you.'

'Just git.'

She turned away and walked back toward the pickup. There was another roar of laughter from the TV set. Her knees were shaking. She hoped it didn't show. Suddenly there was a scuffle behind her and, before she could turn, the first dog hit her. The impact sent her sprawling onto the dust.

Both of them were upon her, one at her thigh and the other at her ankle. They were snarling horribly, their teeth

169

slashing at her hiking pants. She screamed and kicked out. Harding was running toward them, yelling, calling them off.

They stopped as suddenly as they started. They loped off guiltily. Harding picked up a rock and hurled it after them and one of them yelped as it hit. Helen lay for a moment, in shock. There was a rip in her pants but there didn't seem to be any blood. She sat up.

'You okay?'

The tone wasn't exactly sympathetic. He was standing over her.

'I think so.'

Helen got to her feet and brushed herself down.

'You'll be on your way then.'

'Yeah. I think so.'

She walked to the pickup, all the way keeping an eye on the dogs. She didn't feel safe until she'd opened the door. Her shoulders were shaking not just with shock but with anger now too.

'I'd appreciate it if you'd tell whoever's messing with my traps that they'd better watch out. They could end up in a lot of trouble.'

Even to her own ears the threat sounded feeble. Her voice betrayed how close she was to tears. Harding made no reply.

Helen climbed behind the wheel and slammed the door. It was nearly dark. Harding stood watching while she turned the pickup around. Her headlights panned briefly across him. And, with her heart banging and the tears starting to spill, she headed off down the driveway. She cried all the way home.

13

Hope's fairground had known better days. It lay in a dusty sprawl of pasture at the back end of town and for most of the year played host to cottontails, gophers and occasional parties of high school rebels who used it for illicit midnight drag racing.

The rails around the pens and the rodeo arena hadn't seen a paintbrush in years and the bleachers were so rickety and splintered that only the most bolstered or reckless dared sit on them. Around the perimeter was a straggle of exhibit booths whose roofs had been warped to a matching tilt by winter winds, providing nesting space for various kinds of bird.

In times gone by, the place had been busy all around the calendar with craft markets, gun shows and various parades and rodeos. There used to be an annual Mountain Man Rendezvous, to which fantasists in beards and buckskin flocked from several neighboring states, and a Testicle

Festival, which for awhile enjoyed even greater popularity, except perhaps with the calves who supplied the food, euphemistically served as 'prairie oysters'. COME TO HOPE AND HAVE A BALL, the posters urged. But as the years went by, fewer and fewer did.

One by one, all these events had either petered out or sought more salubrious locations elsewhere. The only survivor of any consequence was the Hope Labor Day Fair and Rodeo and even this had now been forced, by dint of stronger competition elsewhere, to change its name and shift from Labor Day to mid-September, in the process shrinking from three days to a single Saturday.

The fair had always climaxed with a concert and a pitchfork fondue, in which hunks of beef the size of small dogs were speared and cooked in drums of boiling oil. In previous years, the concert had attracted some medium-to-big country music stars. This year, however, top of the bill were Rikki Rain and the Ragged Wranglers, who had come all the way from Billings and, for a few precarious moments, seemed set to go all the way back without playing a note.

They had parked their two customized black RVs by the cattle pens and as they climbed out, the first thing Rikki saw was a poster on which someone had scrawled *who?* right under her name.

Buck Calder and several members of the fair's organizing board who had turned out to welcome her had been treated to some vivid advice on where they could stick their godforsaken, horseshit apology for a fair. The offending poster had been rapidly removed and at last the late afternoon sunshine, a drifting smell of pitchforked steak and some serious Buck Calder sweet-talk seemed to have prevailed.

Eleanor sipped her iced tea beside one of the concession stands and watched her husband across the crowd. He had

172

his arm around Rikki now and she was tossing back her peroxide curls and laughing raucously at something he'd said. She was wearing a black shirt, red cowboy boots and a pair of white jeans so tight that Eleanor feared for her circulation.

'Finest set of dentures I ever did see,' Hettie Millward said, following Eleanor's gaze. 'I reckon she looks a sight more ragged than the Wranglers.'

Eleanor smiled. 'Hettie, you don't need to say that.'

'Well, doesn't she? Anyhow, I didn't think Buck was on the board this year.'

'He isn't. You know Buck, if ever there's a damsel in distress.'

'Some damsel. Look at her shirt all unbuttoned there. Talk about mutton dressed as lamb.'

'Undressed.'

They laughed. Hettie was her best friend, the only one who came close to understanding how it was between her and Buck. She was a big-hearted woman, constantly at war with her weight, though it was a war she seemed happy to lose. Doug, her husband, was a friend of Buck's — and one of Hope's most popular and respected ranchers.

Eleanor changed the subject and asked Hettie about her daughter's wedding plans, which seemed to change every week. Lucy was getting married next spring and wanted it to be the 'wedding of the millennium'. The whole of Hope was going to be invited. Hettie told her the latest idea, which she thought absolutely insane, was to have the whole ceremony conducted on horseback. Bride and groom, best man and bridesmaids, even the minister, for heavensakes, were going to be on horses. Hettie said it was a surefire recipe for disaster.

Then she looked at her watch and said she had better go and find her two boys, who had just won blue ribbons in the

4-H calf classes. Their animals were going to be auctioned and the parade was about to start in the main arena.

'Charlie says he's looking for at least three dollars a pound. I told him if he got three hundred it wouldn't pay for all the misery those animals have put us through. I just want to be shot of them. I'll see you later, honey.'

Eleanor finished her tea then strolled along the row of exhibit booths whose dilapidation was disguised by colored flags and streamers that fluttered in the breeze. There were booths selling anything from dogtags to jars of homemade chokecherry jelly. One had been transformed into a tepee outside which a group of teenage girls stood giggling while they waited to have their fortunes told by a 'Genuine Indian Medicine Man'. Farther along, smaller and noisier children were throwing wet sponges at two volunteers from the town fire department, bravely smiling in cut-out faces of Daniel Boone and Davy Crockett.

It had been many years since Eleanor had last come to the fair, though Buck, whose glory days were well remembered by older folk who watched the rodeo, never missed it. Eleanor had stopped coming after Henry's accident, fearing she might glimpse her dead son's face among the crowds of kids waiting to show their steers or clamoring for hot dogs and soda at the concession stands.

Nevertheless, it had been her idea that Paragon should take a booth and, making her way back toward it, she was relieved to have found no ambush of pain. In fact, she was proud that one of her first suggestions as Ruth's new business partner had worked out so well. The warm weather had brought out the crowds. They had sold as much here in one day as they did in the shop in a whole week and had easily covered the fifty-dollar rental for the booth.

As she came up to the booth, she saw Ruth staring at something across the crowd. She had a strange, almost angry expression on her face. Eleanor followed her gaze and saw that it must be Buck she was looking at. He was still making a fool of himself with that singer woman.

It was touching, Eleanor thought, that Ruth should care.

Buck wished Rikki and the Wranglers all the best and said he'd see them after the show, although he wasn't so sure he would. Rikki had looked a whole lot better from a distance than she did at close range and the wink she gave him as she went off to her van did little for him. With his wife and his mistress chatting away to each other like best buddies at the booth over there, life was complicated enough, thank you very much.

He'd seen Eleanor go off to the concession stand and had been about to head over to grab a quiet word with Ruth, when he'd gotten waylaid sorting out Rikki Rain's ego problem. Now he'd missed his chance. Being a pillar of the community was tough sometimes. He felt Eleanor's eyes on him and headed off in the opposite direction.

Buck loved the fair and rodeo, though it wasn't half the show it had been when he was a kid. In those days the whole county used to turn out, as well as hordes of people from far and wide. Winning a rodeo event back then really counted for something. Some of these kids nowadays hardly knew which end of a horse the hay went in. There was a bigger crowd here today than there had been in years, but it still wasn't the same.

He followed his nose to one of the long trestle tables where the meat from the pitchfork fondue was being carved. As he walked past the arena he noticed a huddle of youngsters, mainly girls, gathered around a tall man in a pale blue shirt and a tanned young woman in a tight white dress.

Both seemed to be signing autographs and, with their backs to him, Buck didn't recognize them. A photographer he recognized from the local newspaper was taking pictures. The

175

man in the blue shirt said something Buck couldn't make out but which was obviously hilarious because all the folk gathered around him roared with laughter. As the couple turned to go, all smiles and little waves, Buck saw it was that TV anchorman fellow, Jordan Townsend, who had bought the Nielsen place for a small fortune two summers ago.

Townsend had his own show on one of the networks (though Buck had never seen it) and apparently flew himself up here now and again from LA, parking his personal jet in Great Falls and helicoptering himself out to the ranch, which some other outsider had been brought in to manage.

He had knocked Jim and Judy Nielsen's nice old house down and replaced it with something ten times the size. It had a huge hot tub overlooking the mountains and a proper thirty-seat movie theater in the basement.

Buck joined the end of the line waiting for food. In the old days the folk dishing it out would have noticed him and brought him a plate stacked high, for free. Not today though. It was being served by two spotty kids he didn't know.

He waited his turn and watched while Jordan Townsend and his cute little wife processed like royalty through the crowd. Townsend was doing his Hollywood best to pass as a cowboy. With his carefully faded workshirt and Wranglers, he was wearing a new Stetson and a pair of handtooled boots which must have cost a thousand dollars or more.

His wife (number three, according to Kathy) had a pair too, but it was her only western concession. Otherwise, in her designer sunglasses and that little white dress she was almost wearing, she was every inch the movie star. Which, by all accounts, was what she was, though no one Buck knew had seen any of her movies. Apparently she had two names: one she was known as professionally and one she liked to go under when incognito in Montana. Buck couldn't remember either.

Rumor had it that she was twenty-seven, exactly half her husband's age, but Kathy said you had to take this with a pinch of salt because most actresses spent several years being twenty-seven. The only other thing Buck knew about her (though, if he tried, he could imagine more) was that her Christmas present from Townsend last year was a small herd of bison.

Buck reached the head of the line and paid one of the spotty kids his three dollars for a plate of steak and chili beans. He stood to one side and took a mouthful while the golden couple glided by, nodding and smiling at the natives, Buck included.

'Hi, how're you doing?' Townsend said. Buck knew the guy had no idea who he was.

'Good. How are you doing?'

'Great. Good to see you.'

And he breezed on past. Asshole, thought Buck.

The steak was tough and greasy and Buck chewed it balefully, watching the sway of the actress's cute little ass as she and Townsend processed toward the parking lot with the righteous glow of local duty done.

It seemed wrong to hate people you hadn't met, but Buck couldn't help it. They and their type were buying up the whole damn state. There were some places you could hardly move for all the millionaires, moguls and movie stars. It seemed you were nobody in Hollywood or New York City unless you had a ranch and a slice of Big Sky country.

The result was that real estate prices had gone so far through the roof that decent, young, born-and-bred Montanans didn't stand a chance. Some of the newcomers kept the land working, or tried to, but most either didn't have a clue or else didn't care. It was just somewhere they could play cowboys and impress fancy friends they invited from the city.

Buck tried the beans and found they weren't any better

177

than the steak. He was looking about for a garbage bin when he saw Abe Harding's troubled face heading through the crowd toward him.

That's all I need, Buck thought.

They'd been neighbors for thirty years and in all that time had never really gotten to know each other. You could fit Abe's place twenty times into the Calder spread and still have space to spare. The land was a lot poorer too and it was well known that Abe had borrowed too much money on it and was always on the brink of bankruptcy. With those eyes peering out from under a frowning shelf of eyebrow, he looked like some kind of paranoid, rock-dwelling eel.

'Hi there, neighbor, howya doin'?'

Abe nodded. 'Buck.'

Abe scratched his nose and darted a look around him like someone about to pull a heist. His jaws moved restlessly on a wad of tobacco and you could see the brown juice at the corners of his mouth.

'Got a moment?'

'Sure. Like some of this food? It's good.'

'No. Mind if we take a walk?'

'Sure.'

Abe led the way, not saying another word until he was sure they wouldn't be overheard.

'What can I do for you?' Buck said.

'You know that wolf that killed your Kathy's dog?'

'Uh-huh. Reckon he had one of our calves too.'

'So I heard. This wolf. He was a big, black fella, right?'

Buck nodded.

'Well, we've seen him again. And he had two others with him.'

'Where?'

'Up on the allotment. We were up there, putting some new salt and mineral down and we heard this howl and Ethan says,

178

"That's the weirdest coyote I ever heard." Then we saw them, plain as day, three of them. This big fella and two gray ones.'

All the while he spoke, his eyes kept on the move, rarely meeting Buck's and then only for a moment. As though he were filled with something itchy and resentful.

'Were they going for the cattle?'

'No, but they sure as hell were thinking about it. If I'd had my gun with me, I'd have had 'em. I left Ethan up there and went home to get it, but they took off. Couldn't even find their tracks.'

Buck thought for a moment.

'Have you told that biologist girl about it?'

'Nope. Why should I tell her? Feds put them there in the first place. Damn woman asked if she could tramp all over my land. I told her what she could do with herself.'

Buck shrugged.

'I tell you, Buck, I can't afford to lose a single calf right now.'

'I know what you mean.'

'I'm not so sure you do, but it's the truth.'

'But you know, Abe, you go shooting them and get yourself caught, you could wind up in a whole lot of trouble. Jail even.'

Abe spat a cheekful of black juice onto the pale grass.

'Goddamn government. They lease you the land, take your money, then let these varmints loose to kill your cattle.'

'Then throw you in jail if you try and protect 'em. Doesn't make a whole lot of sense, does it?'

Abe didn't reply, just narrowed his eyes and looked off across the fairground toward the stage area where the band were unloading their gear.

'Thing is, we're going to gather early and bring the herd down where we can keep a better eye on them. I was wondering if you'd mind lending a hand.'

179

'Sure I will.'

'Appreciate it.'

'You bet.'

'I tell you, there'll be hell to pay if there's any of 'em missing.'

Luke had only come down to the fair because he'd promised his mother he would. He didn't plan on staying long. Rikki Rain and the Ragged Wranglers were one good reason to leave. They'd been playing for an hour now and it seemed a lot longer. Another good reason was that Luke had just spotted a group of kids he had graduated with, including Cheryl Snyder, who he'd had a thing about all through high school.

Her dad owned the gas station and she was one of the nicest and definitely the prettiest girl in the school. As a result, she was usually surrounded by the worst kind of guys, four of whom were now showing off to her and her friend Tina Richie outside the fortune-teller's tepee.

Luke was on his way back to the Paragon booth with some sodas for Ruth and his mother who were busy packing up everything they hadn't sold. Cheryl and the others didn't appear to have seen him and he was about to duck between the booths and take a detour around the back when he heard her call out.

'Luke! Hey, Luke!'

He turned and pretended to be surprised. Cheryl waved and Luke smiled and held up the sodas to show he couldn't wave back, wondering if that was enough and could he still escape. But she was heading toward him, the others sauntering behind. She was wearing blue jeans and a skimpy pink top that showed her midriff. Luke remembered, as he often did, that time they'd kissed at a New Year's party a couple of years ago. She was the only girl he'd ever properly kissed. Which at his age was downright pitiful when you came to think about it.

'Hey, Luke, how are you?'

180

'Oh, hi, Ch–Ch–Cheryl. I'm f-f-fine, thanks.' Tina and the others came up alongside her and Luke smiled and nodded at them and they either smiled back or said hi with varying degrees of enthusiasm.

'I haven't seen you all summer,' said Cheryl.

'Oh, well, I've been w-w-working on the ranch, you know. H-h-helping my d-d-d-dad out.'

He watched their eyes, as he always did when he stuttered, for any hint of laughter or embarrassment or of pity, which was by far the worst. The other two he could handle.

'Hey, Cooks, we saw you on the TV, when that wolf got your sister's dog,' Tina said. One of the boys, a loudmouth called Jerry Kruger, gave a comic howl. He'd made Luke's life a misery for awhile in junior high, until Luke knocked him out cold one day in the yard. Luke's reputation had soared. He'd never had to use his fists again.

'Have you seen it again?' Cheryl said.

'The wolf? No. He was p-p-probably just p-p-passing through.'

'Too bad,' Kruger said. 'Tina was hoping to play Little Red Riding Hood with him. "Oh Grandma, what big bazongas you've got!"'

'Jerry, why don't you grow up?' Cheryl said.

No one seemed to know what to say next and they stood there for a moment, listening to the raucous tones of Rikki Rain. Luke held up the sodas.

'I'd better be g-g-going.'

'Okay,' Cheryl said. 'See you around.'

They all said goodbye. As he went off, Luke heard Kruger laugh and say, 'P-p-probably just p-p-passing through,' and the others telling him to hush.

It was cooler now and Helen wished she had brought a sweater. She was wearing hiking shorts and boots and a T-shirt with the sleeves rolled up. She had Band-Aids over the teeth marks Abe Harding's dogs had made on her legs. Amazingly, the skin wasn't pierced.

Most of the people she had met over the past weeks were here at the fair and, with the exception of the Hardings, she'd chatted with all of them. Everyone had made a fuss of Buzz, who was having the time of his life. She had him on a leash but he'd still managed to forage several suppers among the scraps people had dropped.

She knew it was time she was going. She had a late night ahead of her. But with everyone around her enjoying themselves, she was reluctant to leave. It was partly, she realized, a simple hunger for human contact.

At other times, in other moods, she might equally have let herself feel excluded or envious, the way she sometimes did lately when she saw a pair of young lovers or (God, she was so *pathetic*) women her age with babies. Instead, today, she had simply let herself bask in the banter and bustle of the crowd and felt more at peace with the world than she'd been for a long time.

Observing the people of Hope on this sun-washed September afternoon, she had found herself moved by their sense of community, by the roots that seemed to hold them to this place and to a way of life that, despite years of tribulation and all the mad rushings of the world, endured in its essence unchanged.

Helen's favorite rancher, Doug Millward, seemed the epitome of all this. When they bumped into each other, he had insisted on buying her an ice cream. He bought one for himself as well and they'd stood eating them, watching the high school band parade. He was a tall, soft-spoken man, with kind blue eyes. She knew he didn't much care for wolves but he seemed to have a tolerant respect for what she was trying to do. She confided that someone had been sabotaging her traps

and when he heard what had happened at the Hardings',
Doug sighed and shook his head.

'It probably won't make you feel any better about him, but
Abe's had a tough time of it over the years.'

'I heard he was in Vietnam.'

'Yeah. Saw some bad things, so they say. I've never heard
him talk about it. But I do know he has a lot of trouble
making ends meet. And those boys of his aren't a whole lot of
help. Been in and out of trouble since they were kids.'

'What kind of trouble?'

'Oh, this and that, you know. Nothing too serious.'

She could see he was reluctant to spread gossip. He
watched the band in silence for a moment, as if working out
how much to tell her.

'They hang out with one or two fellas who, let's say, I
wouldn't be happy for my kids to spend time with.'

'Like who?'

'Couple of them work for the logging company. Into all
this militia stuff, you know – antigovernment, big on guns,
that kind of thing. A while back, they and Wes and Ethan
Harding got caught illegal hunting. They cornered a whole
herd of elk in a canyon, just mowed them all down.'

He paused. 'I'd appreciate you not telling anyone where
you heard that.'

'No, of course.'

'And they're the exception not the rule. There's a lot of real
good people live in this town.'

'I know.'

Suddenly he laughed. 'Hey! We're getting a little serious
here, Helen.'

He said he had to go and meet Hettie at the 4-H sale and
after they said goodbye, Helen wandered off, thinking about
what he'd said.

The crowd was thinning now and some of the booths were

183

packing up, which was more than could be said for the band. Rikki Rain was wailing on about her man being out somewhere doin' with someone else what she was doin' without at home. Helen didn't blame him.

The sun had slipped behind an anvil of red and purple cloud above the mountains. But suddenly now it found space among them to set the fairground aglow, turning every face to gold as if casting a final blessing on the day's events. As she walked along the line of booths, a rabble of small children exploded around her and ran ahead, chasing each other and laughing at their giant shadows that raced before them on the grass.

It was then that she spotted Luke Calder talking with his friends. She watched and listened unseen. His stutter came as a surprise. And when that little creep imitated him, she had felt like marching over and slapping him on the face. She was sure Luke must have heard. He was heading off through the crowd and because it was the same way to the parking lot, she found herself following him.

She had only seen him twice since that first day, once in town and once on his horse up in the forest. On both occasions he had seemed shy and avoided talking with her. She knew he was spending a lot of time up on his father's allotment, to keep an eye on their herd. But whenever she was over that way, he was nowhere to be seen.

He was at the Paragon booth now, saying goodbye to his mother and Ruth. Then he set off toward the parking lot and Helen followed.

'Luke?'

He turned and stopped and when he saw her, his eyes seemed for a moment to show alarm. Then he smiled nervously and touched his hat to her.

'Oh, hi.'

As she walked up to him, she realized how tall he was, a

184

good six inches taller than she was. Buzz clearly thought he'd found a long-lost friend and Luke squatted to stroke him.

'We haven't really had a chance to meet yet,' Helen said. 'I'm Helen.' She held out her hand to him but he was too busy being licked by Buzz to see.

'Yeah, I kn-n-know.' He noticed her hand just as she was about to let it drop. 'Oh, sorry, I d-d-didn't . . .' He straightened up and shook hands.

'And your new friend for life here is Buzz.'

'B-Buzz. He's . . . cute.'

Helen was suddenly as tongue-tied as he was and the two of them stood there for a few seconds, smiling at each other like halfwits. She waved an arm in a clumsy gesture that was intended to take in the fair, the mountains, the sunshine and everything she'd been feeling about them.

'Isn't this all great? My first rodeo!'

'You t-took p-p-part?'

'No! I mean, the first rodeo I've ever been to. God no. Me and horses: disasterville.'

'D-disasterville. That's good.'

'You don't ride in the rodeo?'

'Me? Oh. No.'

'You're not staying for the music?'

'Oh. No. I've g-g-got some th-things to do. Do you like it?'

Helen frowned and scratched her head. 'Well . . .'

Luke laughed and his big green eyes softened, giving Helen a glimpse of what he might really be like. But his shy defense was quickly back in place.

'I hear your dad talked them into staying.'

He nodded. 'He's real g-g-good at that k-kind of thing.'

He looked away across the fairground, all trace of laughter gone now and it occurred to her that having Buck Calder for

185

a father wouldn't be easy for any boy. There was another awkward silence. Luke had turned his attention to Buzz again.

'Well, I'm afraid I still haven't managed to find your wolf.'

He looked at her sharply. 'Why *m-m-my* wolf?'

She laughed. 'I don't mean yours, you know, personally. I meant—'

'I never saw him.'

Helen could see his cheeks coloring up.

'No, I know. I was just—'

'I'd b-b-better be g-g-going now. Bye.'

'Oh, okay. Bye.'

Helen stood there a moment, wondering what she'd said wrong. They made their separate ways to their cars. She waved as Luke drove off, but he didn't wave back, nor look in her direction. She followed his car out of town but he was driving faster and when she turned off the pavement, he was only a distant cloud of gray dust ahead of her.

She stopped at the row of mailboxes at the turning up to the lake, even though she had checked hers already on the way into town. It had been empty, as it usually was. Since coming to Montana she'd had letters from her mother, her father and two from her sister. But none from Joel. The last she'd heard from him was a belated birthday card in Cape Cod and in all those long weeks she must have written him five or six times. Perhaps he hadn't received them? Or perhaps he couldn't get letters out? She guessed mail and things like that must be difficult there.

The letters she had written lately had been determinedly cheerful. She described the place to him, told him the detail of her routine, joked about her failure yet to catch a wolf. But sometimes she wondered if a whiff of her true feelings, of her loneliness, of the aching hollow he had left in her, had somehow infected her words without her knowing.

Buzz watched dolefully from the pickup while she opened the lid of her mailbox. It was empty.

186

14

He had watched her ever since she arrived.

Even on those first couple of days when Dan Prior was helping her unpack her things and get the cabin into shape. And that next night when she'd come back late and smoked her cigarette down by the water and did that amazing howl. He had stood in the cover of the trees across the lake, where he was standing now, and had prayed no wolf would answer.

He didn't come here every night and he never stayed long. Sometimes all he would see of her was her shadow looming like a giant's inside the lamplit cabin. If he walked farther north along the fringe of the forest and nearer than it was safe to go, he might get a glimpse of her through the open doorway, sitting at the table with all her charts and her computer or talking on the phone.

Once while doing this, he had stood on a dead branch and the snap set her dog off hollering. She came to the door and he froze with his heart in his throat, but she didn't see him and went inside again. Since then he had been more careful and if the wind was behind him, he didn't come at all in case the dog got a whiff of him.

Luke tried to persuade himself that he wasn't *spying*. It wasn't like he was being a Peeping Tom or anything. All he was doing was trying to stop her getting the wolves. Just like in war you needed to know what the enemy was doing. But as time went by, he was finding it harder and harder to think of her that way.

She seemed so sad. The way she came down and sat by the lake, crying and smoking all those cigarettes, like she was trying to kill herself. He'd wanted to go down there and put his arms around her and tell her to stop and that everything was okay.

Then that time she had suddenly slipped out of her clothes and gone into the water and he was sure she was going to drown herself and had nearly called out. And thank God he hadn't because it turned out she was just going for a swim and the dog went in too and they messed around and he actually heard her laugh for the first time. In the dark, Luke had only gotten the faintest impression of her body, but it was enough to make him feel like a freak and a pervert and he immediately left, vowing he was going to stop.

But he hadn't.

The night before last he had dreamed about her. He dreamed he was lying on the ridge above the meadow where the wolves had denned in the spring. The place was somehow different but the wolves were there, all the adults and the pups, and they were sitting in a circle, like the picture he used to love in that old copy of *The Jungle Book* he'd had as a kid. Then he saw that the woman was sitting in the circle too, like she belonged. And she looked up at him and called out his name and asked him why he was spying on them. Not angrily, just wanting to know. And he stood up and tried to say he didn't mean them any harm and that he too wanted to belong, but he blocked. The words just wouldn't come. And the woman and the wolves all just stared at him. And then he'd woken up.

Somewhere behind him now, in the forest, he heard the deep *hoo-hoo-hoo* of a horned owl. He turned and it took him awhile for his eyes to adjust after staring at the lit windows of the cabin. The owl was only a few yards away, sitting in the dead lower branches of a fir tree, fixing him with its wide golden eyes, so close that even in the dark you could see the tiger stripes on its chest. It was only fair, he thought; the watcher being watched.

He looked back across the lake. There was still no sign of life from inside the cabin. Unusually, she had closed the curtains and the door too. But the lights were on and he knew she was there because her truck was parked outside and he'd heard her dog barking. She was probably reading or something. He was always disappointed not to get a glimpse of her. But she was home and that was all he needed to know. It meant he could safely go about his night's work.

He turned and slipped quietly back into the forest. The owl didn't move, just watched him walk by.

As he threaded his way among the trees and circled down toward the creek, he thought again about meeting her at the fair. He'd expected her to be all morose, like she was up here on her own. But she hadn't been like that at all. And he'd been relieved because he'd been worrying that maybe he was the cause of her sadness, because of what he was doing to her traps.

'*Why m-m-my wolf? I never saw him!*'

God, what a dork he'd been, saying that. He'd been cursing himself ever since. She was real nice, which was part of the problem, like it was with Cheryl or any girl he wanted to

189

impress. He always made such a damn fool of himself. Except, of course, Helen Ross wasn't, like, a *girl*. Whatever, he'd done the same thing, gotten himself all worked up so the stutter clicked in and he wasn't able to say what he wanted to and ended up being precisely the dork that creeps like Jerry Kruger considered him.

It was hopeless. He often wondered how any girl was ever going to find out he wasn't that bad. Or maybe he was. Maybe he was going to end up sad and old and lonely, living on his own and jabbering to the birds like a lunatic.

He'd been surprised by how pretty she was up close. That smile of hers and the way she looked so directly at you with those brown eyes. And, God, she'd looked so good in her baggy khaki shorts and her T-shirt sleeves rolled up so you could see her arms all tanned and golden.

Below him now, through the trees, he saw Moon Eye grazing where he had left him, beside the shallows of the creek that cascaded through a narrow, high-sided passage of rock from the southern end of the lake. Any noise the horse made down here was smothered by the roar of the water. Moon Eye heard him though and looked up. Luke put his face against the white crescent on the horse's face, for which he had named him, then spent a full minute rubbing the animal's neck and murmuring his love. Then he swung himself into the saddle that was laden heavy with all he needed for his night's work and coaxed Moon Eye into the creek.

The water ran fast and broke white around the horse's hocks but his hooves found firm places among the slip of the rocks and they were soon on the other bank and heading down through the forest toward the first of the traplines.

It wasn't that he thought she meant to harm the wolves. Far from it. But once she got collars on them, they wouldn't be free. They could be found and gotten rid of whenever anyone chose. It was weird these biologist people didn't get it. But

190

then maybe in the end they were just like everyone else, unable to stand other creatures being truly wild and forever trying to tame and shackle them.

At the start, Luke had treated the trap thing almost like a game. He had enjoyed shadowing her and the predator-control guy, Rimmer, through the mountains and forest, seeing where they chose to set the traps. He was amazed they hadn't him, but they hadn't. He'd bumped into her that once, about a week later, but luckily it was when he'd finished with the traps and was riding back to his father's allotment, so she wouldn't have thought it suspicious.

He hadn't been able to see where they'd put every single one of the traps and it had taken him a few days to find them all. And then she'd started moving them around which was real tricky, but he usually managed to find them by trailing her when she went to check them. It had been fun seeing her get more and more puzzled at why she wasn't having any luck. And even more fun seeing her dog's reaction.

It had taken Luke awhile to find the right formula.

First off, he'd bought some little green crystals from a pet store in Helena. They were supposed to stop cats and dogs pooping on your lawn. When Luke said he needed a dozen bottles, the storekeeper said he must have one hell of a problem but Luke told him it was just a very big lawn.

He tried it out on the ranch dogs and decided it might not be powerful enough to keep wolves off your lawn, so he went back to town and bought supplies of bug repellent, ammonia and various types of pepper and mixed them into a gooey liquid with the crystals, half expecting to blow himself up.

The result, when he sniffed it, nearly made him pass out and it worked like a dream on the dogs. He could put a piece of steak down, spray a circle of the stuff around it and the poor things wouldn't dare cross the line to get it; they just lay there, whining and slobbering. He even gave his new product a name: Wolf-Stop.

He'd read somewhere that wolves hated the smell of two other things: diesel oil and human urine. The diesel was easy. There was a tank of it down by the barns and he always took a can of it along with him and sprayed it around the traps with the Wolf-Stop. The urine was trickier. For twenty traps he'd need a lot. He wondered, briefly, about whether there was a way to augment his own supply from the restroom at The Last Resort, but he couldn't come up with one. In the end, all he could do was drink a lot and distribute it sparingly, using the delivery method God intended. He'd never drunk so much water nor peed so much in his whole life.

The two traplines she'd laid down toward the allotments were a breeze. Once he'd done them, he barely needed to check them. Both places were like corridors and he had effectively blocked them off by spraying a three-line barrier of Wolf-Stop, diesel and urine at each end. He had sprayed it too around every trap he could find – though not too near in case she noticed.

Then, for good measure, he'd sprayed the traps and the wolf scat she had carefully placed near them with some scent-killer he'd bought from a hunting supply store. The real tedious part was clearing up his footprints afterward.

Hiding behind some rocks one morning, he'd seen the woman's dog come hurtling down the slope just above where he'd laid the barrier. It was like a cartoon, the poor mutt suddenly seemed to hit an invisible brick wall. A sniff and a whimper and he slunk off the way he came. The woman didn't even notice. Luke was laughing so much he had to beat a quick retreat too.

The traps in the high canyon were a different matter. The way the land was up there, you couldn't just block it off. The wolves seemed to move through it almost at random. All he could do was spray around each trap and if she moved one, like she'd been doing lately, without him seeing her do it, he could lose hours trying to find it.

Even worse, a couple of nights ago, he'd dropped his bag with all the Wolf-Stop in it on the way up there and even though he went back and looked, it was too dark to find it. He ended up having to spring some of the traps instead, which he'd only ever done when he ran out of the stuff. It was bound to make her suspicious and it was scary too, because you had to do it without activating the radio collars she'd fixed to them.

Sometimes Luke managed to do the traps in daylight, just after she'd checked them. It sure made life easier, but there was always the risk that she would see him. So normally he did it at night, always going first to check she was back at her cabin.

His excuse for being away from home all night was simple. He suggested to his father that he should camp up on the allotment so he could ride the herd through the night. His mother had said it was ridiculous but his father had been real impressed and backed the idea.

Sometimes it took him so long to see to the canyon traps that instead of going back to the tent, he just found a sheltered spot and curled up in the sleeping bag he always kept strapped to his saddle.

The only night he regularly went home was Tuesday, so he could get a shower and a shave and some decent sleep before his speech therapy the next morning. His mother went on and on about how pale and tired and terrible he looked. She said he looked like a drug addict, though when she'd seen one of them, Luke had no idea.

'It's not right you sleeping out in the open up there.'

'Mom, I'm fine. I like it.'

'It's dangerous. You'll get eaten by a bear.'

'I don't t-t-taste good.'

'I'm serious, Luke.'

'Mom, really, I'm not a k-k-kid anymore. I'm fine.'

But, in truth, it was starting to wear him down. He'd looked in the mirror and thought his mother wasn't wide of the mark. He didn't know how long he could keep it up.

Tonight it took him no time at all to see to the two forest traplines. The sky was starting to cloud over but there was a moon and he hardly needed to use his flashlight to locate the traps and refresh the barriers with a good dousing of Wolf-Stop, diesel and his own pee. Within an hour he had brushed away his tracks and was urging Moon Eye up the long, steep route to the canyon.

Exactly where the wolves were at the moment, he didn't know. Twice in the last week he had gone to the meadow where they had spent most of the summer and neither time had he seen any sign of them. He knew from his wolf books that around this time of year, when the pups were big, they left these so-called rendezvous sites and started to hunt as a pack.

A few nights ago he had heard them howl and though it was hard to tell where it came from, for the mountains played tricks with any sound, he figured it was somewhere up above Wrong Creek, a mile or so to the north. With luck, they might have gotten sick of sniffing all the stuff he'd sprayed around the place.

At last he reached the foot of the canyon and tied Moon Eye to a willow bush beside the creek. The slope above grew thick with sage and he broke himself off a good bushy stem to use as a brush for his tracks. Then he had another drink and, taking the bag in which he carried all his various bottles of Wolf-Stop, diesel and scent-killer, set off along the rocky bank of the creek.

He chose his route with care, making sure to step on rock

and scrub and trying to avoid any patch of dust that might show a footprint.

She had set three of her traps along the upper side of a narrow deer trail that skirted a dense thicket of juniper. Below it, the ground fell away in a steep slope covered with buffaloberry, among which Luke now stopped. He was a few yards short of where he thought the first trap was.

He peered both ways along the trail to get his bearings. He was looking for the telltale tuft of grass or scrub in front of which she had dug the hole for her foul-smelling bait. But he couldn't see it.

The moon was permanently masked by cloud now. From somewhere behind the mountains came a long, low rumble of thunder.

Luke took out his flashlight and walked slowly through the buffaloberry bushes along the lower side of the trail, scanning the other side with the beam. Up ahead he could see something dark on the pale dust and as he got nearer he saw it was wolf scat and knew he'd found the right spot. There, behind it, was the tuft of grass and buried between the two, sprinkled carefully with dirt and debris to disguise it, would be the trap.

He reached into his bag for his scent-killer and, taking care not to step on the trail, crouched down and started to spray it on the scat. The thunder rumbled again, nearer now.

'Just what the hell do you think you're doing?'

It was as if someone had jabbed him with a cattle prod. The voice came from the trees and gave him such a jump that he lost his footing and found himself sprawled on his back among the berry bushes. He'd dropped both the spray and the flashlight and couldn't see a thing. Then he realized his hat was over his face. He could hear someone charging out of the trees toward him. Quickly, he rolled over, scrambled to his feet and launched himself down the slope.

★

'Oh no you don't, you son of a bitch!'

With one leap Helen cleared the trail. Whoever it was had about a ten-yard start on her and was already gaining. He was halfway down the slope, crashing through the bushes in giant strides. Suddenly there was a flash of lightning and she could see him below her, his arms spread wide for balance. He had his hat in one hand and a bag or something swinging wildly from his shoulders. Things were falling out of it.

'You're in big trouble, buddy. *Big* trouble!'

Thunder boomed as if to make her point. The bushes thwacked against her legs as she ran and once she went over on one ankle but her mind was too full of outrage and vengeance to pay heed to it.

He was almost at the foot of the slope now where the land shelved down to the creek through a thick band of alder and willow scrub. Once he was in there she could easily lose him.

'Interfering with federal trapping is a serious offense!' Helen had no idea whether it was or not, but it sounded good.

Then, just as he reached the trees, she heard his boot crack against a rock and he tripped and disappeared headfirst into the undergrowth.

Helen gave an exultant, 'Yes!'

She was there within seconds but it wasn't quick enough, for he was already scrabbling off on his hands and knees through the scrub, trying to get to his feet and, without thinking, Helen just dived like a football tackler and landed full-square on his back. He flattened beneath her and she could hear the breath leave his lungs in a great oomphing grunt.

She rolled off him and got to her knees, too out of breath herself, for the moment, to speak. Then the thought occurred to her: now what? She had just attacked a total stranger, a man bigger than her and no doubt stronger and, God, for all she knew, perhaps even armed! And here they were, out in the middle of nowhere. She must be out of her mind.

196

She got to her feet. He was still spread-eagled beside her, facedown, but suddenly he made a peculiar sound and moved an arm and she thought, that's it, he's going for his knife or his gun and so she gave him a kick.

'Don't you try anything, buddy. I'm a federal agent. In fact, you're under arrest.'

As she said it, she realized he was in no state to try anything. He was on his side, with his knees doubled up and gasping for breath and in another flash of lightning she saw his face, all contorted and covered in dust.

She couldn't believe it.

'Luke?'

He groaned but the sound got lost in a great unfurling of thunder.

'Luke? God, what on earth . . . Are you okay?'

She knelt beside him helplessly while he tried to get the air back into him. And when at last he succeeded, she made him sit up and stayed beside him with her hands on his shoulders until he was breathing evenly again. She brushed the dirt and twigs from his back, then went back with the flashlight and found his hat and his bag which he had dropped in the fall. When she came back she saw there was blood on his forehead where he must have knocked it.

'Are you okay?'

He nodded, not looking at her yet. She took out a handkerchief and knelt beside him again.

'You've cut yourself, just there. Shall I . . .?'

Rather than allow her to do it, he took the handkerchief and wiped the wound himself. It looked painful. Maybe it would even need stitches. He said something which Helen couldn't catch.

'What?'

'I s-said, I'm s-sorry.'

'Is it you who's been doing this all along?'

197

He nodded, still looking down. The thunder was becoming more distant, rolling down the valley away from them.

'Luke, why?'

He shook his head.

'Don't you want me to catch the wolf? Your dad does, I know.'

He gave a little humorless laugh. 'Oh, yeah. *H-h-he* does.'

'But you don't?'

He didn't answer.

'You *like* wolves?'

He shrugged, looking away, still avoiding her eyes.

'That's it, isn't it? You know, Luke, we're not trapping him to kill him or take him away. Just to put a radio collar on him. It'll protect him.'

'There's m–more than one. There's n–nine, a whole p–p–pack.'

'You've seen them?'

He nodded. 'And collars won't protect them. It'll just make them easier to g–get rid of.'

'That's not true.'

'You wait.'

For awhile, neither of them spoke. A sudden gust of wind blew down the canyon, rattling the leaves of the alders. Helen shivered.

Luke looked at the sky. 'It's going to rain,' he said.

And then, at last, he looked at her. And something in his eyes startled her. Something lonely and lost, like a mirrored fragment of herself.

It began to rain, as he had said it would. Large, cold drops that smacked on their upturned faces and on the rocks around them and filled the air with the smell of wet dust that always reminded Helen of long-ago summers when she was a child.

★

198

He sat on a chair beside the cabin stove, with Buzz curled up at his feet and his forehead tilted up toward the light so she could see to clean the wound.

She was standing over him and he watched her face while she worked, noting the way she frowned and bit her lip in concentration. Their clothes were still soaked from the rain and he did his best not to look at how her T-shirt clung to her breasts. She had lit the potbellied stove when they came in and now in the warmth he could see curls of steam rising from her shoulders. She smelled wonderful, not of perfume or anything, just of her.

'This is going to hurt a little, okay?'

He nodded. It was iodine and he couldn't help wincing as she dabbed it into the wound.

'Sorry.'

'It's okay.'

'That'll teach you to go messing with my traps.'

He looked up at her and smiled but his mouth went all askew and it ended up more like a sneer.

It was amazing how well she'd taken it. The way she'd come roaring out of those trees like that had scared him half to death. He thought she was going to kill him. But afterward, walking down through the dripping forest, with her backpack strapped to Moon Eye's saddle, she had actually *laughed* about it. She'd made him get the bottle of Wolf-Stop out and taken a whiff of it which nearly knocked her out. She'd laughed even more, when he told her all the trouble he'd taken making it and testing it out on the dogs.

Once or twice, she said, she'd gotten the feeling someone was spying on her and for a moment he was terrified that she meant down here at the cabin, which he hadn't, of course, mentioned. There was no way he could tell her about that, not without her thinking him a total freak. Luckily it turned out all she meant was when she'd been out checking her traps.

He explained how he had first come across the wolves and how since then he had watched them. And when she tried to convince him that collaring them was the right thing to do, he could see she cared just as much as he did about their survival.

She was sticking a Band-Aid on him now.

'There you go. You'll live.'

'Thanks.'

The pan of water she was heating on the Coleman stove was boiling and she went over and started to make hot chocolate.

'Is that horse of yours okay out there in the rain?'

'He'll be fine.'

'Bring him in if you like. There's a spare bed.'

He smiled and this time his mouth felt okay.

While she busied herself, he looked around the room. It was cramped but in the light of the hissing gas lamps it looked warm and cozy. The floor was cluttered with boxes in which she seemed to store everything from books to wolf traps. A red sleeping bag lay crumpled on the bottom bunk and there was a candle in a jar on the floor beside it and a book whose title he couldn't make out. There was also what looked like a half-written letter and a pen and one of those little lamps on a band that you could fix to your forehead. He imagined her curled up at night writing to someone and wondered who it might be.

Across the other corner she had rigged up a washing line where a towel and some clothes hung to dry. Her cell phone and stereo were wired up to two deep-cycle six-volt batteries below the window. Her computer was on the table, surrounded by a chaos of notes and charts and maps.

There was a bucket in the corner with a tin can strung across it. She saw him frowning at it as she came over with the mugs of hot chocolate and told him it was a mousetrap and how it worked.

'That really w-w-works?'

'You bet. Better than my wolf traps have been, anyway.' She narrowed her eyes at him, putting the mugs down on the table.

'Are you sure you don't want to change out of that wet shirt? Look, there's steam coming off you.'

'I'm fine.'

'You'll catch cold.'

'You sound like my m-m-mother.'

'I do? Catch cold, I don't give a damn.'

Luke laughed. He was starting to relax a little.

'But *I'm* not going to,' she went on. 'So if you'll excuse me, I shall retire for a moment to my dressing room.'

She went over to the wardrobe and, facing away from him, started taking off her T-shirt. He caught a glimpse of the back of her bra and quickly looked the other way, hoping he wasn't going to blush and trying desperately to think of something to say, something casual that would make it seem like it was no big deal to have a woman take off her clothes in front of him.

'Am I still un-un-under arrest?'

'I'm thinking about it.'

She came back and sat down at the table, giving him a sly kind of smile. She'd put on a pale blue fleece which made her face look all golden. Her hair was still wet and shone in the lamplight. She picked up her mug of chocolate, cradling it in her hands, then took a thoughtful sip.

'It depends,' she said.

'On what?'

She put the mug down, gathered up one of the maps and placed it squarely in front of him.

'On you showing me where to catch those wolves.'

15

The old bull moose stood with his head lowered, perhaps to get a better view through the dusk of the forest or perhaps to give a better one of his antlers to the nine pairs of yellow eyes that were watching him. The antlers were full-grown by now with a spread of nearly five feet. At the shoulder he was as tall as a horse and probably weighed the best part of eleven hundred pounds. But he was lame and past his prime and both he and the wolves knew it.

They had found him in a bend of the creek, browsing its bank in a thicket of slender aspens which looked like zebra stripes against the dark brown of his flank. He had turned to face them and stood his ground and for the last five minutes predator and prey had waited, weighing their respective chances.

The pups were just big enough now to come hunting with the others, though they normally hung back with their mother or one of the younger adults. The mother was much paler than her mate, the alpha male, and in the twilight looked almost white. The pups and the two younger adults – one male, one female – were various shades of gray between. Occasionally one of the pups fidgeted or whimpered, as if bored with the wait, and one of the alpha pair, mother or father, would chide it with a look and a quiet growl.

The moose was about twenty yards away. Behind him, the creek gleamed like bronze in the dying light. A cloud of freshly hatched flies pirouetted above its surface and a pair of lace-winged moths flitted like pale spirits against the dark of the pines beyond.

Now the alpha male moved. His tail was bushier than the others' and usually held higher, but he kept it lower now as he went slowly in an arc to the right, keeping the same distance from the moose all the way. Then he stopped and retraced his steps and made a matching arc to the left, hoping to prompt the old bull to make a run.

A moose that stood its ground, even one that was old and lame, was much harder to kill. He could see where his attackers were coming from and aim his defensive blows more accurately. One well-placed kick could crack a wolf's skull. They had to get him running, when he couldn't aim so well or see where the next bite was coming from.

But all the old bull moved were his eyes. They followed the wolf's every step, first one way, then the other. The wolf stopped on the left and lay down. And, on cue, the alpha female now moved forward. She went to the right, slowly, almost sauntering, and farther than the male had gone, so that when she stopped she was down by the edge of the creek and slipping behind the moose and at last he had to move to keep an eye on her.

He stepped backward, turning his head toward her, and at the same time realized he had taken his eye off the alpha male and turned back, taking a couple of small backward steps. And as he moved, the younger female moved too, following her mother through the trees.

The moose shifted uneasily, edging back toward the water, perhaps now wondering if, after all, it might not be better to run.

His first instinct might have been to head into the creek, but when he turned that way he saw the two female wolves had worked their way along the bank below him. Between them and the alpha male there was probably not enough space to escape. The alpha female's paws were in the water and when the moose looked at her, she casually lowered her head to drink, as if that were all she was there to do.

On some silent signal, the younger adult male and the five pups were moving now, heading toward their father. And in so doing, they opened a wide gap which, as he was no doubt intended to, the moose saw.

Suddenly he erupted. He thundered off through the thicket, his hooves churning the damp, black earth and his antlers clacking against the white stems of the aspens, gashing their bark and setting off a shower of leaves in his wake.

As soon as he moved, the wolves were after him. He was partly lame in his right front leg and he ran with an odd rocking motion. The alpha male must have seen this for it seemed to summon extra energy in him. He was gaining on the moose with every bound. The others were close on his heels, dodging in their different routes through the trees and leaping the rocks and rotting wood that littered the forest floor.

Upstream, the bank of the creek was clearer and the old bull headed that way, hoping perhaps to run where his antlers wouldn't hinder him and where with luck he could gain access to the water. But as he emerged from the thicket, the alpha male made a great lunge and fastened his teeth onto the left of his rump.

The moose struck out with his hind feet but the wolf

swung clear of them without loosening his grip and the fraction of speed the moose lost by kicking gave the alpha female her chance. Her teeth flashed and found purchase in the bull's right flank and as he tried to kick at her he stumbled. He quickly found his footing again and plowed on up the clearing with the two wolves locked to his flesh and swinging from him like stoles.

He had gone more than half a mile, through another thicket and out again onto a rocky meadow, when the younger adults got involved. Before, they had seemed content to leave the attack to their parents, but now they started slashing at the bull's other flank. The pups loped along behind, the bolder among them plainly tempted to join in, the others hanging back, preferring to watch and learn.

Up ahead, their father lost his hold and the moose thrashed out and caught him a thudding blow on the shoulder with a hind hoof, sending him cartwheeling into the undergrowth in a cloud of dust. But the wolf was on his feet again at once and, seeing the moose veer toward the creek, raced at an angle to cut him off. Within a few seconds he was alongside and he twisted his body around and at the same time launched himself up beneath the moose's neck and closed his teeth on the long flap of tufted skin that dangled there.

The bull swiped at him with his antlers but the wolf was too quick. The whole pack seemed to sense that however mighty this animal once had been, age had dulled and weakened him and tonight was his time to die.

And as if to show the moose he knew this and how reckless he was thus prepared to be, the alpha male let go and came within an inch of being trampled by the heavy front hooves, but instead bounced like an acrobat off the ground to get a better bite. His teeth sank deep into the moose's throat.

The old bull had run more than a mile and was bleeding heavily at both ends, the blood spattering the faces of the young adults as they slashed at his flanks and his rump. Yet on and on he ran.

He swerved sharply now toward the creek and half ran, half fell down a steep bank of willow scrub to the water, dragging his baggage of wolves with him and setting off an avalanche of mud and rocks.

The water near the bank was barely a foot deep and as the moose hit the bed of the creek his lame leg buckled and he went down on his knees, ducking the alpha male beneath him. He quickly found his feet again and when his neck came clear of the water, the alpha male was still fastened there, blood and water sluicing down his fur.

The pups had reached the top of the bank and they stopped there to watch. The old bull turned his head, perhaps to see what had happened to the others when he fell and, seeing her chance, the young female leapt at his face and hooked her teeth to his nose. The moose lifted his head, thrashing her from side to side like wet laundry, but she didn't let go.

All his efforts focused now on the teeth that were sunk into the black, fleshy splay of his nose. He started to stagger blindly toward the far bank, forgetting for awhile about shedding or kicking at the other wolves that were locked on to him.

The mother and the other young adult seemed to sense it and hacked with added vigor at his flanks and his rump then ducked their heads under him to rip at his belly, while the alpha male at his throat tore another gaping hole.

And finally, just as he reached the other bank, the clamor of pain and loss of blood were too much for the old moose and his hind legs collapsed and down he went.

He kicked and struggled for another ten minutes and once during that time managed to get briefly to his feet and haul his bloody cargo of wolf onto the gravel.

But there he fell again and for the last time.

And the pups who had been watching from the near bank

took it as a cue and cautiously made their way down into the water and waded across to join the feast.

And only when the old bull had stopped twitching and the rising moon glinted its reflection in the sightless black of his eye, only then did the alpha male loosen his grip. And he sat up and raised his blood-soaked muzzle to the sky and howled.

And one by one, all his family joined in and lifted their heads and howled with him, both those who had killed and those who had witnessed.

Where once there had been life, now was death. And out of death, thus, was life sustained. And in that bloody compact, both the living and the dead were joined in a loop as ancient and immutable as the moon that arced above them.

16

The allotments that the Calders and their neighbors leased for summer grazing lay along the shoulders of the mountains like patches stitched by some sedulous giant into the darker green of the forest. Among them, along the creeks and coulees now, seams of yellow, lime and gold were starting to show, as the nights gave a first brush of frost to the willow and chokecherry.

In some years all might by now be blanketed in snow. But summer this year was like a party guest with no home to go to and even the flocks of migrating birds, the only apology for cloud in a constant cobalt sky, seemed hesitant, as if tempted too to linger for a last drink.

Buck Calder sat resting his horse on a bare bluff that leaned out from the forest above his allotment. The horse was a Missouri Fox Trotter, a handsome, deep-chested gray, who held himself every bit as proudly as his owner. In the early morning sun, squinting out at the plains from under the brim of his hat, it occurred to Buck, as it often did, that the two of them cut quite a picture. The kind of thing that would have had old Charlie Russell reaching for his paintbrush.

He looked down over the trees at the double curve of tracks he and Clyde had made in the dew of the pasture and those the cattle had made as they moved away. Beyond, hazed by the low sun, the valley stretched away toward Hope. Along the river a curl of mist shrouded the knees of the cotton-woods. Their leaves too were yellow now and the grass around them cured pale as an old elk hide.

Buck loved the fall. The fences were all fixed and the irrigation work all done and everything was on hold for awhile. It gave a man a moment or two to breathe and take stock before the mid-October frenzy of selling and shipping the calves. In a few days they would be gathering the herd and bringing them down where he preferred them to be, on land that belonged to him rather than the government.

Not that the land he leased was bad. Far from it. Buck's was the biggest and lushest allotment there was. And the rent wasn't bad either. In fact, at under two dollars per cow-calf unit a month, it was cheaper than feeding a cat. But the Forest Service always made you feel they were doing you a favor, letting you use it. They were always laying down the law about some new thing or other and, in so doing, only helped deepen the resentment Buck and other ranchers already felt.

It was the principle that Buck objected to. As a state legis-lator, and before that as a county commissioner, it had been his favorite topic. Many a time he'd banged the table and ranted at the scandal of the federal government owning so much of the West, land he and his forebears and many more like them had watered with their own sweat and blood. It was they who, against all odds, had civilized the wilderness, planted it with decent grass and grown the fillet steaks those goddamn pen-pushers ate – without so much as a thank you – in their fancy Washington DC restaurants.

Most ranchers he knew felt the same way and for awhile Buck had believed it might be possible to get some kind of campaign going to change things. But it didn't take him long to figure it wouldn't work.

That same independent grit which ranchers needed to survive out here also made them the most difficult critters on earth to organize. You could get them to agree, sign petitions, even now and then get them riled enough to come to a meeting. But deep down they were all resigned to the fact that ranching was, and always would be, a kind of cruel joke, devised by God to teach man the meaning of pessimism. Adversity was just part of the deal and the measure of a man was how he faced up to it on his own. And anyhow, when all was said and done, everyone knew that for all Buck's spleen and speechifying, the government would go on acting in the same old high and mighty way and do as it damn well pleased.

Recently though, things had gotten much worse. The federal agencies were forever coming up with new restrictions, cutting down the number of cows you could graze on your allotment, even telling you what you had to do with your *own* land. They came and tested the water in your creeks and told you it was dirty and you had to put fences up so your cows couldn't get a drink. Then they'd come and tell you some rare varmint, some goddamn ferret or owl or something, was nesting on your property and would you mind not ranching it for a few years.

Every damn thing a stockman did nowadays wasn't just his business but the whole world's. If you wanted to blow your nose or take a piss, you had to get the government's permission and they wouldn't give it until they'd consulted the so-called *environmental* groups. And then these goddamn bunny-huggers and Patagonia Patsies, who all lived in the city and knew less than jack-shit about anything, would have their say and the agency goons, who were all just like that themselves anyway, would take it as gospel and come up with some new harebrained scheme for making life more of a misery for ranchers. You could suffocate in all the paperwork they threw at you. There were regulations and limits for this, that and everything, plus a whole bunch of fines if you broke them. It made a man sick.

Well, what the hell. Buck could take it. He knew for a fact that most of the agency guys he had to deal with were scared of him and he enjoyed giving them a hard time. Poorer folk, though, like the Hardings for example, were more vulnerable. It was hard to stand up to the feds when they knew you could be ruined by a fine or simply by the hours you lost in fighting all their bureaucratic bullshit.

When Abe had come up to him at the fair, Buck had felt real sorry for him, not because of his worry about the wolves but because of how hunted and beaten the poor man looked. It almost made Buck feel guilty that he hadn't done more to help him these past years.

That was why he and Clyde were about to head over to Abe's allotment to give him a hand gathering his herd. They had come up to their own lease first to fetch Luke, so he could help too.

Below him now, Buck could see Clyde riding up out of the trees toward him. The two of them had split up so as they could comb the hidden corners of the pasture more quickly. The cows and calves, those he could see anyway, seemed fine but Buck had seen no sign of his son.

'Find him?' he called down to Clyde.

'Nope. Don't look like that tent of his has been slept in neither.'

'Where the hell's the boy at?'

'Beats me.'

Buck shook his head and looked away, his good humor spiked, as it so often was, by thoughts of Luke. He waited while Clyde rode up the slope to join him and then, without saying a word, sharply reined his horse around and set off up the logging trail that traversed the forest to the Harding lease.

It had seemed like a good idea to have Luke keep an eye on the herd. God knows, it was hard enough to find anything the boy could do and not get himself in a tangle. At first Buck had been impressed by how seriously he seemed to be taking it and even more so when he took to staying up in the pasture all night. But now he wasn't so sure.

Whenever Clyde came up here, Luke was nowhere to be seen. He only ever seemed to come back to the house when nobody else was there – except two days ago, when he'd shown up for breakfast with that cut on his face, saying how he'd ridden into a branch or something and set Eleanor off fussing again about how it wasn't safe for him to be out here all night long on his own.

Sometimes Buck despaired of the boy. He knew there was only pain to be had from comparing him to the son he'd lost, but he couldn't help it. When he saw Luke messing some-thing up, in his mind's eye, Buck saw Henry doing it right. Beside Luke's long face, silent at the supper table, he saw his brother's smart grin and heard the echo of his laugh. What glitch of nature could bring forth two such different sons from the same seed?

Although his own mortality did not yet figure largely among his concerns, Buck wondered what would happen to the ranch in years to come. Tradition said it should pass to his only son and heir. But tradition could make a monkey of a man. No one in his right mind could think Luke capable of running the place, even if he'd shown the slightest interest in doing so. And though Buck hadn't put it in writing, nor even really confirmed it to himself, he was thinking more and more

212

that Clyde and Kathy should be the ones to take over the reins when he let go.

That this should come to pass, that the Calder place be run, after all these years, by one who bore a different name, was for Buck a source of shame. He had failed to produce a decent, living, male heir to continue the line and the whole world knew it.

The trail was too narrow for the horses to go side by side, so Clyde rode behind, keeping his thoughts to himself, for which Buck was always grateful. Conversation wasn't Clyde's strong suit; indeed, it was sometimes hard to tell what was. Buck had always felt Kathy could have done better, but then that was how most fathers seemed to feel about their daughters.

Both Clyde's parents had died when he was a boy and he'd been brought up by an uncle and aunt on a ranch near Livingston. They'd apparently been hard on the boy, which maybe accounted for what Buck found most irritating about him: a kind of dog-like ingratiation. He was always so keenly tuned to Buck's mood, always a little too eager to please. Whatever Buck's opinion, it became Clyde's as well and if Buck changed his mind, even if he argued that black wasn't black after all, but white, then Clyde would soon be laboring through paler and paler shades of gray until he got there too.

But, hell, if that was the worst of his faults, Buck should count himself lucky. Kathy had enough brains for both of them and the young fellow doted on her and the baby. He wasn't afraid of hard work either. One day he might even make a decent rancher.

Ahead of them along the trail now Buck heard the whine of engines, like wasps in a window. And as the trees opened up before them, he saw Wes and Ethan, Abe's sons, churning up the pasture on their trail bikes.

'What in God's name do they think they're at?' he said quietly.

A small band of frightened cows and calves was making a break for the trees and Ethan, the younger of the two, was trying to head them off. He disappeared with a whoop into the forest, leaving a wake of blue fumes behind him.

Abe sat watching from his horse at the foot of the pasture, occasionally yelling instructions that drowned unheard in the din of the engines. He gave Buck and Clyde a grim nod as they rode up.

'Buck.'

'Howdy, Abe. Sorry we're late.'

'Don't make no odds.'

'We were looking for Luke.'

'Seen him as we was coming up here, 'bout an hour ago,' Abe said, his eyes back on his sons, dodging feverishly among the trees. 'Heading over toward Wrong Creek with that wolf woman.'

'What the hell's he doing with her?' Clyde said.

Abe turned his head away and spat out a cheekful of black tobacco juice. 'Don't ask me.'

It was awhile before anyone spoke. Buck didn't want his voice to show how mad the news made him.

'So how's it going?' he said at last.

'Four cows so far with no calf. Bags are all dried up.'

'Reckon it's the wolves?' Clyde said

'What else would it be?'

Buck and Clyde made themselves useful and did the job Wes and Ethan had been trying to do. Within the hour, they'd ridden the whole of the allotment and every living cow and calf was gathered at the foot of the pasture. By the time they were done, Abe's count of dried-up cows had gone up to six. Of their calves there was no trace, not even a bone.

Abe hadn't said another word, except to yell at his cows or his sons. He'd grown pale and quivered around the eyes, as if he was having trouble keeping the lid on things.

214

The herd was tiny compared with Buck's and once they were down from the higher trails where the cows could stray into the trees, the going got easy enough for Abe and his sons to manage the rest of the way to their ranch without help. Buck called Clyde and the two of them rode up beside Abe.

'You okay from here on down, buddy? I thought we'd just go and have a look for that boy of mine.'

'Sure. Appreciate your help.'

'No problem. Maybe when the rest of us have gotten our herds down, we should all get together, have ourselves a talk about this wolf business.'

'Don't see what good talk'll do.'

'Can't do any harm.'

'Maybe.'

'Okay. Well, see you, Abe.'

'Yep.'

They cut off along a narrow trail that wound up through the forest to the lake where the wolf woman had her cabin. Buck thought it was worth checking if Luke was there. Even if he wasn't, they could leave a message on her door, telling him to get his ass back home right away. The boy had some explaining to do and whatever his reason for leaving the herd, it better be damn good.

17

Luke waited beside the pickup and watched her while she walked slowly ahead along the trail. She was turning the H-shaped antenna above her head while she thumbed through the frequencies on the little radio receiver that hung in its leather case from her shoulder. Buzz sat watching her too from the passenger seat, ears pricked as if he knew what she was hoping to hear in her headphones.

They were parked to one side of the logging trail that snaked perilously up the south side of Wrong Creek, a forested canyon that had apparently played some cruel trick on whoever named it. Luke looked down over the edge of the trail where the land fell sharply away, thick with Douglas fir. He could hear the whisper of the creek a hundred feet below. This side of the canyon was still in shade and the air was cool and damp. Half a mile away, on the other side, a band of sunlight was deepening, setting ablaze the yellow leaves of the aspens.

It had taken them a day and a half to reset all the traps and now they were out checking them. Wrong Creek was the next big drainage to the north and Luke was fairly sure it was here that the wolves had been when he'd heard them howl that time. It was the first place he and Helen Ross had come, driving up as far as they could in her rusty old pickup, then hiking up beside the creek.

Almost straightaway they'd found fresh wolf scat and tracks. Then a flock of ravens had led them to the carcass of an old bull moose. Though there wasn't much meat left, Helen said the wolves would probably be back. She pulled a couple of teeth from the jaw and said she was going to send them away for age analysis. She said if you sawed them you could age them by the number of rings, just like a tree. Then she sawed herself some bone samples and said she could tell the moose was in poor condition from the way the marrow had gone like strawberry jelly.

Setting the traps had been hard work and Luke had loved every minute of it. She had shown him how to bed them and explained the whole process. The idea of a dirthole set, she said, was to make the wolf think he'd stumbled across some other animal's food cache. The best place was on the upwind side of a trail, so he'd smell it as he trotted past. First he'd get a whiff of the buried bait – which smelled so foul you'd think it might send him packing – then he'd get a whiff of another wolf from the scat and urine and think, Aha! An intruder!

Now you had him interested, but you had to make sure he only had one easy way of approach to get a better sniff. The real skill, she said, was to have him put his foot exactly where you wanted, so you laid sticks or rocks which he would step over and tread right onto the pan.

The previous afternoon, when the traps were all set, he had taken her up to the abandoned den and rendezvous site. At the den she put on her little headlamp and got out a tape measure and slithered right down into the hole like a gopher.

217

She was gone so long he started to worry, wondering what he would do if she got stuck down there. But then her boots appeared and she wriggled out backward, babbling with excitement and covered in gray dust, and handed him the headlamp.

'Your turn.'

Luke shook his head. 'Oh, no. I d–don't—'

'Go on, I dare you.'

So he handed her his hat and down he went. The tunnel traveled straight into the hillside for about fifteen feet and was so narrow he had to hunch his shoulders and use the toes of his boots to inch himself along.

In the beam of the headlamp, the walls looked pale and smooth, as if they had been molded in clay. He had expected the air to be fetid or musty, but it smelled only of earth. There were no bones, no scat, no sign of wolf at all, except a few pale hairs snagged in the tree roots that hung from the roof. The end of the tunnel broadened into a chamber about three feet across and Luke stopped there and lay quite still, panting a little from the effort of the crawl. He thought of the mother wolf curled in this womb of cold earth, giving birth to her pups, pictured her licking their blind faces clean and suckling them.

Then he switched off the lamp and held his breath enfolded in the silence and the darkness, and for some reason remembered something he'd read, about how life was a circular trip from the tomb of the womb to the womb of the tomb. He had never understood why anyone should fear the perfect nothingness of death. He would happily have died right there and then.

He was still thinking about this when he emerged blinking into the sunlight and saw her smiling at him. She said she'd thought he was going to stay down there forever and he just blurted out what was in his head, which was really dumb. But she simply nodded and he could see in her eyes that she understood. It was weird, but two or three times now, he'd gotten the feeling that they were somehow alike. As if they belonged to the same tribe or something.

It was probably just wishful thinking.

She'd helped him brush the dust from his back and shoulders and the touch of her hands felt good. Then he did the same for her, which felt even better. She stood with her back to him while he did it and he couldn't help staring at the nape of her neck, where her hair tapered into a sunbleached down on the gold of her skin.

He watched her now, ahead of him along the trail, still holding the antenna above her head. She was wearing khaki hiking pants and her pale blue fleece. She turned and started walking slowly back toward him, chewing her lip as she always seemed to do when she concentrated.

Suddenly she stopped and stiffened and he knew she'd heard something. Then she gave a whoop.

'Yes!'

'W-w-which one is it?'

'Five-sixty-two. That's the one you set. Down by all that willow scrub, remember?'

She came running back to him, grinning and holding out the headphones so he could hear too. Buzz started to bark inside the pickup and Helen told him to hush. Luke put on the headphones.

'Got it?'

For a moment he heard nothing. Then, as she adjusted the receiver, he heard the steady *cluck-cluck-cluck* of the signal. He grinned and nodded and Helen gave him a punch on the shoulder.

'Hey, trapper, you got yourself a wolf!'

It took them twenty minutes to get to where the trail ran out and Helen drove so fast, it seemed to Luke they were lucky to get there at all. All the way, she kept teasing him about how it was beginner's luck and who did he think he was, anyway, breezing in and beating her to it after all the work she'd put in. Luke laughed and promised not to tell anyone.

They parked at the edge of a clearcut and got out to fix their packs in the bed of the pickup. Across the clearcut, two loggers from the post and pole company were leaning against a half-loaded trailer, having a smoke. Luke didn't know either of them. Helen waved and called hi, but they only nodded and went on smoking and staring without so much as a smile.

Helen busied herself with her pack, carrying on a mock conversation with the loggers which only Luke could hear.

'"Well, hi there, Helen! How're you doing? Caught any wolves? Really? That's terrific! Well, thanks. You too. Bye!"'

'Have you seen them b–before?' Luke asked quietly.

'Sure, they nearly drove me off the road a couple of times.' She fastened her pack and grinned as she swung it onto her back. 'Did you see the nod? Small, but definitely a nod. You wait, soon we'll be best buddies. Inside every logger, Luke, there's a tree-hugger waiting to get out.'

'You think so?'

'Nope.'

They left Buzz in the pickup and set off up the creek.

Even before she had heard the signal, Helen was pretty sure that they had caught one. The dream had never yet lied.

She had never dared tell anyone about it. It sounded too preposterous. And anyway, being a woman in the macho world of wolf research was hard enough without everyone thinking you'd gone *woo-woo*, the term her mother used to scorn everything from astrology to vitamin pills. And in truth, although Helen didn't doubt there were more things in heaven and earth than could be seen with the aid of a microscope, on the *woo-woo* scale she was definitely at the skeptical end.

Except, that is, for her wolf dreams.

They had started in Minnesota, shortly after she first learned to trap. The dream was always different. Sometimes it would be almost literal: she would actually see a wolf caught in a trap, waiting for her. At other times it was more oblique, seemingly about something else entirely. All she would get was a *feeling* of wolf, not even a glimpse or a shadow, just the sense that one was present. It wasn't that she had the dream every time she caught a wolf. She could be trapping for months on end, catching lots, and never have it once. It was that whenever she did have it, the next morning, without fail, there was a wolf waiting for her.

And as if that wasn't *woo-woo* enough, she would often wake knowing precisely which trap she would find it in. Sometimes she would see the actual location and at other times it was more symbolic and all she would get was a clue. She might see trees perhaps, or rocks or water, and from that deduce which trap it was. This part of the dream wasn't fool-proof. Sometimes the wolf would be in a different trap altogether. But such was her trust in her wolf dreams, that when that happened, she didn't assume the dream was wrong, only that she had misread the message.

The scientist in Helen rapped her knuckles for indulging such nonsense. She tried to persuade herself that it was simply a case of autosuggestion or some other trick of the brain, a sort of dreaming equivalent of déjà-vu. For a whole summer, when she'd been working with Dan Prior, she had secretly kept notes of the dreams and checked them against their trapping figures. The correlation was undeniable. But she could never quite summon the courage to tell Dan.

Yet here she now was, confiding it to Luke, whom she hardly knew.

They were making their way up beside the last tumbling stretch of creek before the land leveled into the meadow where the trap was and she didn't know why she was telling him except that there was something about him she trusted. She was sure he wouldn't laugh.

He walked at her side, looking at her now and then with his serious green eyes as he listened, but mainly watching where he placed his feet, for the ground was treacherous. She had told him almost the whole story and he hadn't yet said a word and even though she thought it unlikely that he would mock her, she heard herself switching on the old defense-mechanism and making light of it, just in case.

'It's a real pain, you know? I've tried dreaming about lottery numbers and racehorses, but it never works.'

Luke smiled.

'So w-what exactly did you dream last n-night?'

'Just of a wolf, wading across a stream.' Which was true, but not wholly true because the wolf, in that curious duality permitted by dreams, had also actually been Joel and had walked away from her to the other bank without once looking back and vanished into the trees.

'He wasn't in the trap then?'

'No. The one that got away.'

Helen waited for him to say something, but he just nodded and looked down into the creek where the water roared through a gateway of rock and gushed in thirty feet of foam to a churning cauldron of a pool below.

'So, do you think I'm nuts?' she said at last.

'Of course not. I have some pretty w-w-weird dreams too.'

'Yeah, but do they come true?'

'Only the bad ones.'

'Do you dream of wolves?'

'Sometimes.'

The roar of the water was too loud for them to go on talking and they didn't speak again until they stopped in the trees at the edge of the meadow. The grass up here was still almost

222

green. They stared across it toward the thicket of willow scrub where the trap was, but the only sign of life was a pair of ravens flapping languidly over what was left of the moose.

'Would there still be a signal, even if he's g-gotten free?'

'Could be.'

They set out across the meadow and as they drew near to the trail that ran beside the willow thicket, Helen could see the hole where the trap had been torn from the ground. When they got there they found a long furrow carved by the hook of the drag as the wolf had headed for cover. But although it told them roughly where now he must be, still there was no sound or movement.

For a moment she thought maybe Luke was right and the wolf had managed to get free. Then she heard the clink of the drag chain and knew they had him. He was somewhere in the willows, maybe thirty feet from where they were standing.

Helen whispered to Luke to stay where he was, that she needed to check things out, then slowly followed the drag mark toward the thicket.

She had already explained to him how you always needed to see how good a grip the trap had found on a wolf's leg and how firmly the drag was anchored. This didn't matter so much if you'd caught a pup, a yearling or a low-ranking adult; they usually lay submissively, not even daring to look you in the eye. But if you'd trapped an alpha you had to be careful. They could come right at you and given half a chance would get their teeth into you. Knowing how securely they were snagged and how far they could reach was crucial.

Now, up ahead, Helen again heard the clink of the chain and this time the bushes rustled, shedding a flutter of yellow leaves behind which she saw a flash of pale fur. Luke had told her that the alpha female was almost white and Helen's heart leapt at the thought that this was who they'd caught.

She turned to Luke and mouthed, 'I think it's Mom.'

She was now at the very edge of the thicket and could see the mark the drag had carved as the wolf went in. Helen stopped there, listening and peering through the tangled stems of the willow. She guessed that the wolf could only be five or six feet away but there was no sign of her. Everything had gone still. All she could hear was the trickle of the creek and from across the meadow, the mocking, staccato croak of a raven.

Slowly she lifted her foot, thinking maybe if she took a step into the thicket she might see her. It was as if the thought itself sufficed, for hardly had she moved, when the bush in front of her erupted.

Suddenly, there was the wolf's head, all snarling teeth and pink gums and yellow eyes, lunging at her through the branches. It gave Helen such a shock that she jumped away, lost her footing and fell flat on her back in the meadow. But she didn't take her eyes off the wolf and saw the head jerk and disappear as the drag hooks held fast. She looked up and saw Luke's grinning face.

'I think it *is* Mom,' he said.

'That's standard practice, by the way. Always fall over. It makes them feel at ease.'

Luke laughed and helped her to her feet. He pointed to a slab of rock a little way along the thicket.

'Maybe we could see better from there.'

He was right. It was where she should have gone in the first place.

'Okay. Smarty-pants.'

They waded through the willow scrub toward it, giving the wolf as wide a berth as they could. The rock had sheer sides with no low footholes. Luke climbed up first and then reached down and hoisted her up beside him. She had to hold on to his shoulder to keep her balance and the two of them perched there precariously on the narrow spine of the rock, peering over the thicket.

The wolf was looking right at them, about twenty feet away, curling her lips and growling. She was the color of a rainless cloud, shaded faintly along her back and shoulders with gray.

'Isn't she beautiful?' Luke whispered.

'She is.'

Helen could see the trap jaws clamped on the wolf's front left foot. The hooks of the drag had dug themselves into a thick clump of roots and in her struggle, the wolf had wrapped the chain twice around it.

'She's not going anywhere in a hurry,' Helen said. 'Looks like it's best to come at her from the far side there.'

They jumped down and went back to the packs where they'd dumped them in the meadow and Helen took out her jabstick and loaded the syringe with the right amount of Telezol. Then they circled around the wolf and walked slowly through the thicket toward her from the far side, Helen leading the way.

She could hear growling as they came near and when they parted the last shield of bushes and saw her, she tried to make another lunge at them. But the chain held fast. The wolf snarled and lowered herself slowly to the ground.

'Hi, Mom,' Helen said gently. 'Hey, aren't you gorgeous?'

She was in prime condition, her coat lustrous and almost fully thickened for the coming winter. Helen figured she was maybe three to four years old and must weigh almost eighty pounds. Her eyes glinted a pale, greenish yellow in the sunlight.

'It's okay, baby,' Helen cooed. 'It's okay. We're not going to hurt you. Just going to give you a little snooze.'

In the same soft voice, she asked Luke to walk slowly around to the other side and, just as she'd hoped, the wolf was suspicious and turned, struggling with the weight of the trap, to keep her eyes on him. It gave Helen her chance. She reached out and, like a matador, plunged the jabstick into the wolf's rear end.

As soon as the needle touched her fur, the wolf snarled and whipped around with her jaws. But Helen was ready and kept the jabstick pressed home until the syringe had safely delivered its shot. Then she and Luke moved away and watched from a distance while the wolf's eyes grew bleary and her limbs slackened until at last she slumped like a drunk in a doorway.

Half an hour later, they were almost done. They'd blindfolded her, weighed her, measured her, taken blood and feces samples and checked her all over from teeth to tail. She was free of lice and seemed in perfect health. The trap had made a small flesh wound on her leg but there were no bones broken. Helen smeared it with some antibiotic ointment and gave her a shot for good measure. All they had to do now was clip an identity tag to her ear and fit her with a radio collar.

Luke was kneeling beside her, running a hand along the wolf's silvery side. He had been a great assistant, taking notes and marking the samples for her and passing anything she needed from the folding tiers of the kit-box in which she kept her field processing stuff.

Helen sat back on her heels and watched him. He was totally absorbed in stroking the wolf and his eyes were so gentle and full of such innocent wonder that Helen wanted to reach out and stroke him too.

Instead, she said, 'Isn't her coat amazing? The different layers?'

'Yeah. And the colors. From a d-distance, she just looks white. But up close there's all these other colors. Browns and blacks, even a t-tinge of red.'

He looked at her and smiled and Helen smiled back and again felt something connect between them, though quite what it was, she would have then been unable to say. It was she who broke the moment and looked down at the wolf.

226

'This old girl's going to be waking up soon.'

She clipped the ear tag on and made a note of the number. Then she slipped the collar over the wolf's neck, making sure it was neither too loose nor too tight and that the signal still worked. Helen then removed the blindfold, took some photographs and by the time they had packed up all the gear, the wolf was starting to stir.

'Let's go,' Helen said. 'It's best to give her some space.'

Luke was standing by the wolf, staring down at her. She thought perhaps he hadn't heard.

'Luke?'

He turned and nodded and she saw sadness in his eyes.

'Is something the matter?'

'No.'

'The collar could save her life, you know.'

He gave a little shrug. 'Maybe.'

They moved the wolf out of the thicket and laid her beside the trail near to where she had been trapped. Then they shouldered the packs and set off across the meadow. A coyote was chasing the ravens away from the moose carcass down beside the creek. It stopped when it saw Luke and Helen, then loped moodily off into the scrub.

From the trees on the other side of the meadow, they watched the wolf get groggily to her feet. She took a few faltering steps, then stopped and lowered her head to lick her front paw. Then she lifted her nose and delicately sniffed the air and caught their scent. She turned and stared right at them. Helen gave her a little wave.

'See ya, Mom.'

Then, with all the disdain of a slighted movie star, the wolf turned her back, flounced her tail and trotted away up the canyon.

18

He couldn't take his eyes off her.

She was strolling down beside the stream, talking on the cell phone. She'd taken off her hiking boots and socks and was pointing her toes like a ballet dancer before every step. Moon Eye was down there too, browsing the lusher grass that grew near the water, and she idly ran her hand along his side as she passed. Luke wondered if she had any idea how beautiful she was.

He was sitting on the ground in front of the cabin where they'd eaten the picnic. When they got back from trapping, Helen had spread an old blue blanket on the grass and brought out cheese and fruit, nuts, cookies and chocolate and they'd sat there eating in the sunshine, talking excitedly about what had happened.

The sun had moved around and the shadow cast by the cabin roof was creeping across the blanket, swallowing Luke's body and legs and soon his boots. Beside him, Buzz lay sprawled on his back in seventh dog-heaven while Luke rubbed his tummy, watching Helen all the while. She was talking with her boss who was obviously teasing her.

'What do you mean *luck*?' she said. 'Luck, my ass. It's skill, Prior, sheer skill and brilliance. When have you ever caught two wolves in one hit?'

It had happened right after they'd watched the alpha female trot away. Scanning the frequencies again, they'd heard another signal and in a trap they'd set a few hundred yards farther up the same trail, found a second wolf, this time a young male.

'I tell you, Dan, this place Wrong Creek is like a wolf inter-state or something.'

Luke heard the drone of geese and squinted up at the sky. High above, two filigreed arrows of them were following the line of the mountains south. He looked down again at Helen and saw she was watching them too. Several times now, she had caught him staring at her. He found it hard not to. But she didn't seem to mind, just smiled back at him as though it were the most natural thing in the world.

To begin with, he'd been a little nervous of her and stuttered badly. But she hadn't seemed to notice and soon he'd managed to relax. She was real easy to be with. She talked a lot, all fast and bubbly, and sometimes when she laughed, she'd toss her head back and put her hands through her hair, making it go all spiky.

The thing he liked best was how she sometimes touched him when she was telling him something, just put a hand on his arm or shoulder, like it was the most natural thing in the world. When they'd heard that second signal and knew they'd caught another wolf, she'd put her arms around him and given him this massive hug. Luke had nearly died of embarrassment. His hat fell off and he started blushing like an idiot. That's exactly what he was too, because this was a grown woman and he was just a skinny kid with a stutter.

229

Moon Eye suddenly stopped grazing and lifted his head to look down toward the lake, his ears twitching forward. And the next second Buzz was on his feet and off down the hill barking. Two riders were coming out of the trees down there and Luke's heart sank when he saw who it was.

He and Helen had agreed they would keep his role in the trapping a secret. She hadn't even mentioned it to Dan Prior. And now they'd blown it. He looked at her and saw she was thinking the same. She was finishing her phone call. Luke stood up and watched his father and Clyde steer their horses around the water's edge and up the slope toward them, Buzz barking alongside all the way.

'Morning,' Helen said brightly.

She told Buzz to hush. Luke's father tipped his hat at her and gave her one of those smiles he always used when he knew he had you cornered.

'Ma'am.'

Clyde didn't say a thing, just stared at Luke while they reined their horses to a stop in front of the cabin. He saw his father's eyes travel from the picnic remains to Helen's bare feet, then all the way up her to her face.

'Mighty fine life, working for the US Fish and Wildlife.'

'Oh, it is,' Helen said. 'Beats being on vacation anytime.'

'Picnics by the lake, no boss checking up on you.'

'You got it. Get up around noon, do a little sunbathing . . .'

'Sounds a pretty good deal.'

'And, wow, you should see the size of our paychecks.'

Luke was impressed by her gall but at the same time wanted to warn her how dangerous it was to joke like this. Surely she could see there was no humor in that smile of his and that he was only playing in the way a cat might play with a bird.

He hadn't so much as glanced Luke's way so far. He always liked to keep you waiting before he hurt you. But now at last he turned his head and Luke felt the gray eyes fix upon him, cold and critical.

'Well, son, I'm glad we've found you at last. I was starting to think that old wolf had got you.'

'No, sir, I w-w-was—'

'Because, you know, we were all supposed to be helping the Hardings gather their herd this morning. Like I told you. Clyde and I rode up to the allotment to find you and you weren't there.'

Luke had clean forgotten.

'I w-w-was there. You m-must have just—'

'Oh, so you were?'

'Y-yes, sir.'

'So how come Abe saw you with this young lady here, in her truck, driving up Wrong Creek?'

'I w-w-w—'

Luke's tongue was nailed to the roof of his mouth, which was maybe just as well because he didn't know what to say anyway. His chest hurt like it was being squeezed in a vise and his cheeks were starting to burn. A few moments ago, alone with Helen, he'd felt for once almost like a man. Now he was a stupid, tongue-tied kid again.

He glanced at Helen, just to confirm this was how she now saw him too. Instead, she took his look as a call for help.

'He was with me because I asked him for help,' she said.

Luke's father looked at her. He was still smiling but his eyes were like frozen stone.

'And, thanks to him, you'll be pleased to know, this morning we caught and collared two wolves.'

His father lowered his head a little and raised his eyebrows at her. 'You caught two wolves?'

'That's right. Thanks to Luke, here. He helped me find them.'

Luke's father was silent for a moment, while he considered

231

this. Clyde was watching him carefully for a lead on how to react. His father's horse pawed the ground a couple of times.

'So where are they?'

'Well, as I said, we put radio collars on them.'

'Then what?'

Helen frowned. 'Sorry, what do you mean?'

He gave an arid little laugh and looked at Clyde.

'Well, have you already shipped them out or what?'

'Mr Calder, I think you know what the intention is here. We—'

'You just turned them loose again.'

'Yes, but—'

'Let me get this straight, young lady. I've just been with a good friend and neighbor of mine, Abe Harding, gathering his herd. And this man, who, unlike your bosses back in Washington DC, doesn't have a bottomless barrel of tax dollars to burn, finds six of his calves have gone missing. That's a loss to Abe of, what, three thousand dollars? And you tell me you've just caught two of the varmints responsible and then let them go again? And I should be *pleased*?'

Luke could see Helen was angry. But scared too. There was nobody, in the end, who his father wasn't able to scare. Luke saw her swallow.

'Mr Calder, the whole idea—'

'The whole idea, so you and Mr Prior told us, was that we had a lone wolf here. What was it you called it, a "disperser" or something? Now it turns out there's – how many?'

Helen hesitated.

'You don't want to tell me?'

'I believe there's a pack.'

'Oh, so it's a pack now. How many exactly?'

'Perhaps nine. But five of them only pups and—'

'*Nine?* And you caught two and just let them go again? So they can go on killing our cattle and ruining good men like

Abe Harding?'

'Mr Calder—'

'Thank you, ma'am. I've heard enough.'

He gathered his reins and sharply hoisted his horse's head, turning him in front of them, then looking back over his shoulder.

'Luke?'

'Y–yes, sir?'

'When you've finished whatever your business is here, I'd appreciate it if you'd come down to the house. There's one or two things you and I need to clear up.'

Luke nodded. His father touched his hat at Helen.

'Miss Ross.'

He jabbed his heels into the sides of his horse and loped away down toward the lake, with Clyde at his heels. Luke started to gather up his gear. He felt too small and shamed even to look at Helen. As he was picking up his bag, she put her hand on his shoulder.

'Luke?'

He straightened up, but still couldn't meet her eyes.

'It's my fault. I'm really sorry. I shouldn't have asked you to help me.'

'It's no b–big deal.'

And when he'd gotten all his things together, without another word being spoken, he walked to the stream to collect Moon Eye and swung himself into the saddle. And he rode off down the slope, without once looking back, but feeling her eyes upon him all the way.

Helen spent the rest of the afternoon radio tracking the two collared wolves. Mercifully, the signals stayed high up Wrong Creek and well away from any livestock.

She came back around seven and took a shower. Now that the fall was settling in, the water was so cold it gave her a headache. Soon she'd have to wash herself indoors.

She found herself watching over the shower door, hoping to see Luke's horse appear across the lake. But she knew he wouldn't come, not after what had happened that morning. She wanted to celebrate their success, but there was only Buzz to do it with and, bright as they were, dogs didn't seem to grasp the concept.

Shivering, she ran back to the cabin and quickly dried herself and dressed. Then, after checking her messages (none), she lit a celebratory cigarette (her first in three days) and put on some Sheryl Crow. But she made the mistake of listening to the lyrics and when Sheryl started going on about being a stranger in her own life, Helen dived for the off-button. She wanted to celebrate, for heavensake, not slit her wrists.

She thought of writing to Joel. Another bad idea. And why the hell should she? It was *his* turn. Then, since for once there was a good signal on the cell phone, she decided to call her mother in Chicago. All she got was an answering machine. It was the same with Celia in Boston. And with Dan Prior. Where the hell was everyone?

As if in answer, the phone, still in her hand, rang.

It was Bill Rimmer. He congratulated her on trapping the wolves and said it sounded as if she had won the bet they'd had over who'd catch the first one. He was heading up to the Hardings' to talk about those missing calves, he said. Did Helen want to come along?

'Thanks Bill, but not without full body armor.'

'Then, I tell you what. When I'm through up there, I'll buy you a drink in town.'

They arranged to meet in an hour's time at The Last Resort. Helen figured it might be good public relations to put in an appearance there anyhow. Rumors of the Hardings losses were sure to be flying thick and fast.

It was almost dark when she drove into Hope and saw the

red neon sign of The Last Resort glowing halfway along Main Street. She drove slowly by on the other side of the road, checking out the cars parked there and hoping to see Bill Rimmer's among them. It wasn't.

She didn't much fancy the idea of waiting for him inside, so she drove a little farther along the street, and parked by the laundromat. Two young cowboys were in there, clowning around while they loaded wet clothes into one of the dryers. Helen had used the place herself a couple of times, once to wash clothes and once to wash wolf scat.

It was a method Dan had taught her in Minnesota to find out what a wolf had been feeding on. You tied each scat inside a labeled piece of pantyhose, knotted at each end, then put them in the wash. When they come out all you have left is hair and bits of bone. Other laundromat users aren't too keen on this process, so you had to be a little discreet. The hair in every scat Helen had washed the other night was mixed: some deer, some elk, but a lot of cattle hair too, which didn't mean the wolves had actually *killed* cattle; they might simply have found a carcass and fed on it.

Fifteen minutes later, Bill Rimmer still hadn't arrived. Helen was becoming embarrassed at the looks she was getting from passing cars and especially from the two young cowboys in the laundromat. Maybe Rimmer had parked somewhere, else, she thought. Or maybe he'd phoned the bar to leave a message. She got out and headed across the street.

She regretted it as soon as she stepped through the door. Below the antlered trophies on the walls, a dozen pairs of living eyes swiveled and locked onto her, none of them friendly and none Bill Rimmer's.

She nearly turned around and ran back out to her truck. But then the stubborn streak in her, the one that always landed her in trouble, said why on earth shouldn't she come and have a drink if she wanted? So she took a breath and

235

walked right up to the bar.

She ordered a margarita, settled herself on a stool and lit a cigarette.

Apart from the barmaid, she was the only woman in the entire room. The place was crowded, although the only faces she recognized were Ethan Harding and those two loggers she and Luke had seen up Wrong Creek. She guessed these were the ones Doug Millward had mentioned. The three of them were talking at the far end of the bar. Occasionally they looked her way, but Helen was damned if she was going to smile and give them another chance to cut her dead, so she ignored them, along with all the sidelong looks from those she didn't know.

She felt like a scandalous outcast or a stranger who'd just ridden into town in some corny western. She wanted to flee but didn't want to give them the pleasure of knowing they'd driven her away. She imagined the place erupting in laughter after she left.

She finished her drink and ordered another, pretending to be interested in a basketball game on the TV and wondering how the hell she ever thought coming to this godforsaken dump might be good for public relations. She drank the second margarita too quickly. They were strong and she wished she'd had something to eat first.

Then, in the mirror behind the bar, she saw Buck Calder coming in through the door. That was all she needed.

He eased his way toward the bar, working the crowd like a vote-hungry candidate. Helen watched his reflected progression and couldn't help but be impressed. She wondered what those whose hands he shook and shoulders he squeezed really thought of him. They seemed dazzled by his smile and his wisecracks, by the way he tucked their names into his greetings. She saw him notice her and register her stare and though she immediately looked away, she knew, with a small rush of

236

panic, that he was headed her way.

'I can't imagine what's come over all these fellas, letting a pretty young woman sit drinking on her own.'

Helen gave a laugh that became almost hysterical. He was standing right behind her, looking at her in the mirror.

'They're not normally noted for shyness around these parts.'

Helen couldn't think what to say. The tequila seemed to have numbed her wit. She saw in the mirror how inane her smile looked and tried to adjust it. Beside her, a man was collecting a round of drinks and when he moved away, Calder slipped neatly into the slot. Their bodies were only an inch or two apart and their legs briefly touched. She could smell his lemon-scented cologne and was disconcerted. It was the same kind her father now used.

'May I make amends for their lack of courtesy and buy you a drink?'

'Well, thanks, but actually, I was supposed to be meeting somebody here. I think he must have—'

'What is it, a margarita?'

'No really, I think I'd better be—'

He leaned over and called along the bar, 'Lori? Can we have us a beer and another margarita here? Thanks, sweetheart.'

He turned his head and smiled down at Helen.

'Just want to show there's no hard feelings about this morning.'

Helen frowned, as if she didn't know what he meant.

'I appreciate you've got a job to do. Maybe I was a little harsh.'

'Oh, I was born with a thick skin and broad shoulders.'

'From here, Helen, I'd say they were just about right.'

She smiled. Her mind reeled. Was that a *pass*, for heavensake?

'I think Luke was maybe a little more upset than I was.'

'He gets that way sometimes. Takes after his mother.'

Helen nodded slowly, buying time. It seemed like dangerous territory.

'Sensitive, you mean,' she said.

'I guess that's one word for it.'

'Being sensitive isn't such a bad thing, is it?'

'Didn't say it was.'

There was a silence that was only saved from getting awkward by the barmaid coming to tell Helen there was a phone call for her. She excused herself with Calder and made her way through the crowd to the alcove where the phone was. It was Bill Rimmer, full of apologies for standing her up. He said Abe Harding had given him a hard time.

'Do you still have all your limbs?' Helen asked.

'I haven't counted them yet. Those are some dogs.'

'What about the calves?'

'He didn't find a single bone up there. But he says he knows it was the wolves. Says he's seen them and heard them.'

'What did you say?'

'I had to tell him that to qualify for compensation, he'd need verification that the losses were caused by wolves.'

'And that went down pretty well, I imagine.'

'Oh yeah. He really liked that bit. Anyhow, I spoke with Dan and he says maybe you and he should fly tomorrow, see if you can get a real fix on the pack, now you've a couple of collars on them.'

'Sure, that's a good idea.'

Rimmer apologized again for not showing up, but said he figured she might be better off sweet-talking angry ranchers on her own anyway. Helen told him in a lowered voice that she was having a drink with Buck Calder.

'Well, there you go, Helen. He's your main man.'

'Thanks, Bill.'

Calder was talking to someone else when she got back to

the bar and Helen thought this might be her chance to leave. But he immediately turned his attention back to her. He raised his glass and clinked it against hers.

'Anyway,' he said. 'Congratulations on catching them.'

'Even though I let them go again.'

He smiled and they both drank.

He wiped the froth from his lips. 'As I say, you've got a job to do and I understand that, even though I may not agree with it. I was just mad at Luke for leaving the herd, specially after seeing how many calves old Abe lost. I'm sorry if I was . . . well, discourteous.'

'Oh, that's okay.'

Helen took out another cigarette and he picked up her matches and lit it for her. She thanked him. For awhile neither of them spoke.

'Luke knows the country up there really well,' Helen said.

'Yeah, I guess he does.'

'And he's got a real feel for my kind of work.'

'Yep, he's a born bunny-hugger.'

They both laughed.

'Does he get that from his mother too?'

'I guess. She grew up in the city, anyhow.'

'Where all us bunny-huggers grow up, of course.'

'That's how it seems to be.'

He smiled and lifted his glass to drink, keeping his eyes on her over the rim. And suddenly, despite herself, Helen could see how women might find Buck Calder attractive. It wasn't his looks, which weren't bad, she had to admit, for a guy his age. It was entirely to do with confidence. It oozed from him. The way he focused his attention on you was brazen, laughable even, if you chose to see it that way. But Helen guessed many women might prefer instead to bask in it.

Without asking her, he ordered them both another drink and changed the subject. He got her talking about herself, about Chicago and her work in Minnesota about her family and even about her dad getting married again. And though this was clearly another of his techniques with women, he did it so effortlessly and with such well-measured empathy that Helen had to stop herself spilling secrets that, sober in the morning, she knew she would regret.

'Does it bother you that she's so much younger?'

'Than my dad? Or me?'

'Well, both, I guess.'

Helen thought for a moment. 'Than me, no. I don't think so anyway. Than him . . . well, damn it, yes. If I'm honest, it does. I don't know why, it just does.'

'A man can't help falling in love.'

'Yeah, but why can't he pick on someone his own age?'

He laughed. 'Grow up, you mean.'

'Exactly.'

'My momma used to say men never grow up, they just get grouchier. There's this little boy hiding inside every one of us and he's there till the day we die, hollering *I want, I want*.'

'And women don't want?'

'I'm sure they do. But they can handle not getting it better than men.'

'Oh, is that so?'

'Yes, Helen, I believe it is. I think women see some things a little more clearly than men.'

'Like what?'

'Like, wanting something can be better than getting it.'

They looked at each other for a moment. Finding a philosopher in him surprised her, though as always, what he said seemed to have some other meaning swirling beneath it.

Ethan Harding and his po-faced logging pals went by, on their way to the door. Ethan nodded to Calder but none of them so much as glanced at Helen.

Looking around her, she realized how much the crowd had

thinned. They had been talking for nearly an hour. She said it was time she went home and resisted his efforts to persuade her to have a last drink. She'd had more than enough already, as she could tell by the way the walls moved as soon as she stood up.

'I sure have enjoyed our talk,' he said.

'Me too.'

'Are you okay to drive? I could easily—'

'I'm fine.' She said it a little too quickly.

'I'll see you to your truck.'

'No, no. Thank you. I'm fine.' She was sufficiently sober, thank you very much, to know it wasn't a great idea to be seen leaving the bar with him. There would be enough tongues wagging as it was.

The street was empty and the cool of the night air delicious. She searched in her bag for the keys to the pickup and after emptying its entire contents onto the hood, found them in her jacket pocket. She managed to turn the truck around without hitting anything and drove with great deliberation out of town, already aware that she might have embarrassed herself, though still too drunk to care. Shame and self-loathing, she murkily recalled, only came with the hangover.

Doing her best to follow the meandering pool of her headlights, she remembered she was going flying with Dan and that hangovers and small planes didn't go too well together.

Up ahead now, she could see the row of mailboxes. She hadn't checked hers for three days. Earlier, heading into town, she had feared finding it empty might spoil her mood and decided to stop instead on the way home. She was drunk enough now to take it.

As she got nearer she could see something white lying in the road and, a moment later, realized what it was. She stopped the pickup so that the headlights were on it and got out.

It was her mailbox. The metal stake had been twisted to the ground and the box itself flattened. It looked as if someone had smashed it with something and then for good measure driven over it. The other mailboxes were unscathed.

Helen stood, half lit by the headlights, frowning down at the wreckage and swaying slightly, though more sober with each second. The car's engine spluttered and stalled and for the first time she heard the moan of the wind. It had shifted and was coming cold from the north.

Somewhere in the forest a coyote began to yip then broke off, as if rebuked. She peered along the gray gravel to where her shadow reached the blacker black of the night. For an instant, she thought she saw a flicker of something pale there. But then it was gone.

She turned and walked back toward the pickup. And as she did so, the letter jigged again, only this time unseen. Then it flipped and scuttled away in the wind.

19

Dan Prior was not a religious man. At his most indulgent, he considered faith an obstacle to understanding, an excuse for not sorting out the here and the now. More practically, if something needed fixing, it just seemed smarter to try and fix it yourself than leave it to someone you'd never met and who might not show up in any case.

There were two exceptional occasions however when Dan resorted to prayer. The first was any Saturday night when his daughter was out later than they had agreed and hadn't phoned (which happened so routinely nowadays, God would soon have him down as a new recruit). The second was whenever he went flying. It seemed only logical. At several thousand feet, room for self-help was limited and if there did happen to be Someone up there, you were at least well placed for a hearing.

Today, however, as he tried to hold the Cessna steady in the bruising north wind, Dan didn't pray for his and Helen's safety.

Looking down at the higher reaches of the Hope Valley, he could see that word of Abe Harding's alleged losses to the wolves had indeed spread. All along the mountain front, herds were being gathered from their summer allotments. So instead, in a worrying and psalmic extension of normal practice, Dan asked the Lord that all the ranchers he saw down there, on their horses tiny as ticks, would find their cattle had safely grazed.

He watched the plane's shadow pass over the last of them, then looked ahead again to where the mountains curved away north like a fossilized spine, its vertebrae sprinkled with a first fall of snow. The wind had scoured all residue of summer haze from the sky. It was that kind of limpid, limitless blue that made you feel you could fly to the moon and back if you only had the fuel.

Dan kept his poetry to himself, knowing that in her present state, it would be lost on Helen. She was hunched in the seat beside him, scanning the radio frequencies and hiding her hangover with sunglasses and a faded Minnesota Timberwolves cap. Her face was a grayer shade of green every time he glanced at her.

She had arrived at the airfield in Helena with a large black coffee that she'd stopped for on the way and warned him at once that she was in no mood for jokes. She was in such a fragile state that when they'd picked up the first signal, a couple of miles south-west of Hope, she winced and reached for the volume control.

The signal belonged to the young male and, scanning on, Helen had soon found the mother's. Both were strongest as the plane crossed Wrong Creek, which was good news, because it meant they were away from the cattle. They seemed to be on the north side of the canyon, probably resting up somewhere, about a mile farther up from where Helen had trapped the male. But in the three passes they had so far made, they hadn't been able to spot them.

Apart from a few small meadows, the canyon was thick with trees and though the wind was stripping the aspens of their bright yellow leaves, the green of the pine and fir was impenetrable. Even away from the trees, there were a thousand rocky nooks where a wolf might lie hidden.

They reached the end of the canyon again and Dan climbed toward the sun and banked into another turn. At once the wind caught them and the plane lurched and bumped like a car in a pothole, making Dan grateful he hadn't had breakfast.

'God almighty, Prior!'

'Sorry.'

'I see your flying hasn't improved.'

'I see your hangover hasn't.'

He went lower this time, flying above the southern rim of the canyon and tilting the plane so Helen could get a better view. The signals from the starboard antenna grew stronger and stronger and suddenly Helen called out and pointed.

'There she is.'

'The alpha?'

'Unless there's another pale one. And there are the others – four, no, five others.'

Dan leaned across but couldn't make them out. 'Where?'

'See that shelf of rock above the aspens?'

Helen had the binoculars on them now. 'No, that's her, she's got a collar. And there's the young male we collared. Hey, isn't that great?'

'You say the Calder boy thinks there are nine in all?'

'Four adults, five pups.'

'Any sign of the alpha male down there?'

'No. They're all too gray and too small. Looks like four pups and the two we collared.'

Helen got out her camera and Dan circled again so she could take some pictures on a long lens. The wolves were lounging in the sun and seemed none too bothered about the plane until the third pass when the mother roused them and led them off into the trees.

They flew the canyon and the surrounding area for awhile longer, hoping to see the other three, but there was no sign of them. On the way back to the airfield, Helen made notes of what they had seen, logging the time and the map reference. She was looking a little less green.

'Feeling better?' Dan asked, when she'd finished.

'Yeah. Sorry for being such a grouch.'

Dan just smiled. Neither of them spoke for the rest of the trip. He wondered if something other than the hangover was bothering her. She seemed a little sad and distracted.

They landed and drove in their two cars back to the office. It was the first time Helen had been there since the day she arrived and Donna greeted her like a long-lost friend, congratulating her on catching the wolves. Dan suggested to Helen that they take the film she'd shot to the one-hour photo store and get something to eat while it was being processed.

They walked down the hill to the photo store then on a few blocks to a little coffee shop that did good turkey sandwiches and milkshakes. While they ate they talked about what they'd seen in the canyon.

'I'd feel a whole lot happier if the alpha male had been up there with them,' Dan said.

'Maybe he was and we just couldn't see him.'

'Maybe. My guess is he likes to be lower down, near all those tasty young steers.'

'Come on, Dan. You don't believe Abe Harding's calves were killed by wolves, do you?'

'Who can say?'

'We're not talking about the world's greatest rancher here. I bet he loses that many every summer. Probably doesn't even know how many he had up there in the first place.'

'Well, if these wolves *are* killing cattle, you know we're going to have to take them out.'

'What?'

'Don't look so surprised. Helen, we're working to a set of rules here, not making it up as we go along. Wolves who kill livestock jeopardize the whole recovery program.'

'What do you mean *take than out*? Relocate them?'

'In the old days maybe, not now. There's nowhere to put them. No, I mean lethal control.'

'Shoot them.'

'Yeah.'

Helen shook her head and looked away.

'Helen, wake up. It's the real world. Read the Control Plan.'

They finished their sandwiches in silence.

They collected the photos and looked through them as they walked back up the hill to the office. There were some good ones. Helen said she wouldn't come inside. She'd left Buzz in the cabin and needed to check the traplines. In a vain attempt to lighten things up, Dan said maybe she would find she'd caught the other three, the ones they hadn't seen from the plane. She didn't even smile.

He walked her to her pickup. He'd been looking forward to seeing her again but it had all gone wrong. He felt bad about what he'd said just now. He'd been harsh with her and it was probably because he felt rejected by her. Foolishly, with her coming to Montana, he'd hoped something might happen between them. It wasn't going to and he'd better get used to the idea.

Helen climbed into the pickup and he stood by the open door while she started the engine.

'This thing going okay?'

'It sucks.'

'I'll try to find you something better.'

247

'It'll do.'

'And you? Are you okay?'

'Me? Oh, I'm fine.' She saw he wasn't convinced and softened a little and smiled. 'Really. I'm okay. Thanks for asking.'

'No problem.'

He noticed something beyond her on the passenger seat.

'What's that?'

'My ex-mailbox. I have to go get a new one.'

She told him what had happened.

'That's not good, Helen. Any idea who did it?'

She shrugged. 'Nope.'

Dan frowned at it for a moment, in silence.

'Listen, you take care up there, okay? Promise you'll call me if something like that happens again. Anytime.'

'Dan, it was probably just an accident. Some drunken ranch hand on his way home or something.'

'Promise you'll call.'

'I promise. Dad.'

'Angels on your mailbox.'

She smiled. At least he'd gotten her to smile.

She swung the door shut and blew him a little kiss as she drove off. He stood there watching until the old pickup pulled into the traffic and disappeared down the hill. Then he turned and went up to the office.

He could tell from Donna's face, as soon as he walked in, that something had happened.

'I've had the press on the phone,' she said. 'And that TV reporter. She said some ranchers out in Hope are spitting blood. Say they've lost a whole load of calves to the wolves.'

'How many?'

'So far, forty-three.'

'What! Did they say which ranchers?'

'Yeah. And one of them's Buck Calder.'

20

The meeting wasn't due to start for another half-hour, but already there was a steady procession of trucks coming into town. It was getting dark and most had their headlights on. Some pulled up outside Nelly's Diner but the more popular destination was The Last Resort, which didn't bode well for the meeting. A mud-spattered pickup was stopping there now and Helen watched two men in hats and cowboy boots get out and head into the bar. One of them said something and the other laughed, turning his coat collar up against the wind. It was starting to rain.

She was spying from the window of Ruth Michaels' gift shop, sipping her third double espresso, which was a bad idea because she was nervous enough as it was. All she really wanted was a cigarette. Ruth had put some soothing music on, but it only served to heighten Helen's foreboding of the storm to come.

Stuck to the glass of the door was one of the yellow posters that were all over town.

It was two days since Buck Calder and his neighbors had gathered their herds and feelings were still running high. Helen had spent almost every waking moment trying to restore calm. She'd visited every rancher who claimed to have lost calves – and gotten short shrift from all of them.

Dan had hoped these one-on-one visits would help avoid a public meeting that could get hijacked by a few trouble-makers. But Buck Calder had bounced them into it. He'd announced the meeting two nights ago on TV, saying 'those federal government fellas who let all these wolves loose in the first place' might care to come along and explain themselves to the people who paid their wages.

The TV people were already down at the hall, setting up their lights. Dan had groaned when he saw them because it was the same woman reporter who had drooled over Buck Calder when the dog got killed. That aside, Dan – and Bill Rimmer – seemed remarkably cool. They were both sitting at the little bar at the back of the shop, chatting with Ruth as though they didn't have a care in the world.

As she walked back to join them, Rimmer gave her a grin.

'Helen, you know the one about the horse who walks into a bar and the barman says—'

'"Hey, why the long face?" Yeah, I know that one. You're saying I look like a horse?'

'No, just like you're going to a funeral.'

'Yeah, right. My own.'

'Come on, Helen,' Dan said. 'It'll be fine.'

'Thanks, Prior. I might find that a little more reassuring if

250

you hadn't told me what happened last time they had a wolf meeting here.'

'That was before my time,' Ruth said. 'What did happen?'

'Oh, just guys with guns and buckets of blood being poured over cars,' Helen said. 'Nothing much.'

'That was years ago,' Dan said.

'Yeah, before they had wolves. Ruth, do you mind if I have a cigarette?' She saw Dan's surprise. 'So I smoke, okay?'

'Go ahead,' Ruth said.

They spent the next fifteen minutes rehearsing what Helen was going to say. She'd tried to get Dan to front the meeting, but he insisted it was her show. The audience wasn't going to be wholly hostile. According to the radio news, a militant environmentalist group called Wolves of the Earth (or WOE, as they preferred) was planning to show up as well.

In case things got out of hand, Dan had taken precautions.

Hope had a resident deputy sheriff, a young man called Craig Rawlinson, whom Helen had met a couple of times. There was no mistaking him for a wolf lover. He was the son of a rancher and married to the daughter of another who was among those claiming to have lost calves. So Dan had asked for extra police to stand discreetly by, along with a couple of plainclothes special agents from the Fish and Wildlife Service who were already at work over in The Last Resort, keeping an eye on potential rabble-rousers. He'd also set up a sign outside the community hall that said, PUBLIC MEETING. NO ALCOHOL. NO SIGNS. NO WEAPONS. Someone had already added NO WOLVES.

There were voices now, outside in the street, as people made their way down toward the hall. Helen's nerves were jangling with caffeine and nicotine. Dan stood up and paid for the coffees.

'Well, I guess we'd better be getting down there.'

He put an arm around Helen's shoulders.

251

'I want you to know, anyone pulls a gun, I'm right behind you.'

'Thanks, Dan. I'll remember to duck.'

An hour later, Dan's joke about guns seemed even less amusing.

Helen had been on her feet for about twenty minutes, trying to make a speech that should have taken ten. The heckling was starting to get to her.

The place was packed. There was seating for about a hundred, but easily as many again were standing at the back, which was where most of the heckling was coming from. Beyond the dazzle of the TV lights, Helen could see the hall doors had been left open and there were even people standing outside in the rain. Despite this ventilation, the heat was already unbearable because all the hall radiators were on and no one seemed able to turn them off. As tempers and temperature rose, many had shed their coats or were fanning themselves with the leaflets that had been handed to them when they arrived.

Helen was standing at one end of a long trestle table that had been placed on the rostrum at the front of the hall. Dan and Bill Rimmer sat huddled beside her like war criminals. At the other end, leaning back in his chair and regally surveying the crowd, sat Buck Calder. He was in his element.

Beneath the brim of his hat, there was the gleam of sweat. There were damp patches under the arms of his otherwise spotless pink shirt. He seemed literally aglow. His opening speech had been masterful. For the benefit of those few who hadn't heard it a dozen times, he began by recounting how his baby grandson had been snatched from the jaws of certain death. Then, like a suave prosecuting attorney, he went on to catalog the terrible losses he and his neighbors had since sustained. The only surprise was that it was he who first got heckled.

It had started toward the end of his speech and came from a small group of latecomers at the back that Helen hadn't noticed till then. If she had, she would have known whose side they were on from the number of beards and Patagonia jackets among them. They had to be the WOE people. There were about half a dozen of them and at first Helen had felt heartened by their presence – until she saw how their heckling only served to inflame others.

Calder had handled the hecklers well. One of them, a woman with steel-rimmed glasses and a blue fleece just like Helen's, had called out:

'Wolves have more right to be here than your cows! I say, get rid of the cows!'

There was a rumble of anger and Buck stood calmly smiling while it faded, then said: 'I see we've got some of those city folk here tonight.' The audience roared their approval.

He'd kept the gag going when the time came to introduce Helen.

'Miss Ross comes from the windy city of Chicago, if I remember rightly?'

Helen had smiled grimly. 'Yes. For my sins, I do.'

'Well, sweetheart, feel free to repent those sins here tonight.'

Taking their cue from the pro-wolf people who'd started it, another group at the back had been heckling her ever since. Among the loudest were Helen's favorite loggers and Wes and Ethan Harding. Abe Harding, thank goodness, didn't seem to be there.

Neither did Luke.

Helen had looked in vain for his face in the crowd before the meeting got going. She hadn't seen him since the day they caught the wolf. He hadn't come to the cabin or been around when she'd visited the ranch to be harangued by his father about the missing calves. She'd worried about him and been surprised by how much she missed his company.

She was getting toward the end of her speech now and hoped she reached it before the end of her tether. She'd gone through what was known so far about the wolves, which wasn't much, except that there were nine of them and that early DNA tests on the samples she'd taken showed no relation to any of the wolves released in Yellowstone or Idaho. Then she'd said a few words about the Defenders of Wildlife scheme that compensated ranchers for any verified wolf-kill. When she'd finished, they were going to take questions.

'So, just to recap, we've got two of these wolves collared now and we're going to be keeping real close tabs on them. Any proven killers of livestock will be removed or destroyed. That's absolutely clear.' She glanced at Dan, who nodded. 'I understand how strongly some of you are feeling right now. All we'd ask is that you give it a little time and—'

'What more proof do you need? Wolves kill cattle, period.'

'Well, sir, with respect, there's a fair amount of evidence, both from my own research in Minnesota and here in Montana too, in the Ninemile Valley, north of Missoula, that wolves *can* live in close proximity with livestock and not bother them—'

'Hey, even the goddamn wolves are liberals in Missoula!'

There was a roar of laughter and Helen waited for it to pass, trying to keep her smile in place. It felt more like a grimace.

'Well, maybe. But a biologist there did some pretty interesting research. He fitted radio collars not just on wolves but on cattle as well and he found that the wolves mingled with herds the whole time without—'

'Bullshit!'

'Why the hell don't you just let her speak?' shouted one of the WOE group.

254

'Why the hell don't you go back where you belong and mind your own goddamn business?'

Buck Calder stood up and raised his hands.

'Our city friend back there is right. We asked Miss Ross along tonight and we should do her the courtesy of hearing her out.'

Helen nodded at him. 'Thank you. The fact seems to be that wolves prefer to prey on wild rather than domestic ungulates. Over a period of six years in the Ninemile, they killed just three steers and one calf—'

'So how come they killed forty-three here in a couple of months?' Ethan Harding called out. There was a loud murmur of support.

'Well, we're trying to get verification on precisely how many of those losses were in fact caused by wolves.'

'You calling us liars?'

'No, I certainly am not.'

Buck Calder leaned forward in his chair. 'Maybe you could tell us, Helen, how many of these calves you have "verified" as wolf-kills so far?'

Helen hesitated. It was the question she'd dreaded. Of the forty-three alleged losses, only five carcasses had been found and not one of them was recent enough for the cause of death to be established.

'Miss Ross?'

'We've still got some work to do on that. As you know, the evidence is a little thin on the ground—'

'But, so far, how many can you say for sure were killed by wolves?'

Helen turned to Dan for help. He cleared his throat and was about to speak when Calder cut in:

'I think we should hear this from Miss Ross. How many?'

'Well, as I say, sir, we still have to—'

'So far, though?'

The whole room went quiet, waiting for her answer. Helen swallowed.

'Well, so far. None.'

There was uproar. Everyone started shouting at the same time. Some of those with seats were getting to their feet. Behind them, the fiercest WOE woman was nose to nose with Ethan Harding.

'The wolf's an endangered species, you bozo!' she yelled.

'No, lady, *you're* the endangered species!'

Calder held up his hands and called for quiet. But it had little effect. Helen shook her head and picked up a glass of water. As she drank she looked at Dan and he shrugged, guiltily. Bill Rimmer was craning his neck, peering toward the back of the hall. Something was going on back there. The TV cameraman had turned right around and was clambering up on a chair to get a better shot.

Helen could see a truck had pulled up outside with its headlights pointing directly into the hall. Someone had climbed out of it and was walking toward the entrance, the lit rain sheeting down behind him. He pushed his way through the crowd out in the lobby and slowly it parted to let him through. He was in the hall now, elbowing his way through the hecklers, and as they saw him, they stopped their shouting and stepped aside.

It was Abe Harding.

He was carrying something, a bundle of some kind, over his shoulder. Helen glanced at Dan and they both frowned.

'What the hell's he got there?'

'Looks like a rug or something.'

Harding was clear of the hecklers now and heading down the aisle between the seats where most people had risen to their feet to get a better look at him. He was wearing a long yellow slicker that glistened with rain and made a swishing sound as he walked. He wasn't wearing a hat and his grizzled hair was all bedraggled.

Everyone was silent now and every pair of eyes upon him. He was wearing spurs which clinked with every footstep as he made his way toward the rostrum. He was staring at Helen with a kind of crazed intensity that would have been comical if it hadn't been so scary. Helen hoped Dan's two special agents had their guns handy.

It wasn't until Harding reached the rostrum and stopped right in front of her that Helen noticed the blood rivering down his slicker and realized at last what the bundle of black fur on his shoulder was.

'Here's your goddamn verification,' Harding said.

And he swung the dead wolf from his shoulder and dumped it on the table.

By the time Helen and Bill Rimmer managed to get out of the community hall, Main Street looked like a war zone. It was blocked by four police cars and a fifth was blasting its siren as it tried to push its way through the crowd. Flashing red lights bounced and prismed in the store windows and made the great puddles of rain look like blood. It was coming down like a monsoon. Helen was soaked to the skin within seconds.

A cop with a megaphone was asking people to move off and most were complying, negotiating a route through the puddles to their cars. Across the street now she caught sight of Dan. He and the two special agents were arguing with one of the cops who had arrested Abe Harding.

She could see Harding now, still in his yellow slicker with his hands cuffed behind his back, being ushered into the back of one of the police cars. His sons were yelling at two other cops who were stopping them from getting to him. A little farther along the street, in the sheltered doorway of Iverson's grocery store, Buck Calder was giving an interview to the woman from the TV station.

'You okay?' Bill Rimmer was looking down at her.

'I think so.'

The moment after Harding had dumped the wolf, all hell had broken loose. One of the WOE men had gotten into a fight with the two loggers, but it had been broken up before anyone was hurt. In the ensuing chaos Helen had been shoved against a wall and a large rancher had stepped, accidentally, on her foot. That aside, she was just a little shaken.

'Dan looks like he's got himself a problem over there,' Rimmer said. He hunched his shoulders against the rain and headed across the street and Helen followed.

'You don't have to do this!' Dan was saying to the cop.

'The man assaulted a police officer. Listen, it was you who asked for police backup in the first place.'

'Yeah, but why take him away? He's not going anyplace. All this'll do is make a martyr of him. That's what he wants, for Godsake.'

It was too late anyway. The car Abe had been bundled into was already moving off, sounding its siren to get through the dispersing crowd.

In its lights, Helen suddenly caught sight of Luke. He was coming down the street bur hadn't seen her. He seemed to be looking for someone.

'Luke!'

He turned and saw her. He was wearing a brown waxed slicker, with the collar turned up. He looked very pale and very sad. When he came up to her, he tried to smile and gave a little nod that set the water streaming from the brim of his hat.

'I w-w-was looking for you.'

'Me too. I mean, in there. Did you see what happened?'

He nodded. He glanced over to where his father was being interviewed.

'I c-c-can't stay.' He fished something from his coat pocket and handed it to her. 'I f-found this. By the side of the road.'

258

Helen took it and looked at it. It was a letter. The envelope was mudstained and the ink had run. But she could still recognize the handwriting as Joel's. Her heart gave a little flutter.

'I'd better g-go now.'

'Oh, okay. Thank you.'

He nodded and turned and walked away.

'Luke?' she called.

He turned and looked back at her and she suddenly realized how he must feel about what had happened to the wolf.

'Will you come and see me?'

He shook his head. 'I c–can't.'

And he walked away in the rain and was lost in the crowd.

21

Mwanda Hospital,
Kagambali
16 Sept.

My dear Helen,
So did you catch them yet? No? Okay, well here's what you do:
get a metal pail — only BIG, right? About six feet deep and
eight feet wide should do the trick. Next, you rig a pole across
the top with a revolving oil drum on it, onto which you then
strap: ONE DEAD MOOSE. This method has the Latimer
seal of approval and has been used in North Carolina for
centuries, which explains why there are so few wolves there. Let
me know how it goes, okay?

The cabin sounds cool. My grandmother's old place had a
root cellar just like that, full of spiders and things. I used to hide
in it and spring out like a jack-in-the-box to scare my sisters
(yeah, sorry, that was the kind of kid I was. You'd never guess,
would you?)

Helen laughed out loud. She was sitting in bed, reading it by the light of her headlamp. After Luke had given it to her, as soon as she could, she had left Dan and Bill and the mayhem of Main Street and driven back to the cabin with her heart singing. He had written, at last.

She had delayed opening it for a long time, relishing the anticipation, like a child surveying presents under a Christmas tree. She'd laid it on her pillow and gone about her bedtime routine. She shoved Buzz out for a reluctant pee in the rain, cleaned her teeth, then made some tea. Then she'd undressed, pulled on the big T-shirt she slept in, turned out the lanterns and gone to bed with letter, tea and headlamp. She had briefly considered putting on one of Joel's opera CDs, *Tosca* perhaps, but decided not to push her luck.

She reached for the mug of tea now and took a sip, tilting the headlamp beam to find Buzz who was curled up by the stove, already asleep. Cocooned in her sleeping bag, her back pillowed against the cabin wall and the letter propped on her knees, Helen sat for a moment, listening to the rain beating on the roof and feeling something close to bliss.

Things are pretty crazy here and look like getting crazier. The ACL have started a new round of ethnic cleansing about eighty miles north of here and every day we're getting over a thousand new refugees, all of them in pretty bad shape. There's typhoid, malaria and just about every other variety of tropical horror you ever heard of – though, mercifully, as yet, no cholera.

And, of course, there's nothing like enough medicine or food to go around. Some of the kids that get here (hundreds, maybe even thousands, don't make it) haven't eaten for weeks. They're covered in flies and their arms and legs are just sticks. It's pitiful. The amazing thing is, some of them still know how to smile.

Last night there was high drama in the old hospital gardens where most of the aid group volunteers live. The accommodation is, to put it generously, pretty damn basic, i.e., shacks with no doors or windows, camp beds and a mosquito net with (if you're lucky) only a few holes. Anyway, this young German guy, Hans-Herbert, was feeling tired and turned in early, right after supper. When his roommates went to bed a couple of hours later they saw he'd fallen asleep with one arm hanging over the side of his bed and (I hope you're ready for this, Helen) a twelve-foot boa constrictor had started to swallow it. It had gotten up beyond the elbow, with poor old Hans-Herbert still sleeping like a baby!!

They tried to wake him gently, but, of course, he freaked out pretty badly. They gave him – and the snake! – a shot of sedative and, incredibly, managed to ease it off his arm. The digestive juices had already gotten to work on his hand and fingers and he may have to have some skin grafts, but basically he's okay. The snake less so. They released it (no tags or radio collar, I'm afraid) down by the river but some kids from one of the camps caught it and cooked it this morning for breakfast.

Does that beat the python under that old Georgia couple's house for Best Snake Story? I think so.

A lot of the food (and medicine) that's supposedly being flown in to us doesn't get here. It either gets stolen by corrupt government officers at the airstrip or the trucks get hijacked by the ACL on route to us. Mainly they keep it for themselves, but sometimes they try to sell it back to us and we have no choice but to go along with it.

The last group that came to negotiate were no more than kids, twelve- and thirteen-year-olds, all dressed up in their combat gear and ammo belts. One of them, a tiny kid, who couldn't have been more than ten, was carrying this M16 machine-gun and was almost buckling at the knees with the weight of it. The worst thing is their eyes. You wonder what terrible things they must have seen or done to make their eyes go like that.

So, hey! We're having a ball out here!

Actually, it's not all bad. Mainly because of the incredible
people I'm working with. And Helen, that's really the main
purpose of writing this letter. It isn't going to be easy to
say . . .

Helen felt something turn inside her chest. She was still
holding the tea and for fear of spilling it, put the mug down
on the floor. *Oh, Joel*, she begged in her head. *Don't. Please
don't say it.* Her heart was beating hard and her hands trembled
as she forced herself to read on.

Marie-Christine has been out here six months. She's Belgian
but lives in Paris. By training, she's a pediatrician, though out
here, you kind of have to do everything. We didn't meet right
away because . . .

Helen threw the letter onto the floor. Why should she have
to read this shit? How *dare* he think he could tell her all this,
give her a blow-by-blow account – oh yeah, no doubt cute
little Marie-Christine was terrific in that department too, sex-
goddess and Mother Teresa all wrapped up in one chic little
Parisian bundle – how *dare* he?

She sat there for a moment, staring along the beam of her
headlamp at the circle of light it made by the door. Her
breathing made it rise and fall ridiculously. Then she reached
for the letter – she couldn't help herself – and read on.

. . . because she was taking a few days' break somewhere. But
when we did meet – oh God, Helen, this is so hard to tell
you – but it was like we already knew each other.

That sounded familiar, Helen thought. She scanned ahead,
searching for any reference to 'soul mates', but couldn't see it,

263

which was just as well, for she would probably have screamed and broken a fist against the wall.

Anyway, we ended up working together, running this mobile unit that made daily rounds of all the refugee camps and I got to see how amazing she was with these kids. They just all adore her. Perhaps I shouldn't be telling you all this, but I want to and feel I can, Helen, because of our being so close and sharing so many good times.

The bottom line is, in two weeks' time, Marie-Christine and I . . .

'No,' Helen sobbed. 'Don't, Joel. Don't say that.'

. . . are getting married.

Helen scrunched the letter up and threw it across the room. 'You fucking bastard!'

She kicked off the sleeping bag and stood up, holding her hands over her face. Buzz was on his feet too. He started barking.

'Shut up, you stupid animal!'

She ripped off her headlamp and threw it at him and he whimpered and slunk away somewhere while she stumbled in the darkness to the cabin door and fumbled for the catch. She found it and banged the door open and ran blindly out into the rain.

Her bare feet slipped on the mud and she fell heavily and lay there for awhile with her face pressed into the wet earth, panting and cursing him and herself and the day she was ever born.

And then she sat up and hunched herself and held her muddied hands to her face while the rain streamed down her, and wept.

★

All in all, Buck reflected, it had been a fine night's work. He was relieving himself in the restroom of The Last Resort, with a cigar between his teeth and propping himself against the wall, where he saw some brave historian had already scrawled *Abe Harding for President*.

For the last hour Buck had been holding court at the bar, where everyone had adjourned when the fun outside was over. He'd never seen the place so packed or lively. Even the deer heads on the wall seemed to be having a good time.

The meeting had gone better than he could ever have dreamed. It made him nostalgic for the days when he was a state legislator. He hadn't expected those greeno hippies to turn up, but they'd made such damn fools of themselves that in the end he was glad they had.

And then, old Abe, pulling that stunt with the wolf. Hell, what a performance. Money couldn't buy that kind of publicity. Buck would never forget the look on Helen Ross's cute little face when the wolf landed on the table in front of her. Boy, what a night.

He zipped up and made his way back through the crowd. He handed Lori behind the bar a fifty-dollar bill to buy everyone another drink and then said goodnight, promising the Harding boys he'd make some calls and get their daddy home as soon as possible. Poor old Abe was probably sharing a cell with a load of AIDS-ridden drug addicts down in Helena.

First, though, Buck had other business to attend to.

He'd seen Ruth at the meeting, but she was sitting too near to Eleanor and Kathy for him to have a quiet word. Eleanor's lunatic idea of going into business with her was starting to cramp his love life a little. God, it was nearly two whole weeks since he and Ruth had been able to steal so much as a kiss. She always seemed to have some excuse not to see him and often as not it was to do with Eleanor, going through accounts or whatever.

Well, anyhow, he was going to put that right tonight. Rabble-rousing always got his juices flowing.

The rain was thinning. He drove past the gift shop and was pleased to see it was all shut up for the night. It meant she'd be at home, maybe even hoping he'd drop by. Waiting for him, all naked under that black robe of hers. The thought made his loins stir.

He wove the wet gravel out of town and soon saw the lights of Ruth's house up ahead. He would take her against the hallway wall as soon as she answered the door, like he'd done that other time. As he came nearer, he saw the curtains were open and he swung the car into the driveway and parked in his usual place. She must have heard him because she was opening the door as he got out of the car. She was clearly as hot for him as he was for her.

'Buck, you've got to go.'

'What?'

'Eleanor's coming over. Right now.'

'What?'

'Don't stand there gawping. She'll be here any minute.'

'What the hell's she doing, coming here at this time of night?'

'There's a meeting with the accountants tomorrow and we need to go over the figures. Now, GO!'

'Jesus.'

He stalked sulkily back toward his car and heard her shut the door on him. Without even saying goodnight! It was starting to rain heavily again. Buck stuck his half-smoked cigar between his teeth. It was all wet and had gone out and he flung it angrily away across the driveway, got into the car and slammed the door.

He turned the car, sending the gravel flying, and skidded back out through the gates. So as not to bump into Eleanor, he drove up to the end of the road and waited there, out of

266

sight, with his lights off, until he saw the beam of her head-lights turn into Ruth's driveway.

Buck shook his head. Jesus, he thought. What was the world coming to, when a man couldn't bed his mistress because his wife was with her? Scowling through the rain and darkly detumescent, he drove home.

The house was silent as a morgue when he got there. Luke must have already turned in, he figured. His hunger had shifted from sex to food and he went to the refrigerator, hoping there might be some leftover supper. But there wasn't. He opened a beer instead and took it through to the living room, without turning on the lights. He sat down heavily on the couch and used the remote to switch on the TV. Jay Leno was joking with some unshaven young actor or singer or something, who looked like he'd just climbed out of bed. To Buck's jaundiced eye, they both looked a lot too pleased with themselves.

He'd hardly settled when the phone rang. He killed the sound of the TV, leaned across and picked up.

'Is that Calder?'

It was a man's voice he didn't recognize. It sounded as if he was calling from a bar.

'Buck Calder speaking. Who's this?'

'Never mind who it is. Scum like you deserve to die.'

'Not man enough to give your name?'

'Man enough to wipe scum like you off the face of the earth.'

'You were at that meeting tonight, right?'

'I saw you on the fucking TV and saw what your psycho pal did to that wolf. And we want you to know—'

'Oh it's *we* now?'

'We're going to kill your cows.'

'Oh just my cows?'

'No, pigs too. Pigs like you.'

267

'And I guess you'll do all this in the name of the wolf, the greatest killer of them all.'

'That's right. You've been warned.'

There was a click and the line went dead. Buck stood up and put the phone down. The answering machine was beside it and he noticed there were four messages. He pressed the play button.

'So the wolves killed your calves, huh? Oh, dear!' It was a woman's voice. 'Before *you* had a chance to kill them. That's so unfair! You're a dying breed, pal, and the sooner you die, the better.'

Buck heard a noise and looked up to see Luke standing at the top of the stairs. He was still dressed.

'Did you hear that?'

Luke nodded.

'And the others? Are they all like that?'

'Yes.'

'Jesus.'

He fast-forwarded to the next. It was a man this time and started with a howl.

'This is Wolf. With a message for Buck Calder. You're dead meat, motherfucker.' There was another howl.

The next one sounded like the same man he had just spoken with and the last, another woman, was a screaming tirade he could only partly decipher. Buck shook his head and took a drink of beer.

'Did you see it on TV?'

Luke nodded.

'Speak, Luke, speak.'

'Y-y-yes.'

'Did they show Abe dumping the wolf?'

'Yes. Th-the whole . . . thing.'

'They don't hang about. Did it say what's happening to him?'

268

'He's in j-j-jail, in Helena.'

'Guess I'd better get on the phone. He'll need someone to stand bail for him. Boy, what a night. Who the hell are all these crazy people, calling me like that?'

'I d-d-don't know. I'm g-g-going to bed now.'

'Want a beer?'

'N-n-no, sir.'

Buck sighed. 'Okay, Luke. 'Night then.'

'G-goodnight.'

It was a sad thing when your own damn son wouldn't share a beer with you. Buck switched off the mute TV and went to find the phone book. He slumped himself down with it on the couch, thumbing the pages to find the number of the jail in Helena.

Maybe it hadn't been such a great evening after all. Abe's wolf stunt had seemed pretty good at the time, but now Buck could see it wasn't a smart move. The guy should have just followed the old rule: shoot, shovel and shut up. Well, he hadn't and now they had a war on their hands.

Buck was damned if he was going to be frightened off by a bunch of pot-smoking bunny-huggers, threatening him over the phone. But they'd got him wondering.

Maybe he wasn't playing this wolf business the right way.

Originally, he'd thought the way to go was to make a big public issue of it. That was the whole idea of the meeting. Hell, he was real good at all that publicity stuff. And he'd been sure that if he made life hard enough for Dan Prior and his gang, they'd be forced to take action.

But now he could see that Abe killing that wolf would probably have the opposite effect. They were going to dig their heels in. And if Buck was going to get a stream of abusive phone calls every time he gave an interview, maybe he should think again.

Rather than wage war in public, maybe he should play

things a little closer to his chest; come up with some more subtle stratagems; fight on several different fronts at the same time, like you did in a real war.

He resolved to give it some thought.

The trail up through the forest was frozen hard and where it was steep Moon Eye's feet would sometimes slip and he would check his pace and find a safer route among the rocks. The rain had stopped a little after midnight and the sky had opened to coat the land with the first true frost of the fall. It had come suddenly, seizing the rain that dripped from the trees in a million miniature icicles that now glinted and rainbowed as they began to melt in the slant of the early sun.

Luke reached the creek and rode up beside it toward the lake, passing the place by the shallows where he used to leave Moon Eye to graze before he knew Helen. The grass there now was starched stiff with frost and the horse's feet crunched prints in it. At the creek's edge where the water lingered and eddied, curls of steam rose into the still air.

All the way up from the ranch, Luke had been trying to make sense of what his father had said over breakfast. After what happened last night at the meeting and then all those threatening phone calls, it was almost unreal, so that at first Luke thought it was some kind of sick joke.

'I've been doing some thinking about this wolf business,' his father had said, through a mouthful of bread and bacon. 'And I reckon maybe I've been a little hard on those Fish and Wildlife guys. What do you reckon, Luke?'

Luke shrugged. 'I d–don't know.'

'Way I see it, they're only doing their job. Maybe, it'd be better for us all, if we cooperated a little more. Help sort this wolf thing out. You know, finding them, keeping an eye on them and all.'

Luke didn't say anything. He was always wary when his

father came on all reasonable like this. Sometimes he only did it to lay a trap, tempting you to relax and walk right in and then – snap, he had you by the neck. Luke took a spoonful of cereal and looked at his mother across the table. She was listening as warily as he was.

'You know what that Helen Ross girl was saying the other day? How much she appreciated your help, catching that wolf. Fair singing your praises she was, saying how you had a real feel for that kind of work.'

He paused, waiting for a reaction, but got none.

'And it got me thinking, once we've shipped the calves off to the feedlot, maybe you should give her a hand.' He gave a great laugh. 'So long as you don't put any of those radio collars on our cows!'

Luke looked again at his mother. She raised her eyebrows in surprise.

'Don't think she'll pay you much, mind. But seriously, if you want to help her out some, well, it's okay by me.'

Luke couldn't wait to break the news to Helen. He went right out and saddled up. But although he'd turned it inside and out in his mind, he was still no closer to understanding why his father had said it. Maybe those phone calls had really freaked him. It was possible, but Luke doubted it. There was probably some other, more sneaky motive. But Luke wasn't going to argue.

He came to where the land leveled now and heard Buzz barking. He coaxed Moon Eye out of the trees toward the lake, which lay mirror still and steaming like the creek. Above, on the slope up to the cabin, the sun was already melting patches of green in the silver of the frost. The cabin door was open and Buzz stood on the doorstep, staring at something inside and barking uncertainly.

Helen's truck was there, its windshield all frozen over. He had thought she might have already left to check the traps.

271

Buzz turned and saw him and Moon Eye and came bounding down the slope to greet them.

'Hey, Buzz–dog. How're you doing?'

The dog pranced and circled them, then led the way up alongside the stream. In the frosted grass Luke could see the fresh tracks and droppings of deer who had come earlier to drink there. He expected Helen to emerge from the cabin, but there was no sign of her. He got off his horse and walked to the door.

'Helen?'

There was no answer. Maybe she was around the back, in the outhouse. He waited a few moments outside the cabin door and then called again. And again there was no answer. So he leaned forward and knocked gently on the open door.

'Helen? Hello?'

Buzz, beside him, barked again, then brushed past his legs and ran inside. Luke took off his hat and followed him. It was dark inside and it took awhile before his eyes adjusted. Across the room, he could just make out Helen, lying on the bed.

He didn't know what to do. Perhaps he should let her sleep and come back later. But there was something about the way she looked that made him stay. One of her arms was dangling down, the fingers slightly curled, her nails touching the floor. A mug lay on its side in a pool of spilled liquid. There was an open bottle of pills there too. She lay perfectly still, even when Buzz nuzzled her and whimpered. Luke put his hat down on the table and took a cautious step toward her. He told Buzz to go out.

'Helen?' he said softly.

Closer now, he could see there was mud on her arm and on her hand and he looked farther down the bed and saw where her knee stuck out from the sleeping bag that it too was caked with mud and blades of grass. Another step now and he could see the same was true of her face. But she wasn't asleep.

272

Her eyes were open and she was staring blankly ahead.

'Helen? Helen?'

Then something flickered in her eyes, like life itself being switched on. She looked at him, without moving her head. It scared him.

'Helen, what is it? Are you okay?'

She blinked. Maybe she was sick, had a fever or something, he thought. Tentatively, he stepped closer and reached down to touch her forehead. Her skin felt cold as stone. He lifted the edge of her sleeping bag and saw her T-shirt was dirty and soaking.

'Helen, what happened?'

Silently she started to cry. The tears made tracks through the mud on her face and he couldn't bear to see such wretchedness and he sat on the bed beside her and hoisted her up in his arms and held her. She was so cold and wet and he cradled her and tried to warm her and just let her cry, telling her it was okay, he was there, everything was okay.

How long they stayed like that, he couldn't tell. He felt that her life was but the smallest flame that might be snuffed out if he were to let go of her. Her crying seemed to warm her a little and at last, when she had stopped, he found a dry blanket and wrapped her in it, then went to the stove and lit it, to get some heat going in the place.

Behind the door, when he closed it, he saw a screwed-up piece of paper. It was that same pale blue as the airmail letter he'd found and given to her last night. He picked it up and put it on the table, then lit the little Coleman stove and heated some water to make tea. And all the while she sat hugging her knees, with the blanket over her, shivering and staring at nothing.

He found a washcloth and soaked it with some warmed water and then went and sat on the bed beside her again and, without asking, gently cleaned the mud from her face and from her arms and hands. And she didn't say a word, just let him do it. Then he found a towel and dried her.

Her blue fleece and a longsleeved undershirt were hanging on the little washing line she'd rigged up and he took them down and said maybe she should put them on instead of the wet T-shirt, but she didn't seem to hear him. He didn't know what to do, only that she needed to change, so he took the blanket off her and turned her gently by the shoulders so that she was facing away from him. Then he sat behind her so he wouldn't see her breasts and pulled the wet T-shirt over her head.

Below the band of suntan around her neck, her skin was pale and smooth. And as he pulled the undershirt over her head he noticed the notches of her spine and the faint curve of her ribs and it made her seem fragile, like a wounded bird. He had to lift each arm in turn, feeding them like a doll's into the sleeves. He pulled the shirt down over her body and did the same with the fleece.

He prepared the tea and made her drink, helping her hold the mug and guiding it to her lips. Then he stayed beside her, holding her in his arms, for a long time.

It must have been an hour or more before she spoke. Her head lay against his chest and her voice sounded small and faint, as though it came from a great way off.

'I'm sorry,' she said. 'I'm not worth the effort.'

He knew better than to ask what had happened. Perhaps it was something to do with the letter. Perhaps someone she knew had died.

All he knew at that moment, or cared to know, was that he loved her.

22

The two weeks that followed Abe Harding's arrest were the toughest of Dan Prior's entire career and by a long way the most bizarre. As if in revenge for the killing of the alpha male in Hope, wolf packs throughout the region seemed suddenly to be wreaking havoc.

A sheep rancher north of Yellowstone lost thirty-one lambs in one night to wolves that had wandered out of the park. They ate hardly anything, simply killed them and left them. Another pack killed a pair of thoroughbred foals just east of Glacier. And a lone disperser, from a pack in Idaho, killed three calves near the Salmon River and left a fourth so badly maimed that it had to be put down.

Bill Rimmer was hardly ever out of his helicopter. In ten days he shot and killed nine wolves and darted fifteen more, mainly pups, who were relocated where they would hopefully keep out of trouble. It was Dan who had to sign the death warrants and he did so each time with a sense of personal failure.

He was supposed to be in charge of wolf recovery, not liquidation. He had little choice, however. Being prepared to use 'lethal control' was a firm promise in the plan that had allowed wolf recovery to happen in the first place. And because of what had happened in Hope, the media was watching his every move.

Reporters were calling him every hour of the day. At home he left the answering machine on all the time, except those nights Ginny stayed when she answered for him and pretended to be a Chinese takeout or a home for the criminally insane, which wasn't too wide of the mark. At the office, Donna handled most of the media calls, only putting through to Dan those journalists he knew or those who might be important.

It wasn't only the local media who'd suddenly renewed their interest in wolves, it was national and even international people too. There was one call from a German TV reporter who kept talking about Nietzsche and asking all kinds of deep philosophical questions Dan couldn't understand, let alone answer. More surreal still was the guy from *Time* magazine who said they were thinking of doing a cover story on Abe Harding.

'Is this a joke?' Dan said.

'No, of course not.' The reporter sounded hurt. 'Isn't he, in a way, making a last stand for the values of the Old West? Don't you see him that way, you know, as a kind of beleaguered pioneer?'

'Can I tell you off-the-record?'

'Sure. Go ahead.'

'I see him more as a kind of beleaguered asshole.'

The idea of 'Abe Harding, Last Pioneer', on the cover of *Time* magazine had Dan chuckling and shaking his head for days. Thank the Lord, the piece had yet to materialize, probably because it would require at least a modicum of cooperation from Abe himself; and reporters, on Abe's scale of preferences, would rate only fractionally higher than wolves.

After spending the night in jail, Abe had been charged with killing an animal listed as endangered, namely, one wolf, and of possessing the remains and transporting them. A further charge, of assaulting a police officer, was dropped. He was released by a federal magistrate, without bail.

Schumacher and Lipsky, the two Fish and Wildlife special agents who had been at the meeting, had gone with a search warrant to the Harding ranch, accompanied, at his own insistence, by Hope's increasingly uncooperative deputy sheriff. Craig Rawlinson had caused nothing but trouble by more or less siding with Harding's sons, who had been hostile and abusive. The agents managed to keep their cool long enough to find the loaded Ruger M-77 rifle with which Abe had admitted shooting the wolf. It was duly confiscated.

The wolf spent a night lying on some old pizza in Dan's garage freezer and was shipped the next day to the Fish and Wildlife forensics lab in Ashland, Oregon, where a necropsy showed the animal's heart and lungs had been entirely blown away. There were fragments of a 7mm magnum bullet, the bulk of which had passed on and out through the animal's rear end and was never to be found.

The Ashland scientists did DNA tests which showed the wolf had no connection with any of the wolves released in Yellowstone or Idaho. They discovered a tag in one ear that showed he had traveled from a remote part of British Columbia, more than two hundred miles away. They also discovered he was missing a toe on his right foreleg and had a scar there that suggested he had once been trapped and torn himself free. This might have affected his ability to hunt deer or elk, one the scientists suggested, and led him to the easier option of cattle.

Abe at first claimed he'd shot the wolf when he found it

attacking a calf in a pasture only two hundred yards from his house. He later admitted it hadn't yet attacked, but he knew it was going to. He said there was another wolf with it at the time and he wished he'd shot that one as well. He said he was not guilty and was going to take the case all the way to the Supreme Court to prove it. He refused any legal representation on the grounds that lawyers were just wolves in suits.

Meanwhile, pending ultimate endorsement from *Time* magazine, the Harding boys were doing their bit to turn their daddy into a folk hero.

They had two hundred T-shirts printed with Abe's lugubrious face on the front and SWAT (SHOOT WOLVES ALWAYS TEAM) OFFICIAL MEMBER on the back. They went on sale at The Last Resort for fifteen dollars each and sold out in two days. A second batch of five hundred had almost gone too, though the mugs – ABE HARDING, HOPE'S HERO – were shifting more slowly. Bill Rimmer had bought Dan one of each and though he hadn't worn the T-shirt yet, Dan drank his coffee from the mug every morning.

In contrast to their brethren across the state, Hope's remaining wolves kept their heads down and for this Dan was grateful. He was damned if he was going to let Buck Calder bounce him into taking any kind of action there without proof that the wolves had done the damage. And he had enough on his plate as it was.

For every phone call he got from an angry rancher, accusing him of being soft, he got one from an animal rights activist calling him a murderer, on account of the nine wolves whose death warrants he'd signed. Four separate lawsuits had been instigated, two from livestock associations, seeking an end to wolf recovery because it violated the Constitution, and two from environmental groups seeking injunctions against 'any further illegal act of lethal control'.

The day after the meeting, Wolves of the Earth had dispatched a team of activists to Hope to conduct a door-to-door survey. Dan got a series of furious phone calls. One rancher said if they knocked on his door again, he'd shoot them. He called them a 'bunch of longhair commie terrorists' and when Dan drove out and met the pollsters, he thought the guy had a point. He gently suggested to the group's regional coordinator in Missoula that there was enough woe in Hope as it was and that the wolves might stand a better chance if they were allowed to keep a lower profile.

The last thing Dan needed was more trouble in Hope. And, secretly, he thought Abe may have done them all a favor by killing the most likely troublemaker. It had taken some of the sting out of the ranchers' anger over lost calves and, at the very least, had bought Helen some breathing space. With luck, she could keep tabs on the rest of the pack and avert further trouble.

He hadn't seen her since the night of the meeting and had become a little concerned about her. For three days she had neither phoned nor replied to any of the messages he left for her. He'd been on the point of driving up there when she called to say she'd had the flu but was now okay. She'd sounded a little downcast, but Dan figured she was still getting over her sickness. Calder's son, Luke, had been taking care of her, she said, and had been really sweet.

Dan couldn't help feeling a twist of jealousy.

What he wasn't so sure about was the idea of Luke helping her out with trapping and tracking the wolves. After the hostility of the meeting and her mailbox being smashed, it was good that she wasn't going to be alone up there. But the fact that the helper was Buck Calder's son seemed somehow risky. He'd said as much to Helen on the phone the other day when she first mentioned it.

279

'Isn't it a little like sleeping with the enemy?'

'I'm not sleeping with anyone, if you don't mind.'

'Helen, I didn't mean it literally—'

'He's just helping me out. You ought to be damn grateful.'

'But what if he tells Calder where your traps are or—'

'Oh, give me a break, Dan. That's ridiculous.'

There was an awkward pause. Ever since she was sick, she'd been different, either touchy or distant, whenever they spoke.

'I'm sorry,' he said. 'It's a good idea.'

She didn't reply. He imagined her sitting there, all alone, up there in the cabin, surrounded by nothing but forest and darkness.

'Helen, are you okay?'

'I'm fine,' she snapped back. 'Why?'

'Nothing. Just, you don't sound too happy.'

'Is it obligatory? In my job description? "Temporary federal biologists will at all times be cheerful"?'

'Absolutely.'

He thought he heard a little sniff of a laugh. There was another pause. She went on, more gently:

'I'm sorry, Dan. I guess I'm just feeling a little short of angels.'

'I worry about you.'

'I know you do. Thank you.'

'Okay. Listen, I've found you a snowmobile.'

'Same place as you found my pickup?'

'No. It's new. Well, almost. You're going to be needing it soon. I thought maybe I could bring it up at the weekend.'

'Sure.'

He'd told her to take care and after hanging up, sat there awhile, thinking about her, while Hope's Hero, Abe Harding, scowled at him from his coffee mug.

He would buy her dinner again, somewhere nicer this time. He hadn't had a date with anyone since their meal at

Nelly's Diner. He had eventually summoned enough courage to ask Sally Peters out again, and again been forced to cancel. When he called the next day to apologize, she'd told him he was a sad and pathetic man and ought to get himself a life.

Dan had to concede it was a pretty accurate assessment.

Kathy unbuckled Buck Junior from his car seat and hoisted him onto her hip. Just along the street, Hope's oldest inhabitant, Ned Wainwright, was being interviewed by yet another pain-in-the-ass TV crew. The town had been crawling with them for two weeks and people were getting a little tired of it, Kathy included.

As she headed along the sidewalk toward Paragon, she could hear Ned holding forth on why the federal government liked wolves.

'It's plain as can be. They want 'em to wipe out all the deer and elk, so's there won't be nothing left for us to hunt. Then they'll say, since there's nothing to hunt, nobody needs guns no more and they'll ban guns. That's what it's all about, getting our guns off us.'

Kathy had never heard anything sillier in her life, but the TV reporter was nodding as if it was gospel. As she walked by, one of the crew smiled at her. She didn't smile back.

'Haven't you folks got anything important to cover?' she said and, before he could answer, disappeared into the gift shop.

Her mom had been going on about all the great new things Ruth had gotten in for the run-up to Christmas and, out of loyalty, Kathy had decided to buy as many presents here as possible. It was a little early to be thinking of that, but she liked to be organized. She'd chosen this morning because it was the day her mom went shopping in Helena.

Ruth greeted her warmly and insisted on holding the baby while Kathy had a browse.

'Don't all these TV people drive you nuts?' Kathy said.

'Absolutely not. They buy things. Anything with a wolf on it.'

'I hadn't thought. So at least there's something good about it.'

It took her no time at all to find what she wanted. She got Clyde a fancy leather vest, a wood and brass box for her daddy to keep his cigars in and some pretty silver necklaces for her mom and Lane. She got Bob, Lane's husband, a book on Indian art and a hatband in braided horsehair for Luke.

Ruth wanted to give her a discount. Kathy wouldn't hear of it. But she accepted the offer of a free coffee and settled at the bar with Buck Junior on her knee, while Ruth made it.

'All the wolf stuff we've sold, you know, it was your mom's idea to get it in.'

'Really?'

'Uh-huh. She's so smart.'

'She sure is. Always was.'

'I just adore her.'

They talked about Kathy's mom for awhile and then, over their coffees, moved on to Ruth's parents. Her father had died a long time ago, she said. Her mother remarried and now lived a frantic social life in New Jersey.

'She's the exact opposite of Eleanor,' Ruth said. 'Your mom always seems so calm and collected. Mine's like a tornado. I can remember once, after some terrible row, she ran upstairs and locked herself in the bathroom and I had to go talk her out. I was, like, fifteen or something. And as I was doing it, I thought, hold on a minute, this is all wrong, I'm supposed to be the teenager around here.'

When it was time to go, Buck Junior reached out to Ruth and she held him again. He seemed quite smitten and wouldn't leave her hair alone.

'He loves women,' Kathy said.

Ruth laughed. 'So it seems.'

'Don't you think he's like his grandpa?'

'You mean . . .'

'I mean, looks.'

'Oh.' Ruth laughed. Then she frowned, assessing him.

'You know? I'd say he's more like your mom.'

Buck Calder settled himself at the end of one of the long wooden benches at the back of the auction hall and looked down over the rows of white hats toward the arena where a gaggle of Black Angus heifers had just gone for an absurdly high price and were refusing to leave.

They were big-framed and gawky and Buck couldn't understand why anyone in his right mind should want to buy them. There were some things in life where size surely did count, but cows weren't one of them. All you were paying for was extra bone. It was amazing how some folk still didn't get it. As long as an animal was big and black (the only fashionable cow color nowadays, as with everything), they automatically thought they were onto a good thing.

The young rancher sitting next to him, all dressed up in his best clothes, was grinning. Buck assumed he was thinking the same.

'Thank the Lord for fools,' Buck said and saw the man's grin vanish.

'Huh?'

'Paying good money for bags of bone like that.'

'I raised 'em myself.'

'Oh.'

He tried to think of something to say but the man was already on his feet and pushing past to leave. What the hell, Buck thought, and looked down at the arena again.

It was a sandy space, about twenty feet across and surrounded by high white rails. At the moment, two young cowboys were running around it, trying to oust the reluctant heifers who stood under the spotlights like actors who'd forgotten their lines. The cowboys had long white sticks with orange flags on the end and were using them to thwack and poke the heifers. But the only evacuation it seemed to prompt was of the animals' bowels. One of the cowboys slipped in the product of this and fell flat on his face and the audience roared its appreciation.

In the little booth at the back of the arena, the auctioneer, a suave young man wearing a mustache and a scarlet shirt, leaned toward his microphone.

'Never say we don't put on a good show here, folks.'

Buck only came to the Billings auction yards three or four times a year, but he always enjoyed it. It was a long way to come, a good three and a half hour drive, and the prices you got were no better than at stockyards nearer home. But it was good to get away, check out the market and generally keep up contacts over here. The contact he most enjoyed keeping up was Luke's former speech therapist, Lorna Drewitt.

They normally had lunch and then took a motel room for a couple of hours and that was the plan today. Buck glanced at his watch. It was a little after twelve, which was fine, because the two young bulls he'd brought over in the trailer this morning were up next. They hadn't quite been up to snuff for the annual Calder bull sale back in the spring.

The heifers at last found their way out and, right on cue, in came the first of Buck's bulls. He came charging in so fast that the poor shit-covered cowboy had to dive for cover behind one of the corrugated-iron shields that were there for precisely such occasions. The bull's head made a resounding clang as it struck the metal. The only thing missing was steam from his nostrils. Buck felt like shouting *olé*!

Forty minutes later, he was proudly towing his empty trailer out onto the highway under the big green and yellow sign that said WELCOME TO THE NORTHWEST'S LARGEST STOCKYARD. There was a man on the sign waving his hat and Buck was so pleased with himself and the price he'd got for his bulls that he almost waved back.

The motel where he was meeting Lorna Drewitt was just off Interstate 90 and it only took him five minutes to get there. He tucked the truck and trailer away in a discreet corner of the parking lot, in the unlikely event of it being spotted by someone he knew, then headed into the motel.

Lorna was already there, sitting pert and pretty in the lobby, reading a copy of the *Billings Gazette*. It was about six years since she moved here, after that unfortunate day when Luke had caught them in her office (though the boy was too wet behind the ears to have had any notion of what was going on). Now nearly thirty, Lorna looked sexier than ever.

She saw him and got up, smiling and folding the newspaper while he walked toward her. He put his arms around her and she tilted her head back and let him kiss her neck.

'God, you smell good,' he said.

'You smell of cows.'

'Bulls, sweetheart. Purebred Calder bulls.'

The motel had a restaurant that wasn't too bad. They had steak and a bottle of Napa Valley merlot and kept touching knees and stroking each other under the table until Buck couldn't bear it any longer. Without asking for the check, he laid a hundred-dollar bill on the table and led her off to the room for which he already had the key.

Later, as they lay on what remained of the bed linen, Lorna told him this was the last time she could do this. Buck hoisted himself up on one elbow and frowned at her.

'What?'

'I'm getting married.'

'What? When?'

'Next month.'

'Jesus. To what's his name?'

'Buck, you know his name.'

He did. It was Phil. They'd been going out for four years.

'Well, why does getting married have to change things?'

'Buck, what the hell do you take me for?'

Buck was sure there was an answer to that, but right now he couldn't think of it.

They got dressed and, in the fading light of the parking lot, kissed each other goodbye.

'Don't call me, okay?' she said.

'Aw, sweetheart. At least let me call you.'

'Don't.'

He drove back along the interstate, feeling more and more sorry for himself. Rain clouds the color of granite scudded low across his windshield and the trailer shuddered in the cold north wind.

Everything seemed to be going wrong lately.

First, Ruth going into business with Eleanor and getting all conscience-stricken about it and now Lorna doing the same. Then there were all those wackos who still kept calling him about the wolf thing. In fact, now he came to think of it, everything had been fine and dandy until those goddamn wolves showed up.

Well, it was time to get serious and get rid of them.

The first part of his plan was already in place: Luke was working for Helen Ross. And though Buck hadn't yet managed to glean any information from the boy about where the varmints were, it was only a matter of time. When he got it, he would need someone who could act upon it.

And, along with selling bulls and seeing Lorna, that was what he intended to see to today.

In his scheming, he'd remembered an old trapper who, a long time ago, used to live up on the Hope River. One of those legendary fellows you never came across nowadays.

Buck's father used to hire him whenever they had varmint trouble, usually coyotes, but sometimes a mountain lion or a grizzly that was hanging around.

Buck recalled the guy having a son in the same line of business. But try as he might, he couldn't remember the name.

Then, two nights ago, over a beer in The Last Resort, he'd casually asked old Ned Wainwright, who was ninety if he was a day, if he could remember it.

'Lovelace. Josh Lovelace. Passed away, hell, must be twenty, thirty years ago.'

'There was a son too, wasn't there?'

'Uh-huh. J.J. Moved down Big Timber way. Old Josh went there too when he got too old to cope. That's where they buried him.'

'Does the son still live there?'

'No idea.'

'Must be knocking on a little himself.'

'What're you talking about, Buck Calder? He's a good twenty years younger than I am. Barely out of diapers.'

The old man laughed wheezily and started to cough. Buck bought him another beer then saw him safely home.

He'd found a J.J. Lovelace in the phone book and had called several times. There was never a reply. So, with the address in his pocket, Buck had decided to stop by on the way back from Billings and see if he could find him.

Driving in his black mood toward a black horizon, he saw the sign for Big Timber looming ahead. He indicated right and pulled off the interstate.

He stopped at a gas station and asked the kid behind the counter for directions. Ten minutes later, his truck and trailer were bouncing through the potholes of a winding dirt road.

It was getting dark and starting to spot with rain. After about three miles, the road passed through a grove of cottonwoods, whose last leaves whipped yellow in the wind. Beyond, his headlights found a rusty green mailbox that said 'Lovelace'.

The driveway looked too treacherous for his trailer, so he parked and, hoisting his coat collar against the rain and the wind, set off on foot.

The rutted track rose steeply along one side of a coulee whose tumbling water Buck could only hear, for it was masked by a thick scrub of willow. After about half a mile he saw above him a low wooden house, set among trees on the shoulder of a hill. There was a light on inside. Parked nearby under the trees was a trailer, the kind you could live in. It was silver and had rounded ends that made it look somehow sinister, like an alien spaceship.

He expected dogs to bark. But the only sound, as he climbed toward the house, was the wind and the tap of the rain on his hat.

There were no drapes on the windows of the house and Buck could see the light was coming from a single bulb that hung above the kitchen table. There was no sign of life in there, nor in the trailer. He went to the kitchen door and knocked. While he waited for an answer, he turned casually around – and nearly had a heart attack.

He was looking right down the barrel of a twelve-gauge shotgun.

'Jesus!'

The man at the other end of it was wearing a long black parka with the hood turned up. In the shadow of the hood Buck could make out a bony, graybearded face and hostile black eyes. To clear up any doubts about his identity, all he'd need to do was swap his shotgun for a scythe.

'Mr Lovelace?'

The man didn't admit or deny it, just let Buck hang there. 'Hey, I'm real sorry just dropping by unannounced like this, but I was worried my trailer might not make it up the driveway.'

'You're blocking the lane down there.'

'Am I? I'm sorry. I'll go move it.'

'You're not going anyplace.'

'Mr Lovelace, my name's Buck Calder, from Hope.'

He thought of offering his hand but decided against. The mad monk might think he was grabbing for the gun.

'Your daddy, Joshua, used to do some work for my daddy when I was a kid. In fact, I'm sure you and I must have met, but a long time ago.'

'You're Henry Calder's boy?'

'Yes, sir, I am.'

This seemed to make some impression. Lovelace, assuming that's who it was, lowered the gun a little. It was now pointing at Buck's groin.

'Your daddy's something of a legend in our parts,' Buck said.

'What are you doing here?'

'Well, I understand you're in the same line of business as your father was. Or used to be.'

Lovelace said nothing.

'And, well . . .' Buck glanced down at the gun. 'Mr Lovelace, do you think maybe you might adjust your line of fire there a little?'

Lovelace looked at him for a moment, as if considering whether Buck was worth the price of a shotgun shell. Then he whisked the barrel in the air, clicked the safety on and strode past into the house. He left the door ajar behind him and Buck waited outside for a moment, wondering if this added up to an invitation to follow him.

He decided it did.

Lovelace put the gun down on the table and pushed back the hood from his head. The house was cold, so he kept his coat on. Since Winnie died he could never be bothered to light the stove in the living room. He headed through the house to his trap room at the back and heard Calder following him.

The trap room was really no more than a garage but nowadays that was where he spent most of his time. He'd rigged up a little electric fire and even slept there at night, on a mattress he'd hauled in from the trailer. Not that he slept much. It was more a matter of lying there, waiting for the dawn. He knew it was crazy and that he ought to get used to using the bedroom again without Winnie, but he couldn't bring himself to do in

The bedroom, the kitchen, the whole house were empty without her and yet somehow filled with her presence. He'd tried hiding most of her things away, but it wasn't any use. Everything, even the spaces they left, reminded him of her. It was safer to stay out here in the back room, which had always been his territory and not hers. She used to refuse to come in here, saying it smelled too awful, of trapping bait and dead animals, which he supposed it did, though he himself couldn't smell it. He noticed that this Calder fellow could though and was trying not to look bothered.

Lovelace sat down on the camp stool by the fire, dragged the plastic pail with the deer head in it between his legs and got back to work. He'd been half-done skinning it out when he'd heard Calder's truck slow and stop down in the lane. Not bad, he thought, for an old buzzard of sixty-nine, hearing that.

While he got on with the deer head, Calder told him about the wolf trouble they'd been having up in Hope. There wasn't another chair, so he'd propped his backside against the workbench that ran the length of one wall. As he talked, his eyes kept roaming the room, looking at the walls and the wooden beams of the roof, all festooned with traps and wires and snares and the skins and skulls of animals.

Lovelace remembered the man's father, Henry Calder. His own father used to call him 'King Henry' and joke about how high and mighty he was. Lovelace could remember helping out up at the Calder place one summer back in the early fifties, when the buffaloberries high in the forest had failed and the grizzlies were coming down, sniffing around the cows. He and his father had trapped three adults and shot four or five cubs.

He had no recollection of meeting this man yacking away at him here, but then, back in the fifties, Buck Calder would only have been a kid and by that time anyhow Lovelace was mostly working away from home, in Mexico and Canada. In fifty-six he'd married Winnie and moved to Big Timber and after that he'd rarely visited Hope.

'So what do you think?'

'Killing wolves is against the law.'

Calder smiled knowingly and leaned back, folding his arms. There was something smug about him which Lovelace didn't care for.

'Who's going to know?'

'They'll be watching them like hawks.'

'That's true.' Calder winked and grinned. 'But you'd have inside information.'

He paused for a reaction but Lovelace wasn't going to play games. He waited to be told.

'My boy's helping this biologist woman out. He knows where the wolves are, what they're doing, the whole deal.'

'Sounds like you don't need no help then.'

'No, except the boy sees things more their way than mine.'

'So how come he's going to part with the information?'

'Oh, I'll find some way of getting it.'

The deer head was almost skinned out. Lovelace put his knife down and carefully peeled the skin like a mask from the raw pink face.

'I see you're quite a taxidermist too,' Calder said. 'We hunt a fair bit. Do you do it for other people?'

'Only for friends.'

It wasn't true. The only friends they'd ever had were Winnie's. None of them had called in months. Not that he cared.

'So, Mr Lovelace. What do you say?'

'About what?'

'Will you help us out? You can name your price.'

Lovelace stood up and picked up the pail. He took it over to the stainless-steel sink at the other end of the workbench and poured the blood away. He cleaned the knives while he thought it over.

It was three years since he'd last done a black job, killed illegal wolves. Two years since he'd last killed legal ones, up in Alberta. After nagging him for ages to retire, Winnie had at last persuaded him. And then, just when he was getting used to it, even starting to enjoy it, six months ago, she'd gone and gotten cancer. Found her little frame was riddled with it. Within three weeks she was dead.

The truth was, he now needed to keep himself busy. This was the first offer of work he'd had since the funeral. The traps hanging from the rafters were covered in rust. But he could soon fix that.

He dried the knives and swilled the blood from the sink.

'What's that wire thing over there, with all those little bits of metal on it?' Calder said. 'If you don't mind my asking.'

He was pointing to the far wall, above the freezers, where Lovelace hung his drag chains and hooks and coils of steel wire.

'For catching pups. My father's idea. He called it the Loop.'

23

The fatherless pups of Hope were nearly five months old. Slim and lanky, their fur burgeoning with winter growth, they were only slightly smaller than the three older wolves. Most had lost their milk teeth now and though they still hung back in the hunt and had much to learn in the ways of the wild, every day saw them bolder and shrewder.

Each by now had his or her own ranking in the pack and, at play or in earnest, at rest or at the carcass of a kill, the weaker readily deferred. They would pin back their ears and tuck their tails away and grovel, licking and nipping at the jaws of any stronger sibling who stood, assertive and bushy-tailed, above them.

With their father, the alpha cattle-slayer, dead, it was to their mother that they and the two young adults now looked for leadership. Heedless of the collar on her neck, it was she alone now who roused them from their lazy afternoon rests and mustered them for the hunt. It was she who led them in

293

sinewed file through the autumn gloom of the forest, who stopped to sniff the cold night air for the waft of prey, who chose which lesser life to spare and which to take.

Only the younger female had assisted her father in the killing of calves, though the others had all, at times, shared the spoils. She had been with him that night, when the bullet had ripped out his heart. She had fled in terror and seemed content now to follow her mother's choosing.

And her mother chose, through fear or innate inclination, to keep away from where the humans had herded their dim-witted beasts, and to prey instead upon the elk and deer who were drifting down to their winter range, distracted in their mating. The bull elk battled mightily for their harems and the mountains echoed to their bugling and the click and clack of their antlers.

The wolves weren't alone in their hunting, however.

Human predators too were abroad. For a month now, men in mottled green and brown and faces smudged with dirt had stalked the canyons with bows and razored arrows. They left piles of guts which the wolves would sometimes eat when they had failed, as often they did, to kill for themselves.

Soon, more men, dressed in vivid orange, would come with guns. Some would cruise the forest roads in their cars, shooting from the window whatever strayed within range. The more romantic would soak themselves with deer gland scent or, like sirens of the forest, fake mating calls to lure the lustful into the crosshairs of their scopes.

For a month the world would be a frenzy of coupling and killing, while life was seeded in hot abandon and reaped in cold blood.

The two hunters trudged up the trail. They weren't talking and the only sound was the squelch of their rubber boots in the mud. Above them, a steep bank of Douglas fir disappeared into the blanket of damp, autumn mist that had filled the canyon since dawn.

They were wearing full combat gear and had automatic pistols and long, semi-serrated knives on their belts. Both were carrying backpacks and their magnum rifles were slung over their shoulders. The general hunting season started tomorrow and these two clearly didn't want to miss a minute of it. They were probably going to camp somewhere and be out stalking before dawn.

Helen sat in the passenger seat of the Toyota, idly stroking Buzz's sleeping head on her lap and watching the hunters in the wing mirror as they drew closer.

She and Luke had seen others like them earlier. One, who couldn't have been more than sixteen, had asked what they were trapping and when Helen told him, gave her a wild-eyed tirade about how wolves were going to wipe out all the deer and elk that belonged by right to hunters like him. Something in his eyes made Helen think of the young soldiers Joel had described in his letter.

She saw Luke now, coming down through the trees above the trail, with the traps he'd just gone to collect slung over his shoulder. They had to collect them all; it wouldn't be good for business if a hunter stepped into one, though seeing these two approaching now, Helen didn't find the idea wholly unappealing.

Luke stepped down onto the trail just as the hunters came alongside. Buzz suddenly heard them and sat up barking and growling. Helen hushed him and rolled down the window.

The hunters were eying the traps that Luke was dumping, along with the others already collected, in the bed of the pickup. Helen thought she recognized one of them from the wolf meeting. As they walked by, she smiled and said hi. He made a minimal, unsmiling response. A little farther on, the other one muttered something that Helen couldn't make out and the first one glanced back over his shoulder. Then both of them started to laugh. Luke was climbing into the driver's seat.

'Rambo morons,' she said.

Luke smiled. He started the engine.

'D–did you never hunt?'

'No. But I know plenty of good biologists who do. Dan Prior for one. He used to be a big hunter. We'd have these endless arguments about it when we worked together in Minnesota.'

They were driving past the hunters now. Helen smiled sweetly at them again. Buzz growled.

'Dan used to say, man's a predator and needs to stay in touch with that. He'd say our problem as a species is that we've gotten detached from our true nature. And half of me thinks, okay, I'll buy that, and the other half thinks it's just one helluva good excuse for a whole lot of boys' stuff. Like, "We're natural-born killers, so, hey guys, let's go kill!" The truth is, I'm a lousy shot.'

Luke laughed.

'What about you?' she asked. 'You don't hunt?'

'Once. When I was thirteen.'

Helen could tell from the way his face suddenly changed that she'd touched on something.

'You don't have to tell me.'

'No, it's o–k–kay.'

She listened while he told her about shooting the elk, of finding it wounded in the tree and how his father had forced him to help butcher it. Luke kept his eyes carefully on the road as he talked and Helen watched him over Buzz's head, picturing what he told her.

Since that cold morning when he had found her lying wet and filthy in her cabin bed, there was a closeness between them unlike any friendship she'd ever known. Without him, she knew, she would not have survived.

While she clawed her way out of the pit, a little higher each day, he had taken care of her, making sure she ate and slept and kept warm. He would leave her last thing at night, turning off the lanterns and stoking up the stove, and he would be there again at dawn to let Buzz out and make her coffee.

For the first few days Helen had barely been able to speak. She had been in a kind of waking coma. Instead of panicking or pestering her with questions, he had quietly looked after her, as if she were a wounded animal. As if he understood what had happened without needing to be told.

Only later did he mention that his father had said it was okay for him to help her with the wolves, if she wanted him to. And while she lay in the cabin, or sat outside in the pale sunshine, huddled and blanketed like an invalid, he got to work, checking the traps and tracking the signals of the collared wolves.

In the evenings, when he came back to the cabin, he would give her his notes and, while he cooked her supper, tell her all he had seen and done. Through the mists of her own misfortune, she saw he was in his element.

At times now, his stutter seemed to have vanished, returning only when he talked about his father or got excited. Such as on the morning he had come racing back to tell her there was a wolf in one of the traps.

'You've g-g-got to come.'

'Luke, I can't—'

'You've g-got to. I don't know w-what to do.'

He made her get dressed and gather her gear, then he'd driven her in the Toyota up to a narrow canyon, high above the Millward ranch, where the wolves seemed to be spending a lot of time lately. He drove so fast along the narrow logging trails, she sometimes had to close her eyes.

The wolf they had caught turned out to be one of the pups, a female. Under Helen's instruction, Luke did most of the work, all the measuring and noting, leaving her only to give the shots and take the blood and feces samples. The pup weighed a little over sixty pounds and still had some growing to do, so they fitted her with an adult-size collar and padded it out with foam rubber and duct tape.

For Helen, that day was a turning point. Luke's elation seemed to wake in her a glimmer of hope that life might again be bearable.

She still cried herself to sleep most nights or lay awake, with her head playing movies of Joel at the altar with his flawless Belgian bride. She told herself again and again that it was insane to feel this way, because nothing had changed. It had been all over with Joel from the moment he applied for that job. But try as she might, she couldn't avoid the conclusion that his marriage confirmed her worthlessness.

She'd punished herself by giving up smoking and though she'd been surprised at how easy it was, it occasionally made her aggressive, like on the evening Dan had brought the snowmobile out.

He'd planned to take her somewhere fancy over in Great Falls for dinner, but at the last minute she said she couldn't face it. He'd been all hurt and tried to talk her into it and she'd ended up yelling at him. It was probably just as well; she would only have embarrassed them both by sobbing into her entrée or getting drunk.

With Luke, however, her moods didn't matter. He seemed to understand whenever she was ambushed by a sudden rush of rage or tears. He would simply gather her up and hold her, as he had done that first, frosty morning, until she stopped.

Now, listening to the story of the elk, she marveled at how the son of such a father could have learned such tenderness. It must all, she assumed, come from his mother, a woman whose friendly but formal reserve Helen had never yet managed to breach.

Telling the story had brought Luke's stutter back.

'My f-f-father g-got real mad. He always w-w-wanted me to b-b-b-be like my b-brother. He shot a six-p-pointer when he was t-ten.'

'I didn't know you had a brother.'

Luke swallowed and nodded.

'He d-d-died. Al-most eleven y-y-years ago.'

'Oh, I'm sorry.'

'In a c-c-car wreck. He was f-f-fifteen.'

'That's terrible.'

'Yeah.'

He shot her a grim little smile and she got the message that he didn't want to talk anymore about it. He nodded at the radio receiver on the dashboard.

'W-why don't you try the trap signals? See if we g-g-got lucky up here.'

'You're the boss.'

She reached for the receiver and turned it on. These were the last two traps they had to collect. The chances of having caught another wolf were slim. It was a pity, because Helen had wanted at least four of the pack collared – including, ide-ally, two pups – before the hunting season started.

Most hunters were responsible and law-abiding, but there were always going to be one or two who would take a shot at anything. If the anything in question happened to be wearing a radio collar, they might just think again.

She found the frequency of the transmitter attached to the first trap. It wasn't beeping.

But the second one was.

They'd set the trap in the fork of a deer trail, a little farther down from where they'd caught the female pup. The trail was walled on either side by steep banks, tangled with scrub and young fir trees. Judging by all the scat and tracks they'd found there, it was a kind of wolf version of Grand Central Station.

You could drive right to it, but to cause less disturbance, they left the pickup a few minutes down the trail and went in on foot.

They heard the squealing from a long way off and as they came around the last bend in the trail, they could see the bushes moving in the angle of the fork. They put down their packs and as Helen got the jabstick ready, she became aware of a strange, musty smell, like a wet dog, but much stronger. The squealing sounded strange too, quite unlike any noise she'd heard a trapped wolf make before. Peering cautiously through the bushes, while Luke stood back, she saw why.

'Uh-oh,' she said quietly.

'What?'

'Luke, it's *wolves* we're after. You caught a bear.'

He came up beside her and looked. It was a cub, a male grizzly, maybe eight or nine months old. Helen flicked the syringe on the jabstick and squirted a little sedative out to clear any air bubbles.

'You're g-going to p-put him out?'

'Well, we need to get that trap off his foot and he's a little past the cuddly stage, wouldn't you say? Did you see those teeth and claws? He's not a happy bunny. And we need to be quick. Chances are, his mom's not far away.'

In his efforts to escape, the cub had snagged the drag securely in the bushes, so he hadn't got much room for maneuver. While Luke distracted him, Helen managed to slip behind and got the jabstick neatly into the bear's rump. He yelped and turned on her but not soon enough to stop the sedative being pumped into him.

They stood back to let it take effect. Helen knew she should weigh and measure him and do all the checks she would normally do on a wolf, then hand the data over to whichever Fish and Wildlife people were working on grizzlies. But with the near certainty that the cub's mother was somewhere close, possibly at that moment deciding which of them might taste better, Helen didn't want to hang around.

'Are we going to ch-check him over?'

'You can. Once that trap's off, I'm out of here.'

The cub's snarling had grown drowsy now and as soon as he had settled, they knelt down beside him. Helen sniffed.

'He should definitely change his deodorant.'

'Yeah, my mother says they smell like garbage.'

Helen levered open the trap. His foot was bleeding. With all his thrashing around, the jaws had cut into him. Luke knew the routine and, without being asked, passed her a cloth to clean the wound and then the antibiotic ointment to smear on it.

'I'd better give him a shot too.'

Just as Luke was handing her the syringe, a branch snapped somewhere among the trees above them. They both froze and looked and listened. All was still.

'Time to go home,' Helen mouthed. She quickly loaded the syringe and gave the cub his shot of antibiotic. She remembered an old Dan Prior joke.

'Know what you do if you get charged by a bear?'

'What?'

'Pay up, quick.'

He grinned, but she could tell he was as nervous as she was pretending not to be. She handed him the syringe and checked the foot wound again. It had stopped bleeding. When she looked back at Luke she saw his expression had changed. He was staring up toward the trees and she turned and saw a big grizzly staring right back at them. It was no more than forty yards away.

'That's not his m-mother.'

'You're right. He's too big.'

They were keeping dead still, muttering like ventriloquists.

'If we leave the cub, he'll k-kill it.'

301

Helen knew it was true. Grizzly males would kill any male cub they came across, even their own. Slowly, the bear lifted his front feet off the ground and reared up on his hind legs. He had to be eight or nine feet tall. It looked more like twenty. He probably weighed about eight hundred pounds. He was a pale, yellowy brown, though darker around the ears and throat, where the fur was tipped with silver. He lifted his dish-shaped snout high in the air and sniffed.

Helen's pulse was galloping. She thought of the can of pepper spray Dan had given her for exactly this kind of encounter. It was gathering dust in a corner of the cabin.

'Luke, go get the truck.'

'Y-you go. I'll stay with the c-cub.'

'Listen, I'm the hero here. Go. But slowly. Slow-ly.'

He handed her the empty jabstick.

'Thanks, I'll give it to him to pick his teeth.'

As Luke backed away, she kept her eyes on the bear. She had seen bears many times before, but never till now a grizzly. She'd read a lot about them. *Ursus arctos horribilis* was his formal name and right now it seemed to suit him pretty well. His claws were like kitchen knives. Pale and curved. She couldn't take her eyes off them.

As to what to do when you came face to face with *horribilis*, for every piece of advice, there was another contradicting it. Lie down and play dead or yell and try to scare him off; stand still or roll yourself into a ball or slowly back away and talk in a quiet monotone; climb a tree, don't climb a tree. About the only thing biologists agreed on was that fleeing was a waste of time. A grizzly could run at forty miles an hour. With all this confusion, Dan had said the safest bet was to carry the pepper spray. Which she'd left at home.

Slowly and as quietly as she could, and all the time watching the bear from the corner of her eye, she started to put the kit into her pack.

The bear dropped onto all fours again and took a few paces to his left, walking in a slow rolling motion, his head swinging clumsily from side to side, like a sailor who'd had too many beers. He turned and retraced his steps, looking at Helen, then looking away again, and sniffing the air as if he couldn't quite get the drift of her.

She could see the dark hump on his shoulders and, above them, his hackles starting to bristle and the sight gave her a first stab of pure fear. Suddenly she felt ashamed of all her recent, wretched self-pitying and of all those times she had wished she were dead. Perhaps such thoughts had conjured this prowling nemesis to deliver her. But she wasn't ready. With total clarity, she realized that she wanted to live.

She glanced down at the cub by her feet. He was still flat out. She wondered if Luke had reached the pickup yet and, even more, why the hell she hadn't gone with him. Why was she risking her life for that of another who would happily bite her head off?

She heard the distant sound of the pickup now and saw the big grizzly catch sight of it over her head. He stopped his pacing, but didn't seem scared, just mildly diverted. She tried to work out what to do when Luke arrived and decided they should try to lift the cub into the back of the pickup. And pray that the big grizzly didn't charge.

From the sound of it, the pickup was getting close. She could hear Buzz barking and Luke telling him to shut up. The big bear was taking all this in and, from the way he was laying back his ears, took a dim view of it. Helen knew this was not a promising sign.

She slowly turned her head and saw Luke climbing cautiously out of the truck. He'd left the engine running. Buzz was inside with his front paws up on the dashboard, barking for all he was worth. As Luke came up beside her, she slipped the strap of her pack over one shoulder.

'Let's get this little brute in the truck,' Helen said.

They got either end of the cub and lifted him up. He already weighed about sixty pounds. They both kept an eye on the big male. Suddenly he gave a loud 'woof' and then another. He was swinging his head rapidly from side to side.

'That doesn't look good.'

'It m–means he's g–going to charge.'

'If he does, we drop baby bear here and get our asses into the truck, okay?'

'Okay.'

Suddenly the big grizzly made a loud popping noise with his teeth.

'Here he c–comes!'

Helen turned and saw the bear setting off down the bank toward them. And as she did so, the pack slipped off her shoulder and she tried to hoist it, lost her grip on the cub and dropped her end of him.

'Shit!'

She quickly shed the pack and picked him up again, glancing over her shoulder at the charging bear. The bank was well covered in scrub and saplings but he was surging through them like a snowplow.

They got to the pickup and Helen lunged for the door handle and in the process almost dropped the cub again. Inside, Buzz was on the seat, going berserk.

'Wouldn't it be better to p–put him in the back?'

'No. In here, quick!'

They bundled the bear into the passenger-side footwell and Helen shoved Buzz away across the cab and dived after him. The big grizzly was down on the trail now, only twenty yards away, and coming for them in great rollicking bounds.

Helen got herself into the driver's seat, with Buzz wedged against the window, barking like a maniac in her left ear. Then, to her horror, she saw Luke was going back for her pack.

'Luke! Leave it, get in!'

But he was almost there. The bear was closing on him fast. Luke grabbed the pack, but as he turned to run back, he slipped in the mud and fell.

'Luke!'

She slammed her hand onto the horn and gave a loud blast, but the bear didn't even falter. He was only about five yards away from where Luke was scrambling to his feet. There was no way he'd reach the pickup in time. Helen screamed.

Suddenly, the bear was knocked sideways and for a moment everything was just a blur of brown fur. Then Helen realized what had happened. Another bear, presumably the cub's mother, had charged. The impact sent the big male rolling into the bushes, with the female in roaring pursuit.

'Luke, come on!'

He was almost at the pickup now. But the big male grizzly wasn't going to be so easily deterred. He knocked the mother flying and was after the cub again.

'He's coming! Quick, get in!'

Luke dived into the passenger seat, swinging his feet over the cub. He reached out to shut the door when the big male arrived and saved him the trouble by removing it with a single swipe of his paw, sending it cartwheeling into the scrub.

'G-go, Helen! GO!'

Helen rammed the gearshift into reverse and stamped on the gas pedal and the pickup lurched off down the trail, slithering and snaking as it went, its wheels flinging mud and rocks at the big grizzly who was left standing there, apparently non-plussed for a moment.

'Buzz, will you shut the fuck up!' Helen yelled.

She was swiveled in her seat, looking out the back window and trying to steer and pin Buzz to the door all at the same time.

'Is he coming after us?'

'No—'

'Thank God.'

'Yes.'

'Shit.'

'Both of them. And the c-cub's waking up.'

'Terrific.'

Farther down the trail, about halfway to where they had parked, there was a place Helen recalled might be wide enough for them to turn. The question was whether there would be time enough to do it before the bear got there too. She didn't dare look back at him in case she reversed off the edge of the trail.

'Is he still coming?'

'Yeah. He's g-gaining on us.'

She saw the turning place coming up now and decided to give it a go. She told Luke to hold tight, hit the brakes and swung the rear of the pickup around. The truck lurched and lifted up on two wheels and for a sickening moment Helen thought it was going to topple over. But it came down with a bump and she found herself looking into the face of the grizzly. He skidded and thumped into the driver's side door, cracking the window and making the whole vehicle rock. Buzz took this as a cue to duck under Helen's arm and pounce on the waking cub.

She wrenched the gearshift into drive. The big bear had his face pressed against the window and was showing her his dental work.

'Sorry, buddy, no room,' she said. 'See ya!'

And with Buzz and the bear cub trying to kill each other between Luke's legs, off they went down the trail, leaving the big grizzly to cope with the cub's mother.

Helen drove with one hand, as fast as she dared, at last managing to hook the other inside Buzz's collar, while Luke wrangled the rapidly recovering cub. Two miles down the trail, he'd recovered enough to claw gaping holes in Luke's jeans and bite a chunk out of his boot.

Helen figured they were far enough from the adults by now for the little one to have a fair chance of survival. Hopefully he would hitch up with his mother again. Helen pulled up and they ejected him unceremoniously from the doorless side of the truck. And with Buzz tethered to the steering wheel, still bawling blue murder, Luke and Helen stood side by side and watched the cub lope grumpily off into the bushes.

'Hey, please, don't mention it!' Helen called after him.

She put a hand on Luke's shoulder and leaned on him and he shook his head and gave her a grin.

'Maybe we b-better stick to wolves.'

That evening, it started to snow. With no wind to drift it, it fell in heavy, floating flakes which settled on the cabin windowsills while inside Helen and Luke cooked and ate and laughed about the day's events.

After supper, before he went home, they wrapped up warm and took the snowmobile high into the forest with the snowflakes flitting like uncharted galaxies in the headlight. Luke sat behind her, holding on, as you had to, with his arms encircling her and it felt warm and comforting to be held that way. They drove to where they thought the wolves might be and just as they got there, the snow stopped and the clouds opened on a sliver of moon.

She turned off the snowmobile engine and they stood for a moment listening to the perfect muffled silence of the forest. Then they took the flashlight and the radio receiver and walked a little way along the trail, their boots crunching in the snow.

They found the signals right away, clucking clear in the crystal air, and they knew the wolves were very close. In the beam of the flashlight, they found tracks no more than minutes old.

Helen turned off the light and they stood quite still and listened. The only sound was the soft thud of snow falling, now and then, from a tree.

'Howl,' she whispered.

He had heard her do it several times, without success, but had never yet attempted a howl himself. He shook his head.

'Try,' she said softly.

'I c-can't. It w-wouldn't . . .'

He made a little gesture with his fingers toward his mouth and she realized that he was afraid his voice might not come, that it would betray him, and leave him mute and embarrassed as so often it did.

'It's only me, Luke.'

For a long moment he looked at her. And she saw in his sad eyes what she already knew he felt for her. She took off her glove and reached out and touched his cold face and smiled. She felt him tremble a little at her touch. And as she lowered her hand, he put his head back and opened his mouth and howled, long and plaintively, into the night.

And before the note had time to die, from across the snow-tipped trees of the canyon, the wolves replied.

WINTER

24

Nobody witnessed the wolfer's return to Hope.

His silver trailer slid into town like a ghost ship in the dead of the night before Thanksgiving, when the plowed snow lay like unmarked graves along the roadside and the blacktop glistened with salt.

J.J. Lovelace sat alone in the old gray Chevy pickup he always used for hauling the trailer and as he came toward the junction by the old school, he turned off the headlights and slowed to a halt.

Behind the trees on the other side of the street was the graveyard where the mother he'd never known was buried. But Lovelace didn't look that way or even think of it. Instead, he squinted sideways through the darkness along Main Street and was pleased to see it was deserted. He pulled away from the junction and, driving on his sidelights, cruised slowly through the town.

It was much as he remembered. Except for the modern cars

parked there, with their windshields masked against the frost. Some of the names on the storefronts had changed, the gas station had new pumps and there was a new red traffic light swinging in the wind on a wire across the street, flashing pointlessly at no one.

Lovelace had no special feelings for Hope, one way or the other. And no memories, good or bad, were stirred by this witching passage through a place he'd once called home. To him, it was just another faceless town.

Buck Calder had mailed him a map of how to get to the Hicks house, where he was going to be based, but Lovelace didn't need it. He remembered the route well enough. It would take him past his father's old house on the river. And he wondered, as he headed out that way, whether he would feel anything when he saw it.

He had told Calder he would be arriving late and there was no need for anyone to wait up for him. With jobs like this, it was best to come unseen and stay unseen. That was why he had waited for the hunting season to end and the mountains to clear of prying amateurs.

Once he was out of town, he turned his headlights back on, but kept them dimmed. For five miles, following the snow-rutted gravel, the only sign of life he saw was an owl, sitting on a fence post, watching him with saucered yellow eyes.

The gateway to his father's old house was overgrown with scrub and drifted deeply with snow. Lovelace stopped the truck so that the headlights angled toward the house. If he'd turned the engine off and wound down the window, he would have been able to hear the sound of the river. But he didn't. It was a clear night and freezing hard and his bones were too brittle.

He could see the house plainly enough through the bare branches of the cottonwoods and he could tell right away it had long been derelict. A shredded screen hung askew from the window of what was once the kitchen and a wrecked mobile home stood in the yard with its roof agape. Snow had filled the inside so that the windows looked as though they were hung with shrouds.

Lovelace knew such moments called for nostalgia. But try as he might, he couldn't summon any. The best he could do was a mild surprise that some city-type hadn't knocked the place down and built a fancy summer vacation house instead. He turned the steering wheel and headed on up the valley.

At last he saw the epic gateway of the Calder ranch with the steer's skull looming above it, capped with snow and watching all who approached. A mile farther and he saw the ranch house. There were lights on above the yard and he could see cars parked and a pair of dogs running from one of the barns, then stopping when they saw him veer left and on up the road toward the Hicks place.

When he got there, he parked the trailer, as instructed, under some high trees at the back of the barns, where Calder said it couldn't be seen, even from the air. Hicks and his wife were the only others who knew he was coming and what his business was, Calder had assured him.

He felt the blast of the freezing air as soon as he got out of the truck. It had to be fourteen or fifteen below. He pulled the flaps of his fur cap down over his ears and walked back to the trailer, past the snowmobile loaded in the bed of the pickup. The rimed crust of the snow cracked loudly under his boots. An old dog was barking inside the house.

He stopped by the trailer door and looked up at the sky. It was milky with stars, but Lovelace didn't pay them any heed. He wanted clouds that might bring some respite from the cold and he knew there were none.

In the trailer, he lit a lamp and heated some milk on the

kerosene stove. He sat on his bunk to wait, shivering and jamming his gloved hands under his arms and hugging himself. When the milk was ready, he filled his mug and warmed his hands on it and felt each hot swallow disperse without effect in the cold cave of his body.

There was a wood stove but he hadn't the energy to get it going. The trailer was built for work, not comfort. It was like a smaller version of his trap room at home, about eighteen feet long with a narrow aisle of linoleum running from the bunk and galley at the front to a table and workbench at the rear. Instead of hanging exposed, his gear was concealed in wooden cupboards all around the trailer's interior.

Lovelace had made and fitted them himself and he alone knew of the secret panels behind which he stored the things that could betray his true trade: the traps and snares and pots of bait and the collapsible German 'sniper' rifle with its screw-on silencer and laser nightscope; the radio scanner that he used for tracking collared wolves and the M44 cyanide gas 'getters' that exploded in their faces, which were the only concession he'd ever made to poison and which (knowing how his father would have disapproved) he rarely used. It had taken him most of a month to get everything back into working order.

He gulped the last of the milk now and felt just as cold as before. He swung his legs up onto the bunk and lay down, still wearing his coat and cap and boots and gloves, and heaped himself with his wolfskin rugs and the old log cabin quilt that Winnie had once sewn for their bed. Then he reached out and turned off the lamp.

He lay quite still and tried to distract himself from his shivering by thinking about the job that would start in the morning. It was awhile since he'd worked, but he had no doubt he could do it. Even though he was getting old, he was still as handy as some men half his age. Maybe his heart wasn't in it, like it had been before, but then hearts were treacherous things at the best of times. At least, the work would keep him busy.

As his eyes grew accustomed to the dark, he saw how the trailer's frosted rear window had been turned by the glow of the starlit snow into a blank screen of silver. And the wolfer lay beneath his wolfskins watching it, as though a movie were about to start, and waited for the dawn.

'Shall we all join hands?' Buck Calder said.

Everyone was seated at the long table that had been set up in the living room. Ribbons of steam curled from the giant golden turkey that held pride of place, amid a multitude of other dishes, at its center. Helen turned to Luke, who was sitting beside her, and held out her hand. He smiled and took it in his and they lowered their heads for his father to say grace. For a moment, the only sound was the crackle of the great logs that blazed on the hearth.

'Dear Lord, we thank thee for leading our forefathers in safety across this great land and for helping them overcome the many perils and hardships they faced in making this, our home, a place of safety. May their courage and thy spirit guide us and make us worthy of the fruits of thy love laid before us this day. Amen.'

'Amen.'

Everyone started talking at once and the Thanksgiving feast began.

They were fifteen in all, including Kathy Hicks' baby who sat regally between his parents in a high chair, bolted to one end of the table. Luke's sister Lane and her husband, Bob, had come over from Bozeman. Lane was a high school teacher, who not only looked like her mother but had the same gentle dignity too. Bob seemed only to be able to talk about real estate prices. He was doing so now with Doug Millward, who was here with Hettie and their three children. Apart from Helen, the only other 'outsider' was Ruth Michaels, who had arrived late, looking even more apprehensive than Helen.

Helen had only accepted the invitation because Luke insisted. She had been wary of how his father might behave toward her and didn't know if she had recovered enough confidence to lock horns with him. She needn't have worried. Buck Calder had been charming. And so had everyone else.

Before lunch, Helen had helped Kathy lay the table and they'd had their first real chat. Helen was impressed by how bright and funny she was, though quite what she saw in Clyde remained a mystery. As Helen knew from her own experience, there was no accounting for some women's choice of partner. By the time they sat down to eat, fortified by Luke's quiet presence beside her, Helen was glad she had come.

It was warming to be part of a family occasion and in a proper home, even if it wasn't her own. And it was the best meal she'd had in months. She had three helpings of turkey and Doug Millward, who was sitting on her other side, made a big joke of it and kept passing dishes to her.

It wasn't until her plate was finally clear that anyone mentioned wolves.

'So, Buck,' Hettie Millward said. 'Did you get yourself an elk this season?'

'No, ma'am. I did not.'

'He never was much of a shot,' Doug Millward said to Helen in a stage whisper. Everyone laughed. Then Clyde piped up:

'I was talking to that outfitter fella, Pete Neuberg, you know? Says it's been one of the worst hunting seasons in years. Elk and deer numbers are way down, he says. He blames the wolves.'

Kathy raised her eyes to the ceiling. 'I hear they're to blame for the weather too.'

'How can wolves be to blame for the weather?' little Charlie Millward said.

His sister Lucy gave him a shove. 'It was a joke, dumbo.'

There was a moment of silence. Helen saw Buck Calder was staring at her across the table.

'What do you think, Helen?' he said.

'About them being to blame for the weather?'

She regretted the smart remark as soon as she'd said it. The laughter it prompted subtly changed Calder's smile. Helen was aware of Luke shifting uneasily in his seat. She hurried on.

'Well, they're certainly killing elk and deer. That's what they mainly feed on, so their being here is bound to have an impact. But not a huge one.'

Clyde sneered quietly, earning himself a narrow-eyed look from his wife. Luke leaned forward and cleared his throat.

'W-we've seen a l-lot of elk and deer the l-last few weeks.'

'That's true,' Helen said. 'We have.'

No one spoke for a moment. Eleanor stood up to clear the dishes.

'Well, I don't know,' she said. 'At least they're not eating cattle anymore.'

'They never ate any of mine,' Doug Millward said.

Luke shrugged. 'M-maybe yours d-don't taste so good.'

Everyone, even Luke's father, roared and the conversation turned to other matters. When no one was looking, Helen turned to Luke.

'Thanks, partner,' she said quietly.

That secret look and, earlier, the touch of her hand while his father said grace, stayed with Luke for a long time.

He'd been so proud that she should call him her partner. Sitting beside her that day, he'd felt almost as though he was her boyfriend or something. When there were lots of people sitting around the table like that, he normally kept his mouth

317

shut, in case his stutter ambushed him. But having Helen at his side gave him such confidence that, without thinking, he'd spoken up to defend her. Hell, he'd even cracked a joke!

Over the fortnight that followed, it seemed to Luke that they had grown even closer. And yet, in his dreams, it was the opposite. Whenever he dreamed of her now, which was often, she was always with someone else or didn't recognize him or was laughing at him.

Except for the dream he'd had last night.

He was walking with her at the very edge of the ocean on a curve of white sand, palm-fringed and flawless, the kind you see in travel brochures. She was wearing a yellow dress that showed her shoulders. The gently breaking waves were streaming up over the sand and frothing around their bare feet. The water was warm and clear and in the glassed arc of the waves before they broke he could see great shoals of fish.

He pointed them out and Helen stopped and stood, with her shoulder touching his, and they both watched. The fish were of many different kinds and shapes and colors but they moved as one, darting and turning in perfect synchrony.

It was one of those dreams you knew to be a dream even as you dreamt it, the kind that slipped away as the real world seeped in, no matter how hard you tried to cling on. Sometimes though, Luke had found there was a moment, when conscious and unconscious were fleetingly in balance and you could dictate events. And it had been like that this morning. He had willed Helen to turn to him and she had done so. And in the instant before he woke, she had lifted her mouth to his and almost, almost, kissed him.

He thought about the dream while he shaved and showered and he knew he would go on reliving it all day. It had obviously been prompted by Helen getting a letter yesterday from her father, enclosing a plane ticket and a formal invitation to his wedding in Barbados. She was going in three weeks' time, for Christmas, and would be away for more than a week.

Luke got himself dressed and headed down for breakfast.

It was a quarter to eight. Every other day he would have been up two hours ago and out in the forest tracking with Helen. But today was Wednesday: speech therapy. He had already heard his mother's car leave. With Christmas coming up, she was helping Ruth in the store pretty well every day.

His father's office opened directly onto the living room. He always left the door open, so he could monitor the movements of the household. As Luke came down the stairs he could see him in there, sitting in front of the computer, a cigar stuck between his teeth.

'Luke?'

'Yes, sir?'

'Morning.'

'M-morning.'

His father put down his cigar and took off the little half-moon spectacles he used for reading. He leaned back in his big leather chair.

'Not out with Helen today?'

'No sir. It's m-my c-clinic day.'

'Oh, yeah.'

His father stood up and came out into the living room. He had that easy, amiable look on his face, the one that made Luke most suspicious.

'Gonna have some breakfast?'

'Yes, sir.'

'I'll join you for a coffee.'

His father led the way into the kitchen and took the pot off the coffee machine. He filled two cups and took them to the table. Luke never drank coffee, but his father always forgot that. Luke poured himself some cereal and sat down opposite him.

He knew what was coming. These casual, cozy, father-and-son chats about his work with Helen had been happening a lot lately. Only the other day his father had asked a whole load of detailed questions about radio-collar frequencies. It was comical. If the guy had shown any interest in Luke's life before, he might have stood a better chance.

'So, how's the therapy going?'

'It's g-going fine.'

'So poor old Helen has to cope by herself, huh?'

Luke smiled. 'Yeah.'

His father nodded thoughtfully and took a drink from his cup.

'So how'd the tracking go yesterday?'

'G-good.'

'Where are they mainly hanging out now?'

'Oh, they m-m-move around all th-the time.'

'Yeah, but I mean, like yesterday, for example?'

Luke swallowed. He was okay at being evasive, but when it came to straightforward lying, he was hopeless. His stutter nearly always betrayed him. His father was watching him very closely.

'Y-y-esterday, they were way b-back. Right up b-by the divide.'

'Uh-huh?'

'Yeah. Ab-b-bout ten miles s-south of the b-big wwall.'

'Is that so?'

Luke saw his father's face harden and he cursed himself for making such a mess of it. It wouldn't have fooled a gullible kid. For salvation, he looked up at the clock.

'I'd b-b-better be going.'

'The roads are clear. Clyde was out blading first thing.'

Luke got up and put his bowl in the dishwasher. He picked up his car keys and took his hat and coat from the pegs by the door. He knew his father's eyes were on him the whole while.

'Go carefully, Luke.'

The voice was cold and flat. Luke zipped up his coat.

'Yes, sir.'

And he opened the door and fled.

The session with Joan went well.

She told him of a new therapy technique she'd been read-ing about, where you videoed the stutterer and then edited out all the stutters to show him how it looked and sounded when he talked fluently. Joan said it apparently got great results, but she wasn't going to waste the money on him because he'd hardly stuttered once in the whole hour.

When they said goodbye she touched his arm and said how happy he looked. And as he walked to his car, he wondered how it showed. It was true. He'd never felt happier in his whole life. It was like he was, kind of, singing inside.

From the clinic, he drove across town to the supermarket to pick up some things Helen had asked him to get. He parked the Jeep among the mounds of freshly plowed snow and, as soon as he got out, saw Cheryl Snyder and Jerry Kruger head-ing toward him. They had already seen him, so there was no escape. Kruger had his arm around her, making a big show of it, presumably to let the world know he and Cheryl were now an item.

'Hey, Cooks! How're you doing?'

'Hi, Luke.'

They stood chatting for a minute or two, or rather, Luke listened while Kruger rabbited on, cracking jokes that Cheryl didn't even smile at. What on earth she saw in the guy Luke couldn't imagine. Eventually he said he'd better get on with his shopping and they all said goodbye. He was walking away when Kruger called after him.

'Hey, Cooks! Congratulations!'

Luke turned and frowned at him.

'Hear you got yourself laid at last.'

'What?'

Luke could see Cheryl jabbing him in the ribs, telling him to shut up. But Kruger took no notice.

'Aw, come on, don't go all coy. The wolf babe! Everybody knows.'

He howled, just like that day at the fair, and started laughing. Cheryl broke away from him.

'Don't take any notice, Luke,' she said.

'I'm just h-h-helping her. That's all.'

'Yeah, right,' Kruger. 'Oiling her traps, huh?'

Cheryl gave him an angry push. 'Jerry, you're gross. Just shut up, okay?'

Luke walked the aisles of the supermarket in a state of shock. He knew that Hope, like any small town, thrived on gossip. But it was the first time he'd found himself the subject of it.

All he prayed was that Helen didn't get to hear about it.

Eleanor fixed the star to the top of the Christmas tree in the shop window and stood back.

'Let's have a look from outside,' Ruth said.

Eleanor followed her out onto the sidewalk. An icy wind was blowing directly down Main Street, playing havoc with the strings of colored lights that zigzagged between the facing storefronts. The two women stood outside Paragon, holding their hair from their faces while they admired Eleanor's handiwork.

'It looks beautiful,' Ruth said. 'Whenever I do Christmas trees they always end up looking Jewish.'

Eleanor laughed. 'How can a tree look Jewish?'

Ruth shrugged. 'I don't know. They just do. You're a Catholic, huh?'

'Born, raised and lapsed.'

'It shows. I mean, the born and raised bit. Catholics do good trees.'

Eleanor laughed again. 'Ruth, I'm freezing to death out here.

They went inside and while Ruth served some customers who'd been looking around for ages, Eleanor got on with decorating the rest of the store.

She had brought some greenery and a stepladder from the ranch that morning. It had been years since she had put up Christmas decorations. They never bothered at home anymore and doing it now gave her a nostalgic, almost childlike pleasure. It was getting dark outside and the lights on the tree in the window glowed warmly.

When the customers had gone, Ruth came to help her hang a big gold streamer across the front end of the store. Ruth held one end while Eleanor went up the stepladder to tack the other to the picture rail.

'So, is Luke still helping Helen Ross out with the wolves?'

'Yes. We hardly ever see him.'

'I like her.'

'I do too. I think Luke's got a bit of a crush on her.'

'How old is he now?'

'Eighteen.' She pushed in the tack.

'He's so handsome! Makes me wish *I* was a few years younger, anyhow.'

Eleanor looked down at her and Ruth seemed suddenly embarrassed.

Eleanor smiled. 'Shall we fix the other end now?'

'Sure.'

They moved the ladder to the other side of the shop and up Eleanor went again. For awhile they were silent.

'So how come you "lapsed"? If you don't mind me asking.'

Eleanor didn't answer right away, not because she minded, but because no one had ever asked her. Ruth's direct manner was one of the things she liked about her. Eleanor took the box of thumbtacks from her pocket and got one out.

'Well, maybe you don't know, but our oldest child died in a car wreck.'

'I do know.'

'Well. All my life, I'd been a regular churchgoer. Gone to mass and confession – and I tell you, around this time of year, living out where we do, it wasn't always easy. Buck used to tease me about it. He'd say, what on earth did I have to confess? When did I do all these wicked things? And that I should tell him, so he could be around. But then Buck's not a Catholic, so he never understood.'

She glanced down at Ruth and smiled, then tacked the streamer to the rail.

'There.'

She came down the ladder and the two of them stood staring up at the streamer.

'Looks good,' Ruth said.

'Mmm. Where shall we put the other one?'

'At the back?'

They moved the ladder and repeated the process, while Eleanor went on with the story.

'Anyhow. After Henry died, I started going more than ever. Hardly missed a service. Like a lot of people do, I suppose, when something dreadful happens in their lives. You know, you're looking for a reason, I suppose, or a little sign or something, that the one you've lost is somewhere else and happy. And then one day I just realized, well . . . He wasn't there.'

Ruth was frowning at her, trying to understand.

'You mean, your son?'

'Oh, no. He's there okay. He's fine, I know that. I mean *He* with a capital H.'

'So you're saying, you believe in heaven, but you don't believe in God?'

'Exactly.'

By now the second streamer was in place. Eleanor came down the ladder to inspect it.

'What do you think?'

She looked at Ruth and was surprised to find she was staring at her and not the streamer.

'You're a great woman, Eleanor. Do you know that?'

'Don't be silly.'

'I mean it.'

'Well, I think you're pretty good too.'

Ruth gave a little, mock curtsy. 'Thank you, ma'am.'

'Can I ask you a personal question now?' Eleanor said, lightly, as she folded up the ladder. It wasn't fair, she knew, saying what she was about to and she felt a little mean doing it. But there were some moments in life that you simply couldn't let go by unused.

'Of course.'

'How long have you been sleeping with my husband?'

25

Baby Buck Hicks guzzled at his mother's breast as though it were the last meal he'd ever get. Clyde had been going on at Kathy for weeks that she should get the boy onto bottled milk. He'd read some article that said it ruined a woman's shape to breast-feed too long. But Kathy was in no hurry. She enjoyed it as much as little Buck did. And, for heavensakes, he wasn't even a year old yet.

Clyde was just jealous and anyway, what the heck he was doing, reading articles like that, Kathy couldn't imagine. It was probably something he'd seen in a cow magazine and gotten all mixed up in his head.

She'd been up awhile but was still in her pink quilt dressing gown, sitting on the couch in the little living room and idly flicking through the pages of *People* magazine, while the baby had his feed.

There was a three-page spread about Jordan Townsend and Krissi Maxton, with pictures of them in cowboy clothes, posing in front of some bison on their 'dream ranch' in Hope, Montana. Krissi was quoted as saying it was the only place she ever felt 'centered'. But she still looked as if she didn't want to get too close to the bison. There were more pictures of them, dressed up to the nines at the premiere of Krissi's new movie. *SpaceKill III*. Krissi was wearing a sliver of sparkling dress, that showed pretty well everything she had to offer. Jordan seemed to have had a face-lift. It made him look about a hundred and five.

Kathy yawned and shifted the baby to her other breast.

It had snowed again in the night. Clyde was out with the plow, clearing the road down to the ranch. The morning sun was flooding in through the doorway from the kitchen, almost touching the toes of Kathy's sensible sheepskin bootees. The radio was playing that song again about the guy who'd lost his sweetheart and was spending Christmas alone with his horse.

Suddenly, in the corner of her eye, Kathy saw a shadow pass across the patch of sunlit floor. Then she heard the clump of feet on the steps and two sharp knocks on the kitchen door. She got up and made herself decent and right away the baby began to cry. She put him over her shoulder and patted his back while she walked through into the kitchen.

The face she saw when she opened the door gave her such a shock she almost dropped the baby. Everything about it was gray, from the fur of the cap to the frosted tips of the beard. Even the skin, tight and translucent over the man's jutting cheekbones, had a grayish hue. All except the eyes, which were glaring at her like a pair of angry black bugs.

It was the first time she had met the wolfer, though he'd been there more than two weeks. He hardly ever seemed to be around. She had caught a glimpse of him now and then, heading up toward the forest on his snowmobile across the top meadow. Once she'd waved to him but either he hadn't seen her or had chosen to ignore her. Clyde and Buck had gone to his trailer to talk with him a couple of times and Clyde had come back saying he was odd and grouchy and she shouldn't go bothering him.

Little Buck was bawling in her ear and the wolfer was staring at him as if he'd never seen a baby before. Then he seemed to remember Kathy was there too and touched his cap.

'Ma'am.'

'You're Mr Lovelace.'

'Yes, ma'am. Your husband said—'

'Come in. Nice to meet you.'

She held out her hand and he looked down at it as though he didn't understand why it was there. Then he slowly took off his heavy glove and then a thinner glove beneath it and by the time he was ready to shake hands, Kathy was embarrassed and wishing she hadn't bothered. His hand felt cold and gnarled, like the limb of a frozen tree.

'Your husband said—'

'Mr Lovelace, would you mind coming inside. I don't want this little monster catching cold.'

He hesitated and she could see he would prefer to stay where he was. But she held the door open and reluctantly he stepped into the kitchen, his eyes fixed again on the crying baby.

'Can I get you some coffee or something?'

'Is he yours?'

Kathy laughed. This was one strange old guy. Whose baby did he think it was?

'That's right. Though, times like this, I'm open to offers.'

'What's he hollering about?'

'He's hungry, that's all. I was just feeding him.'

'How old?'

'He'll be one come the end of January.'

Lovelace nodded, considering this. Then, abruptly, he took his beetle eyes off the baby and fixed them on Kathy.

'Your husband said I could borrow the chain saw, cut me some firewood.'

'Oh, sure, that's fine.'

'He said it was in the barn, but it's not.'

He looked down. The chain saw was on the floor, right by the door, among all the boots. Clyde had filed and oiled the chain at the kitchen table last night, while lecturing her for the umpteenth time on how she shouldn't go telling anyone about the wolfer.

'Can I take it?'

'Oh, yes. Please.'

He bent and picked up the chain saw, then opened the door.

'Won't trouble you again.'

And before Kathy could say it was no trouble at all and was he sure he didn't want that cup of coffee, the wolfer had gone.

Lovelace had been looking for the wolves for fifteen days now, combing the canyons and forest for tracks and scanning the air for signals. But he'd seen no sign of them, nor heard a single howl.

He'd started from the north, where Calder said he reckoned they were, and worked south along the mountain front, methodically checking each trail, ravine and creek on the map. He knew that the biologist woman and Calder's son would be out radio tracking, so to avoid them he always chose the routes he figured they'd be least likely to use, looping high into the backcountry and dropping down from the west.

The weather was a curse. It had snowed almost every day since he arrived, as if God was on the side of the wolves and trying to hide their tracks from him. And it was the kind of snow that made the going slow and heavy. It was some time since he'd worked country this big in weather this bad and he'd forgotten what a toll it took.

The snowmobile made too much noise to use the whole time. He liked to hear and not be heard. So he only used it to get himself up high and then he would find a safe place to leave it and use skis or snowshoes, depending on the terrain and the condition of the snow.

He had stripped his pack to essentials, but what with the tent and food and the rifle and radio scanner, it still felt heavy as a dead man on his back and at times like this, after a long day's trudging, he barely had the energy to pitch the tent and crawl in.

He lay now in his sleeping bag, looking at the map with his flashlight, working out where he'd go when he'd eaten something and rested and waited for the blizzard to blow itself out. He'd smelled it in the air when it was still light and seen it in the yellow lowering of the sky. It was nearly twenty below outside and after pitching his tent, his hands had been numb and useless. He had the little Coleman stove going to melt some snow to drink and his fingers were starting to tingle and hurt as the blood seeped back into them.

On the map, he saw he was above a place called Wrong Creek. Lovelace remembered the name from when he was a boy. There was a story about how it came to be called that, but he couldn't remember it. High above it, he noticed the crossed pickax symbol of a mine, no doubt disused, and made a mental note to check it out. It might be somewhere he could use for dumping the wolves. Assuming he ever caught them.

He reached into his pack and hauled out the scanner. The cussed thing weighed a ton and was good as useless anyways. Without a clue as to what frequencies they had the wolves' collars set to, it was like looking for a flea in a fur shed. And even if he was lucky enough to stumble across a signal, there was no knowing if it was a wolf. There were sure to be other animals around that had been collared by some biologist or other. It might be a bear or mountain lion, even a coyote or deer.

He switched the scanner on and went through the motions for the tenth time that day. It took him half an hour and, predictably, he found nothing but the mindless rush of static. He switched it off and pushed it away. Next time he went back to the trailer for provisions, he'd ditch the damn thing.

He forced himself to eat some deer jerky and melted some snow on the stove to drink. Then he killed the flashlight and lay on his back, staring blindly at the tent roof until he saw it give the faintest yellow tinge of the dying light outside.

All day he'd been thinking about the Hicks woman's baby. Not yet a full year old. He'd found it hard to take his eyes off the creature. Those tiny pink hands and the little face all screwed up and screaming for his mother's teat. The noise, the energy, the sheer, explosive life in the little thing had quite shocked him.

He had known the young of many species, known what they smelled of and felt like and the different noises they made, be it in life or in the throes of death. But he'd never known a human baby. In all his long years, he'd never held one in his arms nor even touched one. Nor had he ever smelled that warm, sweet, puppy smell he'd smelled that morning.

Early in their marriage, he and Winnie had discovered that they weren't able to have children. She'd been keen to adopt, but he didn't like the idea of rearing another man's child and so they never had.

Whenever possible, he had avoided any contact with children and always steered well clear of babies. Perhaps he feared they might touch some painful spot within him. Like him, Winnie had been an only child and so there were no nieces or nephews who might have come to visit or later to bring children of their own.

Suddenly, and for no reason that Lovelace could then have made sense of, he thought about that last evening he'd spent with Winnie at the hospital.

The doctors had told him in hushed tones outside in the corridor that she was slipping away. And when he went in and sat down beside the bed, he'd thought her already gone. Her eyes were closed and he couldn't see her breathing. She looked so frail and pale and bruised from all the tubes and wires and things they'd stuck into her. But her face was peaceful and after he'd been sitting there some time, she opened her eyes and saw him and smiled.

She started to talk, so softly he had to lean in real close to hear her and it was as if she was in the middle of a conversation that had already been going on awhile in her head. He supposed it was because she was so full of drugs, but it was almost like she was already halfway to heaven and was taking a little rest and looking back on life before she finally left it behind.

'I was thinking, Joseph. About all those animals. I was trying to work out how many it must be. How many do you think?'

'Winnie, I . . .' He took her hand in both of his. He had no idea what she was talking about. Her voice was like a dreamy child's.

'How many? It must be more than thousands. Tens of thousands, maybe. Hundreds of thousands. Do you think it's that many, Joseph?'

'Winnie,' he said softly. 'What animals, dear?'

'Could it be a million? No. No, not a million. Not that many.'

She smiled at him and he asked her again, gently, what animals?

'Why, silly, the ones you've killed. All these years. I was trying to add them up. It's so many, Joseph. All those lives, every one of them a separate life.'

332

'You shouldn't be fretting about things like that.'

'Oh, I'm not fretting. I was wondering, that's all.'

'Wondering.'

'Yes.'

She suddenly frowned and looked at him with great intensity.

'Do you think, Joseph, their life is the same as ours? I mean, what it's made of, that little flicker or spirit or whatever it is, inside them. Do you think it's the same as what we have inside us?'

'No, dear, of course it's not. How could it be?'

Her puzzling seemed to have drained her, for she closed her eyes and sank back on her pillow, with a faint, contented smile on her lips.

'You're right,' she sighed. 'How silly I am. How could it be?'

The blizzard had been blowing for the last two hours. It was coming from the northeast, straight across the lake. Helen listened to it wailing around the cabin like a choir of the unforgiven. She was glad they had decided in time to call off their night-tracking. She levered the lid from the stove and dropped in another log, setting off a small volcano of sparks. The noise roused Buzz where he lay sprawled on the cabin floor, in prime heat-hogging position. He gave Helen a look of disapproval and she knelt and ruffled his head.

'Oh, excuse *me*. I'm *so* sorry.'

He rolled over onto his back so she could rub his tummy.

'Was there ever such a spoiled, ugly mutt in all the world?'

Luke was sitting at the table, with his back to her, putting the last of the day's tracking notes into the laptop. He turned and smiled, then went back to his work.

He knew his way around the GIS software by now as well as she did. He could create new maps or combine them, often in ways that hadn't occurred to her, to show why the wolves might be using a particular route or why they might be spending time in a particular place. Helen had never known anyone learn so fast. It was the same when they were out tracking during the day. He was a born wildlife biologist.

Their routine, now the snow had come, was to go by truck or snowmobile until they found a good signal, then put on their skis and search for tracks. When they found them they would follow them back, sometimes for miles, until they found the wolves' last kill. In the snow it could be a gory sight and the first time, having heard Luke's account of shooting the elk, she had been worried it might upset him.

Backtracking, they had come across a mule deer, a young doe, which the wolves had killed only hours before. They'd brought her down in a clearing and painted the snow widely with her blood. As Helen got down to work, measuring and taking samples, she had watched Luke from the corner of her eye and been surprised by his calm.

That same evening, back at the cabin, they had talked about it while they ate and Luke had explained, without a single stop or stutter, why it was different. When he'd shot the elk, he said, it wasn't for his own survival. Sure, there had been all that pressure to please his father, but in the end he had killed from choice. He had taken a life without needing to. Wolves, Luke said, like the Blackfeet who had once hunted here too, had no such choice. For them it was a matter of kill or die.

Helen watched him now from where she knelt, still stroking Buzz, in the glow of the stove. She treasured these evenings together. It was always dark when they came back from their tracking. Outside the cabin they would stamp their boots and brush the snow from each other's backs. Then one of them would bring in the skis and the rest of the gear from the snowmobile, while the other lit the lanterns and got the

334

stove going. They would keep their hats and gloves and jackets on until the cabin warmed up and the steam was rising off them. If the cell phone was working, Helen would check her voice mail and return any calls and then one of them would cook supper while the other started transferring the day's tracking notes into the computer.

Tonight, they'd eaten Helen's macaroni and cheese, which even though they had it at least three times a week Luke still insisted he adored. In a short while, when he'd finished entering the last of the notes, he would be heading home and Helen would feel the usual, lonely hollowing within her. And if she didn't at once busy herself with something, she would slide inexorably, almost from habit, into a pit of self-loathing and recrimination over Joel.

The stove spluttered. Outside, the blizzard sounded as if it was dying down. Luke clicked on Save and sat back.

'All done?'

'Uh-huh. Come and look.'

Helen got up and went to stand behind his chair, while he showed her on the screen what he'd done.

He had set up a new sequence of maps, showing all the locations where he and Helen had found 'scent posts' – places where the wolves regularly urinated to mark the borders of their territory as a warning to invaders. In other seasons, these were hard to find, but in the snow you could spot them easily and they were finding new ones every day.

His new map sequence showed how the wolves had established a clearly defined territory of about two hundred square miles which they patrolled every few days. Its most northern tip was the foot of Wrong Creek and it spread from there, south and east, to the western edge of Jordan Townsend's ranch.

Luke clicked up a new map and overlaid it.

'Look, this is funny. It's like, every weekend they go down to the Townsend place.'

'Well, of course they do. He's got that movie theater.'

Luke laughed and she suddenly realized that, all the time she'd been standing there, her hands had been resting on his shoulders.

'Maybe he puts on one of his g-girlfriend's movies for them.'

'Right and serves them bison burgers.'

'Those bison are real mean. If I were a wolf, I'd stick to deer.'

Helen tapped her hands lightly on his shoulders.

'Well. Nice work, professor.'

He tilted his head back and smiled up at her and she had a sudden urge to lean down and kiss his forehead and only just stopped herself in time.

'You'd better be getting home,' she said.

'I guess.'

His car was down on the road, about a half-mile below the lake, which was where Helen left her pickup too now that the snow had come. Some evenings, if it was late, she drove him down on the snowmobile.

'Want a lift?'

'It's okay, I'll ski.'

While he got himself ready, Helen went busily around tidying things, hoping to conceal her confusion over what she had felt when Luke looked up at her.

What kind of kiss, exactly, had she had in mind? Was it sisterly? Or motherly? Or was it something else entirely? She told herself not to be ridiculous. He was a friend, that was all. A friend, in whose company she felt easy, who – unlike Joel – never judged her or criticized, who'd taken care of her and hauled her back from the brink.

She knew how Luke felt about her. It was obvious from the way she sometimes caught him looking at her that he was a little in love with her. And there were times, she had to admit,

336

such as just now, when she felt something not wholly dissimilar for him. She missed the physical comfort of those times, when at her most despairing, after Joel's letter arrived, he had held her in his arms and let her weep.

But her emotions were still hopelessly shredded and raw. In the flash of a second, she could plummet from elation to despair. In any case, the idea of anything happening between them was absurd. He was ten years younger than she was, just a boy. God, when she was his age, at college . . . well, perhaps that wasn't such a good line of reasoning. In fact, she had dated men much older than she was now. One of them had been in his mid-thirties, almost twice her age. But, it was different that way around, when it was the guy who was older – just look at her father and Courtney. Though she was still having trouble with that.

Luke was at the door now, ready to go.

'What time in the morning?' he asked.

'Eight?'

'Okay. G-goodnight then.'

' 'Night, professor.'

The instant he opened the door, a pile of snow fell in on him, followed by a howling blast of wind. The blizzard hadn't died, as Helen had thought. It had simply muffled its sound by drifting snow right up the front of the cabin. Luke had to shove hard against the wind and all the snow that had fallen in to shut the door and when he'd done it he stood with his back to it, laughing and covered in snow.

'Back so soon?' Helen said.

Luke woke in total darkness and took a moment to remember where he was. He lay on his back, on the lumpy mattress of the top bunk, listening to the muted moan of the wind and wondering what had woken him.

He strained to hear the sound of Helen's breathing in the

bunk below, but all he could hear was the dog snoring and the occasional crackle of the stove. They had stacked it up before turning in and kept their clothes on inside their sleeping bags so as to be warm when it later burned out. He looked at the luminous dial of his watch. It was a little after three.

'Luke?' she whispered.

'Yes.'

'Are you okay up there?'

'Sure, I'm fine.'

The last of the logs shifted in the stove, showering the grate with cinders and briefly filling the cabin with an amber glow.

'I never thanked you,' she said.

'For what?'

'For everything. For looking after me.'

'You don't need to thank me.'

'Why have you never asked me about what happened?'

'I figured, if you w-wanted to tell me, you would.'

And now she did. And he listened, trying to picture places he'd never been and the face of this man she had loved, who Luke figured must be completely out of his mind to have left her. She talked in a level voice, almost matter-of-fact, though sometimes she paused and he could hear her swallow and knew she was fighting tears.

But she kept them at bay. Only when she got about halfway through telling him about the letter, the one Luke had found in the road and given her on the night Abe Harding shot the wolf, did her voice start to crack and he knew she was crying. But she kept on going, even while she told him about the woman that Joel must by now have married. Luke lay in his bunk, above her in the dark, saying nothing.

'I'm sorry,' she said, when she was done. 'I really thought I could do that without blubbering.' He could hear her sniffing and wiping her eyes.

'It's just that I thought this was it, you know? That he was the one. But there you go. You lose some, you lose some. I hope they'll be very happy.' She paused. 'Actually, I hope they rot in hell.'

She gave a little snuffling laugh. Luke wanted to tell her the guy didn't deserve her anyway and that she was well rid of him, but it wasn't his place to say it.

For a long time neither of them spoke. Down by the stove, Buzz was making little whimpering noises, chasing bears somewhere in a dream.

'What about you?' she said at last.

'How do you mean?'

'I mean, girlfriends and all that. I remember I saw you talking with that really pretty girl at the fair.'

'Cheryl. Oh, she's not a g-girlfriend. She's nice, b-but—'

'I'm sorry. It's none of my business.'

'N-no, I don't mind. It's just that, girls . . . Well, you know, with my s-stutter and all, it never k-kind of . . .'

He felt his cheeks coloring up like a child's and was glad she couldn't see him. He hadn't meant it to come out like that, or rather, not come out like that. He couldn't bear the idea that she might feel sorry for him, because it wasn't like that. He'd learned real early on in life that self-pity only made things worse.

He heard the rustle of her bedclothes and suddenly she was on her feet and her pale face was right beside him in the dark.

'Luke? Hold me. Please, hold me.'

Her voice was an urgent whisper, on the edge of tears. He sat up and pulled off his sleeping bag and slipped down from the bunk to stand beside her. She reached out and put her arms around him and he put his around her and held her head to his chest. And the feel of her body against him almost took his breath away.

'Y-y-you're . . .'

He blocked. He couldn't say it. She looked up at him,

339

though in the dark her face was only an impression, like the shadowed side of the moon. And still he couldn't say it, couldn't tell her that she was the only one he had ever loved or ever would love. Then he felt her arms release him and her hands reach up and softly take hold of his face. He saw the unfathomable pools of her eyes and her mouth lifting toward him. And he bowed his head and closed his eyes and at last, after all his long imagining, felt the touch of her lips.

She kissed his forehead as if in blessing, then lightly traced the tops of his cheeks and kissed the lids of his closed eyes. She rested her cheek against his and it was cool and damp and for a moment they stayed like that, quite still. Then he opened his eyes and kissed her face in the same way. He could taste the salt of her tears on her cheeks and in the corners of her lips.

And when at last their mouths met, he felt his whole body quake and he breathed the smell and the taste and the feel of her, drinking her down into his lungs as if he would willingly drown.

26

The Christmas bazaar and pie sale looked as if it was still going strong when Buck got into town. Feeding the cattle had taken so long, he'd worried it might be over, but the street outside the community hall was lined with parked cars and there were still folk arriving.

Hettie Millward and the other women who organized it seemed to have made more of an effort this year. They'd decorated the front porch and rigged up a Christmas tree with colored lights outside and with the sunshine and the fresh snow, it looked real pretty. Hettie had even managed to persuade Eleanor to get involved for the first time in years. She was in there now, at least that's what Buck was counting on.

He'd had a job getting her out of the house, what with her fretting all night about Luke being lost in the blizzard. She'd been about to call Craig Rawlinson to get a search party out when, just after breakfast, the boy had phoned to say he was fine and had been holed up with Helen Ross all night in her cabin.

What a waste, Buck thought. There was no accounting for the perverse way God sometimes chose to bestow his gifts.

He drove past the community hall and on up Main Street, slowing as he drove past Paragon to see if he could get a glimpse of Ruth, but the window was too cluttered. He parked a little short of Nelly's Diner and walked back, glancing casually around in case anyone was looking. There nearly always was, but today everyone seemed to be down the street at the bazaar.

Ruth was at the till, serving the schoolteacher, Nancy Schaeffer, when he came in. And when the bells on the door clanked, she looked up. He could tell she wasn't too pleased to see him.

'Morning!' he called out brightly to both of them.

'Hi, Buck,' said Nancy. 'Merry Christmas!'

'And a Merry Christmas to you.' He nodded and smiled at Ruth.

'Ruth.'

'Mr Calder.'

She turned right back to Nancy and they went on talking about some school thing. Buck strolled to the back of the store, pretending to browse. There were no other customers.

He hadn't seen or spoken with Ruth in over a month. She was wearing a tight brown sweater. She looked fabulous. At last Nancy was going. He called goodbye and the door clanked shut, with the same odd little echo Buck had heard when he came in.

'Buck, what the hell are you doing here?'

She was stalking back through the store toward him.

'And a Merry Christmas to you too.'

'Don't play games.'

'I'm not playing games.'

She stopped and stood scowling at him from a safe distance, with her arms folded. He held up his hands.

342

'Ruth, it's Christmas, for Christsake, when people buy each other gifts. This is a gift store. I'm allowed to be here.'

'Buck, in case the message hasn't gotten through that hat of yours, it's all over with us. Okay?'

'Ruthie . . .'

'No, Buck.'

'I miss you so bad . . .'

He moved toward her but she backed off. Suddenly there was a loud sneeze. It made Buck jump and he turned and for a moment couldn't see anyone. Then he looked down and saw a baby sitting in a little bouncy chair thing, staring back at him.

'Who the hell's that?'

'Don't you recognize your own grandson?'

'What's he doing here?'

'You don't know a thing do you? Kathy's helping Eleanor down at the bazaar. I'm babysitting.'

'Oh.'

The baby's steady stare made him uncomfortable. It was like he'd been caught red-handed.

'Now, go.'

'Listen, all I—'

'After all that's happened, I can't believe you'd do this.'

'What do you mean, "after all that's happened"?'

Ruth narrowed her eyes. 'You mean, she hasn't told you?'

'Told me what?'

'She knows everything, you stupid bastard! About us.'

'She can't—'

'She can. She does.'

'You *told* her?'

'I didn't need to. She knew anyway.'

'But you admitted it?'

The door clanked and they both looked around. Baby Buck mimicked the sound.

343

'Mrs Iverson!' Ruth called cheerily. 'How are you doing?' She looked back at Buck and said through her teeth, 'Go. Now.'

Buck left without saying goodbye, even to his grandson. He walked to the gas station to buy some cigars and lit one on the way to his car, thinking all the while about what Ruth had said. He was so distracted, he almost pulled out into the path of an eighteen-wheeler. The blast of its horn nearly gave him a heart attack and he dropped his cigar in panic and singed his pants.

Eleanor had never said a word. Not that they ever talked much anyway. But you'd think she might have mentioned it, Ruth being her business partner and all. There were so many questions he would have liked to ask Ruth and hadn't been able to because of the Iverson woman coming in. Like, how the hell did Eleanor find out? And how come she and Ruth were still in business together? It didn't make any goddamn sense at all.

He drove back out to the ranch, his mind flicking from one grim thought to another and settling where it usually did nowadays, with the wolves, who were to blame for everything.

He hadn't seen the old wolfer for a few days now and so when he got to where the road forked below the ranch, he bore left and kept on up toward Kathy's place.

Maybe Lovelace had some news to cheer him up.

The wolfer steered the snowmobile down through the trees and out into the open snow of the top meadow above the house. It was bumpy and it hurt his back which already ached from all the snow he'd had to shovel off the tent and then off the snowmobile. But he was used to aches and pains and they did nothing to dampen his spirits. It had been some years since he'd had to bivouac in such a blizzard and though it was

344

only a matter of having good gear and a little gumption, he was pleased he could still handle it.

More to the point, he now knew where the wolves were.

When the wind had died, around four in the morning, he'd heard them howl and when it got light, he'd found tracks, only a hundred yards from his tent. It was as if they'd heard he was there and had come to check him out. Now he knew what kind of terrain they were in, he was coming back to the trailer to work out a plan and pick up the things he would need for killing them.

Below him now, at the foot of the meadow, a row of black cows were feeding on the hay that had been scattered on the snow for them. Beyond them, Lovelace could see Buck Calder's car parked beside the Hicks', outside the house.

As he came onto the flatter land and veered toward the barn, he saw that the door of his trailer was open. Then, a second later, he saw a man step down out of it. It was Buck Calder. And now his son-in-law was climbing down too, shutting the door behind him. Hicks looked kind of sheepish, but Calder smiled and waved and waited while Lovelace steered the snowmobile up alongside them and stopped.

'Mr Lovelace. Good to see you.'

Lovelace turned off the engine.

'What are you doing in my trailer?'

'We were just looking for you, seeing if you were okay.'

Lovelace didn't say anything. He stared at Calder for a moment then got off the snowmobile and went to the trailer. As he passed them, he saw Hicks pull a face, like a naughty kid. Who the hell did they think they were, he thought, as he climbed inside. Snooping about like that, uninvited. He looked around, checking if they'd touched anything. It all seemed to be as he'd left it. He went back to the door and looked down at them.

'Don't do that again,' he said.

'We knocked and when there was no answer, we got worried that—'

'If I need your help, I'll ask.'

Calder held up his hands. 'Hey, I'm real sorry.'

'Yeah, sorry, Mr Lovelace,' Hicks chimed, like a parrot.

Lovelace nodded coldly.

'So how's it going?' Calder asked, all friendly, as if nothing had happened. 'Did you catch 'em yet?'

'When I'm ready to tell you, I will.'

And he shut the door in their faces.

Baby Buck was sitting on the edge of the kitchen table, while Kathy tried to zip him into his snowsuit. He wasn't enjoying it and was letting the whole world know. The poor little mite had a cold and his face was all red and streaming. Eleanor sat at the other end of the table, chopping onions.

It was Tuesday, the one evening in the week when Luke came home early and the only one when she made any real effort with the supper. They were having fish pie, for two good reasons: it was one of Luke's favorites and his father couldn't stand it.

The baby let out a piercing scream.

'He wants to stay with his grandma,' Eleanor said. 'Don't you, honey?'

'Hey, you can have him. Will you keep still, you little monster! Was I ever like this?' Kathy asked.

'Worse.'

'There's *worse*?'

She was just getting his gloves on when the headlights of a car panned across the kitchen windows. A few moments later, while the baby was gathering breath for more bawling, they heard Luke coming up the path to the house. He was whistling a tune. Eleanor had never heard him do that before.

'At least somebody's happy,' Kathy said.

346

The baby started crying again.

Luke came in and said hi and after he'd shed his hat and coat and boots and given Eleanor a kiss, he picked up little Buck and took him on a tour of the kitchen. The baby stopped crying at once.

'Want a job?' Kathy said.

'I've got one already.'

'One that has him out in blizzards all night,' Eleanor said.

'Mom, we were fine.'

Eleanor watched him waltzing the baby around while she finished the onions. It made her glow inside to see him so happy. Driving back from the bazaar, Kathy had told her people were starting to gossip about Luke and Helen Ross. Eleanor dismissed it as nonsense.

Luke handed little Buck back to Kathy and went off to his room and soon Kathy took the baby to the car and went home, leaving Eleanor alone with her cooking.

She had no idea where big Buck was. He was probably hiding somewhere, trying to work out how to play it when he came home. The thought made Eleanor smile.

Ruth had told her about him coming by this morning. The poor woman still couldn't quite fathom Eleanor's attitude. Betrayed wives were supposed to be vengeful about 'the other woman', even murderous. And Eleanor knew Ruth was still slightly suspicious of how calmly she had taken it all. That it seemed to threaten neither their friendship nor – more importantly – their business arrangements still clearly mystified her. Which, to Eleanor, made it all the more enjoyable.

In fact, Ruth's affair with Buck hadn't even been mentioned since the day Eleanor broke the news that she knew about it. There was really nothing more to be said. She sometimes felt a little ashamed of the way she had brought the matter up, asking Ruth, point blank, how long she'd been

347

sleeping with him. Eleanor hadn't been quite honest, for she was fairly sure the affair.had been already over by then.

To her credit, Ruth hadn't tried to deny a thing. But she did ask how Eleanor had found out.

'You were married once, weren't you?' Eleanor asked.

'Yes.'

'How long?'

'About five minutes.'

'Well, that's probably not long enough. But after awhile, you just kind of know about these things. And Ruth, I'm afraid to say, I've had a lot of practice.'

She spared her the details of how she'd found out this time. Of how, on that first day when she'd come into the shop and offered to get involved in the business, she'd found Ruth's scent oddly familiar and later realized it was the same she smelled when Buck came home and tiptoed fatuously across the bedroom, thinking she was asleep. Of how she'd heard his car that night outside Ruth's house and then found one of his cigars in the driveway.

'There's always some woman somewhere,' Eleanor went on. 'Sometimes several at the same time. Though often I don't know who. And frankly, Ruth, I don't really care anymore.'

'I can't believe that.'

'It's true. Of course, I used to care. And after I got over that, I'd care about people feeling sorry for me, when really it was Buck they ought to feel sorry for. But even that doesn't bother me any longer. People can think what they like.'

'Why do you stay with him?'

Eleanor shrugged. 'Where else would I go?'

Poor Ruth had been quite shaken. And even though Eleanor had assured her their business arrangement remained entirely unaffected, Ruth had treated her ever since with caution and respect. Back at the shop, after the bazaar, Ruth had told her in a nervous whisper, while Kathy was in the bathroom changing the baby, that Buck had been in and what they'd talked about.

So now he knew that Eleanor knew of their affair. And as she finished preparing supper, she allowed herself the smallest pang of pleasure over how he must now be feeling.

It was another hour before she heard his car. When he came in, she was busy laying the table. She glanced up and saw that he looked contrite and edgy and gratifyingly pale.

'Something smells good,' he said.

Eleanor smiled and told him they were having fish pie.

27

They had only kissed. Kissed and lain in each other's arms on her bunk and talked until dawn paled the drifted windows. That was all. Where was the wrong in that?

It was the question Helen had harassed herself with ever since Luke had gone home the previous evening and left her alone in the cabin with the nascent specter of her own guilt. So far, with varying degrees of success, she had refused to allow it substance. Her needs and Luke's, she kept insisting, had been equal. And if each had found comfort in what had happened, why not? How could some modest discrepancy of age and, all right, of innocence too, make it wrong?

She had almost managed to convince herself.

Joel once told her she must have majored in guilt rather than biology and that her true vocation should be the construction industry, so deftly did she build prisons for herself. Luke, it emerged, was the same.

In their huddled confession that night, she had told him of

the guilt she felt for her parents' loveless marriage. And Luke had then told her of his own for his brother's death. With much passion and to no effect whatsoever, they had assured each other how absurd their respective guilts were. The absurdity of other people's prisons was always so much easier to see.

Today, they had come to Great Falls to buy Helen a dress for her father's wedding. She was due to fly to Barbados the day after tomorrow. In a modest emulation of Caribbean weather, a chinook was blowing from the mountains and the snow was melting fast.

They came in separate cars and met as arranged, like furtive lovers, in the mall parking lot. Helen arrived early, anchoring in the gray ocean of slush, and for ten minutes sat watching the highway for Luke's Jeep. He was coming up from Helena after his therapy. Waiting for him, she started to worry that it might be awkward between them after what had happened. But when he arrived, he was sweet and natural and, albeit briefly, put his arm around her as they went into the mall.

All the stores were decked out with Christmas lights and glitter and the walkways of the mall rang with piped carols. All they could find anywhere were winter clothes and Helen was starting to wonder how much of a dash she would cut in Barbados in a parka and ski pants, when Luke spotted some- thing on a bargain rail. It was a simple, sleeveless yellow dress, in a size eight. She went into the fitting room, with no great enthusiasm, to try it on.

It was four months since she'd last seen herself properly in a mirror and it came as a shock. Her haircut had grown out, giving her the look of a poorly stuffed scarecrow. And she hadn't realized quite how much weight she'd lost. Her face was all cheekbones and in the harsh fluorescent light, her eyes looked ringed and cavernous. It was worse still when she took off her clothes. The skin was stretched so tightly over her ribs and her jutting hips that she fancied she could see through it to the bone. The dress had straps at the shoulder and she needed to try it on without a bra. Her breasts, when she unhooked it, seemed several sizes smaller. God, she thought, I look like one of Joel's famine victims. She pulled the dress quickly over her head to banish the sight.

Incredibly, it looked okay. It was too long and gaped slightly under the arms and she looked a little comical, all pale except for her wind-burnt face and the faded remains of a tan on her arms. But the color suited her. With a little make-up, or a lot, she might almost look passable.

Luke was waiting outside the entrance to the fitting room, studying his boots and looking a little uncomfortable while two young women nearby discussed the merits of a sweater one had tried on.

'Luke?'

He looked up and saw her and she walked toward him in her bare feet, feeling exposed and embarrassed, like a girl in her first party frock. She stopped in front of him and did a little self-conscious pirouette. When her eyes came back to him, he was frowning and shaking his head a little.

'No? You don't like it?'

'N-no, I mean, I do. It's just that—' He looked down for a moment and took a breath, as he did sometimes when he blocked, waiting for the words to come free. Then he looked up at her again.

'It's good,' he said simply.

But the way he smiled touched her heart.

Lovelace sniffed the night air like a wolf.

For the last hour he had been worried that the wind was shifting back around to the west and would suck his scent down into the canyon and over the creek where he'd set the carcass. If it did, he might as well pack up and go. But it had

352

held and steadied on a northerly and would be drifting the smell of the deer's blood down the canyon, exactly where he wanted.

The chinook had blown till early afternoon, hauling slate-gray clouds down from the mountains and sending them hurtling away over the plains. All morning the forest had dripped and the rocks streamed and you could hear the snow crack as it melted and shifted and settled again. Twice he had seen avalanches and he had heard the boom of several more, rolling like muffled thunder through the higher canyons. Thus rearranged, the world had frozen hard again.

It was nine o'clock. He'd been waiting nearly four hours.

He was lying on his belly in his sleeping bag, wedged under a high fissured shelf that ran along the wall of the canyon. Below him was a sheer drop of at least two hundred feet, with almost the same again above him on the overhang.

He'd had to slither like a lizard to get there but it was worth it, both for the shelter and for the view it gave him of the ice-crusted creek. The earth in the cave was dry and littered with shards of bone and the air smelled of mountain lion.

Through the rifle's nightscope now, he scanned the canyon again, letting its ghostly green circle of light travel slowly down the creek and the trail beside it which the wolves would likely use if they came. He saw a movement among the trees and his pulse quickened. But it was only a bobcat, picking its way among the snow-caked blowdown. As Lovelace watched, the cat sensed something and froze, its eyes glowing like head-lights in the altered aura of the scope. Then it moved rapidly off into the trees and was gone.

Lovelace panned the scope back up the creek until he found the slabbed island of rock where he'd laid out the young deer. The carcass hadn't been touched. He had shot it at dusk farther up the creek, then dragged it downstream, wading through the water in his rubber boots, so as not to leave any tracks. The rocks on the creek bed were slippery and the shallows treacherously iced. The effort had drained him and he'd had to keep stopping to get breath into his aching lungs.

On reaching the rock, he had carefully cut out the bullet, then opened the deer's belly and its throat so the blood ran into the water. Then he arranged the guts around it on the rock to help the scent carry down the canyon.

The chances of it working this first time were slim. He knew from tracks he'd found that morning that the wolves had been around here last night. But by now they might be twenty miles away. He could lie here every night for weeks on end and still draw a blank. And even if they did show, the shot was far from easy.

He'd measured it when he found the place yesterday. The creek was about two hundred and seventy yards from the foot of the cliff, which was a fair enough shot in daylight. At night it was a long one. He had sighted in the rifle to allow for the right amount of bullet drop but the angle made it tricky. The crosswind made it trickier still. It was blowing a good twenty miles an hour. He'd have to allow for at least two feet of drift.

Lovelace was almost sure the woman and the boy weren't out night-tracking, and if they were, they couldn't get up here without his hearing their snowmobile or seeing its light coming up the canyon. But there was always a chance that someone else might be around to hear the pop of the silencer. Maybe, after all, he should have set snares instead.

For the first three hours, he'd kept himself alert. But now he was tired and his feet were getting cold. He put down the rifle, resting his head on his elbow, and closed his eyes

When he opened them again and looked at his watch, he saw a whole hour had passed. Cursing himself, he snatched up the rifle and switched on the nightscope. The deer hadn't been touched. But as he panned a fraction to the right Lovelace saw a shadow step right into his invisible spotlight of green.

354

There were two of them, three now, four. Trotting in single file around a bend in the trail, their eyes glowing as though there were a phantom fluorescence burning in their skulls. The one in front must be almost white, he figured, though in the scope it looked a kind of milky green. From its size and prime position and from the height of its tail, Lovelace guessed it was the alpha female. He could see the collar on her neck and on the neck of the one behind her too. The other two were slighter, not quite full-grown.

Lovelace's heart started to thump. He couldn't believe his luck. Silently, he slid the safety and switched on the laser sight.

According to Calder, there were eight in the pack, so he kept his eyes on the bend of the trail, waiting for the others to show. But they didn't. It was unusual, he thought, for them all not to be hunting together, but at least he had two to go for. He was going to leave the collared wolves until he'd killed all the others. So long as their signals kept chiming, the woman would likely think the whole pack was okay. Also – if he could only find the damned frequencies – they could lead him to the others.

The wolves stopped now, where the trail dipped through a mound of willow scrub, about twenty yards downstream of the deer. The white one stood quite still with her nose raised and Lovelace worried that she might have picked up his scent on the wind. He settled the red dot of the laser on her chest. Maybe he should forget about the collar and take her now. Trouble was, the two uncollared wolves were largely masked by the willow. He'd only end up scaring them away. But now the white one was coming on again, more slowly, and the others followed.

It took her ten minutes of pacing to and fro along the bank to decide it was safe to cross the ice and water to the altar of rock where the deer lay. Lovelace could have shot them each a dozen times, but he waited and watched. He wanted them all on the carcass and to eat enough of it for anyone finding it to think they'd killed it.

Only when they had feasted, did he get ready to shoot. The two uncollared wolves were side by side, their heads deep in the deer. Lovelace leveled the laser dot on the nearer one who was showing more chest. The wolf lifted its head to swallow. Lovelace could see a green gleam of blood on its muzzle.

He pulled the trigger.

The impact of the bullet lifted the wolf backward, clean off the rock and into the water. He'd only reckoned on getting one. The others, he thought, would spook and run. But they didn't. They simply stopped feeding and stood staring down at the one he'd shot, who was now out of sight behind the rock. The old wolfer quickly levered another bullet into the chamber.

He shot the second clean through the head and it dropped stone dead beside the deer. This time, though, the other two wolves leapt like singed cats. In a flash they were splashing through the water, scrambling the icy bank and crashing off through the trees.

It took him almost an hour to wade down the creek and drag the dead wolves back through the water by their hind feet. They were only pups, but they still weighed sixty or seventy pounds apiece and after loading them on the back of the snowmobile and driving up to the mine, he could barely summon the strength to climb off.

He dumped them beside the overgrown airshaft he'd found the previous day and carefully levered aside the rotting pine logs that had once been laid to cover it.

One at a time, he hoisted the wolves over the edge of the shaft and lowered them gently in by their tails. He listened as they tumbled down in a clatter of rocks and landed with a distant splash in the belly of the mine below.

He stood there a moment, listening to the silence.

'Do you think, Joseph, their life is the same as ours? I mean, what it's made of, that little flicker or spirit or whatever it is, inside them. Do you think it's the same as what we have inside us?'

'No, dear, of course it's not. How could it be?'

The wind had dropped. It was starting to snow again. By dawn his tracks would be gone.

It was still hard to believe she was going away.

Her flight was due to leave at six o'clock the following morning. Despite her protest, Luke had insisted he was going to drive her to the airport. Her bag lay already packed on her bunk.

Her father had sent her a brochure which showed the hotel they were all going to be staying in. It was called the Sandpiper Inn and it looked like heaven. There were palm trees and lawns going right down to the beach and this amazing, pale blue ocean, even better than the one in his dream, which he'd never told her about. The dining room was open at the sides and surrounded by exotic plants. He'd been trying not to fantasize too much about being there with her.

With such an early start in the morning, he should have gone home long ago, but he couldn't bear to and was pretending to be doing something important on the computer. Helen was sitting across from him on the other side of the table, biting her lip and concentrating hard on her sewing, so it was easy to look at her. Sometimes she looked up and caught him, but it didn't seem to bother her. The new haircut she'd gotten in Great Falls after buying the dress made her look younger.

She'd already taken the dress in at the sides and was nearly done shortening the hem. Earlier, after supper, she'd tried it on with the new shoes she'd bought and stood on a chair in the middle of the cabin while he pinned it up for her. It took forever, partly because he'd never done anything like that before but mostly because neither of them could stop laughing. It seemed kind of a funny thing to be doing in a mountain cabin in the dead of winter. To make things worse, Helen deliberately kept leaning one way, then the other, and would then complain that he hadn't pinned it straight.

She would be gone ten whole days.

They'd worked it all out. While she was away, Luke was to stay up at the cabin to look after Buzz and keep the tracking going. Helen said if he was good, she would allow him a couple of hours off on Christmas Day. His parents were okay about it and Helen had cleared things with Dan Prior who said it was fine, provided it was all 'unofficial', which Helen said really meant, provided it didn't cost him anything. Dan had offered to take him flying one day next week and do some aerial tracking.

She was finished now and broke the thread with her teeth. She held the dress up to inspect it.

'I can't get over how clever you were, finding this. The only summer dress in the whole of Montana.'

'I guess I was born to shop.'

She laughed. Buzz suddenly started barking loudly. He'd probably sniffed some passing animal outside the cabin. It often happened. Helen told him to hush. She got up and took the dress over to the bed, folding it for packing.

'Aren't you going to try it on?'

'You want me to?'

Luke nodded. She shrugged

'Okay.'

He turned away and pretended to study the computer screen, as he'd done before when she changed, as he always did. He'd never found it easy, listening to her taking off her clothes, picturing it and feeling aroused and ashamed at the same time. Now, since the kiss, it was a kind of exquisite

358

torture, almost more than he could take. It was all so con-fusing. How was he supposed to know what she felt about him?

He had next to no experience in these matters, but he wasn't dumb. He could tell from the way she'd kissed him that they were already more than just good friends. But what now? What was he supposed to do?

Maybe when they'd been lying with each other afterward, he should have taken the lead and done something. Maybe she'd expected him to. But he'd never done it before and wasn't sure how it all got to happen. The result was nothing had happened, then or since, and Luke had a dismal, almost desperate feeling that, now she was going away, it never would.

He heard the clunk of her new shoes now, coming up behind him.

'Will you do me up?'

She turned her back to him as he stood up. When she'd tried the dress on earlier she had kept her bra on, but he could see that now she'd taken it off, like she'd done in the store. He fastened the zipper and fought the urge to kiss her bare shoulders above it. She walked away to where Buzz was lying by the stove and turned and struck a little self-mocking pose, waiting for the verdict.

'Well?'

'You're so b-beautiful.'

She laughed. 'No, Luke, I think not.'

'It's true.'

He took from his pocket the present he'd bought her. The woman in the store had put it in a little box for him and wrapped it prettily in shiny gold paper. He stepped closer and held it out to her.

'What's this?'

'It's nothing. Just . . . Here.'

She took it and he watched while she unwrapped it. Inside the box, carefully folded in white tissue, was a little silver wolf on a silver chain. She laid it on the palm of her hand, staring down at it.

'Oh, Luke.'

'It's just a little thing—'

She was still staring at it, with a strange look on her face. Maybe she didn't like it, he thought.

'They'll ch-change it. I mean, if you d-don't—'

'No, no, I love it.'

'Anyway.' He smiled and nodded. 'M-merry Christmas.'

'I didn't get you anything.'

'That doesn't matter.'

'Oh, Luke.'

She put her arms around his neck and clung to him and he held her, feeling her bare back under his hands. He bent and gently kissed her shoulder.

'I wish you weren't going.'

'I don't want to go. I'll miss you.'

'I love you, Helen.'

'Oh, Luke. Don't say that.'

'But I do.'

He held her away from him now so he could look into her eyes.

She frowned. 'I'm too old for you. It isn't right. The other night, I should never have—'

'W-why isn't it right? You're not much older than me. W-what does it matter anyhow?'

'I don't know, but—'

'You still love J-Joel?'

'No.'

'He hurt you. I could never hurt you.'

'But I . . .' She stopped.

'What?'

'I might hurt you.'

They looked at each other for a long time. Her mouth was slightly open. His whole body sang for her. He drew her toward him and felt the touch of her breasts against him and he kissed her. For an instant, he thought she was going to pull away, but she didn't. He felt her mouth soften and open. She took a little gasp of air and he felt her fingers tighten on his arms.

'I don't care,' he breathed.

An hour later, when they said their goodbyes and Luke left for home, it was snowing heavily. Had he looked, he might still have been able to decipher the half-filled footprints outside the cabin window. But his head was soaring elsewhere with his heart.

28

Courtney Dasilva was as good at being a bride as she was at everything else. She was the kind of bride that makes grown men swoon and less charitable souls – among whom Helen, with only a modicum of shame, counted herself – feel like throwing up in envy.

The dress, an off-the-shoulder creation in ivory satin, was sculpted to afford a tasteful yet tantalizing glimpse both of bridal knee and cleavage. It had been made, at mind-searing expense, by an Italian designer on Madison Avenue whose name had everyone oohing and aahing but to Helen meant nothing whatsoever. The overall effect suggested someone had put dear Courtney in a blender, then poured her into the dress like a banana daiquiri. She was the cream and even a vacationing Martian would have recognized Helen's father, with his permanent dreamy grin, as the cat who was at it.

They were married on Christmas morning, to give the couple, and those special guests who'd flown in early, a few days to get their tans in order. The ceremony, conducted with a deft mix of mirth and solemnity by the Reverend Winston Glover, took place in a flower-clad gazebo overlooking the bay. Over the rims of their champagne glasses afterward, they watched a Barbadian Santa Claus come skidding over the turquoise water on a jetski. He parked on the beach and strode with dripping, bare legs among them, wishing everyone a merry Christmas and handing out gifts. They were wrapped in paper from Saks Fifth Avenue where they had been carefully selected for each guest by Courtney herself. Helen's was a case of cosmetics. In fake lizardskin.

There were twenty guests and, apart from her sister Celia, Bryan and their children, the only ones Helen knew were her father's younger brother, Garry, and his serial-bore of a wife, Dawn. Helen and Celia had spent most of the past three days avoiding them, a custom at which they were skilled.

Garry had never been able quite to grasp the role of uncle. Since their early teens, he had always flirted with them, kissing them on the lips instead of the cheek when he greeted them and making suggestive remarks, which Dawn, for some elusive reason, seemed to find hugely amusing. Privately, the sisters always referred to them as Ego (Eyes Glaze Over) and Grope.

It was good to see Celia again, and to have time alone with her, for Bryan spent most of the day being the dutiful dad to Kyle and Carey. He was always off swimming or sailing or waterskiing with them, while the sisters lazed on their recliners, reading and talking. Apart from the occasional stroll to the sea to cool off, the most strenuous thing either had done was wave to Carl, the handsome young beach waiter, for another rum punch.

It hadn't occurred to Helen, of course, to bring a swimsuit, so she had bought one in the hotel gift store, a rash, black bikini. Celia had taken one look at her in it and announced a personal mission to fatten Helen up. For the first couple of days, she was forever ordering cookies and sandwiches and ice creams and forcing Helen to eat them. At dinner she would veto anything under a million calories and kick her slyly under the table if she didn't clean her plate. Thanks more to Helen's tan than the few extra pounds she'd gained, the campaign seemed now to have eased a little.

The yellow dress was much admired, though the only remark that stuck was from Courtney, who observed how 'comfortable' it looked.

At the end of a hard day's reclining, the sisters would take a leisurely swim to a small pontoon anchored two hundred yards from the shore and sit there, dangling their legs in the balmy water to watch another extravagant sunset. It became their evening ritual and the only concession they made on Christmas Day, with the wedding party still going strong on shore, was to swim out clutching glasses and a bottle of champagne.

'You don't like her, do you?' Celia said, pouring it.

'Courtney? She's okay. I don't know her.'

'I like her.'

'Good.'

'And, you know? I think she really loves him.'

'Whatever the hell that means.'

Helen always played the cynic with Celia and such a remark would normally elicit some gentle reproof. But Helen had told her two nights ago about Joel's letter and perhaps that was why she now made no reply. The silence soon had Helen feeling a little ashamed. She looked at her sister and smiled.

'Sorry. Sour grapes, I guess.' She sipped her champagne.

'It'll happen,' Celia said simply.

Helen laughed. 'What me? "My prince will come," you mean?'

'I know it.'

'You *know* it.'

364

'I do.'

'Well, that makes two of you. Our new stepmother told me last night she was sure I was going to go back to Montana and get swept off my feet by Marlboro Man.'

'What did you say?'

'I told her he'd died of cancer.'

'Helen, you're terrible.'

'Actually, I already met him.'

Celia didn't say anything. Helen stirred the darkening water with her legs. You could still see the anchor chain curving down to the sandy bottom. A shoal of small, silvery fish was swirling around it. She turned and saw Celia staring at her, wide-eyed and waiting.

'I hate it when you look at me like that.'

'Well, you can't just leave it at that.'

'Okay, he's tall. And dark. And slim. And he has the most beautiful green eyes you ever saw. He's the son of a big rancher and he's sweet and kind and caring. And he's completely besotted with me.'

'Helen, that's—'

'And he's eighteen years old.'

'Oh. Well—'

'"Well,"' Helen mimicked. Celia had her prim schoolmarm face on, always guaranteed to bring out the worst in Helen.

'I mean, is it . . .' Celia went on, still searching for something appropriate to say. 'Did you—'

'Did I fuck him?'

'Helen! You know perfectly well I didn't mean that.'

'Well, the answer's no, I didn't.' She paused. 'Yet.'

'Why the heck do you always assume I'm going to be shocked by things like that? Am I really such a tight-assed, straight-laced bitch? Is that how you see me?'

'No, of course I don't.' She reached out and put a conciliatory arm around her sister's shoulders. 'I'm sorry.'

365

They sat in silence a moment watching the horizon. The rind of the sun was giving a final fiery blaze as it dipped behind the indigo edge of the ocean.

'I mean, why are we here?' Celia said at last.

'Hey, sis, that's the big question.'

Celia exploded, shoving Helen's arm away. 'Fuck it, Helen, will you ever stop mocking me!'

The champagne bottle toppled and spilled. Helen had never seen her sister so angry. She'd certainly never heard her use that word before.

'Hey, I'm sorry.'

'I mean, I know you think Bryan and I are just boring, narrow-minded little yuppies and that you're the one who really lives, who's always out there on the edge, where it really matters, doing all these dangerous things—'

'I don't think that. Really, I don't—'

'Yes you do. And it's always, like, you're the only one who has real feelings, the only one who knows about passion and pain, the only one who suffered when Mom and Dad broke up and I'm just Little Miss Goody Two-Shoes, always smiling, with my nice little family and home and my nice little life. But it's not like that, Helen. Sometimes, the rest of us feel and get hurt too, you know?'

'I know, I know.'

'Do you? Two years ago, I had breast cancer.'

'You *what*?'

'Don't worry, it's fine. I caught it early, I'm all clear.'

'My God, Celia. You never said—'

'Why should I? You don't have to wallow in it. You get on with your life. That's the difference between us. I only told you now to make you see that you don't have some sort of monopoly on pain. So, please. Don't expect us all to feel so darned sorry for you the whole time.'

'I don't.'

'You do. You really do. It's like you think you've got this tragic destiny or something. But it's bullshit. Things didn't work out with Joel and that's very sad. But maybe it wasn't supposed to work out. In fact, maybe you're darned lucky to have found it out now. Mom and Dad lost nineteen years of their lives finding out.'

Helen nodded. She was right. About everything.

'You're only twenty-nine years old, Helen. What the hell's the problem?'

Helen shrugged and shook her head. She was close to tears, not of self-pity, but of shame. About Celia having had cancer, about every other item of truth she'd spoken. Celia seemed to sense she'd touched a nerve. She softened and smiled and it was her turn now to put an arm around Helen. Helen laid her head on her sister's shoulder.

'I can't believe you never told me.'

'Why go worrying everybody? I'm okay.'

'They cut it out?'

'Yeah. Look.'

She pulled down the top of her swimsuit. There was a small pink scar below her left nipple.

'Neat, huh? Bryan says it's sexy.'

'You're amazing.'

Celia laughed. She covered herself again and picked up the champagne bottle. There was still a little left, but neither of them wanted it. She set it down and put her arm around Helen's shoulders again. The air was growing cooler.

'What's his name?'

'Who?'

'Marlboro Man Junior.'

'Luke.'

'Luke.'

'Uh-huh.'

'Does he have cool hands?'

367

'He has beautiful hands.'

'What about his body?' Celia said in a dirty voice. 'Is that beautiful too?'

'Yup.'

They both laughed.

'He gave me this.' She showed Celia the little silver wolf. She had worn it around her neck ever since he gave it to her.

'It's pretty.'

Celia cradled her, stroking her hair, as Helen had seen her do with her children. In silence, they watched a pelican come gliding in to land beneath the palm trees farther along the beach.

Celia said, 'You know, when I said just now, why are we here, I meant, what are we doing right now, here in Barbados?'

'What?'

'The wedding, for heavensake. Courtney's twenty-five, Dad's, what, fifty-six? Okay? What's all the fuss about? If they make each other happy. You know he's become a Buddhist?'

'Dad! A Buddhist? You're kidding.'

'No. They both are.'

'She works for a bank, for heavensake! She really turned him into a Buddhist? Oh, boy. Does Mom know?'

Celia laughed. 'That he's gone *woo-woo*? Absolutely not. But seriously, Helen. Courtney's the best thing that ever happened to him. You know what he said to me last night? He said, "Courtney has given me the secret of life."'

'Is he going to share it with us?'

'He said, she's taught him to "*be*".'

'To be what?'

'Don't joke. It's important. Just to *be*. To live in the moment. And you know what? She's dead right. And if anyone in the whole world needs to do that, it's you.'

'You think so?'

'I *know* it. So. As your sister, therapist and Buddhist counselor, I say, give yourself a break. Have a little fun. Just live in the moment and let things be. Go back to Luke and, well, you know . . .'

'Fuck him?'

'Helen, you're impossible.'

Helen's room was on the end of a long, two-story building. It had a balcony with a view of the bay. That night, after the party was over, she left the doors open and lay listening to the swish and draw of the waves on the beach. She toyed with the silver wolf around her neck while she thought about her sister.

It had been a revelation. Helen felt guilty for having always underestimated her and a little daunted at finding herself so accurately understood. What Celia had said about her 'tragic destiny' and self-indulgent wallowing had the cold truth of a scalpel.

As to her advice about Luke, Helen was less sure. Celia had offered it flippantly, but Helen knew she meant it. The problem was, it was based on only half the picture. It took account of Helen's needs, but not Luke's.

In all Helen's relationships with men, until now, *she* had always been the one waiting to get hurt and rejected. It seemed to be her life's allotted role. And, without fail, it happened, time and again. It was probably self-fulfilling, she thought. Men seemed to sense these things. Now, though, with Luke, all this had changed.

Perhaps it was simply because of his age, she didn't know, but she had not the slightest foreboding that he would hurt or reject her, only the other way around. Yet when she had tried to warn him, he had told her he didn't care. So why should she? Was it not enough simply to love and be loved? For she did love him, she knew, and not simply for rescuing her from despair. She loved him for himself, but in a way that was new to her and oddly liberating.

Furthermore, to her own surprise, she found that she wanted him, physically, almost as much as he clearly wanted her.

On that last night in the cabin, she had let him unzip her dress and kiss her breasts and, instead of being sensible and gently stopping him, she had wantonly unbuttoned his shirt and led him to the bed. And deliberately blocking all admonishing thought, she had guided his hand between her legs and unbuckled his belt and held him, hot and hard, in her hands. And he'd come in a rush and then been all ashamed and she'd kissed and cradled him and told him not to be. It was beautiful, she'd whispered, and wonderful for a woman to feel so wanted.

Outside now, the palm trees stirred and clattered and the rhythm of reggae music floated on the warm breeze from a party somewhere along the bay. Helen turned on her side and shut her eyes, wishing Luke was lying there with her and picturing him, three thousand miles away, in the cold and the snow until she drifted into a dreamless sleep.

Luke had never heard more than a few bars of opera in his life, usually on public radio when he was looking for another station. In general, he had nothing against classical music. Some of it was okay. But the idea of people singing to each other instead of talking had always seemed to him a little dumb. Sometimes they talked as well, which only made it funnier when they burst into song again.

Since he'd been staying on his own in the cabin, he had gotten into the habit of putting on some music when he came back from tracking. Normally he chose one of the albums Helen normally played, Sheryl Crow, Van Morrison or Alanis Morissette, which all somehow made him feel she was there. But today, looking for something different, he had found her box of opera discs and out of simple curiosity put on the first that came to hand, *Tosca*.

He lit the lanterns, got the stove going and put some snow on to melt for a hot drink. After a whole week, being with Buzz in the cabin almost seemed normal, though scarcely a minute went by when he didn't think about Helen. She had called her voice mail on Christmas Day and left him a long message, telling him lots of things about the wedding and her new stepmother. She'd ended by saying how much she missed him and wishing him a merry Christmas.

Christmas at the Calder ranch had been about as merry as it ever managed to be. His older sister Lane had gone to her in-laws, so it was just Kathy and Clyde and Luke's parents. His father was in a bad mood and locked himself away in his office. The women talked in the kitchen and Clyde got drunk and fell asleep in front of the TV. Luke spent most of the time playing with the baby, until he felt he could make an excuse of having to feed Buzz and check Helen's voice mail and escaped back up to the cabin. He'd played her message back a dozen times.

She hadn't called since. He checked for messages again now, but there was only one from Dan Prior. They were going flying in the morning and Dan wanted him at the airfield by seven. He also said he'd at last got the results of the DNA test on the young collared male and that they were interesting because they showed he had different genes from the others, which meant he was a disperser.

By the time Luke had made himself some tea and had a piece of his mother's Christmas cake, the cabin had warmed up and the opera was in full swing. The Italian lady, who sounded the sort you didn't mess with, was all worked up about something and really letting rip. Even though Luke couldn't understand a word, he found himself enjoying it.

He took off his parka and had just sat down on Helen's bunk to untie his boots when he heard a note which, at first, made him think someone in the orchestra had goofed. Or

371

maybe the CD player was on the blink. Then it stopped. Buzz had clearly heard it too and seemed oddly excited.

'It's *Tosca*,' Luke confided, going back to his boots. 'In Italian.'

It was only when he heard the sound a second time that he recognized it. He went to the window and looked out. The first stars were just starting to show in a clear, pink sky. There was still enough light for him to see the wolf.

It was the alpha female. She was at the edge of the forest on the far side of the frozen lake where once, what now seemed a lifetime ago, Luke had spied on Helen. The wolf's white coat stood out against the dark of the trees. He could see her collar quite clearly and, as he looked, she lifted her head and howled. It was different from every other howl he'd heard, starting with a series of barks, just like a dog's. Luke quickly went to fetch Helen's binoculars.

Buzz was all in a lather. He gave a little whimper and Luke told him to hush, though it probably didn't matter because the Italian lady was singing loud enough to drown out everything. Luke gently turned down the lanterns and decided to try and get a better view by gently opening the door a little. He'd barely opened it an inch when Buzz pushed past him. Before Luke could get a hand to him, the dog was outside and heading hell for leather down toward the lake. Luke stepped out after him.

'Buzz! No!'

But there was no point in yelling. The wolf stopped her howling and stood quite still, with her tail held high, watching the dog draw near. Buzz was probably a goner anyway, but if the whole pack was there, they would surely tear him to shreds.

Through the glasses, Luke quickly scanned the trees. If the others were there, they weren't yet showing themselves. He started running down the slope, but he broke through the snow to his knees. There was no way he could get down there fast enough to be of any use. He struggled to his feet and looked again through the glasses.

Buzz was almost across the ice of the lake now and the wolf was still standing there waiting for him. What the hell was the dog doing? It wasn't like he was angry or anything, more like he was going to greet an old friend. He was bounding up the far slope now, only about ten yards below the wolf and suddenly the wolf started slowly wagging her tail. Buzz slowed and went the last few yards getting lower and lower until he was slithering on his belly. And when he got to her, he flipped right over and lay on his back beneath her and the wolf just kept on waving her tail to and fro like a flag, looking down her nose at him.

Luke was waiting for her to pounce and rip the dog's throat out. But she didn't. She just watched Buzz grovel. He was hoisting his muzzle and licking at her, as Luke had seen the wolf pups do in the summer, when they were begging food from the adults. Surely he knew he was more likely to be a meal than get one?

Then suddenly the wolf went down, flattening her chest to the snow and putting her head down on her outstretched paws, still wagging her tail. Luke couldn't believe it. She wanted to play. And as soon as Buzz got the message, she was off, running in teasing circles around him, her tail tucked comically under her and the dog trying in vain to catch her. Then the wolf stopped and crouched down again and Buzz did the same and then one of them made a move and off they went again, only this time it was the wolf's turn to do the chasing.

They took turns like this for several minutes and soon Luke was laughing so much he had to sit down in the snow and prop his elbows on his knees to keep the glasses steady.

Then, abruptly, the wolf veered away and headed for the

trees. Buzz stood there a moment, looking a little lost. Luke got up and called him, but the poor animal was having too much fun and, instead, off he went in hot pursuit and vanished into the forest.

Behind, in the cabin, *Tosca* boomed on regardless. Night was falling fast. Suddenly, the wolf's game didn't seem so funny anymore.

The wolfer heard the music too. He was higher up the valley, on his way to the place where he'd killed the third wolf on Christmas Day.

For several days, he'd followed the boy's tracks, taking care to place his skis and poles precisely inside them, so that only a skilled trail reader such as he would know that more than one had passed that way.

There was a pleasing irony about being led to the wolves by one who was seeking to save them. Before, when the woman was around, Lovelace had thought it too risky. Some of these biologist folk could be pretty smart. The boy was only an amateur, but he wasn't bad. In fact, he hardly missed a thing.

Lovelace could always see where he had stopped to pick up scat or check out a scent mark or something. He had to be careful in case the boy ever doubled back, but it hadn't happened yet and even if they came face to face, he wouldn't guess what the wolfer was up to. Most likely, he'd just think him some mad old buzzard out for a walk in the woods. Better, though, to stay unseen.

The boy's work pattern was pretty much the same as when the woman was around. He worked the same hours, went night-tracking on the same nights and was doing the same kind of work, backtracking to find kill sites and taking samples from the carcass. Not once, so far, had he or the woman returned to the same site. And it was this simple fact that had gotten Lovelace his third wolf.

A pack of wolves could strip a carcass at a single sitting, leaving only scraps for the ravens and coyotes. Occasionally, though, for some reason, they might leave it half eaten or cache chunks of meat beneath the snow and come back later for another meal. It was a kill like this that Lovelace had been hoping to find and on Christmas Eve, unwittingly, the boy had led him to one.

It was an old bull elk. The boy had done what he always did, pulled a couple of teeth, sawed himself some bone and then left. Lovelace found where the wolves had cached some of the meat and set foot-snares on the likely approaches. He'd have preferred to use neck-snares, but even if you crimped a stop on them, they could still sometimes strangle a wolf and he didn't want to risk killing the collared ones yet.

The place was a little too close for comfort to the woman's cabin but Lovelace figured it was worth a try. He spent the night, camped a mile downwind and when he skied back in at dawn, he found Santa Claus had been real generous, leaving him not just one wolf, but a pair: a female pup and the young, collared male.

They cowered, watching him furtively while he took off his skis and pulled his ax and two black sacks from his pack. As he came toward them, neither one dared look him in the eye.

'Hey, wolf,' Lovelace crooned to the pup in a soothing singsong. 'Ain't you a pretty young thing? Ain't you just?'

He stopped a little way short of her, for a cowering wolf could sometimes make a lunge. He raised the ax above his head and as he did so, the pup looked up at him and something in her golden eyes made him hesitate. But only for a moment. He slammed his mind shut to whatever it was that he'd seen there and with two swift blows, cleaved her skull.

With her paws still twitching, he quickly wrapped her head in one of the sacks, so her blood wouldn't stain the snow. He took the snare off her leg and stood over her, coiling the wire in his hands, his quickened breath rising in clouds around him. The caw of a raven grated the silence of the forest dawn and the wolfer lifted his eyes and saw two black shapes circling above him in the scaled, fish-belly silver of the sky.

He looked down at the collared wolf.

It was half turned away, watching him from the corner of its eye. It was older, two or three years old, Lovelace figured. It was bleeding heavily from where the wire of the snare had worked into its front leg in its struggle to get free. Once he had killed it, the collar would start transmitting a different signal which would be sure to raise suspicion. Lovelace could smash the thing and get rid of it, so the signal would simply disappear. But that might worry the boy too and certainly worry the woman when she came back. It might make them change the way they worked, start doing things he couldn't predict.

It was a sorry affair, on Christmas Day of all days, to look a gift wolf in the mouth, but he'd decided to leave the three collared ones till last and he was going to stick to that. Their turn would come.

He threw his second sack over the wolf's head and roped its muzzle, so it couldn't bite him. Then he sat astride it to pin it down while he loosened the snare. The wire was buried to the bone above the wolf's left paw. He could see where the animal had gnawed at himself to get free. Another hour or two and he might well have bitten his own foot off. Lovelace had seen it happen before.

It took him awhile to pull the wire from the wound but he managed it. Then he untied the rope, stood clear and pulled off the sack. The wolf scrambled to its feet and fled into the trees, limping badly as it went. Just before it disappeared, it stopped and looked back at him for a moment, as if making a mental note.

'Merry Christmas,' Lovelace called.

376

The meat caches were untouched. There was still a chance the wolves might be back. He reset the snares, then took the dead wolf directly to the mine and sent her down the shaft to join her brothers.

Three dead, five to go.

That was two days ago. Since then, he'd checked the snares at dawn and dusk and each time found them empty. The place by now was too spoiled by his scent and it was time to remove them. He was on his way to do that, when he heard the music.

He stopped to listen and in that same moment heard the wolf bark and start to howl along with it. It was an unlikely duet for a twilit forest. Then he heard the boy calling the dog and sensed something was wrong.

Quite how wrong, Lovelace didn't discover until half an hour later when he got near to the kill site and heard the yelping. It didn't sound like a wolf and when he found it in his flashlight beam, it didn't look like one either.

The dog had run into the same snare that had snagged the wolf pup two days ago. It must only just have happened for he was still flailing around like a thing possessed, tightening the wire on his paw. Then the ugly mutt saw him and started wagging its tail.

Lovelace quickly killed the flashlight. Likely the boy was already out looking for it and the tracks would lead him right here. If he was anywhere near, he'd already have heard the yelping. Maybe it would be best to get the hell out of it. But then the boy would find the snares and the whole damn thing would be blown. The wolfer cursed himself. He should never have risked using snares. Who'd have guessed he'd catch the damn dog?

Then he heard the boy calling somewhere in the forest below him. Peering down through the trees, he caught a glimpse of a moving flashlight. If the dog barked now, he was in trouble.

There was only one thing to do. He clicked the bindings of his skis and stepped out of them. The dog gave a little whine.

'Hey, dog,' he said, in the same gentle singsong he used when walking up to kill a trapped wolf. 'There's a good dog, now. There's a good old dog.'

29

She looked for him as she came out of the gate behind the other passengers and saw him standing in front of the giant stuffed bear, exactly where Dan had been waiting when she had first arrived.

He was wearing his hat and jeans and boots, with the collar of his old tan wool jacket turned up, and it made Helen smile to herself that he looked every inch the young cowboy her sister had imagined. He stared right at her and for a moment didn't seem to recognize her.

'Luke?'

'Hey!'

They walked toward each other and suddenly Helen had a flutter of nerves. She didn't know whether to throw her arms around him or what. Perhaps it would embarrass him. They stopped and stood shyly facing each other, with the crowd streaming past. A couple beside them were kissing and hugging and wishing each other a happy new year.

'Y-y-your hair's gone all b-blond.'

She shrugged self-consciously and put a hand through it.

'Yeah. It's the sun.'

'It looks nice.'

She couldn't think what to say. It was already too late to embrace him, so she just stood there, grinning inanely.

'Shall I t-take your bag?'

'Oh, no, it's okay.'

He took it anyway. 'Is th-this all there is?'

'Yep, that's all.'

'Shall we . . .?'

'Yeah, sure. Let's go.'

They didn't say another word all the way to the parking lot.

The wind was whipping snow from the mounds left by the plow, spinning it in swirls between the rows of crusted cars. Buzz was in the front seat of the Jeep and when he saw her he started to go crazy. When she opened the door he almost knocked her over. She saw the bandage on his front paw.

'Hey, dog, have you been messing with bears again?'

'W-wolves.'

'Are you serious?'

As they headed out on to the interstate, he told her about putting the opera on and all that happened afterward. Finally, he told her how he'd been following the tracks up into the forest with his flashlight when suddenly Buzz came limping down the trail toward him.

'He was bleeding real bad and I figured the wolf must have b-bitten him. But I took him straight to Nar Thomas's place and he said it looked like a wire wound. He said he reckoned Buzz had gotten himself caught in a snare or something.'

'A snare? Do people set snares up there?'

'Yeah, sometimes. P-poachers, folk like that.'

'Did you find anything?'

380

'No, I was g-going to have a look the next day. But it snowed in the night and by morning all the tracks were gone.'

He was about to go on, but then seemed to change his mind.

'What?' she said.

He shook his head. 'Oh, nothing.'

'Tell me.'

'It was just that . . . Well, I g-got the feeling that night, that there was someone up there. In fact, once or twice lately, I've felt it.'

'What do you mean? Who?'

'I don't know. Just someone.'

He changed the subject and told her how he and Dan Prior had gone flying and seen five wolves, including the three who were collared, feeding on a deer above the Townsend ranch. Dan had said the other three were probably there too, but they were deep in the timber, so it was hard to get a proper look.

'Hey, and g-guess what?'

'What?'

'I applied to the University of M-Minnesota.'

'You did? For the fall? Luke, that's terrific!'

Dan and he had talked about it when they got back to his office, he said. The university had a web site and the two of them had sat in front of Dan's computer and gone on a 'virtual tour' of the campus. They'd downloaded all the application stuff and Luke had sent it off. He'd almost finished writing a long piece about his wolf work and planned to send them that too.

'Dan's going to put in a good word for me with the people he knows in the biology department there.'

'Aha. Pull a few strings, huh?'

'Absolutely.'

She stared at him in silence for a few moments, thinking how good it felt to be with him again. He took his eyes off the road for a moment and beamed at her.

'What are you grinning at?' she said.

'Nothing.'

'What? Tell me.'

He shrugged and said simply, 'You c-came home, that's all.'

They were off the interstate now and heading west over the rolling white tundra. The sky was a crystalline blue. She thought about what he'd just said. She didn't know where or what home was anymore. If it was about belonging, all she knew was that, at this moment, she felt she belonged here with Luke, more than anywhere else. The empty road stretched ahead of them and in the far distance she could see the snow on the mountains glinting pink and gold in the sun.

'Luke, would you pull over for a moment?'

'Sure, why? What's the matter?'

'There's something I need to do.'

He drove onto the hard shoulder and stopped. Helen unbuckled her seat belt, then his, and then moved across the seat toward him. And she guided his face toward her with her hand and kissed him.

The new year baptized itself lavishly. For three weeks, it thawed and rained, then froze and snowed, then thawed and rained again. The forest roads transformed themselves into rivers of mud and the river, in its lower reaches, into a wide, brown ocean, divided by irrelevant fences and the meander of bare grey cottonwoods that traced its vanished banks.

Hope stood marooned, teased by a catastrophe that daily failed quite to arrive. The encroaching water bided its time just beyond the first buildings at the lower end of Main Street, deciding whether the last few feet were worth the effort. Doorways were packed ready with sandbags, while inside, carpets were rolled and things of value stowed upstairs or on the tops of cupboards.

Every few hours, Mr Iverson, the town's self-appointed

382

Noah, would drive down from the grocery store and set sail through the flood to check the calibrated flood posts down by the bridge. On sailing back, he would report, with his long face and voice of relished doom, that the water had risen another three inches, dropped another two, had risen another six. It was only a matter of time, he would say, shaking his head and walking away into his store; only a matter of time.

The town hadn't flooded in over twenty years and because of the million dollars' worth of culverts that had been installed afterward, it probably never would. But thriving in the face of adversity was a western tradition and Hope indulged it to the full. Every night, The Last Resort and Nelly's Diner were thronged with heroes, each with some small triumph to recount: a stranded cow rescued, a neighbor helped, a child ferried through the flood to school.

Those who lived at the higher end of the valley had only the mud to contend with. There was enough of it, however, to keep most of them at home. Only the major logging roads were passable and in some places, even on these, you needed more than an average four-wheel-drive to avoid getting stuck.

Three times, J.J. Lovelace had ventured up into the forest on foot and on each occasion been forced to turn back. He spent days alone in his trailer, thankful of the rest.

He ached all over from his recent efforts. His joints seemed to set solid if he stayed still for any length of time and would crack like a dead branch when he moved again. He was tired. Painfully dog-tired. But try as he might, he couldn't sleep. It seemed he'd forgotten how to. He would lie awake all night, fighting thoughts he'd rather not let into his head. During the day, he would often nod off, but whenever he did, his body would jolt as if warning him, as if sleep posed some kind of danger.

He'd never been much for reading. The only book he kept in the trailer was the leatherbound bible Winnie had given him when they got married. In the old days, he used to enjoy some of those Old Testament stories. Like poor old Job; or Daniel getting shoved in with the lions; or Samson losing his eyes and pulling down the temple on everyone. But now when he tried to read them, he'd get a few lines in and his mind would start to wander and he'd find himself reading the same thing over and over again.

Apart from cutting wood for the stove and forcing himself to eat and drink, the only thing that passed the time was carving his antlers. He'd done it for years. Winnie always used to say he could have been a famous sculptor or something. She'd had them on display all over the house. But he'd seen better in gift stores.

Elk was the best to work with. Sometimes he just carved buttons and belt buckles from the cross-section. But what he liked best was to use a whole length of antler and carve animals as if they were chasing each other along it: big ones at the base, like wolves and bears and elk, then getting smaller and smaller until, at the tips of the tines, it was just little bitty chipmunks and mice.

The one he was finishing now had taken him most of three weeks. It wasn't one of his best, but it wasn't too bad. All he had left to do was carve the name on the underside. He turned the lantern up a little and sat forward to get more light on it. It was only four o'clock but dark already and raining again too. He could hear it drumming on the tin roof of the barn and dripping from the trees onto the trailer.

An hour later he was plodding through the puddles toward the Hicks' kitchen door. There was music playing inside. He knocked and waited and in a few moments the woman came to the door. She always looked a little shocked at the sight of him.

'Mr Lovelace! I'm afraid Clyde's not back yet.'

She obviously thought he'd come for the box of provisions her husband was picking up for him in town.

'That's not why I came.'

He'd wrapped the carved antler in an old rag and when he held it out to her she jumped, as though he'd pulled a gun.

'Oh, what . . .?'

'It's for the boy.'

'For Buck Junior?'

He nodded. 'You said his birthday was coming up.'

'Yes, it's tomorrow. Why, that's really so sweet of you.'

She took it from him. It was raining hard now.

'Please, come in.'

'No. I got things need doing. Just wanted him to have that.'

'May I look?'

She opened the rag. He should have gotten some paper to wrap it in. She held up the antler. He could see she was thinking it was a peculiar kind of present for a baby.

'Oh, it's lovely. Did you do this yourself?'

He shrugged. 'It's just a . . . thing. Maybe, when he's older. See, it's got his name on it.'

'Oh, that's so pretty. Thank you.'

He gave her a nod and walked away.

Buck sat waiting in the driver's seat while Clyde hauled the last of the hay bales from the bed of the truck and spread it out on the ground in front of a row of forlorn-looking cattle. The rain was beating on the cab roof and coming down so thick and fast that it sliced the beam of the truck's headlights like a silver curtain.

As it was getting close to calving time, they were feeding in the afternoons now. The theory, worked out by some smart rancher up in Canada, was that a cow that was fed in the afternoon would have her calf in the morning and so make life easier for the calving crew. It mainly worked, but there always seemed to be enough cows who took delight in keeping you up all night whatever time you fed them.

Calving was tough, whichever way you played it. And this

385

year, if the goddamn rain kept on, it was going to be a regular nightmare. Buck could see them ending up doing what those loony Russian women did a few years back and have the cows give birth under water.

Clyde was climbing back into the cab now, huffing and blowing, the water spouting from the brim of his hat all down his mud-spattered slicker. He slammed the door loudly. Maybe it was just the weather and Buck's black mood, but everything the guy did irritated him at the moment. Buck bit his lip and eased the truck forward, trying not to give the wheels a chance to spin and bed down.

Before he'd gotten out, Clyde had been talking about Jordan Townsend's house, which the ranch manager had given him a tour of yesterday. Clyde had been going on about it ever since.

'Anyhow, one of these guys apparently asked old Jordan why he had a thirty-seat movie theater up there and you know what he said?'

'I have no idea.' Nor did Buck remotely care.

Clyde laughed, annoyingly.

'He said, "Why do dogs lick their balls?"'

'*What?*'

'"Because they can!"'

Clyde rocked forward in laughter.

'What's so damn funny about that?'

Clyde was laughing too much to reply. Buck shook his head.

They slithered and bumped out of the pasture and down onto the road. Clyde got out to shut the gate. The clock on the dash showed it was coming up to five-thirty. They were an hour late for Buck Junior's birthday party.

'Is Lovelace still sitting in his trailer all day?' Buck asked, as they headed for home.

'Yep. Says it's too wet.'

'It's too wet to feed the damn cattle, but someone's got to do it.'

'If you ask me, he's past it. Way too old.'

'I didn't,' Buck snapped.

'What?'

'I didn't ask you. If you're so damn smart, you go find someone better.'

'Hey, I'm sorry, I—'

'You're not paying him, I am. He killed three of them. If he gets the rest before we start calving, that's fine by me.'

Clyde held up his hands. 'Okay, okay.'

'And don't "okay, okay" me either. Jesus!' He slammed a fist on the steering wheel.

Neither of them spoke again during the twenty minutes it took to get back to the ranch house.

Kathy, Eleanor and Luke were all waiting for them. There were balloons and streamers hung across the kitchen and paper hats which Kathy insisted everyone, including Buck and Clyde, put on. Things were getting a little tense because Buck Junior was hungry and as soon as they'd got their boots and coats off, Kathy put him in his high chair and lit the single candle on his birthday cake. It was in the shape of a six-shooter. She'd made it and frosted it herself.

'Bam!' said the baby and everyone laughed and said it too.

They all stood around him and sang 'Happy Birthday'. Kathy helped him blow out the candle and then had to light it again because he started to holler. A few more times and he got bored and eventually everybody got a cup of coffee and a slice of gun.

'So what's this young son of a gun had for his birthday?' Buck asked.

Kathy went through the list while the baby tried to shovel chocolate cake into his mouth. Most of it seemed to end up on his face or the floor.

387

'And Lane sent him a fabulous romper suit, all white and silver. Clyde said he looks like Elvis in it.'

'He looks completely ridiculous in it,' Clyde chipped in.

'He does not, do you, honey? And, what else? Oh, yeah, and Mr Lovelace, would you believe it? He brought over this funny antler thing with animals carved on it.'

There was a moment of silence. Clyde darted a look at Buck.

'Who's Mr Lovelace, for pete's sake?' Eleanor asked.

Kathy suddenly realized what she'd done and seemed to be trying to think of something to say. Clyde beat her to it.

'Oh, he's just an old guy we've got doing some joinery work for us up at the house.'

Eleanor frowned. 'That name rings a bell. Where's he from?'

'Over Livingston way. Used to do a lot of work for my uncle. Hey, Kathy, look! That cake's going all over the place.'

The danger passed. Luke didn't seem interested and Eleanor didn't ask anymore questions. She asked Luke to fetch some more milk and went off to the other end of the kitchen to make more coffee.

'What the hell do you think you're doing?' Clyde hissed at Kathy over the baby's head.

'I just forgot, that's all.'

'It's okay,' Buck said quietly. 'No damage done.'

He walked over to join Eleanor and Luke. What with his wolf work, the boy had been keeping strange hours and Buck had hardly seen him lately. He looked different somehow, more grown up. But kids his age were like that. Look away and they grew an inch taller.

'Well, stranger,' Buck said, clapping him on the back. 'How're you doing?'

'I'm f-fine.'

'Getting much wolf-tracking done in this weather?'

388

'It's a little m-muddy.'

'So what are you and Helen finding to do up there?'

Clyde sniggered. Luke turned to look at him.

'I'm s-sorry?'

Clyde made an innocent face. 'Nothing.'

Kathy groaned. 'Clyde, don't make a fool of yourself.'

'I didn't say a word!'

Buck had heard the gossip himself, only the other night at The Last Resort, about how Luke and Helen Ross were supposed to be having an affair. It was preposterous. He didn't even like to think about it, with his own love life in ruins. Luke had never shown the slightest interest in girls. His dead brother was the one who'd gotten all those particular Calder genes. In fact, at times, Buck had worried that Luke maybe batted for the other side.

The boy ignored Clyde's idiot smirk and turned again to Buck.

'We're c-c-collating all the tracking data we've got so far.'

Buck took a mouthful of cake. 'So where are they hanging out nowadays?'

'Well, j-j-just lately, we haven't been d-doing much tracking—'

'Sure, but I mean, the last time you did.'

Luke looked him right in the eye. The boy plainly didn't trust him at all and it stirred Buck's temper to see it.

'Oh, they g-g-go all over the place.'

'Think I'll go tell Abe or something?'

'N-no, sir.'

'Well, why the hell can't you tell your own father?'

Eleanor, infuriatingly, as always, came to the boy's rescue.

'He can't give away classified information, can you Luke? He's working for the US government, remember? Now who's going to eat the rest of this cake? Here, Clyde, more coffee.'

Buck hadn't thought of it that way before. His own son

389

working for the goddamn feds. And for free too. It did little to improve his mood. He suddenly realized he was the only one still wearing the damn fool paper hat. He ripped it off and chucked it on the table. In grim silence, he stood finishing his cake, while the two women twittered on about something.

'I hope that Ross woman knows you're going to be needed here full-time once calving starts,' he said at last.

Everyone heard the chill in his voice. The room went quiet. Luke gave a little frown and started trying to speak. Buck cut him off. He'd had enough. The sight of the boy's stuttering face enraged him.

'That's not a suggestion. It's an order.'

And he clacked his plate down on the table and left the room.

With the human world beset by mire, the Hope wolves had the forest to themselves. Though much of the snow had melted, the deer and the elk had grown weak contending with it and were easy prey, even for a pack that had only two full-grown adults.

The death of an alpha male and the ensuing rivalry over who should replace him could cause a pack to fragment. But not this one. There was never a doubt over the succession, for there was only one other adult male: the collared disperser who had joined the pack as a yearling, two falls ago.

After the death of the old black killer of dog and calf, it had taken the other wolves awhile to acknowledge him. But in time they had all happily deferred. They had approached him with lowered heads and tails tucked under and rolled in fealty on their backs before him, licking up at his jaws while, haughty and benign, he stood above them.

It was the new leader's right and duty to mate with the white alpha female. Even if there had been other adult wolves capable of mating, it would not have been permitted. Only the alpha pair of any pack could breed.

But the new king was now a cripple. The month-old wound made by the wolfer's snare had festered and the wolf had lain for many days among rocks and rotting timber in a cluttered creekside crevice, licking his foot and daily growing thinner and weaker.

Perhaps because the alpha female and the three remaining pups knew that their survival as a pack depended on him, they tended him and stood watching him and brought him food back from their hunts.

And as January drew to a close and the weather grew cold again, the alpha female started to bleed in readiness and would lie with him in the cave and lick his face and, if he let her, his wound as well. And he would lick her too and sometimes struggle to his feet and go with her to the creek to drink and they would stand there and he would nuzzle her and place his swollen, seeping paw across her shoulders.

Had another male disperser passed through, he might well have laid claim to the stricken pack and its alpha female. And she might well have allowed herself to be wooed and won. But none came.

And in the first week of February, with the windless world again freezing hard and the snow falling in feathered flakes upon and about them, the white queen coupled with her maimed king and they stood tied together for a long time, while the three surviving pups watched silently from across the creek.

On that same night, away across the blanketed forest, Luke and Helen lay naked and entwined in the candlelit cabin.

She was sleeping, curled like a fetus upon him. Her head was on his chest and he could feel her breath, warm and soft and slow, on his skin. Her left leg lay across the top of his thighs and he could feel the gentle rise and fall of her belly against his hip. He was aware of every inch of her, of every textured nuance of her flesh. He would never have guessed his body could be so thoroughly and so constantly alive.

His earliest attempts to be her lover had been fumbling and feeble. In those first few days after she came back, after their kiss in the car, it was always over as soon as it had begun. He'd felt infantile and wretched and wondered why she didn't laugh at him or tell him to go and get lost, which was what he thought women always did to men who couldn't hack it.

But she'd told him it didn't matter and helped him to relax and, after awhile, he found he could do it. And it was more wonderful than he'd ever dreamed or dared imagine. And not just because of the vivid, flesh-quaking feel of it, but because it made him see he wasn't just a useless, stuttering boy anymore and that maybe he was ready, at last, to step into life. And all this, as well as so much more, he owed to Helen.

The candle on the chair beside the bunk had burned low and the flame began its final throes, making their joined shadow leap and bob on the cabin wall beside him. He reached out, carefully, trying not to wake her, and snuffed it out between his fingers. Helen stirred and murmured. She tucked her hand for warmth into the hollow of his arm and moved her leg and then settled again into sleep. He pulled the sleeping bag up over her shoulders and wrapped his arm around her, holding her to him securely and breathing the warm and wondrous smell of her.

He thought of that day in early fall when he'd taken her to where the wolves had denned and how she had gotten him to slither down into the hole as she had done. He remembered lying there alone in total darkness, and thinking it was a perfect place to die.

And now he knew he was wrong. This, here, now, in darkness just as black, but with this other living creature in his arms. This was the perfect place.

30

The trial of Abraham Edgar Harding took place in late February and its third and final day was drawing to a doleful and predictable close. It was too warm to snow and too cold to rain and a compromise of sleet angled unforgivingly on the sorry band of Harding supporters who trudged up and down in the leaden light outside the Helena federal district court building.

From the Saharan warmth of inside, Dan stood surveying them through a corridor window, while he waited for Helen to come back from the restroom. The jury had been out for half an hour and he wondered what on earth could be taking them so long.

Outside, there were only eight demonstrators left and even as he counted, one more broke away and headed forlornly for his car. Spurred by his defection, the others boosted the volume of their chant, though from inside, it was like the dying drone of a bee in a bell jar.

What do we want?
No wolves!
How do we want them?
Dead!

On the first morning there had been fifty or sixty of them there, corralled by almost as many police at a safe distance from a smaller but equally voluble band of 'pro-wolfers'. To the evident satisfaction of the assembled pack of photographers, press and TV reporters, the two sides heckled, chanted and brandished placards of varying degrees of wit and literacy.

Some of the slogans had a pleasing symmetry: NO WOLVES, NO WAY! was mirrored merrily across the street by WOLVES, WAY! Some were more sinister, such as the one being touted by a dourly bearded young man whom Dan thought he remembered from the night of the meeting. He wore a camouflaged hunting cap and jacket and boots laced up to his knees. His placard said, FIRST WACO, NOW WOLVES.

Many of the pro-Harding placards seemed to have been penned by the same hand or at least by hands similarly tutored, for the word *federal* was consistently spelled *fedral*, except on one where the *d* was missing too. WOLVES = FERAL TERRORISM, it proclaimed. Dan couldn't decide if it was a mistake or represented some new, esoteric line of thought.

Abe had arrived that first morning like a celebrity who'd left his charisma at home. Still valiantly lawyerless, he had been chauffered to court – and no doubt coached all the way – by star defense witness, Buck Calder. Abe stood on the court steps, flanked by his grinning sons, and grimly repeated over and over again through tobacco-stained teeth to every question that he was an American citizen (which no one had doubted) and that he was here this day to defend his 'alienable rights' to Life, Liberty and the pursuit of Wolves.

Perhaps to indicate that the second of these rights might

indeed prove alienable, federal judge Willis Watkins had urged Abe to reconsider both his plea of not guilty and his decision not to be represented by an attorney. But Abe would have none of it. It was a matter of principle, he insisted. As a result, twelve patient Montanans had sat through three days of tedium and testimony, waiting to reach a conclusion that only Abe's most diehard fans could fail to deem foregone.

Dan and Helen had given evidence the previous morning and were then cross-examined by Abe in a style that was staccato and surreal. He gave Dan the easier ride, shuffling through several high stacks of notes and leaving such epic pauses that twice Willis Watkins intervened to ask if he'd finished. His first question to Helen was whether, like he, she had fought for her country in Vietnam. When she pointed out that she had only just been born when the war ended, he gave a loud *Aha!* of triumph, as if the point were proven.

He seemed to be under the impression that Helen had personally released the Hope wolves as part of a secret government program, whose purpose was to breed and train wolves to eat cattle so that ranchers went out of business and the government could grab their land. He tried to get her to admit that he'd caught her snooping on his property, carrying out a clandestine survey with that intent. He suggested to her that she was an 'interfering bitch' and got himself a stern rebuke from the bench. Helen handled it all with polite restraint and a face as straight as a marine on parade.

Buck Calder did his best to put a shine on Abe's breastplate, testifying to the man's ranching prowess, neighborliness and generally fine character. But Abe was beyond help. Declining to take the stand himself, he proudly declared in his final speech to the jury that he had deliberately killed the wolf, knowing it to be one. Which was pretty well all the prosecution had to show. He wound up by saying his only regret was that he hadn't killed the other wolf he'd seen and maybe a few bunny-huggers too. If it was a joke, it didn't go down too well with Judge Watkins.

The streetlights were coming on outside now and Dan saw two more demonstrators had lowered their placards, long illegible with sleet. They were calling it a day.

'Dan!'

He looked around and saw Helen hurrying down the corridor toward him.

'The jury's coming back in,' she said.

It didn't take long.

Abe Harding was found guilty on all counts. No one gasped or shouted or sobbed. A few supporters muttered and shook their heads. Abe stared steadily at the ceiling while Willis Watkins berated him in measured tones for wasting many thousands of dollars of taxpayers' money. Sentencing would come later, said the judge, pending reports. He left the court in no doubt however that Abe faced several months in jail and probably a substantial fine as well.

Wes and Ethan Harding turned and glared venomously at Helen but either she didn't notice or pretended not to.

'Let's go get a drink,' she quietly said to Dan.

They got out of the building fast but not quite fast enough to avoid the media gang that had miraculously rallied in the short time since the verdict. TV crews were busy canvassing reaction from the sleet-sodden demonstrators and their drier, less devoted brethren who had materialized from their cars to join them.

'Mr Prior? Mr Prior?' a woman's voice called out.

It was Buck Calder's favorite TV reporter.

'Just ignore her,' Helen said.

But the woman caught up, only steps ahead of her cameraman. Dan could see from the little red light on the camera that he was already being taped. To be seen ducking and running on the local news never looked good. He stopped and smiled warmly, hoping but doubting that Helen was doing the same.

'I was wondering,' the woman panted. 'How do you feel about the verdict?'

'Well, justice, I believe, was done. But it's not a happy day for anyone, humans or wolves.'

'Do you think Abe Harding should go to jail?'

'Fortunately, that's not for me to decide.'

The woman shoved her microphone in front of Helen now.

'What about you Miss Ross? Don't you think a man's got the right to defend his own cattle?'

'I'd rather not comment,' Helen said.

'Should he go to jail?'

'I'd really rather not comment.'

'How did you feel when he called you an "interfering bitch"?'

'How do you feel when people call you one?'

Dan intervened. 'We've got to go now. Thank you very much.'

He steered Helen off through the crowd.

'Why don't you get yourself a proper job?' someone yelled. Dan recognized the camouflage cap of the Waco poster man.

'Hey, buddy, if you're hiring, I'm available.'

'Wouldn't hire you to wipe my ass.'

'Lucky you only use it for talking then,' Helen said quietly, without looking at him. But Dan could see the guy heard.

They got clear of the crowd before either of them spoke again.

'Who the hell is that?' Dan said.

'One of my logger buddies. Works for the post and pole company. We share reflective moments together in the forest.'

They both had cars and drove separately to a bar Dan thought none of the Harding supporters would be likely to choose for drowning their collective sorrows. Everything the place served was organically grown, from the corn chips to the beer, and the clientele were mainly students, vegetarians or both. The music was strictly New Age and there wasn't an antlered head to be seen anywhere on the walls.

They found a booth and ordered two wheat-beers on tap, from which Dan had to fish a large chunk of lemon. He could never understand why they put it in.

'Has Luke heard back from the university?' he asked.

'Not yet. He sent them this great paper about the GIS work he's been doing.'

'They'll take him okay.'

'Yeah. All he has to do is tell his father.'

'You're kidding. He hasn't told him yet?'

'Nope.'

Helen took a drink.

'You know, I can almost have a drink now without wanting a cigarette.'

'How long since you quit?'

'Four months.'

'That's pretty good.'

They were silent for a moment or two. Dan was wondering how best to broach a tricky subject that he'd been putting off mentioning for several weeks now. He took a long draught of beer and put down his glass.

'Helen, there's something I have to tell you.'

'Going to fire me? It's okay, I quit.'

He smiled. 'No.' He paused. 'It's just that we've been getting these calls at the office.'

She frowned.

'It sounds like a different person each time and they never give their names and I'm sure it's just somebody trying to stir some shit on account of this Abe Harding business, and frankly, I—'

'Dan, for Godsake, will you stop blathering and tell me?'

'It's not easy, okay? It's about Luke.'

He saw her stiffen slightly.

'What about him?'

'Well, I know he has to spend a lot of time up at the cabin, what with all the night-tracking and stuff you have to do. And that sometimes he has to stay over. But some folks are clearly getting, well, you know, the wrong idea.'

'Oh. And what might that wrong idea be?'

'Come on, Helen. You know what I'm saying.'

'I'm sorry, I really don't.'

Dan was starting to lose patience.

'Okay, I'll spell it out. They're saying you and Luke are having . . . some kind of affair or something.'

'Or something?'

Dan looked away and cursed under his breath.

'And you want me to tell you if it's true or not?'

'No,' he lied. 'You know damn well that's not what I'm saying.'

His cell phone started to ring.

'Shit.'

He rummaged for it and tugged it out of his coat pocket. The call was from Bill Rimmer. Some wolves had killed three calves near Boulder, he said. The rancher, who Dan knew well, was spitting blood. Bill said it was important that Dan come at once to try and calm things down.

'Helen, I'm sorry. I've got to go.'

'Fine.'

She watched him put on his coat and finish his beer. He felt mean and guilty over what he'd said.

'I'll call you in the morning.'

'Fine. I'm going to have another beer.'

'I'm sorry. I got that all wrong.'

'Hey, no problem.'

He turned to go and as he stepped away she called his

name. He stopped and looked back at her. She looked hurt; and beautiful.

'In case you're wondering,' she said. 'It is.'

'What?'

'True.'

He drove to Boulder with his head whirring and his heart sinking slowly to his stomach.

Helen was at the bottom of her second beer and thinking about a third when she heard the voice behind her.

'Sure is a sorry thing when a pretty woman has to celebrate on her own.'

That's all I need, she thought. She turned and saw Buck Calder standing by the booth, leering down at her. There was snow on his hat and the shoulders of his jacket.

'Why should I be celebrating?'

'You got the verdict. Old Abe looks like he's going down for awhile. I figure that's what you wanted.'

Helen shook her head and looked away.

'Mind if I join you?'

'Mind if I ask what you're doing in here?'

'Well, I was heading home and I saw your pickup parked out there and thought I'd stop and say hi.'

'Oh. Well. Hi.'

The waitress appeared and Buck ordered two wheat-beers.

'Thanks, Mr Calder, but—'

'Buck.'

'Yeah, well, anyway. Thanks, but I ought to be going.'

He turned to the waitress. 'It's okay, sweetheart. Bring two. I'll drink them both.'

He eased himself onto the bench on the other side of the booth. Helen warned herself to go easy. However much she might dislike the man, he was Luke's father. To upset him wouldn't be good for either of them.

400

'I wanted to talk about Luke,' he said.

Helen gave a little laugh. Here we go again, she thought.

'Why do you laugh?'

'Oh. Nothing.'

He looked at her for a moment, with a faintly knowing smile.

'I want you to know, whatever idle tongues may be wagging—'

'Mr Calder—'

'Buck.'

'Buck. I really don't have any idea what you're talking about.'

The waitress arrived with the beers. He thanked her and waited for her to leave before he went on.

'What I wanted to say was, just how grateful Eleanor and I are for all you've done for the boy, letting him work with you and all. Of course, it means we don't see to much of him right now, and I have to say, I'm going to need him around now we're getting into calving, which I hope you'll understand.'

Helen nodded.

'But his mother was only saying the other night that she's never seen the boy so happy. He seems at last to have grown up a little. Even his stutter seems to have gotten better. So, thank you.'

He took a drink. Helen didn't know what to say. As usual, the guy had taken her by surprise. Perhaps she should curb her natural urge to flee and instead, while the going was good, broach the subject of Luke going to college.

'You handled yourself real well, up there on the stand,' he said.

Helen shrugged and smiled.

'No, I mean it. You were impressive.'

'Thank you. So were you.'

He nodded graciously. Neither of them spoke for a moment. The music they were playing was that stuff they made for insomniacs, a soothing blend of electronic waves and the moan of killer whales. It always made Helen feel edgy.

'You know, I reckon if you and I hadn't gotten off on the wrong foot, we might have been friends.'

'Hey, we're friends. As far as I'm concerned.'

'Okay, then. More than friends.'

She pretended to look puzzled. He gave her a slow smile. Then he reached beneath the table and put his hand on her leg. Helen took a deep breath and stood up.

'I'm sorry. I'm going home.'

She put her coat on and got some money from her bag to pay for the drinks. He was sitting back watching her, smiling, totally unfazed. He was just making fun of her. She thought about throwing the untouched glass of beer over him and only narrowly decided against.

'Bye,' she said and walked away.

It was snowing hard. Hurrying across the parking lot, she slipped and nearly fell. She was so shaken and angry that it took her a long time to find her car keys. How *dare* he? She wanted to kill him.

As she put the key in the door, she felt a hand on her shoulder and gave a little yelp of fright.

He turned her around and took hold of her arms below the elbows, pinning her against the truck.

'Why settle for a boy when you can have a man?' he said.

She tried to keep her voice steady. 'Get your hands off me. Now.'

'Come on, we both know you're hot for it.'

He leaned his face toward her and she felt his warm, beery breath on her face. She brought her knee up sharply between his legs and shoved him hard in the chest. He reeled backward, slipped in the snow and fell heavily, his hat rolling off to one side.

Helen climbed quickly into the pickup, slammed the door and locked it. Thank the Lord, the engine fired first time. He was still lying there, moaning and clutching his crotch. She lowered the window.

'Don't *ever* touch me again.'

She hit the gas pedal and the Toyota slithered off. Suddenly, through her shock and outrage, something he'd once said came back to her. She braked hard and skidded to a stop, then reversed back so that she was looking right down on him from the window.

'Wanting something can be better than getting it, remember? Think of it as a favor.'

And she drove off, showering him with wet snow from her wheels as she went.

They finished supper in silence. Or rather, Luke finished his while she shifted hers around on her plate. The plan had been for Helen to get something fresh in town after the court case finished, but she'd forgotten, so Luke had cooked the usual pasta and mixed in a can of tuna, some cheese, then a can of sweetcorn. He still wasn't much of a cook, but it tasted okay.

He could tell something was wrong as soon as she came in, but whatever it was, she wasn't letting on. Maybe she was still upset about what Abe had called her in court yesterday. About what had happened there today, she had told him little more than the verdict and the encounter afterward with their logging friend. Luke had figured on telling her his worries that something funny was going on with the wolves, but it didn't seem the right time. She pushed her plate away.

'I'm sorry,' he said. 'It wasn't great.'

'No, it was fine. I'm just not hungry.'

'When I get to college, I'm going to take cookery class too.'

403

She tried to smile. He got up and went around to her side of the table, stepping over Buzz who was in his usual place, flat out by the stove. He squatted beside her and took both her hands in his.

'What's the matter?'

She shook her head and bent forward and kissed his forehead.

'Tell me.'

She sighed. 'Luke, I don't think you should stay up here anymore.'

'W-why?'

'You know what people are saying.'

He nodded. 'I d-didn't know if you knew.'

She gave a wry laugh. 'Oh, I know all right.'

She told him about the anonymous calls to Dan's office. Luke wondered who it could be, but couldn't think of anyone that mean.

'So are you saying we should stop seeing each other?'

'No. Oh, Luke, I don't know.'

'If it's making you unhappy . . .'

She stroked his face. 'I couldn't bear not seeing you.'

'Does what other p-people think change what we have?'

'I don't know.'

'How can it?'

'Luke, there are just some people who always try to destroy what they don't understand or what they can't have for themselves.'

'B-but if you listen to them, they win.'

She smiled down at him. Sometimes, with just a look, she could make him remember how young he was and how much he had yet to learn of the world's hurtful ways.

'I love you.'

'Oh Luke, please—'

'It's okay. Y-you don't have to say it too.'

404

'The last guy I said it to left me. For a Belgian bimbo.'

'I don't know any B-belgian b-bimbos.'

It almost made her laugh.

'Listen, I'm not going to be able to come up here much anyhow for a few weeks. My f-father wants me to help with the calving.'

'He told me.'

'You spoke with him? What did he say?'

She shrugged. 'Just that.'

The wolf lay halfway up a narrow gully, wedged between two rocks like a piece of flood-jammed timber. His nose was stretched out on his paws as if he were about to pounce and his eyes were open and frozen a solid, dull yellow. His fur was covered in a thin blanket of spindrift that had swirled down the gully. How long he had been dead, it was hard to say.

They had picked up the signal shortly after dawn, not the usual, intermittent beep, but a single sustained note that told them something had happened.

'It doesn't necessarily mean he's dead,' Helen had said, as they loaded their skis and the rest of the gear onto the snow-mobile. 'The collar might just have come off. It happens.'

But she didn't believe it. They'd gone on the snow-mobile as far as they could up the trail that ran beside the creek, the signal getting louder all the time. Both of them were aware it was the last time they would be tracking together for a month or more and they hardly spoke. When the going got too dif-ficult, they put their skis on and threaded their way through the trees and rocks. There were fresh wolf tracks but only the one, unbroken signal. The pack had moved on.

It was Luke who saw the body first. When they climbed up through the rocks they found a crevice, littered with scat and pieces of bone. It seemed the wolf had sheltered there for some time. In a patch of fresh snow among the rocks, they

405

could see the tracks of several wolves. Perhaps they had come to pay their last respects.

His body was frozen hard and it took them a long time to lever him out from the rocks without damaging him further. They laid him down beside the creek.

'Look at his foot,' Helen said. 'That's what's killed him.'

They knelt down to examine it. The whole paw was stripped of fur and was swollen to at least three times the size of the others. There was a deep open gash which went all the way around it.

'You poor old fella. What have you been up to, huh? It looks like he's been caught in a trap or something.'

'Or a snare, like Buzz,' Luke said. 'Same f-foot too.'

Helen took off the collar and stopped the signal. She stood up and sighed.

'And then there were seven.'

'I don't reckon there's that m-many anymore.'

She looked at him. 'How do you mean?'

'Remember when Dan and I w-went flying, how we only saw five of them? And he said the others were p-probably in the trees or somewhere? Well, these last few days, while you've been in court, I've g-gotten the feeling that's all there is now. Maybe not even that many. I know a lot of the time they go in each other's tracks, b-but when they separate, it looks like there's only three or four of them, far as I can tell. And I heard them howl and it wasn't the same. K-kind of thinner.'

They carried the dead wolf to the snowmobile and took it back to the cabin. Helen called Dan and he said he would have Donna drive out right away and pick it up. He'd get Bill Rimmer to have a look, then send it up to Ashland for a full necropsy report. Helen told him it looked like a snare wound.

'Luke thinks someone's trying to get rid of them,' she said.

'Poachers set snares for all kinds of animals. Poison's still the best way to kill a wolf.'

406

'Except it kills lots of other animals too and tells the whole world you're there.'

'So does a snare. I think the boy's being a little fanciful.'

Helen told him what Luke had said about never seeing more than four or five sets of tracks. When Dan replied, his voice had gone hard.

'Helen, I don't want to sound ungrateful for Luke's help, but you're the goddamn biologist. It's you we're paying, not him.'

It was stupid of her, but until that moment, it hadn't occurred to her that Dan was jealous. She'd lost him. Luke was now her only ally.

31

As a young girl, Kathy had always loved calving time. It was the most exciting time of the whole ranching year. She and Lane would hear her daddy and the calving crew guys down in the kitchen in the middle of the night, laughing and fixing food for themselves, and lie awake listening to the moan and bellow of the cows down by the corrals. The girls used to stand on tiptoe at their bedroom windows, peering down at the men working under the arc lights, hauling the calves out of their mothers, all squirmy and covered in blood and slime and laugh out loud as the little things tried to stand and totter on their spindly legs.

When the girls got older, sometimes their daddy would let them come outside and help, even when they had to be up early for school and their mom had said they couldn't. He would come and get them when she was asleep and make them wrap up warm and tiptoe down the stairs.

Kathy remembered them both crying one time, when a calf

came out dead and their daddy had told them not to be silly because it was just God's way of dealing with those who were too weak for the world.

Their mom had some crocus bulbs growing in a pot in the kitchen and the two girls snipped all the flowers off and drove up to the dump with one of the hired hands on the old red John Deere and the three of them had stood and said a prayer over the poor little body and then scattered the crocuses over it. The next morning, when she found her flowers all beheaded, their mom had been furious.

Now, since moving up to the red house, Kathy didn't like calving time at all. It meant that, for more than a month, Clyde would be sleeping down at the main ranch house, working his shifts on the calving crew. Kathy saw him when she drove down to help her mother fix the men's midday meal or whenever he dropped home for a change of clothes. Generally he was too frazzled to pay anyone proper attention, though he often seemed to expect Kathy to jump straight into bed with him, even when she wasn't remotely in the mood.

Calving had been going for little over a week now, but already she was bored and lonely, especially on those long evenings when there was nothing good on TV. So if she saw a light on in the wolfer's trailer, she would find some excuse to go over and visit with him.

She would take the laundry she'd insisted on doing for him or take him some leftovers, soup or maybe some cookies she had baked. And if the baby was awake and not hollering, because she knew the old man liked him, she would take him along too.

Of course, old Mr Lovelace wasn't everyone's idea of company. The first time she went, he didn't even ask her in and when at last he did, the trailer smelled worse than a hog pen. But she soon got used to it, simply for the sake of having someone to talk with. And despite his grouchy way, there was something about the old man that she liked. Or maybe she just felt sorry for him. Whichever it was, anyhow, she could tell he'd taken a shine to her.

He'd been away for a couple of days, up in the forest, and after she'd noticed he was back, she'd given him a short while to get settled, then carried over a bowl of stew. He'd shoveled it down in about two minutes flat and was now mopping the bowl clean with some bread she'd also brought.

Kathy sat on a wooden stool with Buck Junior on her knee, on the other side of the trailer's narrow table, its top stained with things she didn't dare imagine. The old man ate ravenously, almost like a wolf himself, she thought. The lamplight cut crags and hollows in his ancient, grizzled face. Little Buck sat still and silent, his eyes just above the level of the table, following every move the wolfer made.

'That was good.'

'Like some more? There's plenty.'

'No, ma'am. I'm done.'

He poured himself some coffee, not bothering to ask her if she wanted one because she always turned it down. She didn't like the look of the mugs he used. They sat in silence while he stirred three spoons of sugar into it, all the while watching the baby, like he always did.

It was often hard to tell when he might be in the mood to talk. Sometimes he barely said a word and Kathy ended up doing all the talking. She had learned early on the subjects to steer clear of. Once she'd made the mistake of asking him about his wife and he'd clammed right up. The same had happened when she asked how many of the wolves he'd managed to catch.

At other times though, you couldn't stop him. It was like taking a cork from a barrel, just kept flowing, especially when he got onto the subject of his daddy. Kathy had always enjoyed hearing about the old times. In her head she pictured old

410

Joshua Lovelace looking like the old 'griz' hunter in *Jeremiah Johnson*. Usually, if she was going to get him talking, all it needed was a little prompt and she tried it now.

'You know you told me about that thing your daddy invented?'

'You mean, the loop?'

'The loop, that's it. What exactly was it?'

He went on stirring his coffee for a moment.

'Want to see it?'

'You've still got it? Really?'

'Still sometimes use it.'

He got up and went to one of his cupboards. He had to get down on his knees to reach deep inside it and pulled out a coil of wire with small, slender cones of metal attached to it. He brought it back to the table and laid it in front of her. He stayed standing while he undid the two leather thongs it was tied with. Then he uncoiled a few feet of wire. The baby reached out toward one of the metal cones.

'No, honey,' Kathy said. 'Don't touch.'

'That's right, don't you go touching. These things may look like toys, but they ain't. I'll show you.'

There was a piece of bread left on the table and he picked it up and started to slide it carefully over the point of one of the cones.

'My daddy used to say chicken was best, and that's what I use if I can get hold of some. But pretty much any kind of meat'll do. So you have to imagine this bread here's a chunk of meat. And what you do is lay the loop of wire around the den, just when the wolf pups are about three weeks old and thinking about venturing out into the world. And then . . .'

He stopped and Kathy, who'd been watching what he was doing with his hands, looked up at his face and saw he was staring in a strange way at the baby. Buck Junior was staring right back at him.

'And then . . .'

'Mr Lovelace? Are you okay?'

His eyes shifted up to look at Kathy and it was as if he had no idea who she was or what she was doing there. He looked down at his hands again and it seemed to make him remember what he'd been saying.

'So. The pup smells the bait. And 'cos he don't know no better, he takes this into his mouth, the narrow end first. That's important, 'cos you don't want him triggering it till it's gotten right down . . .'

He was looking at the baby again.

'Right down?' Kathy prompted.

'Right down . . . Right down into his throat. Then, the moment he closes his mouth on this wide bit, just here . . .'

He gave it a little squeeze with his fingers and there was a sudden loud snap and three barbed hooks, like a small grappling iron, shot out through the bread, making it explode all over the table.

Buck Junior jumped in fright and started to bawl. Kathy hugged him and tried to soothe him, but he wouldn't stop. She stood up and held him to her, patting his back, but it was no good.

'I'm sorry, I better take him home.'

The old man didn't reply. He just stood there, staring at the hook in his hands.

'Mr Lovelace?'

Kathy didn't know if she should stay and make sure he was all right, but the baby's hollering was becoming unbearable. She went to the door and turned to say goodnight. But he didn't seem to hear.

She would never be sure, for the lamp was behind him and half his face was in shadow, but as she closed the door, Kathy thought she saw, on the old wolfer's cheek, the glint of a tear.

In the dead of night, lying in her bed with the baby asleep

beside her, she heard him start his snowmobile and she went to the window and saw its light going away across the top meadow and up into the forest.

It was the last time she would ever see him.

The Calders liked to get most of their first-time calvers over with first, before the main herd started calving. Luke's father prided himself almost as much for breeding good mothers as he did good bulls and most of his heifers squeezed their calves out easy as soap in a bathtub.

There were always a good few though who needed help. And whereas it was fine to let the older cows have their calves down in the pasture, the first-timers stayed up in the corrals where it was easier to keep an eye on them.

Their times of insemination had all been recorded and as their due date approached, each one of them was doused for lice and given shots against scours and overeating disease. Now, in the second week of calving, they were coming at a rate of around twenty a day and things were getting frantic.

It was made a lot worse by the weather. Sometimes in late March it could almost feel like spring, but not this year. Every day a new blizzard rolled in and the temperature rarely poked its head above ten below. As soon as a heifer looked like starting they had to whip her up to one of the stalls in the calving barn. And if she'd already lain down and started, immediately the calf popped out, they would bundle it into a wheelbarrow and get it out of the cold before its ears froze up. Sometimes, if the mother didn't lick the ears out quick enough you had to thaw them out with a hair-dryer, because if you didn't, you ended up with a load of disfigured beasts no buyer worth his salt would touch.

Space in the barn was at a premium now and as soon as a calf was sucking and the mother looked like she knew what was going on, out they went into the cold again, some of the

413

poor little mites with duct tape on their ears so they didn't freeze up again. Turning them out that quick was a risk because they might not have paired up properly and a day or two later you could find a cow feeding the wrong calf.

The men worked through the night in two- and three-hour shifts, none of them getting more than four hours' sleep. Luke had taken over from Ray at four a.m. and had a fairly easy time of it. The only drama had been when he spotted a pair of coyotes sniffing around the corrals. They could nip in real quick and take a calf before the mother knew what had happened and there was always a rifle at hand in the barn for just such a thing. His father and Clyde would have shot them but Luke just chased them off, thanking his lucky stars that they weren't wolves. He only hoped they were steering clear of the other ranches too.

He finished cleaning the barn then headed down to the corrals to have another look at one of the heifers who was overdue. In the last hour she'd been looking a little troubled and Luke was starting to think something might be wrong. As he walked down there, he thought again of Helen and their sad encounter the day before.

He hadn't seen her in over a week. And knowing she was so close, he missed her even more than when she'd been thousands of miles away. He'd been on his way into town to pick up some more Scour Guard, when he had seen her pickup heading out toward him. They pulled up, window to window, and talked for a few minutes. Not like lovers, more like friends, who'd somehow grown awkward.

'I'd have come up, but I can't get away,' he said. 'My d-dad—'

'It's okay, I understand.'

'Have you been out t-tracking?'

'Yes. And I think you're right. There don't seem to be more than three or four of them now. Not so many kills either.'

'Have you f-found any snares or anything?'

'No, but I think there's somebody around up there.'

'Why?'

She shrugged. 'Tracks and things, I don't know. And I found this place where someone had been camping out. It's probably nothing.'

She said that from the signals, it seemed the wolves were moving down, getting close to some of the ranches, as if checking out the calving.

'Inc-cluding ours?'

'Including yours.'

She made a sad, wry face and for awhile they stayed silent. There was both too much to say and nothing at all.

She shivered. 'I'm tired of the cold.'

'Are you okay?'

'No. Are you?'

'No.'

He reached out and they held hands for a moment. It was then that he noticed the door of the pickup. Someone had scratched WHORE in large letters, right across it.

'Oh, God,' he said.

'Nice, huh?'

'When did that happen?'

'Last night.'

Luke saw a truck heading out of town. They were block-ing the road. Helen saw it too and quickly let go of his hand.

'Did you tell the sheriff's office?'

'That's where I've just been. Deputy Rawlinson was very sympathetic. He said it was probably city kids, come out to party in the forest. He said if I was worried, I should get myself a gun.'

Luke shook his head. The truck was nearly up to them.

'Anyway,' Helen said. 'I'll see you.'

'I'll find some way of g-getting up there.'

'It's okay, Luke Maybe it's better not to for awhile.'

The truck sounded its horn. They said a sad goodbye and drove off their different ways.

He was down at the corral now and he stood on the fence and searched over the rail with his flashlight for the heifer he wanted to check.

'How's it going?'

He looked around and saw Clyde, who was taking the next shift.

'Okay. There's one here I'm a little w-worried about. She's been acting kind of fidgety. I think she may have got a t-twisted uterus or something.'

Clyde asked him to point her out.

'No way,' he said dismissively. 'She's okay.'

Luke shrugged. He told Clyde about the coyotes, then left him to it and went back to the house to get an hour of sleep before sun-up.

He overslept. When he'd showered and dressed, the others were already having breakfast in the kitchen. He could tell right away that something had happened. You could cut the atmosphere with a knife. Ray and Jesse were eating in silence. His father had a face like a thunderhead.

His mother caught Luke's eye in warning as she filled his glass with milk. For awhile no one said a word.

'So how come you let that heifer die?' his father said at last.

'W-what?'

'Don't you w-what me, boy.'

'Which heifer?'

He looked at Clyde, but Clyde was keeping his eyes on his plate.

'Clyde found a dead heifer in the corral. Had a twisted uterus.'

Luke frowned at Clyde with disbelief.

'B-but I showed her to you.'

416

Clyde glanced up briefly and Luke could see the fear in his eyes.

'What?'

'I showed you the heifer and y-y-you said she was okay.'

'You did not. Jesus, Luke!'

'Come on, boys,' Luke's mother said. 'We always lose one or two—'

His father cut her off fiercely. 'You keep out of this.'

'I even t-told you what I thought was wrong with her. And you said she was okay!'

'Hey, look, kid. Don't you try and pin this on me.'

Luke stood up. His chair grated on the floor.

'Where do you think you're going?' his father said.

'I-I-I've had enough.'

'You have? Well, I sure as hell haven't. You sit down.'

Luke shook his head. 'No, sir.'

'You damn well sit down if I tell you to.'

'No, sir.'

For a moment, his father didn't seem to know what to do. He wasn't used to defiance. Ray and Jesse got up, looking at their boots, and quietly left the room.

'You damn well stay put till I've had my say. Your mother tells me you think you're going off to college in Minnesota, is that right?'

Luke's mother stood up. 'Buck, for heavensakes, not now—'

'Shut up. To study bunny-hugging or something. Is that true?'

'B-b-biology.'

'So it is true. And you don't think to consult your own father about this?'

Luke could feel his legs starting to shake. But it wasn't through fear. For the first time in his life, he wasn't afraid of the great bull face glaring across the table at him. All he felt

417

was a pure anger, distilled over all these years. It was almost exhilarating.

'Have you lost your tongue?'

Luke looked at his mother. She was standing by the sink, fighting hard to keep herself from crying. He turned again to his father. *Have you lost your tongue?* He took a deep breath and felt a surprising calm rising in his chest. He shook his head.

'No,' he said simply.

'Then you'd better damn well explain yourself.'

'I d–d–d . . .'

His father smiled in satisfaction.

It was the moment. There was a white bird loose in the room and all Luke had to do was reach out and gently take hold of it and he would be free. He took another breath.

'I didn't think you'd be interested.'

'Oh, really?' His father smiled sarcastically and leaned back in his chair.

'I knew you w–wouldn't approve.'

'Well, you were wrong the first time and right the second. I *am* interested and, sure as hell, I don't approve. You'll go to Montana State, boy, and see if you can learn how to be a good enough rancher not to let good heifers die.'

'If he's too much of a c–coward to admit it, I don't care. And I'm not going to M–Montana State, I'm going to M–Minnesota. If they'll have me.'

'Oh you are, huh?'

'Yes, sir.'

His father stood up and came toward him and for a moment Luke felt his courage falter.

'And who the hell do you think's going to pay for it?'

'I'll f–f–find a way.'

'I'll pay.' It was his mother who'd spoken and they both turned to look at her.

'I told you to keep out of it.'

'W–wh–wh . . .' *Oh God*, Luke thought, *don't desert me now. Don't let the white bird go.*

'Ww–ww–ww . . .' his father mimicked.

Luke felt a river of cold anger sweep the words out of his mouth.

'Why do you have to go on b–bullying everyone? Haven't you done enough damage? We all have to be just like you want us to be, don't we? Anything you c–can't understand, you have to hurt. Is it because you're scared or something?'

'Don't you dare talk to me like that.'

'Is it?'

His father took a step toward him and hit him hard across the face with the back of his hand. His mother screamed and covered her eyes. Clyde was on his feet now too.

Luke could taste blood starting, salty and metallic, inside his mouth. He stared at his father, who stood glaring back at him, his massive chest heaving and his neck flushed with anger. It reminded Luke of the grizzly who'd chased them in the forest. Luke wondered briefly why the sight no longer scared him.

'I'm going now,' he said. He felt blood trickle from the corner of his mouth and he saw his father notice it and maybe just the faintest flicker of doubt in his cold gray eyes.

'You get back to work.'

'No, sir. I'm going.'

'You do and you'll never set foot in my house again.'

'I don't b–belong in it anyhow. I never did.'

And he nodded to his mother and walked out of the room.

Upstairs, he fetched two long canvas bags from the closet and packed some clothes and a few favorite books and one or two other things he thought he might need. He heard the kitchen door slam and out of the window saw his father stomping through the snow to the corrals, with Clyde at his heel. It was getting light. All the while, Luke wondered if the calm would suddenly desert him, but it didn't.

419

As he came to the top of the stairs, he looked through the open doorway of his parents' bedroom and saw his mother was packing a suitcase on the bed. He put his bag down and walked to the door.

'Mom?'

She turned and the two of them stood looking at each a moment. Then she came toward him with her arms outstretched and he went to her and put his arms around her too. He didn't speak until he felt the shudder of her sobs subside.

'W-where will you go?'

She was wiping her eyes. 'I called Ruth. She said I could stay with her for awhile. You'll go to Helen's?'

He nodded. His mother lifted her head from his chest and looked at him.

'You love her very much, don't you?'

He shrugged and tried to smile. For some reason, suddenly, he wanted to cry too. But he didn't.

'I don't know,' he said. 'I guess.'

'Does she love you?'

'Oh, Mom, I . . .'

'I'm sorry, it isn't my business.'

She gave him a final little hug and kissed his cheek.

'Promise you'll come see me?'

'I promise.'

He dumped his bags in the living room and went to the gun rack in his father's office and took down the .270 Winchester that had become his when his brother died, though he had hardly ever used it. There was a box of cartridges in the drawer below and he took them and put them with the rifle in one of the bags. From their hooks in the kitchen, he collected his coat and hat and slicker and took a spare pair of boots, then carried everything out to the Jeep.

As he pulled away from the house, he looked down across the pasture and saw Moon Eye standing with the other horses near the tree that grew from the old Ford. They were too far away for Luke to be sure, but the horse seemed to be staring back at him.

When he drove under the skull of the gateway, he looked over his shoulder toward the ranch. His father and Clyde were moving some heifers up to the barn. Clyde turned and stood there a moment, watching him go. But his father kept on walking.

Before he died, the wolfer wanted to say sorry but there was no one to say it to.

The only person who'd understand was Winnie and she was dead. He wondered how long she'd known about 'that little flicker', as she'd called it, and why she hadn't told him before, though he knew in his heart he'd never have listened.

He had thought of going to the biologist woman's cabin and saying sorry to her. But he didn't know her and he was too ashamed to tell her what he'd done. And anyhow, it wasn't just this he needed to apologize for. It was a whole lifetime. In the end, he'd come straight to the mine. It was as good a place as any.

When he'd first gotten here, his mind was racing so crazily that he thought maybe the pup he'd shot the night before might not be dead after all and if he could only find the entrance to the mine, he might yet be able to save it. He'd hunted all around, but he couldn't find it and in the end he'd come to his senses and remembered the damage the bullet had done.

Now he sat naked, with his back propped against a tree at the edge of the clearing where the covered airshaft was. He'd thrown all his clothes down there and imagined them lying on top of the wolves. His withered skin was almost as pale as the snow. He watched the stars grow dim and disappear one by one in the dawn sky.

The cold was taking possession of him. He felt it creep up his legs and up his arms, closing in stealth upon his heart. He felt it coalescing on his scalp like a cap, while his breath slowed and froze and stiffened in his beard.

He was so cold that he wasn't cold at all. In fact, a dreamy kind of peace was settling on him. And as it did, his thoughts began to play tricks. He thought he heard Winnie calling him and he tried to call back to her, but his voice was frozen inside him. Then he realized that all he'd heard was a pair of ravens, flapping across the salmon sky above the clearing.

He had dealt in death all his days and thus had little fear of it. And when at last it came, there was no clamor or fanfare of pain, nor any vengeful recitation of his sins.

Instead, in his reverie, he saw a baby's face, by the light of a candle, staring at him. Perhaps it was the baby down at the house, though it seemed somehow different. Perhaps it was the child he and Winnie had never had. Then, suddenly, the wolfer knew it was his own young self. And in that moment, the shadow of his unknown mother leaned toward the candle flame and gently blew it out.

SPRING

32

The second thaw of the year came with more discretion than the first. There was no sudden, ardent wind to melt the snow in a rush and the Hope River, satisfied perhaps with earlier extravagance, confined itself, brimming but benign, within its banks.

By now, the first week in April, the snow had left the plains to dry dun-colored in the watery sun and had retreated like a tide up the valley. It lapped awhile from the fringes of the forest and reached in streaks of foam into the shaded folds and runnels of the higher ranches. It was too early yet for any tree to trust this wasn't merely another trick of winter, and though the forest's warmer clearings clicked and fluttered and pre-pared to unfurl, the cottonwoods that ribboned up along the valley would stay cynically gray and leafless for at least another month.

The clock that ticked in the womb of the white wolf, how-ever, would brook no such delay. Three weeks ago, she had found a deserted coyote den at the foot of a clearcut and while her two surviving pups looked on bemused, she had dug for hours on end until it was remodeled to her taste.

Her belly bagged heavily now and in the melting snow she found it ever harder to hunt. The two pups were now full-grown yearlings. But although they had the weight of adults, they lacked the wiles and wisdom. They had helped in many a kill but never until now had to clinch one themselves. And with their mother grown so slow they were a poor match even for the weakest winter-wasted deer.

Together, a dozen times a day, they stalked and tested and chased and failed. Sometimes they would catch a rabbit or a snowshoe hare and share it with their mother, but the meal was rarely worth the energy it cost. Rangy and restless, they would follow the scent of carrion and plunder food from lesser predators.

It was a different scent one day that led them to the drifted edge of a clearing where an old man sat propped against a tree. His bare toes poked through the snow which was marked at a wary distance by the tracks of coyotes and bobcats. The wolves were warier still for there was something fearful yet familiar in his smell and something worse by far in the air of the place where they had found him. They slunk away with their ears flat and their tails tucked beneath them and left his carcass for the waking bears.

The smell that wafted on the warming air from the valley ranches was more tempting by far. The main herds were calving now and the wolves had already found those places where the ranchers dumped their dead. They had chased off coyotes and eaten undisturbed. Traveling the cracks and coulees of the land, they witnessed the birth of these creatures whose flesh they had sampled and they saw how slow-witted and vulnerable they seemed.

Now the white wolf's hour was approaching and she disappeared alone into her den. The two yearlings waited all night and all the next day for her to emerge. They paced to and fro and lay for hours with their heads on their paws, watching the mouth of the den. Sometimes they would put their heads into the hole and whine and a growl from below would warn them to keep out. And on the second evening, when still she failed to emerge, hungry and impatient, they wandered off.

And while their mother bore six new pups, they followed in their dead father's footsteps, stole down from the forest and, with consummate ease, slew their first calf.

Their choice was impeccable: purebred Calder Black Angus.

It had seemed like a good idea when she set off from the cabin. But now, as she parked and looked across the street toward the gift store, Helen wanted to turn right around and drive off again. It was probably too late. Luke's mother might have already seen her through the shop window.

She had told Luke she was coming into town to pick up some supplies from Iverson's. She was pretty sure he wouldn't like the idea of her going to see his mother. But Helen felt she owed the woman some kind of explanation. Quite what she was going to say, she didn't know. Sorry I stole your son, perhaps? Sorry I stole his virginity? She found it hard enough to explain it to herself, let alone anyone else.

How could anyone begin to understand how she'd felt that day, when he'd shown up at the cabin with those two big bags and said he'd left home and could he maybe 'stay for a few days'? She had just put her arms around him and they'd stood there for a long time, holding on to each other.

'You'll be safe now,' he'd said. And that's how she felt.

And to be living with him in that tiny place, which was their world and no one else's, seemed the most natural thing

427

imaginable. Luke joked that they lived like wolves. And in a way it was true, for there was a kind of unashamed animality about them. At night, before they went to bed, they would often heat a tub of water on the stove, then take off their clothes and wash each other's bodies with a cloth. Never had she known a lover so tender and never, even with Joel, had she felt so physically needful.

With Joel, there had been passion and pleasure, and friendship too, but only now did she realize that there had never been real intimacy of the kind that she shared with Luke. With Joel, she had become watchful of herself, careful at all times to be the kind of woman she thought he wanted and would want to keep.

It seemed to her now that true intimacy was only possible when two people were simply themselves, not constantly monitoring. And with Luke, that's how she could be. He made her feel wanted and beautiful and, most important of all, for the first time in her life, completely unjudged.

But how could she begin to say anything remotely like this to his mother, for heavensakes? Maybe, after all, she should give it a miss and drive home. Instead, she mentally crossed herself and got out of the pickup.

Its freshly painted door looked almost as bad as it had with the writing on it. Luke had found the right shade at a Toyota dealer in Helena and done a great job painting it out. The trouble was, the rest of the vehicle was so faded and rusty that the door stood out like a bare billboard, tempting someone to do it again.

The door of Paragon clanked loudly as she went in. Thank God there were no customers, just Ruth Michaels at the till.

'Helen, hi! How're you doing?'

'I'm fine thanks. You?'

'You bet. Now all that snow's gone.'

'I know. Is Mrs Calder here?'

428

'Sure, she's out back. I'll go get her. Want a coffee?'

'No thanks.'

Helen waited, humming a nervy little tune under her breath. She could hear the two women talking, but not what they were saying. Ruth came back, putting on her coat.

'I have to go out for awhile. I'll see you later Helen, okay?'

'Okay.'

The door clanked again and she noticed that, as Ruth went out, she flipped over the OPEN/CLOSED sign and clicked the catch.

'Hello, Helen.'

'Hi, Mrs Calder.'

Helen hadn't seen her since Thanksgiving and she was struck again by how like Luke she looked; the same pale skin and beautiful green eyes. She smiled.

'What can I do for you?'

'Uh. Well, I . . .'

'Come back here and we can sit down where no one can see us.'

Helen followed her to the little coffee bar and perched herself on one of the stools. Eleanor Calder went behind the counter.

'Can I make you a coffee?'

'Not unless you're going to have one.'

'I think I'll have a Why Bother.'

'Then I'll have a Bother. A large one, with an extra shot.'

Helen was still trying to figure out where to start. She watched in silence while Luke's mother deftly made their coffees. She marveled at how a woman could be married to a man like Buck Calder for so long and yet retain such grace and dignity.

'I came to explain about me and Luke – not *explain* exactly, just . . . let you know that . . . oh, shit.'

Mrs Calder smiled. 'Let me make it easier for you.' She put

429

Helen's coffee in front of her and went on making her own. 'You've made Luke very happy. As far as I'm concerned, you've done him nothing but good.'

She came around the counter and sat down, thoughtfully stirring her coffee. Helen was stunned.

'Thank you,' she said, fatuously.

'As to him moving in with you, all I'd say is, some of the folk around here are a little old-fashioned. But that's your decision. And in all honesty, I don't know where else he'd go.'

'You moved out too, Luke says.'

'Yes.'

'I'm sorry.'

'Don't be sorry. I should have done it years ago. I guess I only stayed because of Luke.'

They talked for awhile about Luke's college application and then about the wolves. Helen said there were probably only three or four of them left now. Out of superstition, she didn't mention that only yesterday they'd lost the alpha female's signal too. Though, with luck, that might mean she was denning.

'What's happened to the others?'

'Don't know. Someone's killing them off, maybe.'

Eleanor Calder frowned.

'You know, I forgot to tell Luke and maybe I shouldn't say a word. But my son-in-law has got someone working for him up at his place, called Lovelace. I couldn't figure out where I'd heard the name, but then I remembered. There was a famous old trapper called Lovelace used to live here in Hope. A "wolfer", they called him.'

Dan could see straight away that this time Calder and his son-in-law had followed the stockgrowers' association guidelines to the letter. They had covered the two dead calves with weighted tarpaulins and then carefully laid lengths of plywood

430

over the tracks and the scat that the wolves had left as a calling card.

Luckily, this time they hadn't called the TV station, but Clyde Hicks was doing a pretty good job himself. He'd had his video camera rolling as soon as Dan and Bill Rimmer drove into the pasture. As usual, Dan had brought his camera along to shoot the necropsy, but Hicks wasn't taking any chances.

'You government people can edit stuff in and out and have the pictures say whatever you want,' he said. 'We're gonna make sure we got our own record.'

He clearly fancied himself as something of an artist and kept panning and zooming and changing angles so that he could film not only the necropsy but Dan filming it too. All he needed was a third camera and he'd have himself a film-within a film-within a film.

Calder hadn't even said hello. His silence was deafening. When he'd called Dan at the office to tell him what had happened, he'd stuck to cold facts. The only thing he'd added was a warning to Dan not to bring Helen Ross. He didn't want her on his property, he said. Dan had left a message on her voice mail, telling her.

Now Rimmer had the second calf skinned out on the tailgate of his truck. The teeth marks and hemorrhaging left no doubt that the first had been killed by a wolf or wolves.

Calder stood watching, with his arms folded. There was none of the crocodile charm he'd oozed on the two previous occasions they'd been summoned to his ranch. He looked pale and drawn and he had the dark rings under his eyes that most ranchers got during calving time. He kept clenching the muscles in his jaw. It was like a finger itching on a trigger.

Dan knew something was wrong when Bill Rimmer went quiet. There were teeth marks but almost no hemorrhaging. He was opening up the calf's chest now.

431

'Well,' he said at last. 'They certainly fed on this little fella too.' He straightened up and shot a glance at Dan before turning to face Calder. 'But they didn't kill him.'

'What?' Calder said.

'The calf was stillborn.'

Calder looked at him for a moment.

'We don't have stillborn calves,' he said icily.

'Well, sir, I'm afraid this one was. His lungs haven't opened, I can show you, if—'

'Get out of here.'

Dan tried to mediate. 'I'm sure there'd be no problem getting full fall market price compensation for them both, sir. Defenders of Wildlife are very understanding—'

'You think I'd touch their blood money?'

'Sir, I—'

'Now get the hell off my property.'

Luke almost got lost in the labyrinth of logging roads. He didn't dare risk driving up past the ranch in case anyone saw him. The only other way was through the forest and it was a long time since he'd used it.

He had set off as soon as Helen got back and told him. It was midday and Kathy would be down at the big house, cooking lunch for the calving crew. But time was ticking away fast. She normally went home about three. He only had about half an hour.

At last he found the trail he was looking for. It was muddy and potholed and once he had to stop and haul a fallen tree out of the way. But at last he knew, from the lie of the land, that he was above Kathy's house and he parked and went the rest of the way on foot.

From the top of the pasture there didn't seem to be anyone around. There was a silver trailer and an old gray Chevy tucked away behind the barn. He knew neither belonged to

432

Clyde and Kathy. When he got down to Prince's grave, Maddie, the old collie, came barking around the side of the house, then recognized him and came, squirming and wagging her tail, toward him. While he bent down to make a fuss of her, he kept an eye out to see if anyone had been alerted by her hollering. Everything was quiet.

Just to make sure, he knocked on the kitchen door and called out around the barn. There was nobody there. He walked quickly around the back to the trailer and knocked on the door and when there was no reply he tried the handle. It wasn't locked.

It didn't take him long to figure out that it wasn't the home of any carpenter. The smell alone told you. There was a wolf-skin on the bed, though that didn't mean much. Then he found the hidden cupboards. Two were packed with traps and wires and snares and things he'd never seen before. In another one he found bottles, all numbered but not named. He uncorked one and sniffed it. It smelled just like the stuff Helen had. Wolf pee.

Then he heard a car pulling up.

He quickly put the bottle and one of the snares in his coat pocket and put everything back as he'd found it. He stepped down from the trailer and tried to shut the door quietly, but it made a loud click.

'Mr Lovelace?'

Luke froze and cussed under his breath. It was Clyde. He was coming around the barn.

'Mr Lovelace?'

When he saw Luke, his face switched in an instant from friendly to hostile. Kathy appeared behind him, holding the baby.

'Luke!' she said.

'Hi.'

'What are you doing here?' Clyde said.

433

'I w–wanted to see my sister.'

'Oh, yeah? How did you get here, fly?'

Luke nodded up toward the forest. 'I p–parked up there.'

'You've got a nerve, snooping around other people's property.'

'Clyde, for pete's sake,' Kathy said.

Clyde's eyes flicked to the trailer.

'You been snooping in there too?'

'No, I j–just knocked. There's n–nobody there.'

He felt himself flushing. When the hell was he going to learn how to lie properly?

Clyde nodded. 'Is that so?'

Luke shrugged. 'Yeah.'

'Get your ass out of here.'

'Clyde!' Kathy said 'He came to see me!'

'Well? He's seen you, ain't he?'

'Don't you dare speak to me like—'

'Shut up.'

Luke saw his sister flinch.

'It's okay, Kathy. I'll g–go.'

He walked past them and gave Kathy and the baby as brave a smile as he could manage. She seemed close to tears and she turned and walked away. When he reached the dog's grave, Luke started to run. And he didn't stop till he'd got all the way back to his car.

It didn't take him as long to get back to the cabin and when he arrived he saw Dan Prior's car parked outside next to Helen's pickup. Buzz came bounding through the mud to greet him.

From the tense silence, he knew as soon as he stepped inside that they had been arguing. Dan nodded to him.

'Hi Luke.'

'Hi.'

Luke looked at Helen. She seemed very upset.

434

'Dan wants to kill the rest of the wolves,' she said.

'Helen, come on—'

'Well, it's true, isn't it? Or are we all supposed to call it, what was it? Oh yeah, "lethal control".'

Luke looked from one to the other. 'Why?'

Dan sighed. 'They killed one of your father's calves.'

'So Dan's going to let himself be bullied into doing exactly what your father wants: get rid of the wolves. No wolves, no way – all you have to do is shout loud enough.'

'Helen, you just don't understand simple politics do you?'

'Politics!'

'Yeah, politics. Let this thing get any worse and the whole wolf recovery program could get knocked back years! These wolves have had enough goddamn chances already. Sometimes you have to lose a battle to win the war.'

'That's bullshit, Dan. You're just letting Calder push you around. Remember what you said? About Hope being the real test? If you don't take a stand against people like him, you'll never win the war.'

'Helen, you've just got to face it. Hope isn't ready for wolves.'

'You do this and it never will be. I don't know why the hell you ever asked me to come here in the first place.'

'You know something? I ask myself the same question.'

'You used to have balls.'

'You used to have brains.'

They stood glaring at each other. Luke reached into his pocket and brought out the snare and the bottle of wolf pee. He put them on the table.

'Does this m-make any difference?'

Buck had driven right up as soon as Clyde called him. The two of them went straight to Lovelace's trailer.

'How long since you last saw him?' Buck asked.

435

'Must be near on three weeks. Kathy saw him going off on his snowmobile in the middle of the night. She's been worrying about him because he's never been gone that long before. She thinks something's happened to him.'

If it had, Buck wasn't going to grieve too much. It had taken the old fool a hell of a long time to kill a handful of wolves and cost Buck a small fortune. And still the damn things were killing cattle.

They checked inside the trailer. It didn't look as if Luke had touched anything. If he had, he'd been real careful.

'You're sure he was in here?'

'I think so.'

Buck thought a moment. For Luke to have come sneaking around, he must have had his suspicions. For all Buck knew, the boy might go right back, tell Dan Prior and in no time at all there'd be a bunch of feds coming up the driveway.

'We'd better get rid of the trailer,' Buck said. 'And his truck too.'

'What, burn them or something?'

'Clyde, sometimes you're so slow, I almost give up. No not burn them. Take them somewhere and leave them.'

'Right.' He paused. 'What if the old guy comes back?'

'Then we tell him where they are. Okay?'

They got busy at once. While Clyde tidied up and secured things inside the trailer, Buck walked over to the house to call Ray. He told him something urgent had cropped up with the wolf business and that he and Jesse would have to do an extra calving shift. Ray grumbled a little but agreed.

'If Mr Lovelace has had an accident or something, shouldn't somebody be up there looking for him?' Kathy said.

'Sure they should. I'll have a quiet word with Craig Rawlinson about it. But, you know, sweetheart, we've got to be careful what we say. He was sorting out some coyotes for us, right? Don't breathe a word about wolves.'

'Dad, I'm not that stupid.'

'I know that, sweetheart. You're my top girl.'

He gave her a hug. He said he and Clyde were going to move the trailer out, just in case Luke had gone blabbing to his Fish and Wildlife pals. If anyone came while they were gone, she was to say she didn't know a thing.

Back at the barn, Clyde had found the keys to the wolfer's old Chevy and together they hitched it up to the trailer. They made sure they hadn't left any of the wolfer's things lying around, then took off. Buck drove the wolfer's pickup, while Clyde followed in his own.

They dumped the chevy and the trailer at a big truck stop, some forty-five miles east of Hope. It would be awhile, Buck thought, before anyone noticed.

When Kathy first heard the cars, she thought it must be Clyde and her daddy come back from wherever it was they'd taken the trailer. But a few seconds later, through the kitchen window, she saw two beige-colored trucks she'd never seen before pull up across the yard next to her daddy's. There were two men in each vehicle, all of them wearing hats. She suddenly felt very scared.

They all got out and two waited by their vehicle while the other two headed over to the house. Kathy went to the door and as she opened it, one of them, a tall man with a large mustache, showed her some ID. She was too flustered to read it.

'Mrs Hicks?'

'Yes?'

'I'm Special Agent Schumacher from US Fish and Wildlife Service Law Enforcement Division. This here's Special Agent Lipsky.'

'Uh-huh.'

Kathy recognized them. They'd been at the wolf meeting

437

last fall in the community hall. As Schumacher put his ID away, she caught a glimpse of a pistol holstered inside his jacket. She tried to look casual, forced a smile.

'So what can I do for you?'

'Ma'am, your husband would be Mr Clyde Hicks?'

'That's right.'

'May I have a word with him, please?'

'He's not here right now. Is there something wrong?'

Kathy noticed how Agent Lipsky and the other two were all staring over toward the barn.

'Ma'am, we've received information that someone's been doing some illegal trapping work on Forest Service land, possibly involving the taking of animals listed as endangered.'

'Oh, is that right?'

'Yes, ma'am. And the informant had reason to believe the person or persons involved were operating out of here.'

'Really?' She tried a little laugh, but it came out all wrong. 'I'm sure there's some mistake.'

Then she saw Clyde's car come over the ridge, followed by another that she soon recognized as Deputy Sheriff Rawlinson's. Her daddy was sitting beside him. The agents turned and stood waiting.

As Clyde got out, Kathy could see the anger in his eyes and she prayed he wasn't going to act like a jerk and get himself into trouble. She was thankful her daddy was there to take charge. She stood to one side while Agent Schumacher went through it all again.

Her daddy heard him out in silence. From the look on Craig Rawlinson's face, he didn't like the look of the agents either. Clyde tried once to interrupt but got himself a stern look that quickly shut him up.

'I think someone must have gotten their wires a little crossed,' her daddy said when Agent Schumacher had finished.

'Have you had anybody staying up here lately, in a trailer?'

Her daddy frowned and looked at Clyde. 'That old fella who was up here awhile back, sorting out those coyotes, he had a trailer didn't he, Clyde?'

'Yeah. Think he did.'

Agent Schumacher nodded, thoughtfully chewing his mustache.

'Mind if we take a look around?'

Clyde erupted. 'Yes, I damn well do.'

Kathy's daddy put up a hand to silence him.

'I don't believe we can be of any further assistance to you Mr Schumacher. And I might add, that as a former state legislator, I take exception to any suggestion that I might be harboring a criminal.'

'Sir, nobody has suggested that. We're simply following up information received. Just doing our job.'

'Well, it's done. And I'll thank you to leave.'

The agent reached into his pocket and pulled out a piece of paper. 'Sir, this is a warrant that says I can search the premises.'

Kathy's daddy lifted his chin. Craig Rawlinson stepped forward.

'You guys are way out of line,' he said. 'Do you know who you're talking to here? Mr Calder is one of the most respected members of our community. He also happens to have lost thousands of dollars' worth of calves to these damn wolves you're so anxious to protect. They killed two more last night. I say, if someone's killing them, good for him.'

'I never mentioned wolves, Sheriff,' Schumacher said. 'All I said was, "animals listed as endangered".'

'We all know what you're talking about,' Clyde said.

'Sir, we'd like to search the premises.'

Kathy saw her daddy's eyes flash, the same look that used to have them all diving for cover when they were kids.

'You'll do it over my dead body,' he said in a low voice.

439

Kathy nearly called out. Let them look, what the hell did it matter? The trailer wasn't even there anymore. She knew better, though, than to open her mouth.

There was a cold silence. Schumacher looked toward the three other agents. None of them seemed to know whether to take the next step. Kathy saw Craig Rawlinson gulp. Then he stepped into line alongside her daddy and Clyde, all three now facing the agents.

'This is my jurisdiction. And as sheriff of this county, it's my duty to keep the peace. You guys had better leave. Right now.'

Schumacher looked at him, his eyes just dipping for a moment to the gun at Craig's hip. Then he turned and looked at Lipsky, who hadn't said a word all this time but somehow seemed to be the one who called the shots. After a moment or two, he gave a little nod.

Schumacher pointed at Craig Rawlinson.

'You're the one who's out of line, mister,' he said. 'I'll be calling your boss.'

'You do that, pal.'

The agents got back in their cars and no one said a word until they'd disappeared over the ridge. Clyde punched the air.

'Yes!'

Craig blew with relief and Kathy's daddy grinned and clapped him on the back.

'Son, I'm proud of you. That's how the West was won.'

He turned to Kathy. She wanted to cry, not with relief, but rage.

'You okay, sweetheart?'

'No, I'm not! You men can tell your own damn lies from now on.'

And she turned her back on them and headed for the house.

33

The Red Bell Jet Ranger came bursting out of the canyon, the *thwock* of its blades making the air shudder and the tops of the trees buckle and wave like fevered fans at a football game.

Through the binoculars, Dan watched it bank steeply and head up the mountain front toward them, perhaps two hundred feet lower than where he and Luke stood watching. As it passed below them, it tilted and they saw Bill Rimmer, sitting with his legs dangling from the helicopter's door.

He was held in by a nylon harness, but from here you couldn't see it, and in his red suit and helmet, he looked like a skydiver getting ready to jump. Helen was in there with him too, but Dan couldn't make her out. The sun flashed on the helicopter's windshield and briefly too on Rimmer's mirror sunglasses as he reached behind him for his rifle.

Dan handed the binoculars to Luke.

'Here, take a look at my budget burning up.'

They were leaning against the hood of Dan's car at the top of a cliff, looking down over a mile of undulating forest toward the Hope Valley. Over the radio, Dan had just given the helicopter pilot the map reference of where the collared yearling was. They'd found her signal earlier, then worked out the reference by telemetry.

Luckily, she was on Forest Service land, somewhere above the ranch that belonged to that TV anchorman, Jordan Townsend, so they didn't need anyone's permission to shoot or land. It was around there that Luke and Helen thought the alpha female might have denned. They hadn't picked up even a whisper of her signal in two days, so by now she probably had a whole new litter of Hope wolves. It was all Dan needed.

The helicopter circled below them and then dipped its nose and fell away east. The pilot must have punched the map reference into his Global Positioning System scanner and all he had to do now was follow it to the wolf and any others that were with her. The shooting would be all over by the time he and Luke got down there.

'Shall we go?' Dan said.

'Okay.'

'Varmints at two o'clock!' the pilot called.

Helen looked ahead and saw only treetops rushing madly by below them and then suddenly the trees were gone and the helicopter was chasing its own shadow into a wide clearcut, scarred with sliprock and a crisscross of felled lodgepoles.

Then she saw them. Two of them, sunning themselves on an outcrop of rock. And as she looked, she saw them stir and gaze up at the roaring red dragon that was swooping from the sky toward them.

She could just make out the collar on the paler one. They scrambled to their feet and started to trot, then lope, up toward the trees, glancing over their shoulders at the helicopter. Bill

Rimmer already had the barrel of the Palmer gun sighted on them. Helen heard him click the safety catch.

'That's as low as I go, boys and girls,' the pilot said into his headset microphone. He was a large, bearded guy with a ponytail and a lot of gold rings. All morning, he'd been telling good but politically incorrect jokes, but was now, thank heavens, in earnest.

'It's okay,' Rimmer said. 'I got him.'

Helen looked ahead. They were flying up the middle of the clearcut at no more than about fifteen feet above the ground. There were trees three times that height racing toward them at the top of the slope.

'Going up in five,' said the pilot. 'Four . . . three . . .'

Helen saw Bill Rimmer's back jolt as he fired and she quickly looked down and saw the uncollared wolf cartwheel as he was hit and then she lost him because the pilot wrenched the helicopter into a steep climb, missing the tops of the trees by what seemed only inches.

The pilot whooped. 'My man! Nice shooting!'

Rimmer grinned. 'Can't say I disagree. Nice flying too. Hey, come on, Helen! Don't look so worried, it's only a dart.'

Dan had only granted the wolves a reprieve at the last minute. Even after Luke had shown him the bottle of wolf urine and the snare, he'd still been adamant that all the remaining wolves except the alpha female must be killed. She and any new pups would be evacuated to Yellowstone, he said.

Helen had argued and shouted and pleaded with him, saying the alpha would starve to death in her den and all her pups die too if there were no others to bring her food. But Dan wouldn't listen. It was only when he got back to the office and heard from Schumacher what had happened up at the Hicks place that he'd changed his mind.

He'd been angry enough already, but Buck Calder's open

defiance of federal agents sent him ballistic. Schumacher said they had checked out Lovelace's place in Big Timber and it looked as if no one had been there in a long time. After talking to the county sheriff, they'd gone back again to the Hicks place this morning, but all they'd found behind the barn was a pen of feeding cows. The ground was so churned up, there was no telling what might have been there before.

Dan said it was time to make a stand. Instead of killing however many wolves remained, they would dart and collar them, then monitor their every goddamn move. And if anyone so much as sneezed on them, he would personally throw the bastard into jail by the balls. Helen resisted making any smart remark about Dan's sudden rediscovery of his own.

The pilot was now taking them in a wide circle, so they could keep an eye on the wolf and know exactly where he was when the tranquilizer took effect.

'You reckon two is all there are now?' Rimmer called out.

'I'm afraid so. Plus the alpha. Do you think those rocks where they were lying could be the den?'

'Could be.'

If so, it was far from ideal. Although the land below was steep and thickly timbered, the den itself was exposed and could easily be seen from the logging road that ran along the top of the clearcut. Helen saw Dan's car stopping there now.

The wolf was almost at the edge of the clearcut but just as he reached the trees, he tottered and fell. The collared one had already fled ahead into the forest.

'Okay, boys and girls. Going down. First floor, ladies' underwear and varmints.'

It took Helen and Rimmer about half an hour to do all that was necessary with the wolf. Dan and Luke walked down and stood by, watching. The yearling was skinny and in poor condition and they had to give him a thorough dusting of lice-killer as well as the usual worm pill and shot of penicillin.

444

'Looks like he's having a hard time of it,' Rimmer said.

'Yeah. His sister's probably the same. Maybe we should have darted her too.'

Luke turned to Dan. 'Is that w-why they've started killing cattle again?'

Dan shrugged. 'Could be.'

Once they'd tagged his ear and activated and tested his collar, Rimmer said goodbye and went back to the helicopter. They wanted it out of the way so as not to frighten the wolf again when he woke up. Helen packed her kit and walked back up the slope with Luke and Dan. The air between her and Dan was still strained and no one spoke all the way to the car.

While they waited for the wolf to stir, Helen showed them, with the help of Dan's binoculars, the rocks where she thought the alpha female might have dug her den. It was only about two hundred yards down the slope.

'Maybe we should get the Forest Service to close this road off,' Helen said. Dan nearly jumped down her throat.

'What the hell are you talking about? It's public land, Helen! *Public*. Get it? If she's dumb enough to den beside a road, frankly, that's her problem.'

'Okay, okay.'

'We can't just go around closing down public roads.'

'Dan, I understand. I'm sorry.'

'I mean, for Godsake.'

Luke was looking through the binoculars, trying to pretend he wasn't there.

'He's g-getting up.'

The wolf staggered a little, then shook himself and sneezed. The anti-lice powder had probably gotten up his nose. He stood there a moment, perhaps trying to figure out what had been done to him and whether that red dragon had only been a dream. He sniffed the air and turned to give them a long and

445

scornful look. Then, at last, he trotted off into the trees, the way his sister had gone.

Dan drove them back to the cabin. No one spoke the whole way. A flock of snow geese had settled on the lake, taking a rest on their long journey north. Dan turned off the engine and the three of them sat for awhile in the car, watching.

Then Luke said he had to go into town to see his mother and fetch a few things. Helen knew he was only making himself scarce so she and Dan could have a few words alone. They watched him walk to his car and drive off.

'I'd better be getting along too,' Dan said, not looking at her.

'Okay.' She opened the door and got out.

'Dan?'

He turned and looked at her. His eyes were hard. 'Yeah?'

'I'm sorry.'

'Sorry for what?'

Helen shrugged. 'I don't know. For everything, I guess. It feels like we're not friends anymore.'

'That's ridiculous.'

'I know you disapprove. Of me and Luke, I mean.'

'Hey, Helen. It's your life.'

'Yes.'

He sighed and shook his head. 'Oh shit. It's just . . . Well, you know.'

She nodded. He looked away, down toward the lake again and Helen followed his gaze. The snow geese were taking off. She could hear the thrum and whine of their ink-tipped wings.

'Ginny found this thing on the Internet a couple of nights ago,' he said. 'All about the south pole and how some scientist has worked out that it isn't where everybody always thought it was, but a few feet over to one side. So all these years, people have been slogging over the ice and dying and risking their lives, just to plant their flags in the wrong spot. Even poor old Amundsen, he never really got there.'

He gave her a sad smile. 'Anyway, there you go.'

He restarted the engine. She reached into the car and he took her hand in his and held it a moment

'You know where I am,' he said.

'I know where you are.'

Perhaps it was dread of the red dragon that did it.

Or a sudden rush of good sense. Whatever the reason, for more than two weeks, the two collared yearlings behaved like model citizens. It probably had most to do with the weather. For although some nights still brought frost, the days were growing warm and there was easy prey to be found among the many smaller creatures waking from their winter sleep.

The wolves' best efforts were still no match for the elk who were moving slowly back to the higher sunny slopes and canyons. Even though the bulls had shed their antlers now, they watched these two novice predators with regal contempt. Several times, however, the pair managed to fell a young or weakened deer and they bore proud morsels back to the den.

Only when Helen and Luke witnessed this did they know for sure that the mother and her new litter must be down there. They spied unseen from higher ground to one side of the clearcut, sometimes together, sometimes alone, and only ever when the wind was right. At night they used an infrared scope that Dan had lent them. And whenever they came, they were careful to leave their vehicle well hidden a mile to the south and went quietly the rest of the way on foot.

From their lookout in the trees, they could see the road that ran along the top of the clearcut and were glad to find how rarely it was used. Once, at noon, they saw a logging truck go by while a yearling lounged in plain view on the rocks above the den. They held their breath, but the driver didn't slow or seem to look.

Down in the cool, dark earth, unseen by all, the white wolf suckled her pups. The scraps of meat the yearlings brought were barely enough to keep her milk flowing. And though all six of her pups still lived, they were smaller and weaker than her last year's litter.

Their smoke-blue eyes were open now and their ears were unfolding and straightening. The bolder ones were already exploring the den's nesting chamber, but as soon as they started to wander into the tunnel, their mother would gently take them in her jaws and carry them back to safety. In a day or two, their milk teeth would be breaking through and they would start to need meat. And only then would she let them wander from the den.

It was after eight and Kathy was about to shift from irritated to downright mad. She was in her best dress, Buck Junior was in bed, supper was in the oven, but where the heck was Clyde?

Calving was all but over and it was their first evening alone together at home in over a month – or supposed to be. Since her mom moved out, Kathy had been cooking supper for the whole crew down at the big house. But tonight everyone was going into town to eat at Nelly's, so that she and Clyde could have a cozy, romantic supper and get to know each other again. He had probably gone for a drink with them first.

Things had been a little cool between them since all that trouble with the federal agents. Or to be more precise, she'd been cool and he'd been cautious, for, if she let herself, Kathy could still get angry about it. Why men always had to turn everything into a contest over who had the biggest dick, she'd never understand. Anyway, she'd made him suffer and now it was time to make up.

448

To that end, she had spent the entire afternoon preparing a fancy French meal. She had even printed out a little menu on the computer: *Vichyssoise* soup, followed by *Boeuf en Croûte Napoléon*, followed by *Pie Pécan* (which, okay, wasn't really French, but happened to be Clyde's favorite). And now the whole thing was going steadily to ruin.

To keep herself from smashing something, she was wrapping Lucy Millward's present. The wedding was tomorrow afternoon and the whole town was going to be there.

Kathy had bought her a painting at Paragon. It was by a young artist who lived up Augusta way and who Ruth said looked a little like Mel Gibson. It showed the sun setting over the mountains, which, come to think of it, wasn't all that appropriate for a wedding present, but Lucy wouldn't mind. She was marrying a man from Great Falls called Dimitri. He was in the oil business and seriously rich.

Kathy had just finished writing Lucy's card when Clyde's headlights lit up the kitchen window. When he came in, he looked so sheepish that she almost forgave him on the spot for being late, though she wasn't going to show it. She let him kiss her cheek. He smelled of drink.

'Sorry, honey.'

'Shall I stab you now or later?'

'Whichever.'

'Later then. Light the candles and sit down.'

The food wasn't completely spoiled. Clyde was sober (or drunk) enough to say that it was the best he'd ever tasted. And by the time they got to the *Pie Pécan,* after a couple of glasses of wine, Kathy was starting to feel mellow. The first mouthful had Clyde frowning at the menu and saying it tasted a little like pecan pie. She explained it was similar, but made with French nuts.

Then he had to go and spoil things by bringing up those lousy wolves again. He said that earlier on, down at The Last

449

Resort, he'd been talking with two of the guys from the post and pole company who'd told him they knew where the wolves were denning.

'So, unless someone does something about it, there'll be a whole new pack of the critters. It's unbelievable. World's gone plumb crazy.'

Kathy got up and started clearing the dishes. She didn't want to hear another thing about wolves. And it made her think of poor old Mr Lovelace and that awful afternoon when those federal agents showed up. Clyde got up and went into the living room. She could hear him rummaging around for something in the closet.

'Clyde, are you going to finish up or not?'

'I'm coming, I'm coming.'

When he reappeared, he had something in his hands. It took Kathy a few moments to realize what it was. It was the wolfer's loop.

'Where the hell did you get that?'

'It's the thing he showed you, right?'

'You stole it from his trailer?'

'I just borrowed it.'

'Clyde, for heavensake!'

'All I'm asking is you show me how it works.'

He laid it on the table and came and put his arms around her.

'Come on, honey. Help me. I want to do it for your daddy.'

34

The letter had arrived in Helen's mailbox that morning. It came in an important-looking envelope, marked *University of Minnesota, Twin Cities Campus, Office of Admissions* and offered Luke a freshman place, starting that fall, at the College of Biological Science.

Helen screamed and hugged him and told him how smart he was. Luke wanted to tell Dan right away and because the cell phone had again refused to recharge, they drove into town to call him. He insisted they come on into Helena so he could buy them both lunch to celebrate.

'The wolves seem to be behaving themselves okay,' he said. 'It won't hurt to leave them without a nanny for a few hours.'

It was Lucy Millward's wedding day and Luke felt bad about not being there. Both he and Helen had been invited, sent separate presents and pretended they would try to come

451

if wolf work allowed. The truth was, neither of them fancied bumping into Luke's father or Clyde, both of whom would be there. They accepted Dan's offer.

He took them to a place he liked called the Windbag and they all ate and drank far more than they needed. Dan was in a much better mood than the last time they saw him and seemed to have made his peace with Helen. Luke and Helen drove back out to Hope, into the lowering sun, neither of them talking much, just feeling dreamy and good and together.

When they got back to the cabin, they walked down to the lake and Luke threw sticks into the water for Buzz to fetch, while Helen lay in the grass by the old boat and watched. When the dog grew tired, Luke went and sat with her and she lay with her head in his lap, looking up at a sky that was swirling with red and orange and purple clouds.

'When I was little I liked to hide,' she said.

'D-doesn't every kid?'

'No, I mean, *really* hide. In our living room there were some glass doors that led out to the backyard and they had like, these long, red velvet drapes. And once, when I was eight years old, I got back from school early and crept into the house and hid there. For five hours.'

'Five hours?'

'Yep. I just stood there, dead still. Hardly breathed. My mom and dad just went nuts. They called the school, the neighbors, all my friends, and when no one had seen me, they were convinced I'd been kidnapped and called the police. There was a river not far from the house and a woman said she'd seen a little girl down there, so the police got divers and they searched the whole river.

'And when it got dark they had floodlights out and helicopters combing the neighborhood with searchlights. It must have cost hundreds, thousands of dollars. And I could hear all

452

these phone calls being made and my mom crying and screaming and everything and it was so . . . so terrible, what I'd done, that I couldn't come out.'

'So what happened?'

'I wet myself and my sister saw it under the drapes and they found me.'

'What did they do?'

Helen took a breath. 'Well, they were pretty cut up about it. Kind of relieved and angry all at the same time. And I said, "Why on earth didn't anybody look behind the drapes before getting into all that?" I mean, all these highly trained cops and social workers and everyone, and not one of them looks behind the drapes!'

'Did they p-punish you?'

'Yeah, they sent me to this shrink woman for a year. And she said I had a "problem with reality" and that's why I liked to hide so much.'

'And what do you think?'

Helen looked at him. 'Hey, you know, you'd make a pretty good shrink yourself. That's what they say: "And what do *you* think?"'

Luke smiled. 'Well?'

'I think she was dead right.'

Luke almost started to tell her about his hiding. How he'd hidden and watched her from up there in the trees, when she first came here. But he decided not to. Then he suddenly understood why she'd told him all this.

'Y-you think that's what we're doing, don't you? Hiding f-from reality.'

'Uh-huh.'

'It f-feels pretty real to me.'

Helen reached up and stroked his cheek.

'I know.'

'Look, I've been thinking. W-we could go spend the

453

summer traveling. Go up to Alaska or somewhere. Then in the fall, you can come to Minneapolis with me.'

She laughed.

'W-why not? You could finish your thesis.'

'Oh, Luke.' She sighed. 'I don't know.'

'Tell me. Why not?'

He peered down into her shadowed face. Her eyes gave no reflection of the darkening sky now. He lowered his head and kissed her and she reached for him and pulled him gently down beside her and he felt their mouths and limbs stir with that mutual, miraculous hunger.

It was their way now, he realized, his as much as hers. To answer with their bodies those questions too brutal for their heads.

As he went inside her, a picture flashed across his mind of a small girl, standing like a statue behind a crimson curtain. And then, as the night enshrouded them, it was lost. Melted with all fear and all sorrow in the oblivion of their mingled flesh.

Lucy Millward looked a whole lot more comfortable on her horse than her husband-to-be did on his. Doug and Hettie had made sure to give him the calmest they had on the ranch, a dark brown gelding whose proper name was Zack, often lengthened by Lucy to Prozac. Whether or not Dimitri had been thus informed wasn't clear, but he sat there as if the animal were merely taking a short breather from the apocalypse and might at any moment bear him straight to hell.

'He's a city boy,' Hettie had quietly confided to Eleanor, when earlier they had watched everyone mount up. 'But who needs horses when you own a hundred oil wells?'

Everyone was in the corral now, sitting on pews of baled hay and watching the proceedings. At the western end of the corral, against a backdrop of mountain and reddening sky and beneath a high gateway, entwined all around with red, white and blue ribbon that fluttered in the evening breeze, Lucy and Dimitri were declaring their love.

Their horses stood side by side, facing the minister's mare, whose tail flicked from time to time as if to emphasize the gravity of the vows. Lined up on either side were the brides-maids and the pageboys, three of each, all appropriately mounted. The girls wore white dresses, the boys black suits and hats, except for Lucy's younger brother Charlie, whose hat had twice blown off and was now lying where it wanted to be, under the feet of his Shetland pony.

Lucy's blond hair was woven with lilies and her white satin gown billowed gracefully to show white patent boots. Despite his obvious discomfort, Dimitri looked quite the part. He was wearing a black flat-brimmed hat, a black three-piece suit with a long jacket, boots and spurs and a black ribbon tie with a wingtip collar. Apart from the video cameras and some-body's mobile phone going off, the whole thing was like a living tableau from the Old West.

Eleanor was sharing a bale with Kathy, while Clyde sat with Buck on the next. It was the first time she and Buck had seen each other since she'd walked out and it wasn't as awk-ward as she'd feared.

She and Ruth had gotten here early to help Hettie prepare the food. When Buck arrived, he'd made a point of ignoring her. He'd gone around greeting everyone else and joking and Eleanor knew it was all for her benefit. It was almost like watching a stranger. He looked different; paler and older, as if the shine had been rubbed off his skin. There were red rims around his eyes. When they all filed down from the house to the corral, at last he acknowledged her.

'Eleanor.'

'Buck.'

She smiled but he didn't smile back, just gave her a nod.

And that was all. It was fine by her. In a way, it made it easier. Everyone else made a real fuss of her, asking how she was with such concern it was as though she'd just had major surgery. In a way, perhaps, she had.

The truth was, she hadn't felt so good and in control of her life for many years. Living out of a suitcase at Ruth's house, she felt free and young and that the world once again held promise, though of what, she had no idea.

Ruth had turned out to be a real friend. In their long, late-night talks, she had a way of coming up with things that gave Eleanor new insights, even on her own marriage. She had always assumed Buck's philandering simply stemmed from an overcharged love of women. Ruth, however, believed almost the opposite. She thought it might perhaps be prompted by some underlying contempt or even fear of women and that sex was his way of proving his superiority.

Not all their discussions were so intense. In fact, Eleanor hadn't laughed as much in years. Sometimes she went to bed aching from it.

All she missed of her old life was Luke. But he came to see her every few days and had once even brought Helen to supper. Eleanor had done her best to persuade him to come to the wedding, but she knew he wouldn't and understood why.

'You may kiss the bride,' she now heard the minister say.

'He'll fall off his horse,' Charlie Millward muttered and all around him laughed. Lucy leaned across and spared poor Dimitri the risk and the congregation cheered.

Often, on such occasions, the bride and groom would gallop off together, but today, in case death parted them pre-maturely, Lucy and Dimitri confined themselves to a stately walk around the corral. Then, for the next half-hour, they posed for photographs, while everybody else adjourned to the next corral for a drink.

It was all decked out for the party. There were rows of long tables and benches and a wooden dance floor had been laid in the middle. Nelly's son Elmer, in his best *Bikers for Jesus* T-shirt, was playing away on his fiddle and the sun was going down in a picture-book blaze, just like in the painting Kathy had bought. The colored lights around the rails were starting to look pretty.

And then it happened.

It was Doug Millward who heard it first. The photo session was over and he was coming in from the other corral, behind the bride and groom, when Eleanor saw him stop and turn to gaze up toward the pasture. He was frowning and asked those around him to hush and it took awhile for the word to get around and for someone to tell Elmer to quit playing his fiddle. But when he did, and everyone was quiet, you could hear it, quite plainly on the breeze.

The bellowing scream of cattle in distress.

The night was clear and crisp and a three-quarter moon threw their shadows down the slope as they loaded their gear into the pickup. They were wrapped up warm and though neither of them was hungry after their lunchtime blowout with Dan, they had made sandwiches and a flask of coffee for later.

Luke said he was going to stay down at the clearcut all night if necessary. It was twenty-three days since the alpha female had denned and he was convinced that tonight they would get to see the pups.

Buzz still hadn't got the message that he didn't come on these vigils and Helen had to get him out of the pickup and haul him by the collar back to the cabin. She was just locking the door when she saw the beam of headlights angling up through the trees.

It was an unusual time for anyone to come calling and since her truck had been defaced, she was wary of visitors. She went back and stood beside Luke and they both waited in silence to see who it was.

The car was traveling fast, the headlights jagging as it came over the bumps and furrows of dried winter mud. Neither of them recognized the car and only when it came right up to them and stopped did Helen recognize Ruth Michaels at the wheel and Luke's mother beside her. They both got out and Helen knew, even before they spoke, that something was wrong.

'Mom?' Luke said, going to her. 'What's going on?'

'The wolves have killed some of Doug Millward's calves. Your father shot them.'

'Shot the wolves?'

'Two of them. He just grabbed a gun from one of Doug's ranch hands and shot them both. Doug tried to stop him but he wouldn't listen. And now he's getting a whole crowd together and they're going up to the den to kill the rest of them.'

'They know where the den is?' Helen said.

'Clyde says it's up above the Townsend place.'

'They've gone down to The Last Resort to pick up the Hardings and some of Clyde's logger pals,' Ruth said. 'Then everybody's heading up there. They'll all have had a few drinks.'

Luke was shaking his head in disbelief. Helen tried to think.

'I'll call Dan.'

She grabbed a flashlight and ran to the cabin. She snatched up the cell phone and punched in the number. She waited, hissing curses that it was taking so long to connect.

Luke's mother and Ruth were standing in the doorway now and Luke was lighting a lantern. Eleanor's eyes roamed the cabin. It was the first time she'd seen her son's new home. Then Helen realized that all this time on the phone she had been listening to total silence.

'Shit!' She slammed it down.

'It still hasn't re-ch-charged?'

'No. Shit!' She thought for a moment.

'Luke, you go down to the clearcut with your mom and Ruth and try and talk some sense into them. I'll go try and get the pups out.'

'Helen, these guys are pretty fired up,' Ruth said.

'He w-won't listen to us anyway.'

'Then block the road. Do anything. Just stall them, try and buy some time.'

'Helen, you're the only one they might listen to,' Eleanor said.

'I'll g-get the pups out.'

'You've never done it before. You have to crawl right down into the den. With the mother down there, it can be dangerous.'

'I'll manage.'

'Luke, come on—'

'Helen, I can do it!'

She hesitated. He was probably right.

'C-come on, let's go!'

'You'll need something to carry them in. Those bags of yours, the canvas ones.'

Luke ran across the cabin, hauled them out from under the bunk and started emptying them.

'Ruth, we need to get hold of Dan. Could you go into town and call him?'

'Sure.'

Helen scribbled his home number on a piece of paper and handed it to her.

'Call the police too, the Forest Service emergency line, anyone you can think of. Tell them we're at the big clearcut above the Townsend ranch.'

'You bet.' She was off at once, running to her car.

Luke had the two empty bags. He was loading his rifle.

'You won't need that.'

'No, but you might.' He checked that the safety was on and held the rifle out for her to take.

'No.'

'Take it.'

She did as she was told. She picked up the chain saw, locked Buzz in the cabin and followed Luke and his mother to the cars. Ruth was already driving away. Helen dumped the gun and chain saw in the pickup and took the jabstick and another flashlight over to Luke, who was climbing into his Jeep.

'Go down into the den slowly. And be ready, she could come right at you.'

'I know.'

'Keep the jabstick out in front of you. She'll threaten you, but in the end she'll make a break for it.'

'Okay.' He fired the engine and turned on the headlights. 'Shall I bring the p-pups back here?'

Helen hadn't thought about it. But the cabin would be the first place anyone would look.

'Take them to Ruth's house,' Eleanor said.

'Okay.'

'And Luke?' Helen said.

'What?'

'Be careful.'

He smiled and nodded then slammed the door. As he swung the car around, Helen and Eleanor climbed into Helen's pickup. For a moment she thought it wasn't going to start. But at the third try it did and soon she'd caught up with Luke and was following the glow of his tail-lights down through the winding corridor of trees.

'Thank you,' Helen said. 'For coming to tell us.'

Without taking her eyes off Luke's car, Eleanor reached across and gently touched her on the shoulder.

35

The white wolf paused in the mouth of the den while the two biggest and bravest of her pups tottered between her legs and out into the moonlit world.

The excavated earth around the den was packed solid as cement from the pacing of the two yearlings and was strewn with scat and bone shards. One of the pups tried his new teeth out on a piece but then dropped it, unimpressed. There was something near at hand that smelled better.

The mother had smelled it too, all day. Perhaps she thought it was something the yearlings had brought, though they hadn't been back since the humans came the previous night. Perhaps the humans had left it there. She had caught their scent long before she heard their voices and she'd lain still and listened to the scuffle and tramp of their feet outside the den. She'd heard the clink of something too and could still smell it out there, mixed with the waft of fresh meat. It had the same harsh, unnatural tang as the thing that had once snapped shut on her paw.

461

It was a scent unknown to the two pups however. All they smelled was the meat. All day they had tried to leave the den and time and again she had stopped them and carried them back. But after so many hours of waiting in vain for the year-lings to bring food, and with six greedy mouths tugging at her teats, she was starving and at last relented.

The first of the pups staggered with great purpose toward the smell and his mother followed, nudging the other pup before her to his first proper meal. Behind her, two other pups stood in the mouth of the den, blinking at the moon.

There was a lump of pale meat and now she could smell and see others, the same, a few yards to either side. The tang she had smelled came from a line, a thing of humans, that ran between them. She hesitated, sniffed the air.

By now the pup was sniffing the meat. He nudged it with his nose and nipped it, pulling it along the ground. As he tugged, his mother saw the line move and she shied, as she might at a rattlesnake. There was danger here, she now knew. And it was no snake. In a bound she was beside the pup.

But the meat was already inside his mouth and he bit on it.

Luke waved as he forked down off the road and Helen, behind him, flashed her lights and kept on toward the clearcut. He left the car in its usual hiding place, took the bags and the jabstick and headed off at a run through the trees.

The going was tricky. He kept the beam of the flashlight low and ran in the pool it made. There were rocks and roots and tangles of blowdown and several times he caught a foot and fell headlong in the bushes.

He tried to work out how much time he had.

If they set out from The Last Resort, they would be coming from the north. They would use the road that ran from town due west alongside the Townsend property all

462

the way to the forest, then turn left onto the logging road. But without knowing when they had left, it was pointless trying to calculate. All he knew was that he had to keep running.

At last, through the trees ahead of him, he saw the moon-lit glow of the clearcut. He turned off the flashlight and fished in his pocket for Dan's nightscope, while he walked to the forest's edge. He stopped there and switched it on and just as he found focus, the wolf started to bark.

It was the alpha female. She was a few yards from the entrance to the den and barking right at him. There was a movement behind her and it took Luke a moment to realize it was the pups. They were scurrying down into the den. They were much darker than their mother and he couldn't count how many there were. The mother was shepherding them in, but she didn't seem to want to follow them.

When the last one had gone, she started pacing to and fro, all the while looking toward Luke and barking. Every now and again, she kept going back to the same place and lowering her nose to sniff something. Then she would lift her head and bark and now she ended each burst of barking with a howl. Luke willed her to shut up. She was telling the whole world where she was.

He put the nightscope away and stepped into the clearcut. The wolf was about fifty yards away and as he got closer, she seemed to grow less sure of herself. She kept running off a few yards, lowering her tail, and then seemed to get her courage back and turned and came back, barking and howling at him. In the moonlight, Luke could see something dark in the place that she kept returning to. And now, in a pause of her barking, he heard a whine and a whimper that he knew didn't come from her.

As he walked the last few yards to the den, the mother ran off. She stopped about twenty yards away and stood watching

463

him. She was suddenly silent. There was another whimper. He switched on the flashlight.

'Oh God,' he murmured.

Helen had parked the pickup across the road and hidden the keys under a rock nearby. On its own, it wasn't much of a roadblock, but the tall Douglas fir she'd cut down in front of it with the chain saw made it better. Now she was cutting a second and the chips were showering into the beam of Eleanor's flashlight.

In a minute she was through and she stood back and yelled for Eleanor to do the same. The tree leaned and creaked and toppled exactly where she wanted it and the forest repaired its bruised silence around them.

They were a mile and a half north of the clearcut. Helen had chosen the place for its view of the road that wound up from the valley below in a series of steep bends. Any approaching headlights would be seen a long way off. So far there were none.

Helen put the chain saw in the bed of the pickup. Eleanor handed her the flashlight.

'Mind if I switch it off and save the batteries?'

'No. I like the dark.'

She seemed perfectly calm and Helen wondered how she managed it. Her own heart was on a rollercoaster. The two women stood in silence for awhile beside the pickup, staring at the moon. Somewhere far above them in the forest, an owl was calling.

'Are you warm enough?' Helen asked.

'I'm fine.'

'I'd give anything for a cigarette.'

'I used to love to smoke.'

'Well, they say only the best kind of women smoke . . .'

'And the worst kind of men.'

'So if we quit, does that disqualify us?'

'Absolutely not.'

They both laughed and then fell silent again.

'Maybe they're not coming,' Helen said.

'Oh, they'll come.' She frowned. 'What is it, do you think, about these animals, that makes people hate them so much?'

'About wolves? I don't know. Maybe they're too much like us. We look at them and see ourselves. Loving, caring, social creatures who also happen to be terrific killers.'

Eleanor considered this awhile.

'Maybe it's envy too.'

'Of what?'

'That they're still part of nature and we've forgotten how to be.'

She seemed about to go on, when something down in the valley caught her eye.

'Here they come,' she said.

A pair of headlights was coming around the first bend. Helen's heart climbed back on the rollercoaster The women stood watching while another vehicle, then another came into view. And now they could hear their engines and dogs barking. There were more trucks coming now. Five, six . . . eight in all, winding up the road in convoy.

'Well, here we go,' said Helen.

Buck hadn't counted but he figured there were about twenty of them, including a good few he'd rather not have had along. The two Harding boys and the loggers they'd been drinking with in the bar were pretty far gone. Some had brought liquor along and he'd had to stop on the way up and tell them to quit whooping and singing or they could turn around and go home. On the other hand, there was safety in numbers. No one was going to put the whole damn town in jail.

He and Clyde were leading in Clyde's truck, with one of

the loggers sitting wedged between them to make sure they didn't get lost. He was one of the guys who'd come up here with Clyde last night to lay that damn fool loop thing. They should have just stuffed some poison down the hole or poured gasoline in it or something. Anyhow, they'd put that right when they got there now.

Buck's anger had refined itself. Shooting those two wolves, he was so fired up he'd hardly known what he was doing. It was like something bursting into flames in his head, an explosion of all the pressure that had been building inside him, months of being slighted, rejected and thwarted. But now the smoke had cleared and his anger glowed white-hot within him like a branding iron, searing and still.

'Hey, look,' Clyde said. He was peering up ahead. 'There's somebody already got here.'

They were coming around the last bend and the road was leveling out. A couple of hundred yards ahead of them, there was someone with a flashlight. Then, in the headlights, they saw trees had been felled across the road and a truck parked behind them.

'What the . . .?' Clyde said. 'It's the wolf woman. Who the hell's that with her?'

Buck had already seen who it was. And now Clyde recognized her too. He looked at Buck.

'What's Eleanor doing here, for Christsakes?'

Buck didn't answer. She must have gone and told Helen Ross what was happening. His own damned wife.

'Stop here,' he said.

They stopped about fifteen yards short of the roadblock and as they did, Helen Ross stepped over the trees and came toward them, shielding her eyes against Clyde's headlights. Buck got out and walked slowly around to the front of the car. He stood with his back to the hood, waiting for her. All the other men were piling out of their trucks and coming up

466

behind him to see what was going on. Abe Harding's dogs were barking their heads off.

'Hello, Mr Calder.'

He just stared at her. He could tell the little bitch was scared.

'I'm afraid, sir, this road has been closed.'

'Uh-huh? On whose authority?'

'The US Fish and Wildlife Service.'

'This is a public road.'

'I know that, sir.'

Eleanor was coming up behind her now. No doubt thinking she could make a monkey of him in front of everyone. He didn't look at her.

'Craig?' he called out, keeping his eyes on Helen Ross. 'Is Craig there?'

'Yeah!' Craig Rawlinson pushed his way through the crowd.

'Buck?' Eleanor said. He ignored her.

'Sheriff Rawlinson. Does this woman have the authority to close a public road?'

'Not unless she's got a piece of paper to prove it, she hasn't.'

'Buck,' Eleanor said again. 'Please. It's time to stop.'

'Stop?' He laughed. 'Honey, I haven't even gotten started.'

The Ross woman turned to Craig Rawlinson.

'I can't believe you're going to help these men commit a crime.'

'You're the only one who's committing a crime around here, far as I can see. You're obstructing a public highway.'

Ross pointed at Buck. 'This man has just shot two wolves . . .' Everyone laughed '. . . You should be arresting him, not helping him kill more.'

'I don't know what you're talking about. Now turn around and get your truck out the way or I'll arrest you.'

He reached out to take her by the shoulder, but she lashed

out and gave him a shove in the chest that made him stagger back. One of the loggers cheered sarcastically.

'Feisty little thing, ain't she?' Wes Harding called out.

Everyone laughed again.

'Why don't you all just grow up?' Helen shouted.

Eleanor stepped forward and put a hand on her shoulder.

'What's the matter with all you boys?' Eleanor said. 'I've known some of you since you were kids. I know your mothers. I think you'd all be better just going home.'

The sound of her voice, the calm reasoning tone, made Buck's blood seethe.

'Will someone shut those damn dogs up? Clyde?'

'Yessir?'

'Get those fucking trees off the road.'

Luke had tried for ten minutes to get the hooks out of the pup's mouth, but all three barbs were deeply bedded in and he couldn't loosen them without doing more damage. He managed to get all the meat out of the poor little thing's throat so it didn't choke, but that was all. In the end, he knew it was going to bleed to death and if he wasted anymore time, maybe all the others would be lost as well, so he put it back on the ground where he'd found it, attached to the line like a drowning fish.

All the while, the mother wolf had been barking and howling at him from across the clearcut, pacing up and down, thinking no doubt that he was murdering her pup. He could even hear her now that he was down in the den.

He was inching along the tunnel on his belly, pointing the flashlight ahead of him. It was narrower than the one he and Helen had gone down last summer and it seemed longer too, with bends where the digger had come up against rock. There was a faint smell of ammonia and the farther he went, the stronger it got. He guessed it was from the pee of the pups and that he must now be getting near to the nesting chamber.

468

He held the jabstick out in front of him, in the beam of the flashlight, just in case the mother came in through the other entrance below the rocks. He had no idea how many pups he would find. Helen said there could sometimes be as many as nine or ten.

Then suddenly he heard them whining and a moment later, as he slithered around the final bend, he saw them in the beam of the flashlight. They were in a dark furry huddle at the far corner of the chamber, squinting and mewing at the light. He couldn't tell how many there were. Five or six at most.

'Hey, there,' he said softly. 'It's okay. Everyone's going to be okay.'

He put down the jabstick and the flashlight and pulled out the canvas bag that he'd stuffed down the front of his shirt. He opened it up and elbowed his way toward the pups. There were five of them and he wondered if he could take them all in one go. But the tunnel was narrow and he didn't want to risk hurting any of them. He decided to take three first, then come back for the other two.

He reached out and plucked up the first one. Its fur was soft and all fluffed up. It mewed at him.

'I know, I know. I'm sorry.'

'Move your truck,' Buck Calder said.

'No.'

Helen stood facing him, with her arms folded, trying to look tough and official. Her head came about halfway up his chest. She could feel her knees going wobbly. She had her back to the driver's door and was wishing she'd locked it before hiding the key. She'd lost all track of time. All she knew was that Luke would need longer than he'd had to get the pups out.

Eleanor had given up on her husband and was now trying to make her son-in-law see reason while he supervised the removal of the second tree. The first had already been towed off the road by the Harding boys. Hicks stood there, shaking his head, not looking at her.

'Hey bitch!' someone yelled. 'Move your fucking truck!'

Helen glanced at him and saw it was her bearded friend from outside the courthouse. He and some of his buddies had guns out now and others had broken off branches and were busy wrapping rags around them and dowsing them with kerosene.

'Hey! That's great, guys,' Helen said. 'Are we going to set a cross on fire too?'

'You offering to be on it?'

'Craig!' Buck called. 'Does this truck constitute an obstruction?'

'It certainly does.'

Buck turned back to her.

'Are you going to move it?'

'No.'

He looked over her shoulder into the pickup.

'Give me the keys.'

He held out his hand and Helen only just resisted the urge to spit in it. Over his shoulder she could see Eleanor talking to Abe Harding, telling him he was already in enough trouble as it was and would end up going to jail for a long time. He wasn't listening. The second tree was being dragged away behind his sons' truck, in the back of which the two dogs were tethered, still hollering.

The torches were being lit.

Buck Calder tried to reach around her for the door handle, but Helen moved back to block him. She suddenly remembered the last time he'd had her backed up against her truck and he seemed to remember it too, for he edged away a little, out of range of her knee.

'Clyde? Get a rope on this thing.' He walked away.

470

'On her or the pickup?' Ethan Harding called out.

They all laughed. Someone handed Hicks a rope and he started to walk toward the pickup. Helen turned and wrenched open the door. She reached behind the seat and pulled out Luke's rifle.

She pointed it at Hicks and cocked it. He stopped in his tracks and everything went quiet. Buck Calder had his back to her and, slowly now, he turned and saw the gun. Helen swallowed hard.

'Go home. All of you.'

Everyone stood frozen, staring at her. For the first time, Eleanor looked frightened. Calder was frowning at the gun and as he stepped toward her she swung the barrel so it was pointing at him instead. He faltered. But he kept on coming.

'Where did you get that?'

Helen didn't answer. She was breathing too fast and knew her voice would show, if it wasn't already obvious, how scared she was. He walked right up to her, until the barrel was an inch from his heart.

'You dare,' he whispered. 'You *dare* point my own dead son's gun at me?'

And he closed his hand over the barrel and took it from her.

The mother wolf was right at the mouth of the den when he came out with the first bagload of pups and he thought for a moment that she was going to attack him. She backed away, barking and snarling at him, showing her teeth and gums. Luke yelled and swung the jabstick at her and only then did she run off.

But she was still only twenty yards or so away, still barking and Luke worried that if he left the first bag of pups outside the den she might come and carry it off while he was down getting the others. Maybe, to be safe, he should take the first

471

lot to the Jeep. But he probably didn't have time and anyway, she might nip into the den while he was gone and make off with the others.

He wedged the whimpering bag of pups into a crevice between the rocks and then hunted around for smaller rocks to stack in front of it. It wouldn't stop her getting at them, but it might buy him enough time. All the while he was doing this, he tried to block his ears to the screams of the pup who was hooked to the wire which, he now discovered, stretched in a wide circle all around the den.

What kind of mind, he wondered, could ever have devised such a thing?

In the end, he couldn't bear the screaming any longer. And although he knew he shouldn't waste precious time, he had to have another go at getting the hook out of the pup's mouth, while its mother ran around him in demented circles. But still he couldn't get it out.

Then the mother stopped hollering and Luke heard another sound. A first distant rumble of engines and a dog barking. And looking up the clearcut, he saw headlights pan the sky.

He put the pup down, grabbed the flashlight and the empty bag and dived back down into the den.

The cars and trucks all pulled up in a line along the top of the clearcut and everyone climbed out. Most of them had guns and those who didn't were holding flashlights or flaming torches. Abe had his dogs on leashes now. They were barking more crazily than ever.

Buck stood by Clyde's truck with Henry's gun in his hands. His blood was still simmering at the sight of that little whore-bitch pointing it at him. He felt like smashing her cute little bunny-hugger face in. It was just as well Craig Rawlinson had been there to take her aside while they shunted her shit-heap of a truck off the road. He'd felt pretty much the same about Eleanor, siding up with the bitch against her own husband like that. It was unbelievable.

Tactfully, Rawlinson had said he'd stay down there with the two of them. Buck knew he'd then be able to plead ignorance about what they were all about to do.

'So, where is it?' he said.

Clyde pointed down the clearcut.

'Plumb in the middle there. Couple of hundred yards down. See the rocks?'

'Uh-huh.'

'Den's right under there.'

'Look!' Wes Harding yelled. 'There's one right there!'

He was pointing toward the edge of the clearcut. Every flashlight they had was at once pointed the same way. Few of the beams could reach that far, but enough could for them to see a white wolf, brazen as day, standing there staring right back at them. And as they looked, she had the nerve to start howling at them.

Buck was just lifting his rifle when three or four others beat him to it and a volley of shots rang out.

How many hit her, it was impossible to tell, but it was enough to lift her clean off her feet. She was dead before she landed.

'Listen up!' Buck called out. 'I've got a job to finish here. I've killed me two of these critters today and if anyone's going to jail it's me, okay? If another one shows, it's mine. You all understand?'

There was mumbled agreement.

'Abe and me are going to be cellmates. Ain't that right, Abe?'

Abe didn't smile.

'Okay. Got the shovels and the gasoline?'

The loggers called out to confirm that they had.

'Then let's go.'

It wasn't as easy a walk as it looked. There were felled trees that they had to climb across and stumps and root holes to snag their feet. Buck let Clyde lead the way with the flashlight. He kept the safety catch of Henry's rifle off and his eyes locked on the den. He wasn't going to have one of these drunken jerks beating him again if another wolf showed its face.

They were about halfway down the clearcut now and he could see the black hole of the den showing clearly in the pale moonlit earth. Suddenly he saw its shape alter. It was another wolf. He didn't want to yell because he knew, despite what he'd told them, all the others would take a shot.

Instead, he whispered to Clyde to stop.

'There's one coming out. When I tell you, shine your light.'

He raised his gun and centered the crosshairs on the moving shape emerging from the mouth of the den.

'Now!'

At exactly the same moment that the flashlight beam found its mark, Buck pulled the trigger and the shot rang out.

There was a cry. Sharp and terrible.

And Buck and all who heard it knew that it wasn't from a wolf.

'Luke? Luke?'

It was the moon calling him and he couldn't understand why or what it might want. And he couldn't understand why it kept getting lost in a whirl of red clouds and then suddenly bobbing out again. Except they were more liquid than clouds and closer too, almost as if they were actually in his eyes. And now he found he was in control of them, because when his eyes filled up and the moon went red, all he had to do was blink and everything would clear and there was the moon, all clean again, calling him.

'Luke? Oh God. Luke?'

It sounded like his father, but it couldn't be, because his father didn't want anything to do with him anymore. And there were other voices, voices he didn't recognize, and sometimes their shadows loomed across the moon and he wished they would get out of the way and leave him alone so he could watch it.

He thought of telling them, because he knew he had a voice. Helen had found it for him. But he didn't know where it was at the moment. Perhaps she'd borrowed it. There was a kind of cold space in his throat where it normally was, like a hollow in a snowdrift. It was the only thing he could feel. Except that when he blinked, one of his eyes felt funny and he wasn't sure he was looking through it anymore. It seemed to have something wet and lumpy in it that even the blinking couldn't clear.

Thwuck-thwuck-thwuck.

Now there was another moon coming across the sky. Or maybe it was a star or a comet. But it was lower than that and really, really bright. Blindingly bright. It hurt his eye. And he could hear it too now, getting louder and louder and louder.

Thwuck-thwuck-thwuck-thwuck.

And then both it and the moon flooded with red clouds again.

It wasn't clouds. It was curtains, red curtains, closing across the sky. And this time he couldn't blink them open. Someone was trying to do it for him, but they just kept on closing.

Crimson curtains.

Thwuck-thwuck-thwuck-thwuck-thwuck.

Where was she?

He wanted her to bring him his voice so he could talk with her and touch her and feel more than just this cold hollow in his throat. There were so many people now. And there seemed to be some new ones too and they were sticking

475

things into him and putting some kind of mask thing over his face.

But where was Helen?

Just for an instant, he thought he heard her voice, among all the others, calling his name. But they were lifting him up now and away and the red curtains had closed for the last time. Maybe when they opened again she would be standing there. Maybe he'd be there too, beside her.

Two stone statues, hand in hand.

SUMMER

36

Eleanor sat alone in the mall café, sipping a soda and watching the holiday crowds go by. It was the Fourth of July weekend and the place was teeming. The café was on a corner by the escalators and had counters serving food of almost every ethnic kind, provided it was fast and fried. There were troughs of plastic greenery and the tables were of plain white plastic, each with its own blue and white umbrella, whose purpose (since the mall was hermetically sealed to the elements) Eleanor found puzzling. Perhaps they were to protect those eating from any missile thrown from the escalators.

At the next table, a group of teenage girls sat trying out make-up and nail polish they'd just bought. Occasionally they would all erupt in screams of laughter or call out in chorus to someone they had spotted on the escalator. The waitress had already warned them twice to be quiet. Nearby, a young couple was feeding identical blond baby girls, who lounged happily in the most splendid double stroller Eleanor had ever seen.

She looked at her watch. He was ten minutes late. Perhaps he was having trouble finding the place. He'd always hated malls, but when he'd called she hadn't been able to think of anywhere else to meet. It was right across the street from the apartment she was renting.

The prospect of seeing Buck again, after all these weeks, didn't make her feel nervous, only sad. The last time had been at the hospital on the night of the shooting, while the surgeons were trying so hard to save Luke's life. Eleanor hadn't been able to look at Buck, let alone speak to him. She wasn't going to let it be like that today.

When he'd called, his voice sounded so different that she hadn't recognized him. He'd had to say his name and she'd thought, how strange, not to know who it was, after all those years of marriage.

She saw him now, at the end of the avenue of storefronts, walking alongside his reflection. He had his head slightly bowed, his face half hidden by the brim of his hat. His walk was uncertain, awkward almost, as though he didn't belong in such a place. He was wearing a pale blue snapbutton shirt and black jeans that seemed baggy on him. As he got nearer she saw how thin he'd become.

The girls at the next table had paid their check and were sweeping out of the café and one of them, who wasn't looking, collided with Buck. He staggered back and for a moment it seemed he was going to fall. But he didn't. The girl apologized and was whisked away by her friends. Eleanor saw them all giggling and teasing her as they went.

Buck stood by the entrance, adjusting his hat and scanning the faces. She had to wave to make him see her.

'I'm sorry I'm late,' he said as he walked up. 'I got confused with all the different entrances.'

Eleanor smiled. 'That's okay.'

He sat down and the waitress arrived. He ordered a coffee

480

and asked Eleanor what she wanted and she said she was fine with the soda. When the waitress went, they sat in silence for a few moments, neither one of them knowing what to say.

'So,' he said at last. 'You fly tomorrow?'

'Monday.'

'Monday. Right. To London.'

'Via Chicago.'

'Oh. Then . . .'

'We'll have a week in Ireland, then on to Paris, Rome. Then back to London for a few days, then home.'

'That's quite a trip.'

Eleanor smiled. 'You know I always wanted to travel.'

'Yeah.'

'I think Lane's looking forward to it.'

'She is. She told me. Nice for you to have some time together.'

'Yes.'

Buck's coffee arrived and he stared at it and stirred it for a long time, though there was no need because he always took it black, no sugar. It gave her time to study him. He looked almost haggard. There was a patch of gray bristles on his chin that he'd missed with his razor. His shirt looked as if it hadn't been pressed.

'Lane was telling me the house you're buying down in Bozeman is real nice.'

'It's lovely. Small, you know. But I don't need a big place.'

'No.'

'You heard Ruth's moving to Santa Fe?'

'Yeah.' He nodded. 'Yeah, I heard that.'

There was a pause. The music playing in the mall dipped briefly for an announcement about a young boy who'd gotten himself lost. It told the parents where they could find him.

'You know, Eleanor. That thing between Ruth and me, it was never really—'

481

'Buck, don't. It's gone.'

'Yeah, but—'

'It's all gone.'

He nodded and kept his eyes on his coffee. He started stirring it again.

'Anyway,' he said.

'How are things on the ranch?'

'Good. Pretty good. I've handed a lot of stuff over to Kathy.'

'She told me.'

'She's quite something, that girl. Twice the rancher Clyde'll ever be.'

'He'll learn.'

'Maybe.'

'Little Buck's growing so fast.'

Buck laughed. 'Yeah! Yeah, he's coming along good. Give him a year or two and he'll be running the whole joint.'

He took his first sip of coffee. Eleanor asked if he'd heard yet when his trial might take place.

'September, so they reckon. Kathy tell you about Clyde?'

Eleanor nodded. They'd found his fingerprints on that horrible wire loop thing. But, probably because Buck was pleading guilty to everything, charges against Clyde had just been dropped. Eleanor knew that Kathy would never forgive herself for showing him how it worked.

'Do you have any idea yet what kind of sentence you'll get?'

'Nine months, a year, maybe more. Tell you the truth, I don't really care how long it is.'

'Oh, Buck.'

She wanted to reach across the table and take his hand. But she didn't. She saw his face clench up as he tried to fight his tears. As if he hadn't been punished enough, she thought.

'When I think of Luke, I . . .'

'Buck, please don't.'

'No. I know.'

He took a deep breath and held it inside him a moment, then let it come slowly, shudderingly, out. After awhile, he sniffed and looked around.

He forced a laugh. 'Anyway, Abe's boys say it's like summer camp in there. Apparently the old guy's having the time of his life.'

Eleanor smiled. The young couple with the twins was leaving now. She watched Buck's face as he watched the babies being wheeled past. One of them gave him a glorious smile and it seemed to start the tears welling again in his eyes. He was so very near to the edge all the time. Eleanor sat still and let him get over it. And at last he was able to look at her.

'All I wanted to say, was . . . I'm sorry, Eleanor. I'm so sorry.'

By the time they had driven high into the mountains, as far as the last road would take them, a thin band of pink had risen in the eastern sky. Hope, two hours earlier, had been like a ghost town and as they crossed the river, she had looked toward the church and thought about that day, almost a year ago, when Dan had told her about the road of wolf skulls.

This time, he didn't say a word and neither did Helen. And the only pair of eyes that saw them as they drove down Main Street belonged to a black cat that stopped in their dimmed lights to assess them then hurried on across the road.

The van they had hired was dark green and unmarked except for the spattering of mud that their night's efforts had given it. When they were finished, they were going to take it down to the cabin and Dan was going to use it to load it with all the things she didn't want. By nightfall the cabin would be as empty as the day she'd moved in. The mice could have it back.

The road was getting rough now and as they bumped from rut to pothole, the whole van shuddered. Helen could hear the faint rattle of the cages in the back. She hadn't been up this high since the day Luke had shown her the wolves' first den. She remembered the look on his dusty face when he came crawling out and what he'd said about being happy to die down there.

'I figure this is about as far as we can get,' Dan said.

'Seems as good a place as any.'

'Okay.'

The road was being repossessed by newgrown weeds and flowers and seemed to peter out in a short plateau of rock. To the east, it fell away sharply in a narrow, rock-strewn funnel through the trees. Below, in the wakening light, Helen could see a meadow full of colorless flowers and beyond it the white flash of a creek still swollen with snowmelt.

Dan swung the van around so that its rear was pointing to the top of the funnel. He turned off the engine and looked at her.

'You okay?'

'Yeah.'

'Just like the old times, huh? Prior and Ross, alpha wolf team.'

She smiled. 'What are you going to do?' she asked.

'With my life? I don't know. Get a proper job, I guess. My mom always said I should "work with people" and I'd say, okay, I'll be a mortician.'

'So even back then your jokes weren't any good.'

'That's true.'

Dan had handed in his notice the day after Luke was shot. They'd asked him to stay on and insisted he was in no way to blame for what happened but he said he'd had enough; he was 'wolfed out'. He agreed to stay on until they found a successor. The new guy was due to start next month.

484

'I'll probably stick around these parts till Ginny's finished high school, then move on somewhere, I guess.'

They were silent for a moment. Dan peered at the sky.

'It's getting light. Better get this show on the road. Ready?'

'You bet.'

They got out and walked to the back of the van. Helen held the flashlight so he could see to unlock the padlock on the rear doors. Then he pulled the handle and opened them wide.

They pulled off the tarpaulins and the flashlight glinted on two aluminum cages standing side by side. They were similar to the cages that had been used to bring the Yellowstone wolves down from Canada. They were like perforated crates, about four feet long and three feet high, with a sliding door at the front. Poles to carry them with slid out at each corner.

'I hope someone's told these guys what happens to wolves around these parts,' Dan said.

'I thought you said these were vegetarian wolves?'

'They are. But, you know, it could be just a fad.'

Helen wasn't going to ask where they'd come from. Dan had made all the arrangements. All she knew was that they were an alpha pair, untagged, uncollared and untraceable. She and Dan had picked them up just before midnight at a remote spot about ten miles south of the Canadian border. There was no one to meet them. The crates had just been there waiting for them, covered with the tarps and a few branches.

Helen went behind the first crate and slid the handles out.

'Ready?'

'Yep.'

'One, two, three, lift.'

They put it down at the top of the slope, then did the same with the other one. Then they took off the locks and slid up both of the front doors. Behind each was an inner door of vertical square bars through which, now, they could see two pairs of amber eyes, warily surveying them.

'Good morning, folks,' Dan said. 'This is your four a.m. wake-up call.' He looked at Helen. 'One at a time or both together?'

'Together.'

On the count of three, they opened the inner door and for a moment nothing happened. Then, like two Tomahawk missiles, the wolves launched themselves out of the cages. They landed in a clatter of sliprock, but didn't fall or falter, just plunged headfirst down the slope. They were both gray, the color of the shadowed rock they ran down.

'Well, looks like the sedative wore off,' Dan said.

Halfway down the funnel, they stopped and though in the dawn it was hard to be sure, they seemed to look back up toward the van. Helen started to sob.

Dan walked over to her and put his arms around her.

'Hey, come on now. It's okay.'

'I know, I know, I'm sorry.'

When her tears cleared and she looked again, the wolves had vanished.

When they pulled up outside the cabin, the sky had brightened to a perfect, cloudless blue and the sun was drying the dew from the spring flowers that still smothered the slope down to the lake. Buzz came bounding through them and because he didn't know the van, he barked loudly until Helen climbed out and then he came wiggling and wagging toward her in apology. As they walked toward the cabin, they could smell breakfast cooking.

Luke was standing in the doorway.

He was smiling and squinting in the sunshine with his one good eye. The black patch over the other still gave Helen a shock whenever she saw it. In time she was sure she would find it dashing.

He saw that she'd been crying and he stepped out and came to meet them and put his arms around them both and the three of them stood huddled in silence for awhile, their heads bowed in unspoken communion, while Buzz bounced around them, wondering what was going on.

The bullet had hit him in the side of the neck. It had passed right through, then hit a rock, sending a splinter of it, the size of an arrowhead, into his left eye. In the time it took for the helicopter to arrive and fly him to the hospital, he had lost a lot of blood. That he had survived was little short of a miracle.

The neck wound had done little damage. They had operated on his eye for many hours and managed to save it, though Luke would never see much with it. The first thing he wanted to know, when he came around, was what had happened to the pups.

Only the hooked one had died. The others had been taken to Yellowstone and successfully fostered. Luke's father had told the police where they could find the wolfer's trailer. And sometime later, a ranger discovered his snowmobile in a clearing above Wrong Creek. No trace of the old man himself was ever found.

Luke had been keen to come with Dan and Helen last night to collect and release the wolves. But Dan said it was safer, in case anything went wrong, if Luke wasn't involved.

'It went okay then?'

'Like a dream.'

'I wish we could stay to hear them howl.'

'Maybe one day you will,' Dan said.

'I hope you're both hungry.'

'Ravenous.'

They sat on the grass outside the cabin and ate eggs and

bacon and hashbrowns and washed it down with coffee and fresh-squeezed orange juice. They talked about Alaska and some of the places she and Luke were going to visit in the next two months before he started college. Beyond that, they hadn't made plans.

Luke wanted her to come to Minnesota with him. They would find an apartment, he said, and while he went to classes, she could do more research and finish her thesis. On weekends she could show him the wilderness.

Maybe she would. There was plenty of time to decide.

Curiously, for the first time in Helen's adult life, the future didn't seem to matter. It was as though all that had happened here had purged the part of her that had always yearned and nagged and worried. No amount of worry would alter for the better what befell them. Perhaps, as Celia had suggested in a recent letter, Helen had at last learned, along with their rookie-Buddhist father, simply to *be*. All that mattered was *now* and that she was with the person she loved best in all the world.

After breakfast, Dan wouldn't let them help clean up the cabin. They had a long journey ahead of them, he said. So together they loaded the last few things, along with Buzz, into Luke's Jeep. Helen gave Dan the keys to her old pickup.

'You see?' he said. 'It lasted the year.'

'So did I.'

None of them wanted to make a big issue of saying good-bye, so they just gave each other a hug and wished each other well. Dan cracked a joke about them quitting when there was still work to be done. He stood beside the car, with the sun behind him, while Helen and Luke got in and buckled up.

'Angels on your body,' he said.

'Yours too, Prior.'

Driving down beside the river, with the cottonwoods swaying green and silver above them, they passed the derelict house where the old wolfer had once lived. There was a SOLD sign nailed to a tree by the gate.

They saw no one they knew when they passed through town. They turned east and headed out toward the plains.

As they came over the bridge, Helen slowed the car and stopped and they both looked one last time toward the church above the river.

'Look,' Luke said.

He was pointing at the sign on the other side of the road, the one that said HOPE (POPULATION 519). Three narrow beams of sunlight were shining through the bullet holes.

THE END

Also available from Little, Brown Book Group

The Smoke Jumper

by Nicholas Evans

The fire that was to change so many lives started with a single shaft of lightning that struck a mountain ridge on a still and moonless night. The woman who camped nearby with her group of troubled teenagers slept on and heard nothing. Until the deadly inferno engulfed the mountain, and into the flames leaped *The Smoke Jumper*.

His name is Connor Ford and he braves the flames to save the woman he loves but cannot have, for Julia Bishop is the partner of his closest friend, Ed Tully. Julia loves them both but the tragedy on Snake Mountain forces her to choose between them and burns a brand on all their hearts.

In the wake of the fire, Connor travels to the world's worst wars and disasters to take photographs that find him fame but not happiness. Reckless of a life he no longer wants, he dares death to take him, until another fateful day on another continent, when he must walk through fire again . . .

*Read on for a preview of this epic novel of
love and loyalty . . .*

1

The important things in life always happened by accident. At fifteen she didn't know much, in fact, with each passing year she was a lot less clear about most things. But this much she did know. You could worry yourself sick trying to be a better person, spend a thousand sleepless nights figuring out how to live clean and decent and honest, you could make a plan and bolt it in place, kneel by your bed every night and swear to God you'd stick to it, hell, you could go to church and promise properly. You could cross your heart seven times with your eyes tight shut, cut your thumb and squeeze it and pen solemn vows on a rock with your own blood then throw it in the river at the stroke of midnight. And then, out of the black beyond, like a hawk on a rat, some nameless catastrophe would swoop into your life and turn everything upside down and inside out forever.

Skye later reckoned that on the night in question that old hawk must have been outside sitting up on the roof biding his time and watching the rat have a little fun, because it all started in a real low-key kind of way when those two women came sashaying into the bar.

She didn't know who they were but what they were was plain for all the world. They were wearing more make-up than clothes and she could tell from the way they swayed on their high heels that they were already hazed with drink. They both wore tight little tops, one red, one silver and fringed, and the woman in front, who had long black hair and breasts propped up like melons on a shelf, had a skirt so short she needn't have bothered. The music in the bar was thumping loud and the black-haired woman tried a little shimmy to it as she walked and almost fell.

The men they were with were close behind them and obscured, steering them through the crowd. Both wore cowboy hats and from the corner booth across the room where Skye and her friends were sitting, she couldn't make out their faces. Not that she was remotely interested. She was more than a little hazed with drink herself. The lights were dimmed to a dull red glow and through the hanging curl of smoke all she registered was a couple of sad forty-something-year-old guys chasing their youth and doubtless cheating on their wives. Skye looked away. She picked up her beer and drank, then lit another cigarette.

She watched them mostly because she was bored, which was kind of sad too, considering it was her birthday. Jed and Calvin were slumped stoned and speechless beside her, Roxy was still crying into her hands at something Craig had said to her, and Craig was still cussing on and on about his goddamn heap of a car breaking down. Another great night in fun city, Skye said to herself and took another swig. Happy birthday to me.

The bar was a godforsaken dump so close to the railroad that the bottles shook and clinked whenever a train went by.

For reasons that weren't too hard to fathom, the cops left the place alone and so long as you weren't in diapers, the staff turned a blind eye to underage drinking. Consequently much of the clientele was around the same age as Skye. A lot younger for sure than the four who had just walked in. They were at the bar now and stood waiting to be served. They had their backs to her and Skye again found herself staring at them.

She watched the tall man's hands moving on the black-haired woman's hips and on her ass and up her spine to her bare shoulders and saw him lean in close, nuzzling her neck. God, he was *licking* her. How gross some guys were. What was it with women? How could they stand being slobbered over by jerks like him? The whole sex trip was something Skye still didn't get and doubted she ever would. Oh sure, she *did* it. Everybody did. But she still couldn't figure out why it was cracked up to be such a big deal.

The man must have whispered something dirty because the woman suddenly threw back her head, laughed raucously and made a playful attempt to slap him. The man laughed too and swiveled to avoid her and his hat fell off and for the first time Skye could see his face.

It was her stepfather.

In those few moments before his eyes met hers she glimpsed in his face a look she had never seen before, a kind of inner face that was still just a boy's, loose and joyful and strangely frail. Then she saw him recognize her and saw the boy vanish as swiftly as he had appeared. His face clouded and clenched and became again the one she knew and feared and loathed, the one she saw when he came back in the early hours to the trailer seething with drink and fury and called her mother a squaw bitch and beat her until she howled for mercy and then turned his foul attention upon Skye.

He straightened up and put his hat on the bar and said

495

something to the woman who turned to consider Skye with a look that lay somewhere between disdain and disinterest. Now he was heading toward the booth. Skye squashed out her cigarette, hoping he hadn't seen it. She stood up.

'Let's go,' she said quietly.

But she was trapped in the booth. On one side Roxy was sobbing into Craig's shoulder and hadn't heard and on the other Calvin and Jed were still out of it. Her stepfather reached the table, his eyes taking in the evidence: the beer bottles, the brimming ashtrays, the comatose bums she chose to hang out with.

'What the fuck are you doing in here?'

'Come on, it's my birthday.' It was pathetic but worth a try. She even thought of calling him 'Dad' as she briefly had when he and her mom married, before he revealed just what a mean, disgusting sonofabitch he really was. But she couldn't bring herself to utter the word.

'Don't give me that shit. You're just fifteen years old! What the fuck do you think you're at?'

'Aw, give her a break, man. We're only having a little fun.' It was Jed, who had resurfaced. Skye's stepfather leaned across and grabbed him by the throat, hauling him halfway across the table.

'You dare talk to me like that, you little slice of shit.'

Jed's weight made the table tilt and everything on it except for him slid off onto the floor in an avalanche of breaking glass. Craig was on his feet now and he tried to grab Skye's stepfather by the arm but her stepfather twisted himself around and with the hand that wasn't throttling Jed punched the boy full in the face. Roxy screamed.

'For godsake,' Skye shouted. 'Stop it! Stop it!'

She was aware that everyone in the bar was staring at them. One of the waiters was coming over along with the man her stepfather had arrived with.

'Hey folks, let's cool it here, shall we?' the waiter said.

Skye's stepfather shoved Jed back into his seat so hard his head slammed against the back of the booth. Craig was on his knees bleeding from the mouth and Roxy was sobbing over him, trying to help him. Skye's stepfather's chest was heaving and his eyes were narrowed and dark and he turned them on the waiter.

'Did you serve alcohol to these kids?'

The waiter held up his hands. 'Sir, let's keep things calm now, please.'

He was slightly built and about a foot shorter than Skye's stepfather. He had long hair tied back in a ponytail.

'Did you? Did you serve them alcohol?'

'They said they were twenty-one.'

'And you believed that? Did you ask for their I.D.?'

'Sir, could we talk about this—'

'Did you?'

Skye stood up and pushed her way out of the booth.

'Look, we're going, okay? We're going!'

Her stepfather spun around and lifted his hand to hit her and although all her instincts told her to cower, somehow she managed not to and instead stood her ground, glaring at him. She could smell his cologne and it was so cloying and the memories it stirred so foul that it almost made her gag.

'Don't you dare lay a finger on me.'

It was little more than a whisper. But it stopped him or maybe it was all the eyes upon him that did it. Whatever it was, he lowered his hand.

'Get your ass home, you little Indian whore. I'll see to you later.'

'The only whores in here are the two you came in with.'

He made a lunge for her but she ducked out of his reach and ran for the door. Over her shoulder she saw that his friend and the waiter had grabbed his arms to stop him coming after her. She burst into the night and started to run.

497

The air hung hot and humid and she could feel the tears running on her cheeks and it made her almost choke with anger that she should be so weak as to let that bastard make her cry. A freight train was going by and she ran alongside, watching the lights beyond it strobe between the wagons. There were lights on her side of the rails too, strung on a wire above her, each with its own frenzied aura of insects. The train seemed many miles long and from afar, already out of town, she heard the mournful wail of the engine like a verdict on the sorry place through which it had passed. Had it been traveling more slowly she would have climbed on board and let it bear her wherever in the world it was headed.

She ran and ran like she always ran. And it didn't matter where because wherever it was couldn't be worse than where she was and where she had been. She'd run away first when she was five and done it many times since. And it always got her into trouble but, what the hell, what kind of trouble was there that she hadn't seen already?

She ran now until her smoke-seared lungs could take no more, and as she stopped, the train's last wagon went by and she stood slumped with her hands on her knees, gasping and watching its taillights grow smaller and smaller until the night swallowed them as if they never had been. Somewhere way off in the darkness a dog was barking and a man yelled for it to cease but it paid no heed.

'Never mind. You can catch the next one.'

The voice startled her. It was male and close at hand. Skye scanned the darkness around her. She was in what appeared to be an abandoned lumberyard. She couldn't see him.

'Over here.'

He was sitting on the ground, leaning against a stack of rotting fence posts overgrown with weeds and he looked as if he might almost have melted out of it for his hair was long and tangled and so was his beard. He was a white boy, older than

498

Skye. Eighteen or nineteen maybe and very thin. He was wearing torn jeans and a T-shirt emblazoned with a roaring Chinese dragon. A dust-covered duffel bag lay on the ground beside him. He was rolling a joint.

'Why are you crying?'

'I'm not. What the fuck is it to you anyhow?'

He shrugged. For a while neither of them spoke. Skye turned away as if she had other things to do or think about. She wiped the wet off her cheeks, trying not to let him see. She knew she should probably walk away. All kinds of freaks and psychos hung out down here by the railroad. But something within her, some hapless craving for comfort or company, made her stay. She looked at him again. He licked the cigarette paper and sealed the joint, then lit it and took a long draw. He held it out to her.

'Here.'

'I don't do drugs.'

'Sure.'

The car they stole belonged to somebody with small kids. There were little seats fitted in the back and the floor was littered with toys and picture books and candy wrappers. The boy knew what he was doing, for it took him only a couple of minutes to pop the door lock and get the engine going. They stopped after a few miles so he could switch the plates with another car.

He said his name was Sean and she told him hers and that was all they knew about each other except for some common hurt or longing that didn't need uttering. Nothing else seemed to matter, not where they were going nor why.

They drove north until they hit the interstate then headed west with a river to one side and the dawn rearing in a widening red scar over the endless plains behind them. Neither of them spoke for a long time and Skye sat turned in her seat

499

looking back and waiting for the sun to show itself and when finally it did it set the land aflame with crimson and purple and gold and flung long shadows from the cottonwoods and rocks and from the black cattle that grazed beside the river and Skye thought it was the most beautiful thing she had ever seen in her whole life.

On the floor she found a picture book that she remembered from elementary school. It was about a little boy called Bernard whose parents always ignore him. One day a monster appears in the backyard and Bernard runs inside to tell them but still they just ignore him. The monster eats him and goes into the house and roars at the parents but they think it's Bernard fooling around and ignore him. And because they're not scared, the monster loses all his confidence. Skye turned to the last page which always used to make her feel sad. The poor old monster has been sent to bed and is sitting all alone and forlorn in the dark, feeling a total failure.

They pulled off the interstate to get gas. There was a diner there that was just opening and they bought coffee and muffins and settled themselves to eat at a table by the window while an old woman mopped the floor around them. While they ate he asked her how old she was and she lied and told him she was seventeen. She said she'd been born in South Dakota and was half Oglala Sioux, on her mother's side, and he said that was cool but she told him that she didn't think it was and anyhow she didn't know anything about that people or their history except that it was full of pain and misery and she already had enough of both to be getting along with, thanks very much.

He told her he came from Detroit and that his parents and his older brother were all in jail though he didn't say for what and Skye didn't ask. When he was fourteen he had taken off and for the last three years had been traveling all over. He said he had been down to Mexico and Nicaragua and Salvador and said he'd seen things he never could have imagined or believed.

'Like what?'

'Magic. Shamans. People walking through fire and not even being marked by it. People dying on account of being cursed. I saw a dead woman brought back to life.'

Skye asked him about it but he didn't want to tell her. She asked why he had come to Montana and he said it was because he wanted to meet a grizzly bear in the wild. He said he had learned in Mexico that it was his spirit animal and that he had been a bear in another life. She laughed because this skinny kid was about as unlike a bear as a person could get. A stick insect maybe or a giraffe or something, but a grizzly bear? No way. He looked hurt and went all quiet on her and so she apologized and, finding it hard to keep a straight face, asked him how he planned to go about finding a grizzly. He conceded that it wasn't going to be easy but figured they should head for Glacier Park, which he'd been told was a good place to start looking.

Skye nodded, trying to look serious.

'Right,' she said.

'You got a better idea?'

She could think of about a hundred.

'Whatever,' she said. 'I don't give a shit.'

They drove the rest of the day while the sun swung over them, heading like them for the snow-capped mountains that loomed ever larger before them. In the afternoon it got so hot they pulled off the interstate and meandered along narrow roads through a forest humming with insects. They found a creek with a swirling pool and swam naked and unashamed in the cold clear water then lay in a meadow full of wildflowers and dried themselves in the sun while butterflies danced around them. He said she looked pretty and she thought he might want to touch her and half wanted him to but he only

501

stared at the sky and smoked another joint and seemed hardly to know she was there.

By the time they got back on the interstate the western sky was filling with great gray thunderheads among which the sun crazed fitfully, pale and cold and metallic, while lightning flickered from their roiled bellies to the mountain mass below.

She saw the police car before he did. Something made her look back and as she did so the cop turned on his flashing red and blue lights. Sean looked in the rearview mirror and said nothing. He didn't look scared or even worried, just stoned.

The Smoke Jumper
by Nicholas Evans

Available now
£6.99
ISBN 978-0-7515-3938-7